# MOST ELIGIBLE TEXAN

JULES BENNETT

To single parents trying to push through
from one day to the next.
You are somebody's hero and you've got this!

# MOST ELIGIBLE TEXAN

**JULES BENNETT**

# THE BILLIONAIRE'S LEGACY

**REESE RYAN**

MILLS & BOON

First Published in Great Britain 2018
by Mills & Boon, an imprint of HarperCollinsPublishers,
1 London Bridge Street, London, SE1 9GF

*Most Eligible Texan* © 2018 Harlequin Books S.A.
*The Billionaire's Legacy* © 2018 Roxanne Ravenel

Special thanks and acknowledgement are given to Jules Bennett for her contribution to the Texas Cattleman's Club: Bachelor Auction series.

ISBN: 978-0-263-93621-6

1018

**MIX**
**Paper from**
**responsible sources**
FSC™ C007454

This book is produced from independently certified FSC™ paper to ensure responsible forest management.

For more information visit: www.harpercollins.co.uk/green

Printed and bound in Spain
by CPI, Barcelona

*USA TODAY* bestselling author **Jules Bennett** has published over sixty books and never tires of writing happy endings. Writing strong heroines and alpha heroes is Jules's favourite way to spend her workdays. Jules hosts weekly contests on her Facebook fan page and loves chatting with readers on Twitter, Facebook and via email through her website. Stay up-to-date by signing up for her newsletter at julesbennett.com.

**Reese Ryan** writes sexy, deeply emotional romances full of family drama, surprising secrets and unexpected twists.

Born and raised in the Midwest, Reese has deep Tennessee roots. Every summer, she endured long, hot car trips to family reunions in Memphis via a tiny clown car loaded with cousins.

Connect with Reese at ReeseRyanWrites on Instagram, Twitter and Facebook or @ reeseryan.com/desirereaders.

# One

An entire morning of pleasure reading plus an extra-large pumpkin-spice latte with a healthy dose of whip? Hell yes, sign her up.

Rachel Kincaid spotted The Daily Grind across the street and nearly skipped to the door. She had two weeks before she had to dive back into her textbooks and this was her first time out alone since giving birth eleven months ago.

Part of her felt guilty for leaving her precious Ellie, but on the other hand, she knew her baby was in the best hands back at the Lone Wolf Ranch under the care of her friend, Alexis Slade, and the host of staff members they had. The chef had taken quite a liking to Ellie and was always fussing over her.

Alexis had graciously invited Rachel and Ellie to stay in her Royal, Texas, home and Rachel desperately needed the gal-pal time. Alexis and her grandfather Gus had gone out of their way to make the two of them feel like part of the family.

Rachel stepped up onto the curb and pulled her cell from her boho-style bag. She'd just shoot off one quick text to make sure everything was okay. Although she was most definitely looking forward to this break, she was still a fairly new mom and a bit of a worrier when it came to her baby girl.

Just as she pulled up the text messages, Rachel plowed into the door.

No, not a door. A man. A broad, strong, chiseled man.

Large hands gripped her biceps, preventing her from stumbling backward. Rachel jerked her gaze up at the stranger she'd slammed into.

Familiar dark blue eyes stared back at her, no doubt mirroring her own shock.

"Matt?"

"Rachel?"

The last time she'd been in Matt Galloway's arms had been at Billy's funeral, and that had been just over a year ago. Other than a handful of texts immediately following, she hadn't heard a word from her late husband's best friend.

The pain from the void thudded in her chest. Matt had been her friend, too, and she'd wondered where he'd disappeared to. Why he'd dodged her for so long.

"What are you doing in Royal?" she asked, pushing aside the heartbreaking thoughts.

Last she knew he was still in Dallas making millions and flashing that high-voltage smile to charm the ladies.

Matt released her and stepped back.

"Hiding out," he stated with a laugh. "I'm taking

a break from the city for a bit and staying out of the limelight."

Rachel couldn't help but smile. "Ah, yes. I recall you being dubbed Most Eligible Bachelor in Texas. What's wrong, Matt? Don't want all the ladies chasing you anymore?"

Matt never minded the attention he received from beautiful women. In fact, Rachel had been interested in him at one time, but then Billy had asked her out, whisked her off her feet and, well…that was all in the past. She was moving forward now.

"Come in," he said, gesturing toward the door. "I'll buy you a cup of coffee."

"Just like that? As if the past year of silence hadn't happened?"

The words escaped her before she could stop herself. But damn it, she'd needed him and he'd vanished. Didn't she deserve to know why?

Honestly, such a heavy topic was just too much to handle this early in the morning running on little sleep and no caffeine.

"You know, never mind," she amended, waving her hand through the air as if she could just erase the words. "It's good to see you again, Matt."

She wasn't sure what to feel or what memory from their past to cling to, as there were a great many. From meeting him and Billy for the first time at a college party, to the fun times they all had together, to the tragic death that had forever changed the dynamics between them.

Rachel pasted a smile on her face, though. She needed a day out, and running into Matt might just be what the doctor ordered. Even though he'd hurt her, she'd missed him, and she knew Matt well enough to know he had a reason for staying away. She just couldn't fathom what could keep him at such a distance for so long.

"I don't do coffee," she stated as she passed him to enter The Daily Grind. "But you can buy my glorified milkshake."

Matt placed a hand on the small of her back, a simple gesture, but one that had her inwardly cringing. Not because she didn't want Matt to touch her, but because the electric tingle that spread through her was so unexpected. No other man had touched her in so long...

She wasn't affected by him, she told herself. He was her friend, for pity's sake. No, the reaction only came from seeing him again and the lack of human contact... the lack of *male* contact.

Ugh. This was so silly. Why was she letting such a simple gesture from Matt occupy so much of her mind?

"You're going to get something pumpkin-spice with whip, aren't you?"

Rachel smacked his chest as she made her way toward the counter. "Listen, I won't judge you and you won't judge me. Got it, Mr. Eligible Bachelor?"

Matt shook his head as he placed his order for a boring black coffee. Once Rachel placed her own order, the two of them found one of the cozy leather sofas in front of the floor-to-ceiling glass window.

The shop wasn't too busy this morning. A few people sat on stools along the back brick wall, and the bar top that stretched along the brick had power stations, so those working had taken up real estate there.

Even though they were seated in the front of the coffee shop, Rachel and Matt had just enough privacy for their surprising reunion. She still couldn't believe he was here in Royal. Couldn't believe how handsome and fit he still looked. Okay, fine. He was damn sexy and she'd have to be completely insane to think he'd ever be anything but. The past year had been nothing but kind to Matt, while she figured she looked exactly how she felt: haggard and homely.

Rachel eased back into the corner of her seat and smoothed her hands down her maxiskirt. She wasn't sure what to say now, how to close the time gap that had separated them for so long.

More importantly, she wasn't sure how to compartmentalize her emotions. Matt had been her friend for years, but seeing him now had her wondering why she felt…hell, she couldn't put her finger on the exact emotion.

"What are you doing in Royal?" Matt asked, resting his elbow on the back of the couch and shifting to face her. "You're not hiding from some newly appointed title by the media, too, are you?"

Leave it to Matt to fall back into their camaraderie as if nothing had changed between them over the last year. She'd circle back to his desertion later, but for now she just wanted a nice relaxing chat with her old friend.

"Afraid I'm not near as exciting as you," she stated with a smile. "I'm visiting Alexis Slade, my friend from college."

"I'm familiar with the Slade family. Are you alone?"

"If you're asking if I have a man in my life, no. I'm here with my daughter."

Matt opened his mouth, but before he could say anything, the barista delivered their orders and set them on the raw-edged table before them. Once they were alone again, Rachel reached for her favorite fall drink.

"I didn't mean to pry," Matt muttered around his

coffee mug. "I don't have any right to know about your personal life anymore. How are you, though? Really."

"I'm doing well. But you're not prying. We've missed a good bit of each other's lives." She slid her lips over the straw, forcing her gaze away when his dark blue eyes landed on her mouth. "Ew, what is this?"

Rachel set her frosted cup back on the table. "That's not a pumpkin-spice latte."

Matt laughed. "Because that's not what you told them you wanted."

"Of course it is," she declared, swiping at her lips. "I always get the same thing at any coffee shop, especially in the fall. I'm a creature of habit and I'm pumpkin-spice everything."

"That I definitely recall." The corners of his eyes crinkled as he laughed. "But at the counter you ordered a large iced nutmeg with extra whip and an extra shot."

What the hell? Bumping into Matt had totally messed up her thought process. Maybe it was the strength with which he prevented her from falling on the sidewalk, or the firm hand on her back as he'd guided her in. Or maybe she could chalk this up to good old-fashioned lust because she couldn't deny that he was both sexy and charming.

And her late husband's best friend. There could be no lust. Not now. Not ever.

"I'll go get you another." He came to his feet. "Tell me exactly what you want."

"Oh, don't worry about it. I'm just not used to leaving the house alone—I guess it threw off my game."

Yeah, she'd go with the excuse that she was used to carrying a child and a heavy diaper bag. No way would she admit that Matt's touch, Matt's intense stare, had short-circuited her brain.

He pulled out his wallet. "Better tell me your order or I'll make something up. Do you really want to risk another bad drink?"

Rachel laughed. "Fine."

She rattled off her order and watched as he walked away.

Nerves curled in Rachel's belly. She shouldn't feel this nervous, but she did. At one time, Matt had meant so much to her—he still did. Yet she had no clue what to talk about and she certainly didn't want the awkward silence to settle between them.

One thing was certain, though. Matt hadn't changed one bit. He was still just as sexy, just as charismatic as ever. And he was the Most Eligible Bachelor in Texas. Interesting he came back into her life at this exact time.

Matt took his time getting Rachel's drink. He opted to wait at the counter instead of having the barista deliver it. He needed to get control of himself, of his thoughts. Because Rachel Kincaid, widow of Billy Kincaid, was the one person he'd thought of a hell of a lot over the years…and even more so this past year. Yes, he'd deserted her, but he'd had no other choice.

And now she'd want answers. Answers she deserved, but he wasn't ready to give.

He'd thought for sure the absence would get his emotions under control. He'd been hell-bent on throwing himself into his work, into a new partnership with his firm, and forging more takeovers in the hopes that he'd get over the honey-haired beauty that had starred in his every fantasy since they'd met.

Unfortunately, that hadn't been the case. Perhaps that's because he'd kept track of her. That sounded a bit stalkerish, but he'd needed to know she was alright.

Needed to know if she was struggling so he could step in and help. From what Matt could tell, Billy's parents, plus his brother and his wife, had made sure Rachel had all she'd needed. Insurance money only went so far, but Billy came from a wealthy family.

Rachel had sold her Dallas home, though. She'd moved out and now she was here. So what was her next move? Did she have a plan? Was she going to return to Dallas?

Insurance money would run out at some point and so would her savings. Matt couldn't just let this go, not when she might need him. She'd be too proud to ever ask for help...all the more reason for him to keep an eye on her.

So many questions and he'd severed all rights to ask when he pushed her from his life. But for his damn sanity and out of respect for Rachel, he'd had no other choice.

Matt had known she'd had a little girl. She was a few months pregnant at the funeral and had already started showing. He recalled that slight swell against him as he'd held her by the graveside.

He'd honestly had no idea she'd be here in Royal, but like the selfish prick he was, he wasn't a bit sorry he'd run into her. Now was the time to pay his penance and admit he'd dodged her, admit that he needed space. But one thing he could never admit was his attraction. That was the last thing Rachel needed to be told.

"Here you go," the barista said with a smile as she placed the new frothy drink on the counter.

Matt nodded. "Thanks."

The second he turned back toward Rachel, the punch of lust to his gut was no less potent than it had been the first time he'd seen her all those years ago. She'd always been a striking woman, always silently demanded attention with just a flick of her wavy blond hair, a glance in his direction. Hell, all he had to do was conjure up a thought and she captivated him.

And nothing had been as gut-wrenching as watching her marry his best friend…a man who hadn't deserved someone as special as Rachel.

Rachel was, well, *everything*. But she wasn't for him.

Matt wasn't sure what was worse, staying in Dallas dodging paparazzi over this damn Most Eligible Bachelor in Texas title or being in this small town face-to-face with the one woman he could never have—the only woman he'd ever truly wanted.

A group of college-aged kids came through with their laptops and headed to the back of the coffee shop. Their laughter and banter instantly thrust him back to that party where he had first met Rachel. He'd flirted a little and was about to ask her out when Billy slid between them and whispered, "Mine," toward Matt before whisking her away.

If only Matt had known how things would go down between Billy and Rachel…

"One extra-shot pumpkin-spice latte with a side of pumpkin and pumpkin whip on top." Matt placed the drink in front of Rachel and made a show of bowing as he extended his arm. "Or something like that."

Rachel's laughter was exactly the balm he needed in his life. "Thank you, but that wasn't necessary."

"Was the bow too much?"

He took a seat next to her and couldn't take his eyes off the way her pretty mouth covered the pointed dollop of whip or the way she licked her lips and groaned as her lids lowered. Damn vixen had no idea what she could do to a man. He wondered how many others she'd put under her spell.

"So, tell me all about this newly appointed title." She set her drink on the table and tore the paper off her straw. "Are we going to get bombarded by squealing fans or camera flashes?"

"I sure as hell hope not." Matt grabbed his mug and settled back into the corner of the sofa. "And I'd rather not discuss all of that. Let's talk about you. What are you doing here in Royal? Other than staying with the Slades."

Rachel held on to her cup and crossed her legs. The dress she wore might be long, but the thin fabric hugged her shapely thighs and shifted each time she moved. And from the way she kept squirming, she wasn't as calm as her smile led him to believe.

"I'm working on finishing my marketing degree on-line and figuring out where to go from here."

Matt didn't like that there was a subtle lilt leading him to believe she wasn't happy. The thought of her not moving on to a life she deserved didn't sit well with him. Not one bit.

"How much longer do you have?" he asked.

Rachel slid her fingertip over the condensation on her glass. "One more semester and I'm done. The end can't come soon enough."

And being a single mother no doubt added to her stress. Surely she wasn't strapped for cash. Her in-laws alone should've covered anything she needed that Billy's finances couldn't.

She'd been working on her degree when they'd met, but once she and Billy married, Billy had talked her out of finishing. Matt was damn proud she was doing this for herself.

He had so many questions, yet none of them he should ask just yet. Even though she smiled and laughed, he'd seen the hurt in her eyes, the accusation in her question when they'd been outside. Rachel deserved her answers well before he was allowed to have his.

Matt wasn't going to leave Royal without making sure Rachel and her daughter were stable and had what they needed, at least until she got on her feet.

Well, hell. Is that why they were here? Because she didn't have a place to stay? What about the home she and Billy had?

"How long are you hiding from your fan club?" she asked, pulling him back to the real reason he was in town.

Matt clenched his jaw. He wasn't about to get into all the issues he had going on. The disagreements with his partner, the negotiations he had still up in the air, the fact he wanted to sell his 51 percent and start his own company. There really was no way to just sum up in a blanket statement all he had going on.

He would much rather keep their unexpected reunion on the lighter side. And now that they were both in Royal, Matt sure as hell planned to see her again. Fate had pushed them together for a reason and he couldn't ignore that.

"I'm going to be here awhile. My grandfather's old estate is on the edge of town. It's sat empty for several years. Figure I should think about having it renovated and perhaps selling. For now, I'm staying at The Bellamy."

The five-star establishment had been recently renovated into a luxurious hotel. Matt had requested the penthouse and had paid extra to have it ready on the same day he'd had his assistant call for the reservation.

Money might have gotten him pretty much everything he wanted in life, but there was still a void. Something was missing and he had no clue what it was.

Rachel slid those plump lips around her straw again and Matt found himself shifting in his seat once more. He'd been in her presence for all of ten minutes and it was as if no time had passed at all. He still craved her, still found her one of the most stunning women he'd ever known. Still wondered what would've happened between them if Billy hadn't been at that party.

Actually, there wasn't a day that went by that he didn't wonder. If he were being honest, most of the women he'd hooked up with were just fillers for the one he truly wanted.

Matt set his mug on the table, then leaned closer to her. "Listen, Rachel…"

"No." She held up her hand and shook her head. "Let's not revisit the past. Not quite yet."

He stared at her for another minute, wanting to deal with the proverbial elephant in the room, and yet needing to dodge it at the same time.

Finally, he nodded. "Since we're both in town for a while, I'll treat you to dinner tonight."

Rachel laughed. "I'm not the carefree woman I used to be, Matt. I'm a single mother with responsibilities."

"Bring your daughter."

Where had that come from? He'd never asked a woman and her child on a date. Had he ever even dated a woman with a kid?

He hadn't. But none of that mattered, because no other woman was Rachel. Besides, he wanted to see Billy's daughter. His best friend might not have been the world's greatest husband, but he was a good friend and his child would be the last connection to him.

Rachel's smile widened as she reached out and gripped his hand. "It's a date."

Matt glanced down at their joined hands and wondered why he'd just jumped head first into the exact situation he'd been running from. If he stayed around Royal too long with Rachel, he didn't know how long he could resist her…or if he'd even try.

# Two

"From the way you're eyeing those photos, maybe you should consider bidding on your own bachelor."

Smiling, Rachel glanced up from the glossy images all spread out across the farm-style kitchen table to look at Alexis. Each picture featured a single man in Royal who had agreed to step up to the plate and be auctioned for a good cause. All funds would go toward the Pancreatic Cancer Research Foundation, but each woman writing the check would be winning a fantasy date with one hunky bachelor.

Rachel and Alexis were still searching for someone who could be the "big draw" or headliner.

"I think I'll just stick to the marketing and working behind the scenes and not worry so much about getting my fantasy date." Rachel blew out a breath and flattened her palms on the spread of photos. She did some quick figures in her head of what she could donate and still live off of until she completed her degree and got a paying job. "Don't worry, I'll still write a check for the cause. There are so many great guys who agreed to help… I'm just not sure which one we should use as the main event."

Alexis dropped to a chair next to Rachel and started sliding the images around. She picked up one, then set it aside, picked up another, dismissed it, too. There were so many options, from doctors to lawyers, ranchers to pilots. Royal had quite the variety of upstanding men. How were all of these hotties still single?

"The problem is these guys are all fabulous," Alexis stated, her blue eyes searching all of the options. "You can't go wrong with any of them. We do need the final man to be someone spectacular, someone the ladies won't mind writing an exorbitant amount for."

A small white paper with handwritten notes was paper clipped to the top right corner of each picture. The brief stats gave basic details of the bachelor: name, age, occupation. The overwhelming response from handsome, eligible men to help with the charity auction was remarkable. The Pancreatic Cancer Research Foundation would no doubt get a fat check afterward.

Gus and Alexis had done all the grunt work lining up the bachelors and it was Rachel's job to make sure word got out and women flocked with full purses to the biggest event of the year.

"We need to get these framed," Rachel murmured, thinking aloud. "They need to be propped on easels and in sturdy wood frames to showcase all this glorious masculinity."

They'd have to strategically set them around the outdoor garden area at the Texas Cattleman's Club so the women could come early and get an idea of who they wanted to bid on. Once Rachel went to the site, she could better plan all the details of how to arrange things.

She had already made a mock-up of the programs that would be handed out at the door. The program featured the bachelors with their regular posed image, plus she'd requested something playful or something to show their true personality.

"I have a spreadsheet of the order I think they should go in," Rachel stated. "Sorry, I know that's not quite marketing, but I was up late last night and started thinking of the best way to advertise and then I started numbering them and—"

"I get it. Your OCD kicked in and you ran with it." Alexis reached for her girlfriend's hand and squeezed. "I'll take any help I can get, and having you stay here is just like being in college. Well, with a child and less parties, but I love having you at the ranch."

Rachel loved being here, as well. She had been feeling adrift, but when Alexis had invited her to Royal, she figured this was just the break from life she needed. Who knew? Maybe Royal would become home. The big-city feel with the small-town attitude of everyone helping each other was rather nice.

Plus, there was the bonus of her best friend living here. Ellie seemed to have taken to Alexis and Gus.

"Lone Wolf Ranch is gorgeous," Rachel said, beaming. "I'm still excited you asked me to help with this auction. I think it's going to pull in more money than you ever thought possible."

Alexis pulled her hand away and blew out a sigh. "I don't know. I've set a pretty large goal. This fund-raiser means more to me than just money. I want to honor my grandmother's memory and make my grandfather proud of me at the same time. They did so much for me growing up."

Rachel knew this was so much more than a show or a popularity contest. Alexis lost her grandmother to pancreatic cancer and all of the funds from The Great Royal Bachelor Auction would go straight to the foundation in loving memory of Sarah Slade.

"She would definitely be proud of you," Rachel stated. "You're doing great work."

"I think you're doing most of it. I'd seriously be overwhelmed without you."

Rachel pulled all of the photos into a stack and neatened them up with a tap onto the table. "I'd say we make a great team."

The back door opened and Alexis's grandfather, Gus Slade, stepped inside. He swiped the back of his arm across his forehead and blew out a whistle.

"An old man could get used to walking in his back door and seeing two beautiful ladies."

Rachel flashed him a grin. If Gus was about thirty years younger, she'd make him the headliner for the auction. The elderly widower was quite the charmer and his dashing good looks and ruggedness would make him a surefire hit. No woman could resist his thick silver hair and broad shoulders. The weathered, tanned skin and wrinkles around his blue eyes only added to his masculine appeal. Why couldn't women age as gracefully?

"Where is the youngest lady?" Gus asked as he headed to the fridge and pulled out a bottle of water.

"Ellie needed a nap," Rachel replied. "She was rather cranky."

"She's a sweetheart," Gus defended. "I get a little cranky when I need a nap, too."

Rachel's heart swelled at how easily Alexis and her grandfather just took in two stray guests as if they were all one big happy family. Rachel had only been in Royal a short time, but she already felt like this was home. She hadn't really had a sense of belonging since Billy's death. Staying in Dallas in their home hadn't felt right. Especially considering the house they'd lived in had been purchased without her approval. He'd surprised her with it and she'd never really liked the vast space. The two-story home had seemed too staid, too cold.

She'd sold that house not too long ago and moved to a small rental house, much to the shock of Billy's family. Speaking of, life had been even more stressful with her in-laws hovering and making it a point to let her know they'd be willing to keep Ellie for a while so Rachel could finish her degree.

Then Billy's brother and his wife offered to take Ellie to make Rachel's life "easier." What the hell? She didn't care about easy. She cared about her child and providing a stable future.

Ellie was the only family she had and Rachel wasn't going to be separated from her for any amount of time. She'd give up her degree first. Ellie was her world... a world Rachel hadn't even known she'd wanted until the time came.

Billy hadn't wanted children and they'd both been taken by surprise when Rachel had gotten pregnant. Rachel had slid into the idea of motherhood and couldn't imagine a greater position to be in. Billy, on the other hand, hadn't gotten used to the idea before his death. In fact, that was one of the things they'd argued about right before he'd left that fateful day.

Rachel didn't have many regrets in life, but that argument still haunted her.

"Well, I hope you both are saving your appetites for a good dinner tonight." Gus's statement pulled Rachel from her thoughts. "I've got the chef preparing the best filets with homemade mashed potatoes and her special gravy, and baby carrots fresh from the garden."

All of that sounded so amazing. Any other night Rachel would welcome all those glorious calories. In fact, she'd enjoyed each meal their chef prepared over the past several days. If she hung around much longer she'd definitely be packing on the pounds.

"I actually have plans."

Alexis and Gus both turned to her like she'd just announced her candidacy for president. Rachel couldn't help but laugh at their shocked faces.

"I ran into an old friend earlier at Daily Grind and he asked to see me tonight. I'll be taking Ellie, so don't worry. You won't be babysitting."

Alexis waved her hands and shook her head. "Hold up. Forget the babysitting, which I'd happily do. You said *he*. You're going on a date?"

Rachel cringed. "No, not a date. Matt is an old friend."

"Matt who?" Gus asked, his brows drawing inward like a concerned parent.

"Galloway."

Gus's features relaxed as he nodded. "Businessman from Dallas, also a member of TCC. So, he asked you on a date?"

"No, it's not a date," she repeated, feeling like perhaps she shouldn't have disclosed her plans.

"Matt Galloway. Oh, I remember him," Alexis murmured. "A businessman from Dallas sounds perfect. How old is he now? Early thirties, right?"

"A few years older than me. Why do you say he's perfect?"

Alexis's smile beamed and she merely stared. Then Rachel realized exactly where her friend's thoughts had traveled.

"No." Rachel shook her head and gripped the stack of photos. "We have our guys and I'm not asking my friend to do this. I couldn't. We just reconnected after a year apart and he was one of Billy's best friends. It would just be too weird."

Not to mention her heart rate still hadn't recovered from their morning together. Part of her felt guilty for the way she'd reacted. Yes, her husband was gone, but was it okay to already feel a flicker of desire for another man? And one of her friends at that. Surely her sensations were all just heightened over their reunion. Rachel was confident the next time she saw Matt it would just be like old times when they hung out as pals.

And if that attraction tried to rear its ugly head, Rachel would just have to ignore it. A romantic entanglement between the two of them was *never* going to happen. Besides, even though a chunk of time had passed, Rachel still considered Matt someone special in her life. So, no. She couldn't ask him to put himself up on the stage…especially considering he was trying to stay out of the public eye.

"You didn't tell me he was named Most Eligible Bachelor in Texas," Alexis exclaimed.

Rachel blinked and focused on her friend who had her phone in hand, waving it around. An image of Matt in a tux on the red carpet posing in front of some charitable gala had Rachel sighing.

"No, I didn't tell you that. One of the reasons why he's in Royal is to lie low."

"Rach, no guy can look like this and have women ignore him. It's not possible."

"Looks like a perfect candidate for you to bid on, Lex," Gus chimed in with a nudge to his granddaughter. "You're putting in all this work—you should pick out a date, as well."

The idea of her best friend and her other friend hooking up hit the wrong chord in Rachel. But what could she say? She had no claims on Matt, and Alexis was single. They both could do whatever they wanted...but Rachel wasn't so sure she'd like it.

"Poor guy," Gus added, leaning over to look at the photo. "It's hell when the women are all over you and you have no place to hide. I feel his pain."

Alexis rolled her eyes and laid her phone down on the table. "Ignore him. He's a romantic. But let's focus on Matt. Seems like he's the perfect big name for our auction needs. Figured I'd look him up really quick and see how we can market him."

As if he were cattle ready to go to the market. Rachel was fine discussing the other bachelors; in fact, she rather enjoyed using her creativity and schooling to make each guy stand out in a unique way. But something about the idea of Matt up for grabs really irritated the hell out of her.

Perhaps it was because Rachel knew for a fact that the female attendees would bid high on the very sexy, very wealthy Matt Galloway, but she didn't want to give them the opportunity.

First, she'd feel like a jerk asking him when he'd been up-front as to his reasons for being in Royal. He was dodging this new title and clearly not comfortable with the added attention.

Second, the idea of women waving their paddles and

tossing money for a fantasy date with Matt...well, she was jealous. *There.* She admitted it—if only to herself.

Why was she suddenly so territorial? She'd always found Matt attractive, always respected and admired him. How could she throw him into the lion's den, so to speak, and expect not to have strong feelings on the matter? They were friends. She should feel protective, but there were other feelings swirling around inside her, and none of them remained in the friend zone.

"Tell me you'll at least think about it."

Rachel met Alexis's pleading gaze. She was here to help her friend—they were actually helping each other—and this auction was a huge deal to the Slade family. How could Rachel say no when Alexis had opened her home and heart to Rachel and Ellie?

"I'll see what I can do," she conceded with a belabored sigh. "But I can't promise anything and I won't beg."

Alexis squealed. "All I ask is you try."

Gus rested a large, weathered hand on Alexis's shoulder. "My granddaughter is all Slade. When she wants something, she finds a way to make it happen. So, which guy are you bidding on, Lex?"

Alexis rolled her eyes. "Stop trying to marry me off. I'm working on raising money, not finding a guy to put a ring on my finger."

Rachel scooted her chair back and came to her feet. "Well, I'm pretty determined to help bring in all the money possible, but I won't make Matt feel uncomfortable."

"I understand," Alexis said, nodding in agreement. "But, I'll wait up so I can hear all about your date and see if he agreed to be auctioned."

That naughty gleam in her friend's eyes was not

going to last. If Alexis knew all that Rachel, Matt and Billy had been through, she'd understand just how delicate this situation was. But she wasn't wanting to get into all of that now. She didn't want to revisit the ordeal that was her marriage and the gap of time she'd missed Matt.

"Feel free to wait up, but I assure you I won't be out long. I have a baby, remember? Early bedtimes are a must."

"Why don't you leave her here?" Gus suggested. "It's nice having a little one around, and she's no trouble."

Alexis stood up and patted her grandfather's shoulder. "If that's a hint, relax. It's going to be a while before I give you a great-grandchild. I'm a little busy in case you haven't noticed."

Rachel didn't miss the way Alexis's eyes landed on the top photo…which featured the very handsome Daniel Clayton.

Alexis Slade and Daniel Clayton had once been quite an item, but they'd fallen apart and Rachel still didn't know what had happened. Whenever Rachel brought up the topic, her friend not-so-subtly steered their chat in another direction. Eventually, Rachel would find out what was going on between her friend and the mysterious ex.

"What time is your date?" Alexis asked.

Resigned to the fact nobody believed her about the nondate, Rachel shrugged. "We kept it open. He realizes I need to be flexible with a little one. I'll head over to his hotel room later. Once Ellie wakes, I need to grab a shower and we both need to get ready."

"What are you taking?" Alexis asked.

"Taking?"

"A bottle of wine? A dessert? I'm sure we have something the cook has whipped up. She always has breads."

Rachel shook her head. "I'm not taking anything. You're letting that romantic streak show."

"Just trying to help," she muttered.

Rachel patted her friend's arm. "I know, but I've only been a widow for a year. I'm not ready to rush into anything."

Her marriage had started out in a whirlwind of lust and stars in their eyes. Rachel and Billy had lived life to the fullest and loved every minute of it. Then the pregnancy had slid between them and continued to drive a wedge through their relationship. They'd built something on top of shaky ground and hadn't realized until after the fact.

Unfortunately, Rachel would never know if their marriage would've worked itself out. Would Billy have ever settled down and stepped into the role of loyal father and devoted husband?

Pain gripped her from so many angles, but she had to keep pushing forward for her sake as well as Ellie's. Rumored infidelity and ugly arguments weren't how she wanted to remember her late husband.

"I'm going to go check on Ellie," Rachel told them. "She should be waking soon. Lex, I'll get you a list of the order I think we should use for the auction. If Matt isn't onboard, then Daniel might be our best bet as the big-name draw."

Her friend's lips thinned, her jaw clenched. Gus blew out a breath that Rachel would almost label as relief, and he had a satisfied grin. Whatever was going on with Daniel and Alexis—or wasn't going on—was quite a mystery.

One thing was certain, though—Alexis was not a fan of having Daniel up on the auction block. Ironically, Rachel still wasn't too keen on the idea of Matt being up there, either.

Because if that came to pass, one or both of them might just have to grab a paddle and place their own bids.

# Three

Matt tipped the waitstaff a hefty amount for their quick, efficient service and for meeting his last-minute demands. He hadn't known what to have for dinner for Rachel, let alone an infant.

Infant? Toddler? What was the right term for an eleven-month-old? He knew nothing about children and had never taken to the notion of having his own, so he'd never bothered to learn.

But he was interested in Rachel, and she and Ellie were a package deal that he didn't mind. No matter the years that passed, no matter the fact she'd married his best friend, nothing at all had ever diminished his desire for Rachel. He'd hid it as best he could, often gritting his teeth and biting his tongue when Billy would be disrespectful to Rachel's needs.

Once Rachel got pregnant, the two started fighting more, and Billy's answer was to get out of the house so they both could cool off. Those times when Matt and Billy were at the Dallas TCC clubhouse shooting pool and drinking beer or even out on Matt's boat on the lake, Billy never did grasp that running didn't solve the problem. He never once acted excited about the pregnancy. He never mentioned how Rachel felt about being a mother. Billy's life didn't change at all and Matt knew Rachel hurt alone.

He also knew she'd been excited about the pregnancy, but how much could she actually enjoy it knowing her husband wasn't fully committed?

Whenever Matt would mention anything to Billy about Rachel, the other man always told him to mind his own business and that he didn't know what marriage was like. Valid point, but Matt knew how to treat a woman and he damn well respected Rachel.

Matt stepped back and surveyed the dinner he'd had set up on the balcony. His penthouse suite at The Bellamy had a sweeping view of the immaculate grounds, yet was private enough he felt comfortable bringing Rachel out here to talk.

He hoped this setting was okay. For some asinine reason he was a damn nervous wreck. What the hell? There had never been a woman to make him question himself or his motives. Even when he and Rachel had been friends before, the main emotion that always hovered just below the surface had always been forbidden desire.

But she was a different woman now. She was a single mother seeking out a fresh start, not some short-term fling with her late husband's best friend. And he wasn't looking for anything more than exploring the connection and seeing if this was just one-sided.

Matt needed to curb his desire. She wasn't coming

here for a quickie. He'd invited her as a friend...and unfortunately, he feared that was the category she'd try to keep him in. Being near her again only put his desires right on the edge, and he had to retain control before he fell over the line of friendship and pulled her right with him.

Even now that she was single, he still had no chance with her because he was known as a ladies' man, the Most Eligible Bachelor in Texas, and Rachel was a sweetheart who wouldn't settle for anything less than happily-ever-after.

Damn that title. It had been nothing but a black cloud over him since he'd been given the title some men would happily flaunt. He was not one of those men. He hadn't even been able to go on a damn date back in Dallas without a snap of the camera or someone coming up to him asking for his autograph.

The final straw had been when he'd come home to his penthouse and a reporter was lurking outside his door. He'd fired his security guard promptly after that irritating inconvenience.

The one woman he wanted could never be his, even temporarily. Perhaps that was his penance for lusting after his best friend's wife.

Matt looked at all the items he'd ordered. He might not know much about children, but he'd paid his assistant a nice bonus to make a few things happen within the span of a few hours and by just making some calls. Even from Dallas, the woman was working her magic here in Royal and had baby things delivered in record time. That woman definitely deserved a raise. She saved his ass on a daily basis.

With one last glance, he started having doubts. The balcony ledge went up waist-high on him, the wrought

iron slats were about an inch apart. There shouldn't be
a problem with Ellie out here, especially with all the
other paraphernalia to keep her occupied, but seriously,
what did he know about this? Did she walk or crawl?
Did she look like Rachel or Billy?

Nerves pumped through him and he didn't like it.
Not one bit. Matt never got nervous. He'd handled multibillion-dollar mergers and never broken a sweat, so it
baffled his mind as to why he was getting all worked up.

Besides, what did he think would happen here tonight? Did he truly believe they could pick back up
where they'd left off before Billy died? He'd deserted
her due to his own selfish needs and worry he wouldn't
be able to control those wants. He'd had to push her
away for both of their sakes.

Surely he wasn't so delusional to think that she'd…
what? Want to tumble into bed with him? He'd be a
complete liar if he said he hadn't fantasized about her
since the moment they'd met. There was probably some
special pocket of hell for men like him, coveting his
best friend's wife.

But Rachel had always been different. Perhaps it was
her beauty or the way his entire body tightened with
desire when she was around. Maybe it was the way she
could go up against anyone in a verbal sparring match
that he found so sexy.

Hell, he had no idea. What he was sure of, though,
was that having her come to his suite and bring her child
along might have been the worst idea he'd ever had.

No, the worst idea he'd had was letting Billy ask
Rachel out first. That was where Matt had gone wrong
from the start.

The bell chimed throughout the suite and he raked a
hand over his cropped hair as he crossed the spacious

room. There was no going back now, and he wasn't about to keep second-guessing himself. Rachel was a friend; so what if he had her over for dinner?

*Yet you want more.*

He wished like hell the devil on his shoulder would shut up. Matt was well aware of exactly what he wanted from Rachel, but he respected her enough not to seduce her.

With a flick of the lock, Matt pulled the door open and every single best intention of keeping his thoughts platonic vanished.

The formfitting blue shirt that matched her eyes hung off one shoulder. Those well-worn jeans hugged her shapely hips, and her little white sneakers had him immediately thinking back to the younger version he'd first met. But this grown-up Rachel had a beautiful baby girl on her hip…a baby that was a mirror image of her mother right down to the prominent dimples around her mouth.

Matt had always been fascinated by Rachel's mouth and those damn dimples. Every time she smiled, he'd been mesmerized.

"Come in."

Geesh, he'd been staring and reminiscing like some hormonal teen. He was a damn grown man, CEO of a billion-dollar company, and he stood here as if he'd never seen an attractive woman before.

"Wow, this is one snazzy hotel."

Rachel moved into the living area and spun in a slow circle. Her daughter still clutched her little arms around her mother's shoulders.

"I thought the outside was impressive," she stated. "But this penthouse suite is bigger than the apartment I'd been renting."

Matt frowned. Why the hell had she lived in such a small space to begin with? He understood her emotional reasoning for selling the home she and Billy shared, but why an apartment? Could she not afford another home?

He had no right to ask about her financial standing, but that's exactly what he wanted to do. Obviously this wasn't something he'd get into with Ellie here.

"I figure this is a good place to hide while I'm in town," he joked. "I can work from the offices at the TCC clubhouse and come back here and enjoy the amenities of the gym and sauna, and having dinner here is no hardship."

Rachel patted her daughter's back. "Then you can stay up here on the balcony and look down on the peons and paparazzi?"

"Something like that," Matt laughed. "Actually, I had our dinner set up out there if you'd like to head out. The view is breathtaking."

Rachel moved toward the open French doors. "I don't know if it's safe to have Ellie out here."

As she stepped outside, she gasped as she took in everything he'd done. "Matt, my word! What didn't you think of?"

Matt shrugged, wondering if he'd gone overboard. Hell, he hadn't known what to do, so in those instances his default was always to do everything. His motto had always been "Better to have too much than not enough."

"I wasn't sure if she used a high chair," he stated, stepping over the threshold to join her. "When I called my assistant for reinforcements, I told her to ask for the works. The guy came to set all of this up and asked how many kids I had."

Rachel laughed as she turned and surveyed the spacious balcony. Matt couldn't take his eyes off her or her daughter. He wasn't even sure how to feel looking at Billy's child, but when he saw that sweet girl, he really only saw Ellie.

Guilt slithered in slowly from so many different angles. He shouldn't still have been lusting after his late friend's wife, but there was clearly no stopping that. But he also shouldn't be wanting to get closer to Rachel knowing full well that he wasn't looking for a family or any type of long-term commitment.

Being married to a career didn't leave much time for feeding into a relationship. Besides, he couldn't lose Rachel as a friend. The risks were too high that that was exactly what would happen if he pressed on with his pent up desires.

Rachel still hadn't said anything as she continued to take in everything. One area of the stretched balcony looked as if a department store had set up their latest display of baby gear. High chair, Pack 'n Play, play mat, toys, stationary swing…

"I don't know the age for any of this stuff, so if you need something else let me know and I'll call—"

"No." Rachel turned back around to face him, her eyes filled with unshed tears. "This is… I don't even have words. You invited me for dinner and thought of everything for Ellie."

His gaze darted to the child in question. Her wide brown eyes, exactly like Rachel's, were focused on him. She clutched a little yellow blanket against her chest and huddled against her mother for security. Something shifted inside Matt, an unknown emotion he couldn't label and wasn't sure he wanted to explore.

"She's beautiful." Matt turned his gaze back to Rachel as a shimmer of awareness flowed through him. "Just like her mother."

She blinked and glanced away, never one to take a compliment. That had never stopped him from offering them. Even when the three of them had all hung out, back in the day, Matt would tell her she looked nice or he liked her hair. There hadn't been a time he recalled hearing Billy compliment his wife, and Matt hadn't been able to help himself. Billy had been a great friend, yet from everything Matt could tell, he had been a lousy husband.

But really, all of this was a moot point. Because regardless of the state of their marriage, Matt knew he shouldn't be trying to make a play for Billy's wife. He had regrets in his life, but this might be the most asshole-ish thing he'd ever done. Still, Matt had never backed away from what he wanted…and he wanted the hell out of Rachel Kincaid.

"Who else is eating with us?" Rachel asked as she stared at the spread he'd ordered.

"Just us. I ordered all of your favorites. Well, what I remember you ordering in the past, but I didn't know what you were in the mood for."

Rachel wrinkled her nose. "I'm a boring creature of habit. I pretty much stick with pizza, pasta or any other carb. This all looks amazing."

He took a step forward and offered a smile. "You're not boring," he corrected. "There's nothing wrong with knowing what you want. I'm the same way. I see something I want, I make it mine."

Damn it. He needed to calm the hell down. Hadn't he told himself to get control over his desires?

But saying and doing were clearly two different things because he couldn't stop himself. Rachel pulled out emotions in him he couldn't even describe.

Her eyes widened. "Are you talking about food or something else?"

Matt shrugged, forcing himself to take a step back and not get her any more flustered. "We'll discuss food. For now."

Rachel moved to the Pack 'n Play and sat Ellie down. The little girl whimpered for a moment before Rachel pulled a doll from the diaper bag on her shoulder. Damn it, why hadn't he taken that from her?

"Let me help." He took the bag from her shoulder. "Damn, woman, what do you have in here?"

Rachel straightened and turned. "It's amazing how one little person can need so many things. Diapers, wipes, butt paste—"

"Pardon?"

She laughed and went on. "I have an extra change of clothes in case of blowouts, food, snacks, toys, pain reliever for her swollen gums…"

"I don't know if I want any more information about the butt paste and blowouts." Matt set the diaper bag next to the door. "I'll fix you a plate. The restaurant downstairs serves some of the best food I've ever had and I've been all around the world. I ordered their rosemary bread because when I called, they said they'd just taken it from the oven."

"Well, you clearly know me," she said with a wide smile that punched him with another dose of lust. "If it's carbs, I'm in."

"Do you still have a love for key lime pie?"

Rachel rolled her eyes. "If you mean do I still inhale it like it's my job, then yes. I don't even care about the added pounds. Key lime pie is so worth it."

"You're still just as stunning as always, Rachel. No pounds could change that."

She crossed her arms over her chest and tilted her head. "I'm starting to see why you were the recipient of the most prestigious bachelor title. You're still quite the charmer."

He might try to charm other women—well, he didn't try; he flat-out *did* charm them. But with Rachel, he wasn't trying. He always spoke the truth, always wanted her to know her value and how special she was.

*If you cared so much, you wouldn't have let a year pass since seeing her.*

"I've missed you," she stated, as if reading his mind. "I miss our friendship."

Friendship. Yes. That's the only label their relationship could have, because she was a widow, a single mother and she wasn't looking to jump back into anything. Honestly, he wasn't looking to fill the role of Daddy, either, but that didn't stop the fact he wanted Rachel as more than a friend.

Likely she'd thrown that out there as a reminder, but he dismissed the words. He'd respect her if she flat-out wasn't interested, but he had to know. He had to know if she was interested in him. He needed to find out if she burned for him as much as he for her. Would she even want to attempt anything physical knowing he wasn't ready for anything more?

Why did this all have to be so damn complicated? Oh, right. Because he'd spent years building and attempting to ignore these emotions.

"I'd better eat before she starts fussing," Rachel told him as she went to take a seat. "There's always a small window of opportunity and I rarely get warm food because I feed her first."

Matt urged Rachel toward the table and pulled her chair out. "If she fusses, I'm sure I can hold her and entertain her while you finish, or I can feed her. Regardless, you are eating right now while it's warm, and there will be no arguments."

Rachel looked up at him and quirked one brow. "You ready to play Uncle Matt?"

Ouch. That stung. He wasn't sure what he wanted to be called…then again, he hadn't given it much thought. He was having difficulty processing much of anything with that creamy shoulder of Rachel's on display and her familiar floral fragrance teasing his senses.

"I win over billion-dollar mergers before breakfast," he joked. "I'm pretty sure I can handle a little person."

Rachel snorted. "Don't get too cocky. It's harder than it looks."

"I never doubted that for a minute," he corrected. "Now eat. There's plenty."

Once she took a seat, Matt eased it closer to the table. He immediately started filling her plate with rosemary bread and Alfredo over penne and chicken, then filled her glass with pinot grigio.

"You put all of this together pretty quick considering you just asked me today."

Matt set her food in front of her before taking a seat across the table. "Just a few calls and the right connections. Why wouldn't I go all out for a friend I haven't seen in a year?"

Her stare leveled his. "I'd think a cup of coffee or a stroll in the park would've sufficed."

Matt reached across the table and squeezed her fingers. Her eyes immediately darted to their joined hands. "You have every right to be angry with me."

"I'm not angry," she retorted.

Matt raked his thumb across the silky ridge of her knuckles before easing back. He noticed she didn't wear her wedding band any longer and part of him swelled with approval and excitement.

"Hurt then. You can't lie to me, Rachel. Billy's death did something to both of us."

Like the fact he couldn't be the one to console her. He simply…damn it, he couldn't. He'd wanted too much for too long so he'd had to let her go and pray someone else offered the comfort she needed. Because if he'd had to hold her day after day, night after night until her pain had eased…

"I was hurt," she admitted. "I still am, actually. Care to tell me why you just disappeared?"

"I texted."

Such a lame defense, yet the words left his mouth before he could stop himself. Out of everything and everyone in his life, Rachel was the one he'd barely been able to control himself around.

"I don't really want to dredge up the past right now. I want answers from you, but let's not do it tonight." She picked up her fork and offered a typical dimpled smile. "Billy was a big part of my life, but I've worked hard at moving on. I'm trying to make a future for Ellie and me. Always looking back isn't the way to do that."

He had to hand it to her. She'd hurt from her husband's death, from Matt's absence, from being thrust into being a single mother, yet she forced herself to trudge on.

"So, you're finishing your degree," he started, hoping to keep the topic on her life. "Where do you go from there?"

Rachel stabbed a piece of pasta and lifted a shoulder. "Right now I'm helping Alexis with the charity auction for the Pancreatic Cancer Research Foundation."

Impressed, Matt nodded in silent admiration.

"What's the auction? Do you have donations from area businesses?"

Rachel dropped her fork, pulled the napkin from her lap and dabbed the corners of her mouth. "We're auctioning men."

Matt stilled. "Excuse me?"

Those bright, beautiful eyes locked on his across the table. There was that mischievous gleam he'd seen from her in the past. He wasn't sure he wanted to know more.

"We're having a bachelor auction. Care to be Bachelor Fifteen?"

# Four

Way to go. Nothing like blurting out her thoughts without easing into the request. Granted she'd promised Alexis she'd ask Matt for the favor, but Rachel probably could've done a better lead in.

"Bachelor Fifteen."

The words slid slowly through his sultry, kissable lips as he set his fork down and continued to hold her gaze without so much as blinking. She really needed to not stare at his mouth, and she absolutely should not be imagining them on hers.

Rachel cringed. "So, we need another bachelor and we were wanting one that would be fairly popular, and you came to town, we're friends, you've got that new title and…"

He sat still as stone.

"I'm rambling," she muttered. "You don't want the hype or the press. I get it. Forget I asked."

Rachel focused on the potatoes on her plate. Carbs

were always the answer, especially when she'd just verbally assaulted their friendship.

"Is that why you came?" he asked.

Rachel immediately met his gaze. "What? No. I wanted to see you. I wanted you to meet Ellie. Earlier I was working on the auction and Alexis and I started talking and your name came up."

Matt offered that cocky, familiar smirk. "Is that right?"

He was clearly intrigued by the idea of being the topic of conversation, but she wasn't about to feed that ego.

"But don't feel obligated to agree just because we're friends. In fact, forget I asked."

Rachel started to reach for her sweet tea just as Ellie let out a cry of frustration. Pushing back in her chair, Rachel came to her feet, but Matt was quicker. He stood and crossed to the Pack 'n Play, reached down and lifted Ellie out.

Unable to look away, Rachel stared at the way Matt's large hands held on to her daughter. Ellie's little mouth slid into a frown as she stared at the stranger. She reached up and patted her tiny fingers against his mouth.

"Here, let me take her."

Matt shook his head as he made his way back to the table. "She's fine. Enjoy your dinner and we can discuss this auction some more."

Rachel eased back into her seat as Matt sat back down in his own chair. Immediately Ellie's arm smacked Matt's glass over, spilling his drink into his plate of food.

"I'm so sorry." Rachel jumped up and grabbed her daughter before handing Matt her cloth napkin. "Let me go inside and get a towel. Go finish my plate and I'll get this cleaned up—"

Matt grabbed her arm. "Relax. Nobody's hurt here and it's just a spill. Maybe we should go inside where Ellie can play on the floor and we can sit on the sofa and have dinner?"

Rachel wanted to gather her child and their things and leave to save further embarrassment, but she knew that would be rude after all the trouble he'd gone to. So against her better instincts, she nodded.

"I think she's getting hungry," she replied. "Let me feed her and then I'll help clean and carry things inside."

"Take care of her. I'll take care of everything else."

Rachel stared for a moment until she realized he was serious. She couldn't help but think back to Billy, who hadn't wanted kids, who'd been flat out angry over the pregnancy. Yet here was Matt offering to care for Ellie while Rachel did something as simple as eat her dinner.

She shouldn't compare the two men. Sure they were friends, but they'd always been opposite. Billy had been the adventurer, the wanderer, which had been the initial draw for Rachel.

Matt was just around for a good time. He was content in Dallas, happy with life and work. He was well-grounded and only got away to travel to Galloway Cove.

Who wouldn't be happy owning their own island? At this point in her life, Rachel just wanted to own her own home, not the house Billy had bought and not some place her in-laws wanted her to have. She wanted to do life her way.

Several moments later, Ellie had been fed. After cleaning her up, Rachel scooted the coffee table off to the far wall and left an open area for Ellie to play in without hitting her head on the furniture.

Matt came back in and quickly had their food all set up, acting as if an infant hadn't just turned his steak and potatoes into tea soup.

"I'm really sorry about that," Rachel offered as he sat on the sofa next to her.

"Why do you keep apologizing? Just because I don't have children doesn't mean I'm going to get angry over an accident."

Rachel glanced down to Ellie who was quite content plucking the nose on the stuffed toy monkey. "I just never know how people will respond. Some people don't like children."

"I've never really seen myself in the role of a father, but I like kids. I mean, I highly doubt she knocked my glass down on purpose."

Rachel settled her plate into her lap. "You can eat at the table, you know. You don't have to sit here with me."

All of this was too familial, and being in a situation like this with Matt only made her fantasize about things she could never have…at least not with this man.

"Tell me more about the auction," he said, ignoring her previous statement.

"Matt, really—"

"Tell me."

His gruff command had her pulling in a deep breath. "Alright. The bachelor auction is going to raise funds for the Pancreatic Cancer Research Foundation. Alexis's grandmother and Gus's wife passed away from that. When Alexis invited me to come visit, I offered to help with the auction. I'm not quite finished with my marketing degree, but I'm thrilled to be doing something along the lines of where I want to be. Not only am I helping the cause—this will look great on a resume when I finish my degree."

"They're lucky to have you working on this," Matt stated with such conviction she turned to him in surprise .

"You have a lot of confidence for someone who hasn't seen me in a year."

Matt finished chewing before he replied. "I know you, Rachel. Maybe better than you know yourself. You're determined, headstrong and always looking out for everyone but yourself."

His blue eyes locked with hers, causing a warm melting sensation to spread through her.

"Alexis couldn't have chosen a better person for the job. You don't need a degree to have compassion."

She wasn't even sure how to respond to such praise. She hadn't been looking for a compliment. They finished their dinner in silence and Ellie played without interruption.

"Let me take the plates to the kitchen," Rachel said, reaching for Matt's empty dish.

"I've got it."

"You've done enough. I can take care of this."

His suite at The Bellamy was absolutely dreamlike. Rachel couldn't imagine being a guest here. She'd never want to leave.

"I invited you."

Matt took the dishes and headed toward the open kitchen area. Having a sexy man do domestic chores was something no woman could look away from. Added to that, the thin navy sweater he wore stretched beautifully across his broad shoulders, captivating her attention.

"You're not doing anything except telling me more about the auction," he stated. "What do I have to do as Bachelor Fifteen?"

Rachel laughed, more out of shock than humor. "You don't have to put yourself up for auction. We have guys who will bring in the goal Alexis is hoping to raise."

To Rachel's surprise, Matt didn't sit back on the sofa with her, but on the floor with Ellie. With one hand propped behind him, he rested his other arm on the knee he'd drawn up.

"So when a woman wins her dream guy onstage, or however you're doing it—"

"In the gazebo at the TCC clubhouse," she interjected.

He nodded. "Fine. So when a lady's knight in shining armor steps from the gazebo and they gaze into each other's eyes, then what?"

Rachel eased down to the floor as well and couldn't help but laugh. "It's probably not going to be that dramatic. But, the ladies are bidding on a fantasy date. Whatever that might be. One of our bachelors is a pilot, so the winner could also choose to be flown in his private jet to a nice dinner. All of the guys bring something different to the table, which is exactly what we want so we can appeal to a variety of women."

"And their checkbooks."

Rachel smiled and nodded. "Exactly."

"How many bachelors have an island?"

"None."

"Then count me in."

Rachel jerked back. Ellie crawled to her and climbed onto her lap. "Just like that you're offering yourself up?"

"It's one date, Rachel. I'm not marrying anyone. If it's for a good cause, and it is, I'm willing." He handed Ellie her monkey when she wobbled closer to him. "I'll match the donation of the bid made on me, as well."

She couldn't believe how easy this was. "You could

just write a check if you're only wanting to help financially."

"Sounds like you don't want me to be on the auction block," he threw back with a quirked brow.

That's precisely what she sounded like because that's exactly how she felt. But she had no right, and she truly had no motive to keep him all to herself. Matt didn't belong to anyone, especially not his best friend's lonely widow.

"I just want you to be fully aware of what you're getting into."

His eyes held hers and they did that thing again, that thing where he seemed as if he could look right into her soul and grab onto her deepest thoughts. However, it was best for them both that he couldn't see her true feelings.

"I think I can handle myself," he murmured. "Will you be bidding?"

Rachel's heart thudded in her chest. She honestly hadn't given it much thought until the idea of Matt being up for grabs came to light. Could she actually bid on him? What would he think? Would he think she was trying to date him? That she wanted to start something beyond friendship? Or would he think she was saving him from the other women waving their paddles?

"Do you want me to bid on you?"

Why did her voice come out so husky like some sultry vixen? Because she certainly was no seductress. For pity's sake, her child had fallen asleep on her lap and Rachel was acting like some love-struck teen.

Matt lifted a shoulder. "What would your dream date be? We might be able to work out a deal and both get what we want."

What did that mean? Did he want a date with her?

Why the hell was this all so confusing now? When she'd been married to Billy and they'd all gone out with friends and had a good time, she and Matt would joke and laugh and there was never this crackling tension.

Crackling tension. What a great way to say sexual energy, though she had no idea if this was all one-sided or not. Or had this been there before and she'd never noticed? Surely she would've sensed it if Matt had been interested.

"I don't know what my dream date would be," she admitted. "I've never thought about it."

Matt reached over and Rachel thought for sure he was reaching for her, but he slid a wisp of a curl from Ellie's forehead. Rachel's heart flipped. She had no idea what to expect with Matt and his reaction to Ellie, but he'd put her needs ahead of anything else. The baby items on the patio had to have cost a ridiculous amount, and now he sat here acting so caring and doting toward her little girl as if this were the most natural thing in the world.

He settled his hand on her knee and Rachel realized he'd slid even closer. "What about a day out on my boat? You could relax and do nothing but get a suntan and snap your finger for another fruity drink."

Rachel tipped her head and smiled. "Do you honestly think I could relax and do nothing? When have you ever known me to laze around?"

Right now, though, it was getting rather difficult to think of anything because all she could concentrate on was his large, firm hand on her knee. Forget the fact a good portion of her lap had gone numb from Ellie's weight; she could most definitely feel Matt's searing touch.

"Okay, then, maybe a trip to Galloway Cove. You

could swim, have dinner on the beach, get a massage from one of my staff."

Rachel shook her head. "I'm pretty sure I won't be bidding. First of all, I'm not sure I could afford you once the ladies see your credentials. And second, I couldn't leave Ellie for an entire day."

"If you bid on me and win, Ellie could come, too. I have on-site staff at every single one of my homes."

Of course he did. Billy had come from money, but that was nothing compared to the lifestyle Matt lived. Billy partied with his money, but Matt invested. He had homes, jets, an island and who knew how many cars. Most likely he had businesses on the side from the company he ran. Men like him never had just one business going because that wouldn't be smart. And Matt was one of the most intelligent people Rachel had ever known.

"I think I better just write a check to the foundation and stay behind the scenes."

Matt's thumb stroked over her knee. Back and forth, back and forth. The warmth through the fabric of her capris ironically sent shivers through her.

"Matt," she whispered, not knowing what to say but realizing this moment was getting away from them.

"What if I want you to bid on me?" he asked, never looking away from her. "Maybe I want to give you that day you need. Perhaps it's time someone makes you take time for yourself."

Rachel didn't know what to say. She'd seen Matt charm women in the past, but she'd never been on the receiving end. He was dead serious that he wanted her to bid on him. But if she did that, if they went off on some fantasy date, Rachel couldn't guarantee that she'd be able to avoid temptation. Matt had always held a special place in her heart, but she was seeing him in a whole different light now. Getting mixed up with him on a physical level would only end in heartache…and she had plenty of that to last a lifetime.

"You don't have to answer now," he added. He hadn't eased back, nor had he removed his hand. "But I'm all in under one condition."

She was almost afraid to ask.

"And that is?"

That cocky, signature Matt Galloway grin spread across his face. "You're the only one I'm dealing with. As in the photos that need taking and anything else that is needed from me for the auction itself. You're it for me."

That last sentence seemed to spear straight through that tough exterior she'd shielded herself with. Matt had that power, a power she'd always known he possessed, but she'd never fully realized the impact he could have on her until now.

"I'm not exactly a professional photographer," she reminded him.

"I recall your hobby behind the lens and I would bet anything you've kept up with it, especially to take pictures of Ellie." He slid his hand away, but eased forward until their faces were only a few inches apart. "Do we have a deal?"

Rachel simply nodded, unable to speak with him so close. She wasn't sure what she was getting herself into, but Alexis would be thrilled to have Matt as the headliner. Wasn't that the goal?

# Five

Gus closed the tack box and blew out a sigh. He'd worked hard today, but he wouldn't have it any other way. Lone Wolf Ranch gave him the reason to get out of bed each day, especially since his beloved Sarah had passed. That made two women in his lifetime who had left an imprint on his heart. There was only so much heartache a man could take, and Gus had met his quota.

From here on out, he planned on devoting his every single day to his livestock, his ranch and his granddaughter. There was no way in hell his sweet Alexis could hook up with Daniel Clayton. That boy was nothing but trouble and the grandson of Rose Clayton… Gus's first love.

The Claytons were dead to him. He'd rather give up his ranch than see their families merge…and he sure as hell wasn't giving up his ranch.

The years he and Rose spent together all seemed

like a lifetime ago. In fact, it was. They'd been in love and Gus had worked his ass off to make sure he was ready for marriage before he set out to get approval from Rose's father.

Gus had never been so nervous, so excited, so ready to spend his life with the woman of his dreams. But when he'd come back, he'd discovered his beloved Rose had been married the year before to a man handpicked by her father.

Gus wasn't going down that road in his mind again. He'd traveled that path too many times to count, too many times wondering what the hell had happened. But in the end, he'd married Rose's best friend, Sarah, and they'd had a beautiful life together until she passed.

The rap of knuckles on wood had him turning from the stalls. Outlined in the doorway of his barn with the sun setting against her back stood Rose Clayton. He might as well have conjured her up from his thoughts. Lately his mind had been focused on her more than it should, but that was only because they were conspiring with each other…not that they were reconnecting. That love story had ended long ago.

"I hope this isn't a bad time," Rose stated, stepping into the barn.

She always appeared as if she were going to a tea party at the country club, but as she strode through the barn filled with the smell of hay and horses, Gus got a lump in his throat. She looked absolutely beautiful here. Her pale pink capris and matching jacket with a crisp white shirt and gold necklace created quite the contrast to his filthy work clothes. She'd always been that way, though…a vast juxtaposition from him.

Damn it. He needed to focus on the present, and not waste his time dwelling on nostalgic memories.

"I'm just finishing up for the day," he replied, adjusting the tip of his Stetson. "You're lucky Alexis isn't around or she'd wonder what you were doing here."

"I actually just saw her getting out of her car in town so I knew it was a safe time."

The way she looked at him as she moved through the open space, the way she spoke so softly, all of it was so Rose. Everything about her was precise, well-mannered, captivating.

And he'd always been the man who wasn't good enough for her. Being pushed from her life was the last time he'd ever allowed anyone to make him feel inferior.

But he could look and even admit that she was more stunning now than she'd been forty years ago.

"I was wondering how the auction is shaping up," Rose stated, clutching her purse with both hands. "I hadn't heard from you in a few days and I didn't know what Alexis has said."

Why did Rose seem so nervous? She typically had confidence he admired, even though they weren't friends—more like sworn enemies.

"Alexis and her friend Rachel were going over the list of names the other day. Daniel still hasn't fully committed even though he did allow us to put him on the roster. He told Rachel he was still on the fence, so you'll have to nudge him." He released a breath. "Rachel is doing the marketing and has all of his information and the headshot that you sent anonymously, but we'll need him to actually sign the contract."

Rose sighed. "That's what I was afraid of. I've told him he's a perfect bachelor. What woman wouldn't want to go out with a successful rancher? He has his own jet—he could take his fantasy date anywhere."

"But his fantasy date is my granddaughter," Gus reminded her tersely.

Rose pursed her pale pink lips and nodded. "I'll talk to him tomorrow."

"Alexis didn't seem all that pleased to see his name on the list when Rachel was going over it the other day."

"He'll be on that stage," Rose assured him. "We just have to make sure Alexis isn't the one bidding on him."

Gus smiled. "Oh, I'll have her busy when it's his turn. If I have to make up some backstage disaster, Alexis will not bid on Daniel. I've mentioned a few bachelors to her, but I'm pushing her toward Matt Galloway, Rachel's friend from Dallas. He seems perfect for my Lex."

Rose stared at him another moment before giving a curt nod. When the silence settled heavy between them, Gus propped his hands on his hips and tipped his head.

"Something else on your mind?" he asked.

She opened her mouth, then shut it. After a moment, she finally said, "No. That's all. I just want to keep this communication open if we're going to make sure this goes off exactly as planned."

Gus didn't believe her one bit. She could've called or texted. Showing up here was rash and dangerous. They might have ended things decades ago, but he still knew when she was lying.

"Rose."

"Were you happy?"

The question came out of nowhere and left him speechless for a second. From the soft tone, the questioning gaze, he knew exactly what she referred to.

"Of course."

He never understood the term *sad smile* until now.

The corners of Rose's mouth tipped up, but her low lids attempted to shield the pain in her eyes.

"That's all I ever wanted," she whispered.

Gus started to take a step forward, but Rose eased back and squared her shoulders. That fast she'd gathered herself together and whatever moment had just transpired had vanished.

"I'll keep you posted about Daniel."

When she turned to go, Gus couldn't stop himself. "You were happy with Ed, weren't you?"

Rose said nothing as she slowly turned and offered him that same less-than-convincing smile. Then she walked away. Not a word, not a nod of agreement. Nothing but sadness.

What the hell had just happened? What was this cryptic visit all about?

Any time he'd seen Rose and Ed over the years he'd always assumed they were a happily married couple. Sure Gus had been brokenhearted when he and Rose split, but he'd moved on and so had she. They'd turned into totally different people, created their own families and lives.

Gus never got over his bitterness toward how he was treated, how Rose so easily threw aside what they'd had. But marrying Sarah had been the right thing. He'd loved her with his whole heart and still mourned her loss.

And he'd be damned if Alexis and Daniel tried hooking up again. The last thing the Slades and the Claytons needed was to circle back together. He didn't want Rose in his life in any capacity. That might be harsh and rude, but the Claytons weren't exactly friends.

There was a nice young man out there for Alexis... Daniel Clayton just wasn't him.

* * *

"Where's Alexis?"

Rachel glanced around the garden area at TCC, but only saw Gus striding toward her. The wide hat on his head shadowed his face, but she could still catch that smile.

"She couldn't make it, so I told her I'd come help."

"Really?" Rachel asked, then shook her head. "Sorry, that was rude. I'm just surprised you'd want to discuss flowers, seating arrangements and how we'll be setting up the stage."

"This charity is dear to me," he told her as he wrapped an arm around her shoulder. "I'll do anything to help the cause."

After a quick pat on her back, Gus dropped his arm and spun in a slow circle. "Well, this place could use some maintenance."

Rachel had had those exact thoughts as she'd stepped outside. She and Alexis had planned on meeting here so they could figure out various parts of the auction. Rachel was hoping to get some photos to help use for the promotional side of things. Like maybe one of the empty area where the bachelors would be on display. She could use a simple photo like that and change out different catchy phrases for social media.

Unfortunately, Rachel wasn't so sure the gazebo was the best place to show off the hunky men.

"I don't even know where to start," Rachel murmured.

Gus pulled in a deep breath and adjusted his hat. "Well, first thing we're going to do is get a professional in here. You tell me what you want, and I mean every bloom and color, and I'll see that it happens."

Gus Slade wasn't joking. His matter-of-fact tone left

no room for argument and she certainly wasn't about to turn away the help.

"I think everything out here needs to be dug up," she stated, waving her hand over the overgrown, neglected landscaping. "The gazebo could use a fresh coat of paint, too. Keep it white, definitely, and add some nice fat pots at the entrance. Something classy, yet festive. Maybe whites and golds—or should we add some red in the mix? I love the idea of the clean look with white and gold. Oh, poinsettias. We would definitely need those, too."

Gus laughed. "Honey, you better write all that down. I'll make some calls and get a crew out here. We'll get this place fixed up in no time."

"Hopefully they can make it magical on short notice. We only have a few months to get everything ready, and I'll still need to get some pictures to advertise after the work is done."

She wanted to showcase the auction site and make a fairy tale–like poster to entice women and pique their interest before revealing the bachelors. She figured she would do one bachelor per day on their social media sites; that way each man got his proper attention.

Gus rocked back on his heels and pulled his cell from his pocket. "Money can make a whole host of things happen when and how you want it. I'll make a couple of calls right now. Hang tight."

Rachel walked around, making mental notes. She took some random pictures on her phone to use for reference later. In her mind, she could easily see the grand garden area filled with a perimeter of festive blossoms, with white chairs lining the middle. She wasn't sure if any woman would be able to sit once the excitement of bidding started, but there was also a good possibility of some ladies getting weak in the knees. Their bachelor lineup even had Rachel ready to wave a paddle.

"All set."

Rachel shifted her focus back to Gus. "You found someone to come already?"

"I left a message with Austin Bradshaw. He did some work for me a few years back and there's nobody else I'd trust to do this job. I know he's good and he'll make sure it's done in the time frame I want."

If Gus was that confident, and footing the bill, Rachel was definitely onboard. Alexis would be thrilled, too.

"I can't thank you enough." Rachel patted his arm, then adjusted her purse on her shoulder. "So, I'll go back to the ranch and draw up the list in detail. I took some photos so I can remember exactly what I want, and where. I'll get that to you this evening."

"Sounds good. I'm sure I'll hear back from Austin today." Gus narrowed his gaze and grinned. "Do you have your sights set on any bachelors? You've seen each one, so you have an edge on the competition. Daniel Clayton has his own ranch. You seem to love that lifestyle."

First of all, the auction was only bidding for a date. Second, Rachel was pretty sure Alexis would have something to say if her best friend bid on Daniel.

And third…there was only one man from the entire group she'd want to bid on, and she was still torn over what to do on that. Matt had flat out asked her to bid on him. She wasn't sure what to make of his demand, but she certainly wanted to take as much as she was able to from her savings and do just that. If she already had her degree and a job, she'd be able to donate more, but she certainly could spare some to a worthy cause.

"Ah, so there is a man," Gus drawled out. "Well,

he's a lucky guy. And who knows, maybe a date will turn into more."

Rachel laughed and shook her head. "You're a hopeless romantic, Gus. But I'm a widow and a single mother. I'm not ready to jump into the dating pool, let alone make another trip down the aisle."

The older gentleman opened his mouth to speak, but his cell chimed from his pocket. "Hold that thought," he said, pulling the phone out.

Yeah, she wasn't about to keep that topic open. She couldn't bring herself to fully think what would happen if she actually bid on Matt.

A shiver crept over her and she could chalk it up to nothing but pure desire. When she'd had dinner in his suite the other night, she was certain he would've closed the gap between them and kissed her. She'd seen the passion in his eyes and she hadn't missed the way his eyes dropped to her mouth and lingered.

Rachel wrapped her arms around her midsection and attempted to cool her heated thoughts. This kind of thinking was counterproductive, not to mention dangerous. She needed Matt to remain a friend, nothing more. She'd loved him like that for years. Yes, she was still hurt and she still deserved an explanation as to why he vanished, but this was Matt and she couldn't stay mad at him. She realized he'd been hurting, too, when Billy passed.

"That was Austin," Gus said. "He said he'll meet me out here tomorrow morning and look over your list. He'll start as soon as he gets all the supplies in."

"Wow," Rachel exclaimed. "That was fast."

Gus shrugged. "He's pushing a few jobs back for this. I just need to clear everything with the TCC board, but that won't be an issue."

Gus Slade was one powerful man who got what he wanted, when he wanted it. He reminded her of another strong man.

Rachel sighed. Did every thought lately circle back to Matt? Because every time her mind headed toward him, she got that tingling sensation all over again. Hard as she tried, there was no controlling her imagination or this new ache that seemed to accompany each thought of him.

"I truly appreciate this," she told him. "Alexis will be so thrilled."

"You're doing so much more than just marketing," Gus added. "We need to be thanking you."

"Just give me a good reference when I get my degree and need a job."

"Consider it done."

Gus wrapped his arm around her shoulder and started walking back toward the entrance to the clubhouse. "What do you say we grab some lunch? My treat."

"I really should get back to Ellie."

Ellie had been left with a member of Gus's staff. Each person at Lone Wolf Ranch absolutely doted over Rachel's daughter, so there was no doubt she was in good hands.

"Another hour won't matter," Gus stated. "Call and check on her if it makes you feel better."

Rachel nodded. "You're spoiling me and I might never leave."

As he led her toward the restaurant inside TCC, Gus laughed. "You have an open invitation to stay at Lone Wolf as long as you like."

Her in-laws probably wouldn't like that idea, but the longer Rachel stayed in Royal, the more she felt like she'd finally come home.

# Six

Matt glanced at the Halloween-costume party invitation that had been hand delivered to his suite. The board at TCC was hosting the festive event and apparently the entire town was invited.

What the hell would he do at a costume party? Was there a man in his right mind who actually wanted to dress up?

Granted he could always go as a disgruntled CEO or aimless wanderer since he had no clue what the hell he wanted in his life right now. Something was missing, something that his padded bank account couldn't buy. Being back in Royal stirred something in him he hadn't felt in a long, long time. There was a sense of community here and people always looking out for each other…something he didn't see in Dallas.

Tossing the invitation on the counter, Matt grabbed his keys and headed to the elevator just off his living area. He planned to do a drive-by of his grandfather's place today to see exactly what he was dealing with, and then he had to pick up Rachel so she could take some pictures of him for the auction.

Whatever possessed him to agree to such madness? Auctioning himself off sounded absurd, and he preferred to choose his own dates, thank you very much. It wasn't like he had trouble finding female companions. So how did he end up here?

*Oh, that's right.* Rachel had asked. Things were as simple and as complicated as that. He couldn't say no to her, no matter what she wanted. Rachel was...well, she was special and she deserved better than the thoughts and fantasies he'd been harboring for years.

More times than he cared to admit he'd imagined her in his bed, all of them from the island mansion to his Dallas home. He'd pictured her swimming in the ocean wearing nothing but his touch and a sated smile.

Matt attempted to shove thoughts of Rachel from his mind as he drove toward his grandfather's old farm. The place had sat empty for years. After Matt's parents had passed, the land had been willed to him. He had been too busy in Dallas to deal with it, but now, well, he could sure as hell use the outlet.

He and his partner weren't seeing eye to eye, and that was partially due to Matt not being happy in the place he was at in his life. Every day he went to work, and no matter how successful he was, there always seemed to be a void.

Maybe finding a contractor and pushing through some renovations would help. It certainly couldn't hurt.

Matt pulled into the drive overgrown with grass and weeds. The white two-story farmhouse sat back, nestled against the woods. The old barn off to the right actually looked to be in better shape than the house itself.

Swallowing the lump of emotion, Matt stared at the front porch that looked like a good gust of Texas wind could knock it down. He recalled spending his summers with his grandfather, learning all about farm life, about hard work and seeing it pay off. Matt owed everything to that man. Without Patrick Galloway, Matt wouldn't be the successful oil tycoon he was today.

As a young boy, he hadn't realized all the life lessons being instilled, but now looking back, there was no doubt he was being shaped.

Matt smiled as he continued to look at the porch. The creaky swing that hung on one end was gone, but he could easily see it in his mind. His grandfather would sit there and play the harmonica while Matt sat on the top step with two sticks and played faux drums.

Damn it. He missed the simpler times. He missed his parents, his grandfather, those carefree summer nights followed by sweat-your-ass-off workdays.

He'd call a contractor tomorrow. This wasn't something he was going to leave to his assistant, though she was fabulous. Matt planned on handling every bit of this personal project himself.

His cell rang through the speakers of his truck, but he ignored the call when his partner's number flashed on the screen. Matt would call him back later. Right now he wanted to get to Rachel and get this photo shoot over with. She'd requested he wear a suit so she could capture him in his element. Although it was true that business attire was part of his daily life, he'd like to be a bit more casual for this shoot.

Then again, this wasn't his charity and he wasn't the one bidding. Good grief. He was honestly going to stand on a stage and watch women waving paddles around just to go on a date with him.

There was only one woman he wanted to win that bid. He'd have to do some convincing, though. Rachel had seemed a little hesitant and he couldn't blame her. He'd up and deserted her after Billy's funeral, then he'd dropped back into her life unexpectedly, and followed that by making it clear he wouldn't mind kissing her.

Yeah, he saw her lids widen and heard her breath hitch when he inched closer as they sat on the floor of his suite. Had Ellie not been between them, Matt would have pulled Rachel to him and taken a sample of something he'd coveted for far too long. Just one taste. At least that's what he told himself he needed to get over the craving.

Matt pulled out of the drive and headed toward Lone Wolf Ranch. Ten minutes later, he was turning into the sprawling estate with a wrought iron arch over the entrance. This was Royal, small town charm mixed with money, lots of it, and a big-city feel. Matt could easily see the pull to live here, and he was banking on that for when he renovated his grandfather's farm. The real estate market was booming and he knew he'd have no trouble selling.

The thought didn't settle well with him, but he didn't need the place. He had his ten-thousand-square-foot home in Dallas and his own island, for pity's sake. He traveled when and where he wanted. He couldn't hold on to the old farmstead simply for nostalgia.

As he approached the massive main house, Rachel came bounding down the stairs. She smiled and waved. There was no denying the punch of lust to the gut. She wore another one of those long, curve-hugging dresses that she probably thought was comfortable, but all he could think was how fast he could have that material shoved up to her waist and joining their bodies after years of aching to have no barriers between them.

There wasn't a doubt in Matt's mind that the real thing would put the fantasy to shame.

Damn. He seriously needed to get a grip.

Rachel opened the truck door, and had he not been imagining her naked he would've gotten out and opened her door for her.

"Hey." She hopped in and set the camera bag between them. "Are you ready for this?"

A day alone with Rachel? Hell yeah.

"I guess so." He turned toward her slightly. "This suit okay?"

He absolutely relished the way her eyes raked over him. Sure his ego was larger than most, but the only woman he wanted was looking at him as if she wanted him right back.

"It will do."

Leave it to Rachel to knock him down a peg. With a low chuckle, Matt put the truck in gear and headed back down the drive.

"So, where are we going?" she asked.

He'd insisted on the location of the shoot as well as her being the photographer. If he'd told her ahead of time where he was taking her, she would've balked at the suggestion.

"I'll keep it a surprise for now."

Rachel clicked her seatbelt into place and settled back in the seat. "As long as I'm back in time to give Ellie a bath. I was actually ordered by Alexis to go have fun. She thinks we're dating."

Interesting. "What have you been saying about me to your host family?"

Rachel laughed, the sultry sound flooding the small

space. "Gus is a romantic at heart and Alexis, well, she's just excited I'm talking to any man."

Matt gripped the steering wheel. "Surely you've been on a date in the last year."

"Why would you think that?"

He pointed the truck toward the edge of town, heading for the airstrip. "Because you're a beautiful, passionate woman, Rachel."

"I'm a widow and a single mother."

Gritting his teeth, Matt weighed his words carefully. "So you've reminded me before, but that doesn't mean you don't get to have a social life. Do you plan on staying single until Ellie moves out of the house?"

Rachel blew out a sigh and turned to face the side window. "I don't want to argue with you, Matt. It's not like I can just pick up and date anyone I want. I have a child to think about now and she has to come first. We're a package deal, so I can't just bring men in and out of her life."

He didn't say another word, because he also didn't want to argue, but there were plenty of thoughts circling around in his mind. Maybe he didn't want a ready-made family and marriage and picket fences, but he wanted Rachel. He wanted to prove to her that she was still alive, that just because her life had changed dramatically didn't mean she had to give up her wants and needs.

Maybe this bachelor auction was exactly what he needed to make his case. If he was going to put himself on display like a piece of meat, he was sure as hell going to use it to his advantage. Rachel was about to come to grips with the fact that she could still be a mother *and* a woman. A passionate, desirable woman.

"What are we doing here?"

Rachel stared at the small airstrip and the private

plane with a man dressed all in black waiting at the base of the stairs. For the past ten minutes, she and Matt had ridden in silence. He simply didn't understand where she was coming from in regard to her dating life and she wasn't going to keep explaining her situation.

"You wanted pictures, right?" He pulled the truck to a stop and killed the engine. "We're going to Galloway Cove."

She jerked in her seat and faced him. "What? But, you're in a suit and I thought we were doing office-type images since you're a CEO."

Matt shrugged. "You want me in the auction, I'm calling the shots on how I'm portrayed. Don't worry, there's an office in my beach house."

He hopped out of the truck without another word and circled the hood. When he opened her door, Rachel still couldn't believe he was taking her to his island for the photo shoot. She couldn't be alone with him on a secluded island. That screamed *cliché* with all of these newly awakened emotions she had toward him. Was he purposely trying to get her alone?

Anticipation and nerves swirled together deep in her gut. Was he trying to seduce her?

"Why don't we just take some of you standing in front of your plane?" she suggested, trying not to sound as flustered as she felt. "That would fuel any woman's fantasy for the auction."

Because this suit was totally doing it for her.

Matt's striking blue eyes held her captivated as he leaned closer. "Maybe there's only one woman I want to fantasize about me."

Even with the truck door open, there still didn't seem to be enough air to fill her lungs. This was Matt, her friend. Her very sexy, very dynamic friend whose broad shoulders filled out his suit to the point it should be illegal for him to walk around in public.

The stirrings of desire hit her hard. Harder than when she'd wanted him to kiss her in his penthouse suite. Why now? Why did he drop back into her life and make her question the direction she was moving? She didn't have time for desire or kisses or hot, sultry looks from a man who used to be her rock. She wasn't looking for anything akin to lust or attraction right now. Like she had the time to worry about another relationship.

His dark blue eyes slid from her eyes to her lips.

"Don't do that," she scolded.

His mouth kicked up in a cocky smirk. "What's that?"

"Try to be cute or pretend like you want to kiss me."

Matt laughed. "Leave it to you to not skirt around the situation. I'm not pretending, Rachel. I plan on kissing you. You won't know when, but that's your warning."

Well, hell. Apparently the gauntlet she just threw down had awakened the beast. The real question was, how long had he been lying in wait?

Matt leaned across the seat, his solid chest brushing hers, his lips coming within a breath. Rachel inhaled, the subtle movement causing her sensitive breasts to press further against his hard body. She hadn't been aroused like this in so long, she couldn't trust her judgment right now. Her mind was all muddled and her hormones were overriding common sense. But she had to remain in control…at all costs.

"Relax," he murmured.

The click of her belt echoed in the cab of the truck and Matt eased away, taking her hands in his to help her out. He reached back in for the camera bag and flung it over his big, broad shoulder before closing the door.

Finally, she could breathe. Even though he was holding her hand as they walked across the tarmac, Rachel could handle that.

What she could not handle, however, was that promise or threat or whatever he'd issued when he'd warned her of the kiss. The way he'd looked at her, rubbed against her and put naughty, *R*-rated thoughts inside her head.

They shouldn't be kissing. What they needed to do was get photos and focus on the auction…an auction where other women would be writing big fat checks to score a date with this handsome, prominent bachelor. He wasn't hers…not in that way.

"I'm not going to bid on you," she stated, as if that was her mega comeback for the way he'd got her all hot and bothered in the truck, and then strolled along as if nothing had changed between them. "You need to get that through your thick head."

"Of course you will."

Rachel jerked her hand from his and marched onward toward the steps of the plane. Arrogant bastard. Why was she friends with him again?

The pilot smiled and nodded as he welcomed her on board. Rachel climbed the stairs and was stunned at the beauty and spaciousness of the plane. She'd known Matt had his own aircraft, but she'd never been inside it. She'd never been to Galloway Cove, either. When they all hung out, Billy, Matt and her, Matt usually came to her house or they all met at their favorite pub in Dallas.

But Rachel wasn't going to stroke his ego anymore and comment on the beauty of the details or even act like she was impressed.

She went to the dark leather sofa that stretched beneath the oval windows, took a seat on one end and then fastened her safety belt. Matt and the pilot spoke but she couldn't make out their words. Didn't matter. She knew where they were going, knew Matt's intentions, but that didn't mean she would give in. He still owed her answers, and being on a plane with nowhere for him to run was exactly where she planned on getting them.

Rachel shifted and kept looking out the window as Matt came back and took a seat—of course on the same sofa, but at least on the opposite end. It took all of her willpower not to just bombard him with all the questions she'd been dying to ask since he'd disappeared from her life. But she would. She wanted him to get nice and comfortable with his situation first. He thought he was calling the shots, but she was about to flip their positions.

# Seven

Rachel had been quiet during takeoff. Too quiet. Her gaze never wavered from the window. The flight took about an hour and a half from Royal and Matt had to admit, he was worried.

She was plotting something. She was pissed, if the thin lips and the sound of her gritting teeth was any indicator. Perhaps he'd been too forward earlier, but damn it, he'd held out for years and he was done skirting around his attraction. She deserved to know how much he wanted her. He couldn't go at this any slower. At this rate they'd be in a nursing home before he got to first base.

He might want nothing more than to see where this fierce physical attraction went, but perhaps she was on the same page. He knew she was more of a happily-ever-after girl, but perhaps she wanted to just have a good time and not think about commitments for a while.

That was plausible…right? Or was he just trying to justify his actions to himself so he didn't feel like an ass for making a move on his late friend's wife?

"Why don't you just say what you're stewing about and let's move on?" He couldn't stand the damn silence another second.

She didn't move one bit, except her eyes, which darted to him. Oh, yeah. She was pissed.

"Fine. Start with Billy's funeral and your immediate absence after."

Hell. He'd known this was coming—he'd rehearsed the speech in his head over and over. However, nothing prepared him to actually say the words aloud.

"I know you were hurting—"

"Hurting? You *crushed* me," she scolded. "Billy's death tore me apart and I needed you. I was pregnant, scared, facing in-laws who were smothering me, and I just wanted my friend."

He'd crushed her. That was a bitter pill to swallow and he had no excuse other than he was selfish and trying to do what he thought was best at the time. But she'd needed him, and he worried more that he'd take them into unknown territory while she was still vulnerable. He'd been a total prick, but hindsight was a bitch.

"I texted." That was lame even to his own ears. "I just… I needed space."

She turned her attention back to the window. "An entire year," she murmured. Then she shifted in her seat to fully face him, anger and pain flooding her eyes with unshed tears, and she might as well have stabbed him and twisted the knife.

"Would you have contacted me had we not run into each other? Or were you only friends with me because of Billy?"

"No." She had to know that above all else. "What you and I shared had nothing to do with Billy."

And everything to do with him.

"I would've reached out to you, Rachel," he said softly. "I missed you."

"Well, that's something," she whispered, almost in relief.

Matt immediately unbuckled his belt and slid closer, taking her hands even though she tried to pull back. "Look at me, damn it. Did you honestly believe that because he died I was just done with you? With us?"

"What else was I supposed to think? I mean, we were close for so long and then I didn't see you. I went by your house and your housekeeper told me you were on vacation. You answered my texts in short sentences as if I was bothering you. Then…nothing."

Yeah, because he'd hidden away at his home on Galloway Cove until he could go back to Dallas and not risk telling Rachel how he'd felt for years. There were things about Billy she didn't know, and it had taken all of his strength to keep those secrets to himself. But those last few days of his life, Billy hadn't only argued with Rachel. He and Matt had finally had it out and Matt had issued an ultimatum. Rachel didn't deserve to be treated like she wasn't the most important thing in Billy's world. Billy accused Matt of always wanting her, and fists started flying.

"Matt?"

He blinked away from the memories and squeezed her hands. He couldn't tell her about all of that. He sure as hell wasn't going to tell her when Billy died, because she was suffering enough. What would the point be in telling her now that her husband had been unfaithful?

There was no reason at all to drudge up the past and make her feel even worse.

"I had to get away," he croaked out, cursing himself for showing weakness. He swallowed the lump of guilt and the ache that accompanied his desire for her. "I knew Billy's parents and brother would watch out for you. I needed some time to myself."

"I still don't understand why so long." She stared back at him, studying his face as if truly trying to understand his way of thinking. "I missed you."

There was only so much a man could take, and those last three words sliced through his last thread of control.

Matt gripped her face between his hands and covered her mouth with his. For a half second he had a sliver of fear that she would push him away. She didn't pull back, but she stiffened, hopefully from shock and not from repulsion.

*Yes.* That's all he could think as he slid his tongue through the seam of her lips. He'd been right. The real thing didn't even compare to his fantasies. Not only that, no other woman had ever made him so damn achy and needy like Rachel.

The second she relaxed, Matt shifted his body to cover hers as she leaned against the back of the sofa. Her hands came up to his shoulders, her fingertips curling around him as if to hold him in place. Like he was going anywhere after finally getting her in this position. If only he could shut out the rest of the world and stay like this with her until he'd finally exorcised her out of his system.

Matt wanted to rip her dress off, discard this ridiculous suit and lay her flat out, taking everything he'd craved for damn near ten years.

But he couldn't. He respected Rachel, and a kiss

was one thing, but taking it to the next level was another. And if that was the route they were going to go, he wasn't dragging her. No, if she wanted him, she'd have to show him.

At least now she knew where he stood.

Matt pulled back, still keeping her face between his palms. He rested his forehead against hers and fell into the same breathing pattern as her.

"Well, you did warn me."

He laughed. He couldn't help it. "I won't apologize."

Rachel tipped her head back. Heavy lids half covered her expressive eyes, and her lips were plump and wet from his passion. She stared at him for a moment before she seemed to close in on herself, blinking and pulling in a deep breath.

"I didn't ask for an apology," she stated. "We kissed. It's over. We're friends, so this shouldn't be a big deal."

Processing her words, Matt slowly released her and sat back. *Shouldn't be a big deal?* He'd waited to touch her, to taste her for a damn long time, and she just brushed it aside as no big deal? It sure as hell was a huge deal, and she knew it.

"I told you before you're a terrible liar."

Rachel's eyes widened a fraction before she eased away from him and came to her feet. Considering there was nowhere for her to escape, he sat and watched as she paced. She not only paced—she held her fingertips to her lips. The egotistical side of him liked to think she was replaying their kiss—he sure as hell was.

"Let me get this straight." She paced toward the kitchen, then back toward him. "We've been friends since college. I marry your best friend. He passes away. I don't hear from you for too damn long, and now you want to…what? What is it you want from me?"

*Everything.*

No. That wasn't true. He didn't want marriage or children. He'd never considered any of that part of his life plan. Billy hadn't, either, but when he'd married Rachel, he'd been in love. It was the whole family thing that had put him off-kilter.

"Maybe I want to prove to you that you're ready to get back out in the world and date." The thought of her with another man prickled the hairs on the back of his neck and made him fist his hands in his lap. "You returned that kiss, Rachel. Don't tell me you don't have needs."

She snapped her attention back to him, crossing her arms over her chest. "My needs are none of your concern."

They were every bit his concern.

"Sit down," he demanded. "You're making me dizzy watching you pace back and forth."

She narrowed her eyes before turning and taking a seat in one of the two swivel-style club chairs on the opposite side. She crossed her legs and adjusted her dress over her knees, but that did nothing to squelch his desire.

Matt still tasted her on his lips. He still felt her grip on his shoulders. What would she be like when she fully let her guard down and let him pleasure her? Because that moment would happen. Right now she had to get used to the kiss—there would be more—and then he'd slowly reawaken the passion he knew was buried deep inside.

Matt's single-story beach home with its white exterior and white columns along the porch might have been the most beautiful thing Rachel had ever seen.

The lush greenery looked like a painting, and the various pieces of driftwood in the landscaping were the perfect added touch.

Rachel could easily see why he kept this island a secret. Some men would've thrown parties here at the opulent beachfront home, but Matt kept his life more private.

And that privacy was one of the main differences between him and Billy. Her late husband liked to live large, celebrate life every single day by going on adventures or partying.

It was difficult not to compare the two friends, especially now that she'd kissed Matt. No. Correction. He'd kissed her. And boy did he ever kiss. That man's mouth was potent enough she was still tingling. What the hell would happen to her if he actually got his hands on her?

The idea had hit her the moment he'd touched his mouth to hers and part of her had wanted him to take things further.

Which was why she'd had to sit on the other side of the plane for the duration of the flight. Her mind was clouded, that's all. She didn't want her best friend... did she?

Being on the other side of the plane hadn't stopped Matt from staring at her, looking like the Big Bad Wolf deliciously wrapped in an Italian suit. Predators apparently came in all forms and hers was billionaire oil tycoon posing as her friend. Because the way he'd stared made her feel like he could see right through her clothes to what lay underneath.

If he saw her saggy tummy and stretch marks, maybe he wouldn't be so eager. She wouldn't change her new mommy body for anything, though. Ellie was the greatest thing that had ever happened to her.

"Where do you want me?"

That low, sultry tone wrapped Rachel in complete arousal. Damn that man for making her want, making her think things she really shouldn't. She was human, after all, and she couldn't turn off her emotions or her needs. Surely there was some unwritten rule about lusting after your late husband's best friend.

Rachel turned from the wall of windows facing the stunning ocean view and met Matt's gaze from across the living room. He'd told her to look around and see which room would be best, and that had been nearly a half hour ago. She wasn't sure where he'd gone or what he was doing, but even her time alone in this stunning house hadn't cooled her off from that most scintillating plane ride.

"I thought you were calling the shots," she tossed back. "Granted the other guys I photographed didn't care where I put them."

Matt's eyes narrowed. "I thought you weren't comfortable taking my picture for this. You didn't say you'd done the others."

Rachel shrugged. "It saved money and I enjoy it. I never said I didn't want to take your picture, by the way. I simply said I wasn't a professional. You should've asked someone else."

One slow, calculated step at a time, Matt closed the distance between them. "And why is that, Rachel? Afraid of what you're feeling?"

She swallowed and tipped her chin. "I'm not afraid of anything. Now back off and stop trying to seduce me."

He reached out and smoothed her hair from her face before dropping his hand. "I'm not trying to seduce you. When I seduce you, you'll know it."

*When.*

The bold term had anticipation and arousal pulsing through her. This was getting them nowhere except dangerously close to the point of no return for their friendship.

"Are you willing to throw away our friendship for a quick romp?" she countered.

"Oh, honey. It won't be quick. I assure you." He stepped back and spread his arms wide. "Now, where do you want me?"

Why did he keep phrasing it like that?

*Focus.*

Rachel clutched the camera bag on her shoulder and nodded toward the hallway. "Let's start in your office. We'll do some professional shots and then I'll have you take off the jacket and tie, and roll up your sleeves and we'll do some casual ones outside. You've got such gorgeous landscaping and pool, it would be a shame not to grab some there."

"What about the waterfall?"

Rachel shook her head in amazement. "You have a waterfall? I seriously need to get my own island."

Matt laughed. "I'll show you when we're done. Maybe you'll want some shots there, as well."

A photo of this rich, gorgeous oil tycoon posing in front of a waterfall…yup, that would certainly have all the ladies drooling. Not her, of course, but the others who were bidding.

"You might just decide to bid on me yet," he drawled.

"Don't get too cocky."

"If I wasn't cocky, I wouldn't have gotten where I am today. And I prefer to use the term *confident*."

Rachel rolled her eyes and headed toward the other end of the house, where the office was. "And I prefer to leave our friendship intact, so keep those lips to yourself."

"Whatever you want," he murmured as she passed by. But his low, seductive tone indicated she'd want something else entirely, and damn it, he was right.

# Eight

Rachel was going to need to take a dip in the pool to cool off. Mercy sakes. She'd thought Matt adorned in a three-piece suit, leaning against his desk with his arms crossed over his massive chest, flashing an arrogant smirk at the camera was sexy, but that was nothing compared to the images she currently snapped of him in the waterfall.

As in, *in* the waterfall. He'd rolled up his pant legs to his calves, folded his shirt sleeves onto those impressive forearms, and then untucked and unbuttoned the damn thing.

Oh, he was playing dirty and he knew it. It would serve him right if she let some wealthy socialite bid on him and then make him fulfill some fantasy date.

But would he kiss that faceless woman good-night? Would he pour every bit of his body and soul into that kiss like he had with her?

Jealousy didn't sit well with Rachel. She'd experienced it with her own husband in the final days of their marriage when she suspected infidelity, and she sure as hell didn't want to experience it again. Matt was a ladies' man, his newly appointed title made that crystal clear. No way would she ever want to get involved with a player again, and she wasn't sure if she'd ever be ready for another committed relationship.

"I think we have enough," she shouted over the cascading water.

Matt raked his wet hands through his hair, making the black strands glisten beneath the sun. In an attempt to ignore the curl of lust in her belly, Rachel scrolled through the images she'd taken over the last couple of hours.

The only problem she saw with each picture was that each one was absolute perfection, which said nothing of her photography skills and everything of the subject on the other side of the lens.

"Put your camera down."

Rachel glanced up. Matt still remained in the water, the bottom of his pants soaked, his shirt clinging like transparent silk against his tanned, muscular chest.

"What?"

"Get in the water. Work is over."

"Then we should head back."

She could *not* get into that water with him. Then her clothes would get clingy and he'd probably touch her or kiss her again, and at this point she wasn't sure she would be able to ignore the aching need. There wasn't a doubt in her mind Matt would set her world on fire; it was everything that came afterward that worried her.

She'd been without a man for so long…*too long*. She simply couldn't trust her erratic emotions right now.

Matt stalked toward her like some god emerging

from the water. Droplets ran down his exposed skin and she was so riveted she couldn't look away. Part of her even imagined licking each and every one, and that only added fuel to the proverbial flames.

How had he put this spell on her and why was she letting him? Oh, right. Because she was on a slippery slope and barely hanging on.

When he reached for her hand, Rachel set her camera down on a rock. He urged her forward.

"I can't get wet," she protested, though her feet were following him. "I don't have extra clothes."

He walked backward, his eyes never wavering from hers. "Take off your dress and we won't have a problem."

"You're not getting me out of my clothes."

The smirk, that raised brow, the way he kept walking her toward the water's edge…damn it. He took her statement as a challenge.

"Matt, we can't do this."

Cool water slid over her toes, over her ankles, soaking the bottom of her dress. She was losing a battle she wasn't sure she ever had a fair fight in.

"No one is here to tell us not to."

"I'm telling us not to," she argued. "This isn't right."

"Says who? Tell me you're not attracted to me, Rachel. Tell me you didn't kiss me right back and you haven't been thinking of it every second since."

She chewed on her bottom lip to prevent a lie from slipping out…and also to hold the truth inside. But her silence was just as telling as if she'd admitted her true feelings.

"It's just water," he crooned. "Nothing to be afraid of."

"I told you before, I'm not afraid." She pulled her

hand from his and lifted her dress, bunching it in her fist at her side. "Is this how you get all your women? You use that sultry voice, that heavy-lidded gaze and…" She waved up and down at his bare chest.

"All of my women?" he repeated. "Watch it, Rachel. I'll start to think you care about my sex life."

She'd never given it much thought before now. And in the past several hours, Matt and sex had consumed nearly all of her thoughts.

Without thinking, she pulled from his grasp and leaned down, scooped up some water and splashed him right in the face. He sputtered for a second before flicking the excess away. Rachel couldn't help but laugh at his shocked expression, but then that surprise turned to menace.

"You think that's funny, do you?"

In a lightning-flash movement, he scooped her up into his big, strong arms and headed toward the waterfall.

"No!" she squealed. "Don't drench me, Matt, please. I'm sorry! I'll do anything, just don't—"

Water covered her entire body, chilling her instantly. Rachel squeezed her eyes shut and held her breath as she wrapped her arms around Matt's neck and clung tight. She turned her face toward his neck, trying to shield herself from the pounding spray. A moment later, he shifted and the water was behind her.

Rachel blinked the water from her eyes and glanced up. Matt stared down at her with even more raw, elemental desire than she'd ever seen. Billy had never looked at her that way…no one had.

Easing her to her feet, Matt kept an arm banded around her waist and cupped the side of her face with his other hand. Rachel's heart pounded in her chest. She needed to stop this before things went any further, but she hadn't done a very good job at stopping the progress up to this point.

"I want you," he muttered against her mouth. His words were barely audible over the rushing waters.

"I know."

He tipped her back, leaning over her, still very much in control over her body...physically and emotionally. Those blue eyes locked on hers.

"Tell me no and we'll walk out of here and get back on the plane. My pilot is there and ready when we are."

He'd just handed over total control to her and with one word she could end it all...or take what he'd presented to her wrapped in a delicious package.

And there was really no decision to be made here. Because, in the end, she wasn't going to deny herself. She had basic needs—there was nothing shameful about that. Besides, this was Matt. They were friends; he wasn't looking for more and neither was she.

*One time. Just this once, be selfish.*

Rachel gripped his face and pulled his mouth down to hers. In the next instant, Matt wrapped his arms around her waist, filling his hands with her rear. The warmth of his touch through the cool material warmed her instantly.

She slid her hands through his wet hair, clutching onto him as he continued to tip her backward. There was no way he'd let her fall, though. His grip was too tight, his mouth too powerful, his need practically radiating from him. She wasn't going anywhere.

His hips ground into hers and the thin layer of wet clothes might as well have been nonexistent. Except it was and proved to be a most frustrating barrier. She'd never felt this overwhelming need before, never had the feeling of all-consuming passion, like she couldn't control herself.

*It had never been this way with Billy.*

No. For right now she was going to be completely closed off from reality and anything that threatened to steal her happiness. Damn it, she was going to take what she wanted...what Matt wanted. How long had he desired her? Did seeing her again spark something inside him?

*Oh, my.* Had he wanted her before?

"You're thinking too hard," he rasped against her mouth.

His hands came to her shoulders and gripped the straps of her maxi dress. He yanked them down, the clingy material pulling the cups of her bra as well, instantly exposing her breasts.

She didn't have time to worry about her body or what he thought, because his mouth descended downward and Rachel arched against him as he drew one tight nipple into his mouth.

"Matt," she moaned.

"Say it again," he demanded. "I want my name on your lips."

She didn't think he'd heard her over the rushing water, but she definitely heard him. From the command, she had to guess that he was just as turned on as she was at this point.

Rachel yanked on the material of his shirt, but it clung to his biceps. He eased back just enough to remove the garment and toss it in the general direction of the shore.

Instantly her eyes went to the ink over his shoulder. She traced her finger over the eagle's wings that spanned around to the back.

"This is new."

When he trembled beneath her touch, she wondered just how much control she had here. More than she'd initially thought.

When her eyes darted to his face, she noted the clenched jaw, the heavy lids, the blue eyes that had darkened with arousal.

So much hit her all at once that it was like truly seeing Matt for the first time...and recognizing the secret yearnings he'd kept locked up inside for so long. "I never knew."

"Now you do."

Yeah, she did. And she'd have to worry about that later. Her body was humming and zinging and doing all of the other happy dances that accompanied the heady anticipation of having really great sex. But she'd never been this charged before, never wanted a man so bad. Knowing that he wanted her just as much...well, that only fueled her desire.

With more confidence than she'd ever had, Rachel pushed her dress all the way down until it puddled around her waist. She shimmied just enough to let it fall before she stepped out of it. With her bra barely covering her and her panties beneath the surface, she felt more exposed than ever.

Who the hell had sex outside in the middle of the day? The sun shone bright down on the pair, the water rushed beside them and a butterfly had literally just flown by. It was as if she'd already bid on her best friend and was living out the fantasy date she never knew she even wanted.

On a growl, Matt picked her up and headed toward the shoreline. Her legs instantly wrapped around his waist. This was seriously happening. If she deliberated too much about all the reasons this was a bad idea, she might back out, so she cleared her head of all rational thought.

Matt sat her down once again, this time her toes landing on the lush ground cover that ran along the edge of the waterfall. In seconds he'd discarded his clothes, and Rachel was too busy admiring the mouthwatering view to realize he'd gripped the edge of her panties. The material fell away as he gave a yank and they ripped clear off her body.

"Matt," she cried.

"I'm done waiting."

He enveloped her into his arms, gently taking her to the ground, but he rolled beneath her so that she was on top. Instantly her legs straddled his hips. Her hands went up, ready to cover her torso.

"No," he commanded as he took her hands away. "I want to see all of you. Don't be ashamed of something so beautiful."

*Beautiful?* Not how she'd describe her post-pregnancy body, but the way Matt's eyes caressed her skin had her almost believing him.

*We don't have protection.* The thought slid into her mind and she wondered if he'd stop. "I'm on birth control even though I haven't been with anyone since Billy, and even that was a couple months before his death."

The night Ellie had been conceived, actually. But that was a story she didn't want to plunk down right here between them.

"I've never been without protection, Rachel. I know I'm clean, but this is your call."

He gripped her hips, whether to hold her away or encourage her to hurry and make up her mind, she didn't know. But she was sure of this, of him.

Without a word, she lowered herself and joined their bodies. His groan of approval had her smiling as she rested her hands on either side of his head. Matt nipped at her lips before pushing her back up.

"I want to watch every second of this," he murmured.

He might have seduced her, not that she'd put up too much of a fight, but he was handing over total control. Matt wasn't a man who liked to give up his power... which just proved how much he wanted her, wanted *this* to happen.

Rachel would have to analyze that from all different directions later. Right now, she only wanted to feel—and she certainly felt.

Matt's hands roamed from her hips to her breasts and back down. She shifted against him, finding that perfect rhythm. Never once did she shy away from his hot, molten gaze. She couldn't pinpoint that look in his eyes; she couldn't figure out what he saw when he stared at her so intently. But she did know she'd never felt like this, and she wasn't so sure she wanted this to end.

Matt tightened his hold on her as his hips pumped faster beneath her. That strong jawline of his clenched. Rachel leaned over him, her wet hair falling around to curtain them as she covered his mouth.

Then the dam burst. Matt's hands were all over her as he pushed up to a seated position. Her legs curled around his back and her hips continued to rock against his. When the climax spiraled through her, Rachel tore her mouth away, clutched onto his shoulders and arched back.

He murmured something, but she couldn't decipher the words. She clung to him as wave after wave crashed over her. Before she came down from her high, Matt was clutching her against him, his hips stilled beneath her as his entire body tightened and he let the passion consume him, too.

Rachel circled her arms around his neck and buried her face against his moist, heated skin. As Matt's body relaxed, his fingertips started trailing up and down her back. She couldn't lift her head, couldn't face him.

What had they just done? Part of her mind said they'd both betrayed Billy, but the other part wondered how the hell she could ever be with another man after the way Matt made her feel.

At some point, she'd have to face him. More so, she'd have to come to grips with how this changed every emotion she had toward her best friend.

# Nine

**M**att had known she wouldn't want to talk. He'd sensed her emotional disconnect the moment their bodies calmed, even while she was still wrapped around him. They'd still been joined physically, but she'd checked out mentally.

What did he think would happen? That she'd flash that wide smile at him and ask him to take her back to the house for an encore?

Sex with Rachel was everything he'd ever wanted… and nothing like what he expected. No fantasy could've compared to having the real thing.

He stood in his living room and waited on her to dress. They'd walked back to the beach house in awkward silence and he'd given her that gap she'd obviously needed. Knowing Rachel, she was trying to analyze her new feelings, was trying to figure out if she'd just done something morally wrong against her late husband.

Matt had loved Billy like a brother, but Billy was gone. Life moved on and he was done waiting. He was done letting guilt consume him. But where did that leave the two of them?

As soon as they'd reached the house, Matt had taken her soaking-wet clothes and put them in his dryer. He'd told her to go shower in the master bath, which was a wall of one-way windows that overlooked the ocean. Surely the combination of the breathtaking view, the rain head and six jets would relax her.

He'd taken his shower outside surrounded by the lush tropical plants he'd had arranged perfectly to ensure privacy for guests…not that he'd invited anyone here. Galloway Cove was his haven, his private life away from the office and its demands.

Rachel was the only woman he'd ever brought here, and damn it if he didn't like seeing her walk around his private domain. There had never been a doubt in his mind who he would bring here. Having shown her his favorite spot on the island, having made love to her with the waterfall in the background…

Matt turned from the windows and curbed his desire. There was no way he could go into that bathroom and show her just how amazing they were together. She knew. He'd seen that look of passion, desire and want staring back at him earlier.

But she'd been in the bathroom nearly an hour. Her clothes had dried and he'd laid them on his king-size bed. Her delicate bra and that dress that drove him out of his mind were displayed for her to see. He owed her a pair of panties, though.

Matt pulled out his cell and attempted to clear his head by checking work emails. His partner had forwarded one where another firm had showed interest in buying them both out. He wasn't sure how he felt about that. True he wanted…hell, he wasn't sure *what* he wanted. He knew something was missing, and as soon as he could put his finger on that, he'd be better-off.

Selling his share of the company? He'd given his partner the chance to buy his half. But was Eric wanting to sell his own, as well? That was definitely something they'd have to discuss via phone because Matt wasn't about to email all of his thoughts.

Shuffling feet down the hallway had him shoving his phone and his business predicament aside. With his body still humming from being with Rachel, work wasn't relevant right now.

Never in his life had he ever put a woman, put *anyone*, ahead of his career. That's how he'd gotten to where he was, able to take off whenever he wanted, travel wherever, buy anything. Yet all of that still left him with an aching void.

And the only time he'd felt whole was when he was inside Rachel.

Raking his hands over his face, Matt blew out a sigh and wished like hell he could get a grasp on his emotions. He'd wanted Rachel physically for years. What the hell was all this other stuff jumbling up his mind for? He couldn't feel whole with her. She wasn't the missing link. Hell, he'd avoided her for a year to dodge all of the other mess that he worried would come with getting this close to her.

But he didn't have regrets about the waterfall, and he'd only just sampled her. He wanted more.

Rachel appeared at the end of the hall. Her steps stalled as she met his gaze from across the room. With her long blond hair down around her shoulders, her dress clinging to her luscious curves like before, he couldn't prevent the onslaught of a renewed desire even though he'd had her only a short time ago.

She looked the same, yet everything was different. If he wanted to get anywhere with her, to convince her that what they did was not wrong—but *inevitable*—he'd have to try to get her to open up.

"Do you want to talk, or just get on the plane and pretend like nothing happened?" he asked, knowing full well he'd never let her forget. What had happened here today was nothing short of phenomenal.

"I'd say it's best for both of us if we go back."

He started closing the gap between them, totally ignoring the way her eyes widened as he drew closer. "To Royal or to just being friends?"

Rachel tipped her chin, but never looked away. "Both."

"We'll talk on the plane."

He started to reach for her, but she held her hands up and stepped back. "There's nothing to say. I was selfish and took what I wanted. We can't do it again."

Did she honestly think he'd let her just brush him aside like that? If she had feelings she wanted to suppress, well, that was her problem, but she was not going to pretend like he was nothing more than a cheap fling.

Damn it. Since when did he get so emotionally invested? He did flings; he did one-night stands. He moved on with a mutual understanding. But now? Rachel was a complete game changer for him and he had no clue how to proceed from here.

"Listen, I'm just as freaked out." He reached for her, grabbing hold of her shoulders before she could move away again. "You think I don't have feelings about what happened? You think I don't know you well enough to realize you're thinking you betrayed Billy? That we did something wrong?"

Rachel glanced away, but Matt took his thumb and forefinger and gently gripped her chin, forcing her gaze back to his. "I don't know if you're more upset over Billy or the fact that you slept with me. You're allowed to feel again, Rachel. I've wanted—"

"I know what you want." She jerked out of his hold. "I don't want to keep talking about it."

"Well, too damn bad," he threw back. "You deserve to know that I've wanted you for years."

Those bright eyes widened in shock. "Don't say that, Matt. You don't mean it."

"Like hell I don't. I've wanted you since I saw you at that party, before Billy interrupted us talking."

"So you just…what? Stepped aside and let your buddy ask me out? You let him *marry* me? You couldn't have wanted me that bad."

She had no idea. Hell, he wasn't sure he'd had any clue until he'd tasted her. Now he only wanted more. He'd had years to process this, but clearly Rachel was just now getting used to the idea of them being together.

Matt crossed his arms over his chest and took a step back. "Go get on the plane, Rachel."

"What?" she whispered.

"We're done here. I've given you enough to think about."

"No damn kidding." She threw her arms wide. "You've confused me, made me face things I never thought about before…what the hell do you want from me, Matt?"

Honesty was the only way. From here on out, he had to let her into his thoughts. She deserved that much.

"I don't know," he murmured. "I wanted you and

thought maybe that would be the end of it…but I'm not done with you, Rach. Not even close."

Tears welled up in her eyes as her lips thinned. "I don't want a relationship. I've got a baby, a degree to finish, a life to figure out…"

"I'm not looking for long-term, either. I just know I couldn't take another day without you. I'm not sorry for what happened and I wish like hell neither were you."

"I never said I was sorry it happened."

Matt turned and headed toward the door. "You didn't have to."

"What are you going to be for the TCC Halloween party?" Alexis asked, smiling and waving around the invitation.

Rachel glanced up from the images of Matt covering her computer screen. For the past day she'd stared at these, not knowing which one to choose for the bachelor auction.

The petty, selfish side of her wanted to choose the worst one, but the realistic side had to admit there wasn't a single bad picture in the lot. He flashed that panty-melting sexy smile in each and every one. Not once had he blinked in an image. He was game on the second she'd started snapping.

"Rachel?"

She clicked to minimize the screen before she turned her focus to her friend.

"The party?" she asked. "Um, I hadn't thought about it. I saw the invitation on the kitchen island yesterday."

Before she'd left, before her entire life had changed. Before she'd boldly slept with her friend without putting up much of a fight. Despite what Matt thought, she wasn't sorry.

"Are you alright?" Alexis dropped the invitation to her side and stepped on into the office. "I didn't see you much yesterday evening, and the cook said you took yours and Ellie's breakfast up to her room."

Because she just wanted to spend her time with her daughter and not have any contact with people she had to actually talk to—not even Alexis. Rachel couldn't get a grasp on her thoughts and she hadn't slept. Today she looked like a zombie, and her hair wasn't faring much better.

"I'm just tired, that's all." She attempted a smile in an attempt to erase the worry lines between her friend's brows.

"Is the auction becoming too much?" Alexis took a seat on the leather sofa next to the desk. "Dad said he's got Austin starting on the landscaping and gazebo area. I can't wait to see how that turns out. Is there something I can do to lighten your load? Why don't you let me take care of Matt's pictures and getting them printed and ready?"

"No!" She hadn't meant to shout her answer. "No," she said more softly. "I've got it. I think I've narrowed it down to what we need."

She had to go with the one of him in the waterfall. The one right before he'd demanded she come into the water, the one where his eyes had started getting all heavy-lidded and molten with desire.

No woman could resist that—obviously she hadn't been able to. Isn't that what she wanted? Women to throw more money toward the charity? Alexis and Gus were counting on a big check, and Rachel was here to help.

So she'd offer up the man she wanted. There was no denying she wanted him again, and he'd made things perfectly clear he wanted her just as much. But they couldn't sleep together again. She couldn't even look at him on the plane ride home, let alone undress for him again.

Guilt had accompanied her onto the plane. Granted she and Billy had had a rocky relationship, she'd suspected infidelity and he'd pushed her away after discovering the pregnancy. Still, she had been willing to work on their marriage.

But then they'd had that terrible fight and then the accident…and then it was too late to fix their marriage.

"What's going on?" Alexis asked, easing forward on the edge of the sofa.

Even though Alexis was her best friend, Rachel didn't want to get into the events of yesterday. She had to try to figure out how to wrap her own brain around it first.

"I just want to make sure I get everything perfect for the auction," she stated, which was the truth.

Alexis raised her brows and tipped her head. "You're a terrible liar."

So Matt had told her more than once.

"I'm just dealing with a few things," she told her friend. "Nothing to worry about. I'm just not ready to talk."

"Well, I'm here whenever you need me. I can bring wine or ice cream or both. Both is always a good answer."

Rachel smiled. "Thanks. I know you're here for me."

With a nod toward the computer, Alexis came to her feet. "Pull those back up and let's see what we're dealing with. Because from the little bit I could see when I walked in, your Matt is one devastatingly handsome man."

"He's not mine."

Alexis made a sound of disagreement as she came around the desk and clicked on the mouse. "Wowza. Do you see how this man is looking at you?"

Rachel clenched her teeth and stared at the multiple images as Alexis scrolled through. "He's looking at the camera."

"He's looking like he wants to devour you." Alexis glanced over her shoulder and met Rachel's eyes. "I'll assume this is what you're dealing with. Considering you two were at his private island all alone, I'd say you had a pretty good day."

"His pilot was there," she muttered.

Alexis laughed. "In the plane and paid a hefty sum to keep to himself."

Turning, she sat on the edge of the desk and crossed her arms. Her eyes held both questions and compassion.

"Stop staring at me," Rachel demanded. "I'm not talking about it."

"If a man looked at me like that and I was on his own island, you better believe I'd be talking about it."

Rachel pushed from her seat and shoved her hands in her hair, wincing when she encountered a massive tangle. "I need to go check on Ellie. She's resting."

"You have the monitor on the desk and there hasn't been a noise. Why are you running? Because of Billy?"

Because of Billy, because of Matt. Because the only other man in her life she thought she could depend on had turned out to be…more than she ever thought. Shouldn't she feel guilty simply over the fact that sex with Matt had been more amazing than anything she'd ever experienced in her marriage? Forget the fact that Billy had trusted them both?

Then again, she hadn't trusted Billy. Not in the end.

Did he even deserve her loyalty at this point? He was gone and if this were Alexis telling her this story, Rachel would tell her friend there was nothing to feel guilty about.

But still, this wasn't Alexis.

"It's okay to have feelings for someone else," Alexis added. "You're young, you're beautiful, you're going to get a man's attention. What's wrong with your friend, the Most Eligible Bachelor in Texas? Honey, women would die to be in your shoes."

"Then they can have them."

Part of Rachel was glad her friend knew some of what was going on without her having to say things out loud.

"I need a break." She came to her feet and sighed. "What do you say when Ellie wakes up we go shopping? Maybe we can find some Halloween costumes for the party. Which is always difficult because I don't want to be a slutty Snow White or a clown. So…something in between?"

Alexis practically jumped with glee. "Yes. I want to go as a Greek goddess. Care to join me?"

Retail therapy to find a fun costume—sounded like the break from reality she needed. Royal had some adorable little shops, so surely they could find something to throw together. Since the party was adults only, Rachel didn't have to find Ellie anything, but she'd gone ahead and ordered her a little unicorn costume online for trick or treating.

For the rest of the day she wasn't going to think about Matt or the waterfall or the tumultuous feelings she had to face. Unfortunately, those emotions weren't going anywhere and she'd have to deal with them at some point. Damn that man for taking their relationship into unknown territory. She had absolutely no experience with flings or friends with benefits or whatever the hell this was called between them.

But she was certain of one thing. No way could she bid on him during the auction. A fantasy date with Matt Galloway was only asking for more trouble.

# Ten

Matt walked through the old farmhouse, snapping pictures and making notes. He'd been here for hours, taking each room one at a time. There wasn't a spot in this place where he didn't see his grandfather or reflect on the memories of the greatest summers of his life.

This might not have been the grandiose spread that Lone Wolf Ranch was, but the small acreage and the two-story home still meant more to Matt than anything. More than his padded bank account, more than his private beach house on Galloway Cove and more than any relationship he'd ever had.

He'd already put a call in for a trust contractor to meet him at the end of the week and give an estimate of turning the whole place into something new. Matt wanted to keep the old elements as much as possible, like the built-ins and the old fireplaces, but breathe some new life into the home to make it marketable. Royal was a hot spot right now, so Matt had confidence the place would sell fast.

As he stepped back onto the porch, a lump caught in his throat. The thought of his grandfather's home going to someone else didn't sit well. Every time he thought of selling, well, he hated it. Maybe once an overhaul happened and most rooms seemed newer he would feel different. Perhaps then it would feel less like his family's farm and more just like a business transaction.

The wood plank beneath Matt's foot gave way and he jumped back just in time to save his leg from going through the porch. The damn thing was falling apart.

He rolled up the sleeves on his dress shirt and bent down to assess the damage. He recalled many times doing repairs with his grandfather. He'd always kept this place in pristine shape, and summertime was when he'd saved up all the projects to work on with Matt.

A few hours plus ruined clothes and shoes later, Matt had the porch torn apart and had found old, sturdy boards in the barn to prop up the porch roof.

He stepped back and pulled in a deep breath as he surveyed his destruction. Damn, even in the fall the hot Texas sun beat down on him. The moisture from all his sweat had his shirt clinging to his back.

Tires over the gravel drive forced his attention over his shoulder. Rachel's SUV pulled closer to his truck as he swiped his forearm over his forehead.

Confused, Matt crossed to her car. He hadn't spoken to her since yesterday and he honestly didn't think she'd come to him. Was she ready to discuss what happened? What it meant to their relationship?

When he got to the driver's side, the window slid down. Rachel offered a nervous half smile.

"Hey, there!"

Matt leaned down and spotted Alexis in the passenger seat. "Afternoon."

"It's evening now," she corrected with a laugh. "Looks like you ruined your clothes."

Matt glanced to his grimy shirt and back up. "Impromptu demo. What are you all doing out?"

"We went to find Halloween costumes for the TCC party," Alexis stated. "You'll be going?"

With a shrug, his eyes came back to Rachel. "How did you all end up here?"

She nodded toward the back seat. "Ellie fell asleep as soon as we were done shopping, so we took the long way home so she can get a little nap in."

There were various routes to get back to Lone Wolf Ranch. Interesting that she would choose this one.

"We saw your truck and pulled in," Alexis stated with a knowing grin. What had Rachel told her friend?

"Alexis insisted I pull in," Rachel corrected.

A whine from the back had Rachel jerking around and reaching toward the car seat. "It's okay, sweetie."

"Let me take her home," Alexis offered.

"What? No," Rachel insisted. "We're going now."

"Stay."

The word slipped through his lips before he could even think otherwise. From the shock on Rachel's face and the glee on Alexis's, he had to assume they were just as much caught off guard.

"Matt—"

Alexis was already out of the car before Rachel could finish whatever argument she had on her tongue. Matt reached for her door handle as Ellie's whines started getting louder.

"This is crazy," Rachel muttered. "I can take my own daughter home."

"You can," Alexis agreed as she took Rachel's hands to ease her from the car. "But let her come with Aunt Alexis. I'll give her a bath and read her a story. I'll even get her to sleep…you know, if you end up coming home late. Or even in the morning."

The little Matt had been around Alexis back in college, he'd liked her. Now he suddenly felt like he had an ally.

Matt couldn't smother his grin or stop the wink in her direction. She merely raised her brows as if they had some secret bond. Clearly they both wanted Rachel happy, which meant in this situation, Rachel didn't have a chance in hell of winning the argument.

The two of them had to talk and the opportunity wouldn't get any more obvious. Being a businessman, he took every open opportunity to further his steps toward his goals. And Rachel was one goal he wasn't about to get rid of. Now if he could just figure out what to do once he fully had her…other than the obvious need to fulfill.

"Take your time, Rach," Alexis practically sang as she slid into the driver's seat. "Don't worry about Ellie. She's in good hands."

Then Alexis closed the door and Matt reached for Rachel's hand. "Relax," he murmured against her ear. "I won't bite unless you ask."

Rachel threw a glance over her shoulder and rolled her eyes. "I won't ask."

Alexis pulled from the drive and Matt headed toward the house, assuming Rachel would follow since she had nowhere else to go.

He started picking up the mess he'd created, carrying

the broken boards around back and stacking them in a pile against the barn. When he came back from his third trip, he laughed at the sight of Rachel still standing in the driveway with her arms crossed over her chest. She merely stared back at him and raised a brow.

"You find a costume for the party?" he called.

"Shut up."

She was crazy about him.

"I'm thinking of going as a fireman…if you want to hold my hose."

Well, that pulled a smile from her lips. "You're a jackass."

"No, but I do care about that frown on your face." He moved closer to her so he didn't have to keep yelling. "Seriously, at this point I'll be going as a CEO because I have no idea what to wear."

"So you're going?"

He shrugged. "Why not? Sounds fun."

"You don't strike me as someone searching for fun by way of costume parties."

He laid a hand over his chest. "That hurts, Rachel. Maybe you've forgotten the time I dressed up as a pirate."

Rachel shook her head and snorted. "That doesn't count. You did it to get into that bar when we went to New Orleans for Mardi Gras. If I recall, that costume garnered you several beads."

He still hadn't disclosed how he'd acquired those, and at this point he figured it was best she not find out. He'd like to garner a few acts to get beads from Rachel. The images flooding his mind weren't so much fantasies now, but possibilities.

"Well, we got in where we wanted and a good time

was had by all," he stated. "So, are you going to tell me your costume or not?"

"You'll see it at the party."

Was she flirting? Hell, he had no clue. For the first time in all the years he'd known her, he couldn't get a read on her thoughts.

"Want to walk through?" he asked, nodding toward the house.

Her eyes darted to the ripped-apart porch and the two-by-fours propping up the roof. "I'm not sure that's a good idea."

"There's a back door." He grabbed her hand without asking and urged her toward the house. He'd missed her touch. Even though he'd been with her not long ago, the span of time was still too much. "I'm going to have a contractor meet me at the end of the week and discuss renovations."

"So you were trying to save money by ripping into it first?" she joked.

"Not hardly." He led her to the back, where the weeds had nearly overtaken the back porch. "Watch your step."

After helping her up and safely inside, Matt closed the screen door at his back.

"I'm not going to be doing the actual work," he told her. "I was actually getting ready to leave earlier when the boards snapped on the porch. One thing led to another and time got away from me. Demo is a good source to work out frustrations."

"Maybe you should give me a sledgehammer, then."

Though humor laced her voice, Matt knew she was quite serious. "You're more than welcome to help. You might actually enjoy the manual labor."

She glanced down to her jeans and off-the-shoulder

sweater that showcased one sexy shoulder. "I'm not really dressed for renovating today."

Matt held his hands wide. "Clearly I wasn't, either. You up for a little grunt work?"

What in the world had she been thinking? First, she let her friends steamroll her right out of her car and parenting responsibilities, then she'd gone into the house, and now she was sweating like she'd just run a marathon…which was absurd because she'd never run a marathon. Ever. Unless there was chocolate and wine at the end, and even then she'd have to think about it.

Rachel stepped back and surveyed the upstairs master bath. The rubble around her looked like a Texas tornado had whipped through, but her screaming shoulders reminded her she'd smashed everything to bits.

She hoped like hell Matt knew what he was doing by taking everything out. He claimed some of the things in the house, like the claw-foot tub in the guest bath and the old dumbwaiter, would be kept.

Propping the sledgehammer at her side, Rachel smiled. This had been therapeutic…no doubt about it. Maybe she should take up demo work instead of photography for her hobby.

"How's it g—" Matt stopped in the doorway of the bathroom and blew out a low whistle. "Remind me not to piss you off. You do some serious damage with that thing."

Rachel couldn't help but smile, as she was rather proud of herself. "So, what now? I'm a sweaty mess and apparently I have a sitter. Where else do you want me?"

His eyes raked over her body, instantly thrusting her back to the waterfall and making her realize her poor choice in words.

"I already told you that was a onetime thing," she warned, though saying it out loud was more as a reminder to herself than for him.

"You did say that." He remained in place, but the way his eyes drifted over her again only reminded her of yesterday. "Tell me you haven't thought of what happened on my island, haven't played it over and over in your mind, reliving every moment, just like I have. Tell me you can just be done after one time."

Rachel started to argue, but dropped her head and blew out a sigh. "What do you want, Matt? Do you want me to admit that I couldn't sleep for thinking of you? Of us?"

She lifted her gaze, surprised to find him still in the doorway and not right up on her, crowding her and filling her mind with more jumbled emotions.

"Fine," she conceded. "You win. I thought of every single detail from start to finish and then I rewound my memory bank and did it all again. I've thought of you while I'm awake and you've even invaded my dreams. But you know what? Nothing will come of this. You live in Dallas—I'm probably staying in Royal. You're a career businessman and bachelor extraordinaire, and I'm—"

"A single mother and widow. You've reminded me." Now he stepped forward, but didn't touch her. "You want to know how I see you? As a passionate woman who is denying herself because of guilt and misplaced loyalty."

"How dare you," she scolded through gritted teeth.

"What?" he yelled back. "You need to know what I've kept to myself for so long. Why I stayed away for a year. Why Billy was so unhappy."

Rachel shook her head and closed her eyes, as if

she could keep the pain from seeping inside. "Stop it. Just stop."

"I've wanted you for so long." His voice softened, as did her heart at his raw tone. "I watched Billy marry you. I watched him flirt with other women. I watched him disrespect you behind your back toward the end of your marriage. When I confronted him, he told me to stay out of your relationship. When you got pregnant…"

Matt clenched his fists at his sides and glanced down to the floor. He cleared his throat before meeting her gaze again.

"I know," she finished. "He didn't want the baby. We fought all the time. But I wanted her. From the moment I knew I was expecting, my whole outlook on life changed and I was excited to be a mother."

"You're a damn good mom." He smiled as he reached out to her. Cupping her face in his hands, he stepped in to her. "It's time you take back your life. Isn't that your goal? You want to start over? Well, now is the time. You can be a mother, but you also need to move on."

"With you? You don't want a family, Matt. Remember?"

His jaw clenched as he studied her face. "You want honesty? I don't even know what I want. All I know is when I'm not with you, I want you. When I am with you, I want you. I want you, Rachel. Right now."

He crowded her in this tiny room full of rubble. Her body instantly responded—if she was honest, the tingling had started in the driveway hours ago.

"I won't pressure you," he added. "But you need to know where I stand for however long I'm in Royal."

Matt released her and turned, stepping over the mess and back into the master bedroom. Rachel remained still, her skin still warm from his touch, her heart beating fast, her mind rolling over everything he said, everything she felt.

She couldn't deny herself, couldn't deny how Matt had made her feel more alive in the past few days than she had in a long time. Did she want to throw that away because she was confused and scared about the future, or did she want to grab onto this bit of happiness?

Rachel climbed over the mess she'd made. "Matt."

He stopped in the doorway leading into the hall, but didn't turn. His pants were filthy, his dark hair was a complete mess and there was a tear in his shirt on the right sleeve. Her attire wasn't faring much better. They both needed a shower, they both were feeling emotionally raw and they both had no clue where this was going.

There were so many reasons she should let him walk right out that door. But she couldn't do it. Maybe it was time she learned by his example and simply take what she wanted.

"Why is it when I'm with you, my clothes end up ruined?"

Her shaky hand went to the zipper of her pants. As she drew it down, the slight sound echoed in the room. Slowly, Matt turned to face her.

# Eleven

Matt couldn't move, he couldn't speak. Right before his eyes Rachel had turned into the vixen he'd always known her to be. He'd gotten a glimpse of her at Galloway Cove. But this, this woman before him doing the most erotic striptease he'd ever seen, took his breath away.

He didn't miss the way her hands shook. That slight uncertainty, even while her gaze had completely locked onto his, only added to his arousal. She might be nervous about her feelings, but she was taking what she wanted…and that was him.

Matt didn't even bother to be subtle when he ran his eyes over every gloriously exposed inch of her. When she stood before him completely bare, there was no way he could keep this distance between them.

"While you're here, I'm taking this." She shook her long, honey-blond waves back and offered a slight smile. "Whatever is going on, it's between us. I know you're not looking for a happily-ever-after, and honestly, I don't think those exist anymore."

Her words stirred something in his soul…something that irritated the hell out of him, but with a beautiful, naked woman standing before him, he wasn't about to start analyzing his damn feelings. There was only one thing he wanted to analyze right now and it was all of this soft, creamy skin exposed before him.

"If you're waiting on me to argue with your logic, you'll be waiting a long time."

Before he could wrap his arms around her, Rachel was on him. Damn, if that wasn't sexier than her standing naked before him. She threaded her fingers through his hair and covered his mouth with hers. Her sweet body pressed against his and he wished he could just get his clothes to evaporate so he didn't have to step from her arms, from her mouth.

"I'm filthy," she murmured against his mouth. "I probably smell."

He trailed his lips along her jawline and inhaled just below her ear. "You smell amazing and you'll taste even better."

Matt stepped back and stripped down to nothing. He wanted her glorious, silken skin against his; he wanted to be one with her and he damned any consequence that would come their way later.

With his hands full of the woman who'd been tantalizing him for years, Matt backed her up until they fell onto the old, squeaky bed.

He realized the mattress probably wasn't the most comfortable, so he rolled, pulling her on top. But when he looked up at her, she was all smiles, her eyes sparkling with happiness and desire.

"This damn thing is a brick," he growled. "Did I hurt you?"

She shook her head, her hair sliding around her shoulders. "It's not pain I'm feeling right now."

Just like yesterday, Matt held on to her hips as she settled over him. Would he ever tire of this view? All these years he'd wanted her, but he'd never thought of what he'd want once he had her...now he had his answer. He wanted more Rachel.

"I'm yours," she murmured. "Do what you want."

She was his. His.

No. That sounded permanent. What they were doing was...

Damn it. He vowed to worry about this later.

Matt sat up, thrusting his hands in her hair as he came to his feet. She instantly wrapped her legs around his waist and then he turned and held her against the wall.

"Now, Matt."

His name on her lips was all the motivation he needed. How long had he waited to hear such a sweet sound?

With a jerk of his hips, Matt joined their bodies, eliciting a long, low groan from Rachel. Another sweet sound he couldn't get enough of.

Rachel wrapped all around him as he set the rhythmic pace. She fit him perfectly—yesterday wasn't just a onetime epiphany. No woman had ever made him want like this, like he couldn't breathe if he didn't have her, like he didn't want to go a moment without touching her.

Matt reached around to grab her backside and moved faster. His mouth ravished hers as the all-consuming need filled him. He couldn't get enough...and wondered if he ever would.

Rachel's body arched against his; her mouth tore

away as she cried out with her release. Matt couldn't take his eyes from her. Rachel coming apart all around him would forever be embedded in his mind.

His climax overrode any thoughts, but he never took his eyes from hers. She stared back at him now, a soft, satisfied smile on her face as his body trembled. Little minx knew exactly the power she held over him…and he wouldn't have it any other way.

Their sweat-soaked bodies clung together, not that he was in a hurry to release her.

"We need a shower," she mumbled, her head against his shoulder.

"If the utilities were on, we could make use of that bathroom downstairs."

He actually liked her soaking wet, wouldn't mind having her that way again. An image of her in his Dallas home filled his mind. He'd been to his island, now to his family's farmhouse. Where else could he take her?

Matt patted the glossy bar top to get the bartender's attention. He needed another drink and he wanted to try to make sense of these chaotic feelings swirling around his head. Wanting Rachel, having Rachel and then being confused as hell as to what he wanted now was tearing him up inside.

No, the answer couldn't be found in the bottom of his tumbler of bourbon, but it sure as hell didn't hurt.

"Hey, man."

Caleb McKenzie took a seat on the stool next to Matt. Caleb was another member of the Royal TCC and Matt had met him while they'd both been here using the TCC offices just a few weeks ago.

"What's up?" Caleb asked.

"Taking a break from work."

He'd been at his grandfather's farm for the past several days doing more demo work. His contractor had come by and they'd gone over each room in detail, but Matt was finding the demolition rather therapeutic. For now, he'd wait on hiring his contractor. Mainly because he was enjoying the manual labor and getting back to his roots. Another reason was that Matt knew his grandfather would be proud of his work, and that was more important to him than anything when it came to the farm.

He ordered another bourbon and Caleb requested a craft beer. After tipping his Stetson back, Caleb shifted on his seat and rested his elbow on the bar.

"I'm taking a break from wedding planning. Shelby probably appreciates the fact I'm letting her deal with choosing the exact shade of purple for the flowers."

Matt laughed. Caleb had dodged the auction block, but in the end, he'd landed his very own fiancée.

Matt wouldn't be dodging the charity auction, considering he wasn't engaged or looking to be.

"Oh, good. Glad I'm not the only one ready for a drink at twelve-oh-five."

Caleb and Matt turned to see fellow TCC member Ryan Bateman striding toward them. He took a seat on the other side of Matt and adjusted his Stetson.

"It's Friday," Matt stated. "Might as well kick off the weekend a little early."

"Hey, I heard you were the new recruit for the auction." Ryan let out a bark of laughter. "None of us are safe. You've been in town, what? Two weeks?"

The bartender set the drinks down and took Ryan's order. Matt curled his fingers around his tumbler and blew out a sigh. "Yeah, I was added most likely because this guy took himself off the market," he said, nodding toward Caleb.

"I'm a catch," Caleb drawled. "What can I say?"

"I just hope the fantasy date I'm supposed to go on involves steak," Ryan added as he took his beer from the bartender. "Other than that, I don't care."

Matt cared a hell of a whole lot about his fantasy date. If Rachel wasn't on the receiving end, he didn't want to be with anyone else. Sure he dated quite a bit over the years, but lately he wasn't wanting to get mixed up with anyone else. Besides, he knew exactly what she liked…in bed and out. Didn't it just make sense she bid on him? Damn stubborn woman putting an expiration date on their bedroom escapades…

Would she be jealous if he took another woman out? That wasn't a game he wanted to play, but if Rachel didn't bid, then he'd obviously have to wine and dine someone else.

"I have a buddy who would be a great candidate for the auction," Ryan chimed in. "Tripp Noble. That guy is down for anything."

Matt sipped on his bourbon, welcoming the slight burn as the liquid made its way through his body. "I'll let Rachel know. She's been working hard on the social media aspect and getting the headshots ready for the posters. I doubt it's too late to add another, especially if it brings more money."

"Did I hear you and Rachel were at Daily Grind the other day for a date?" Caleb asked, a knowing smile on his face. "You may be off the market, too, if you're not careful."

Matt shook his head in denial. Their coffee "date" had been their first encounter in a year. So much had happened since then and none of it was about to be shared here.

"I'm not looking for a wife," he explained, shaking his head. "I'm just stepping in to help the cause."

"I wasn't looking for a wife, either," Caleb threw back. "These are the mysteries of life."

Oh, there was no mystery for Matt. He wasn't getting married anytime soon. Maybe one day he'd like a family, but he hadn't given it much thought, and he was too busy now to nurse another commitment.

He tipped back the remainder in his glass and came to his feet. After throwing enough bills down to cover all drinks, Matt glanced between his two friends. "I'd best get back to work."

"Are you using one of the offices here today?" Caleb asked.

Matt nodded. "I'll be here another couple hours." Until he traded his dress clothes for jeans, a T-shirt and work boots and headed back to the farm. He needed to get a call into his partner, but Matt's assistant had told him that Eric was out until this afternoon.

It was time to make a decision on the sale of the business…or Matt's half, anyway. Considering he kept feeling a void in his life he couldn't quite describe, perhaps it was time to start liquidating things that didn't fulfill him anymore—like his partnership.

"I'll probably be here later this evening," he added. "The Bellamy has an amazing restaurant, but I'm thinking beer and billiards sounds more like what I need."

"If that's an invite, I'll be here, too," Ryan added. "I'll bring Tripp."

"Shelby is going to some makeup party, so I'm also free tonight," Caleb supplied, dangling the neck of his beer bottle between two fingers. "It's been a while since I played pool."

"Looking forward to crushing all three of you," Matt said with a smile.

"You want to put money on that?" Ryan asked, quirking his brow.

"I can get behind that." Matt adjusted the rolled-up sleeves on his forearms. "But don't whine when I take all your money."

The guys tossed back insults as Matt headed toward the hallway leading to the offices. He loved being a member of TCC in Dallas, but connecting with the guys in Royal made him feel even more welcome than at his regular clubhouse.

Royal was definitely a town anyone would be lucky to live in. But he wasn't so sure it was for him. First of all, once the auction was over and he and Rachel ended their…dalliance, Matt wasn't sure he could stay in a town where he saw her every day. Because he was absolutely positive she'd want to stay here for the long haul.

He and Rachel would go back to being friends, he'd go to Galloway Cove until he figured out what he wanted to fulfill him and Rachel would meet another guy and settle down, just like she was meant to do.

Without him.

A heavy dose of jealousy and fear came over him as he realized he didn't want to see her with another man. Hadn't the years of seeing and hearing her with Billy been enough?

So what now? How did he carry on with his life and career and attempt to figure out what was missing? How did he move on like Rachel hadn't touched something so deeply inside him?

Matt had never been this confused, this out of control of his own emotions. And he didn't like it, not one damn bit.

# Twelve

Rachel tugged at her dress once more. Mercy sakes. Hadn't this dress been a few inches longer? She'd tried this on at the Halloween shop, but being in a dressing room and getting ready to leave your house were obviously two totally different scenarios.

Ellie was down in the family room playing with the chef, who seemed to be doubling as a nanny lately. Since the party was adults only, Gus and Alexis had both demanded Rachel make an appearance because she was working on the auction. Any way they could talk it up and promote it, they would.

So Rachel stood before the floor-length mirror and tugged at her flapper dress once more. Her only saving grace was the added fringe around the bottom. She just couldn't bend over. Or breathe. Or lift her arms.

Really, what could go wrong?

There was no plan B by way of costumes unless she

went as a haggard mother, so Rachel blew out a sigh, adjusted her sequined headband around her forehead, then grabbed her matching black clutch from the dresser.

She did feel a little silly going out with a fringe dress, bright red lips and these stilettos. She should be braless, in her sweatpants and getting ready to give Ellie a bath. That was her routine…save for a few nights ago when she'd been wrapped in Matt's arms once again.

Heat coursed through her and she shivered just as she had at his first touch. He'd been so thorough in their lovemaking—likely because he'd been waiting for so long to have her.

There was no denying that a good portion of her nerves had his name written all over them. He would be at the party and she had no idea how he'd come dressed. No doubt whatever he chose, he'd set her heart beating faster.

As soon as she hit the bottom steps, Mae stood there holding Ellie, who was already rubbing her eyes.

"I really appreciate this," Rachel said, giving Ellie a kiss on the forehead. Well, that was a mistake. Now the poor child had a perfect red lip outline. "Sorry about that."

Mae laughed. "No trouble at all. I'll clean her up, read her a story and get her in bed. She's such a sweetheart."

Rachel loved how this family had so easily taken them in. The family and the staff. They were all so close-knit, so bonded. That's what Rachel wanted for her daughter, for their new life.

"You look quite lovely," Mae stated, glancing to Rachel. "Is there some young man you're meeting at the party?"

"I'm going to talk up the charity auction." Though

if she happened to see Matt, she wouldn't mind sneaking off for a kiss or two. "I don't plan on staying for the entire event, so I shouldn't be long."

"Oh, please." Mae patted Ellie's back. "You're young and stunning and dressed up. Stay for the whole thing. I assure you we are all fine here, and if anything arises, I'll call you."

Rachel smiled. "Thank you. For everything you're doing for us."

"No thanks necessary." Mae started up the steps. "You go have a good time and don't worry about a thing here."

Gus came down the hallway dressed as a pirate in all black complete with eye patch and parrot on his shoulder.

"Well, look at you." Rachel crossed to him and smiled. "You look great."

Alexis came from the back of the house, where her room was, and Gus turned, then glanced back to Rachel. "I'll be walking in with the most gorgeous ladies there tonight. How did I get so lucky?"

Alexis looked absolutely stunning in her white one-shoulder dress with gold sandals, and gold ribbons holding her hair back. The goddess look definitely suited her.

"We're the lucky ones," Alexis stated, giving her grandfather a kiss on his cheek. "Nothing better than a rogue pirate. Are we all ready?"

Rachel nodded and when she stepped outside, the car had been brought around for them. Anticipation curled through her. Even though she wasn't used to being this fussed up, she couldn't deny her excitement about the party or seeing Matt. Being lovers aside, she was glad he'd come back into her life. She'd missed him. But knowing why he stayed away…well, that still left her confused and a little hurt. She wished he'd been up-front with her, but at the same time, she couldn't fault him. Had he come forward after Billy's death and told her he'd had feelings for her, Rachel highly doubted she would've believed him. She certainly wouldn't have been in the frame of mind to hear such things.

Matt was special. What they had was special. She had no clue where they were going, if anywhere, but for the first time in a long time, she was going to enjoy herself and have a good time.

When they pulled up to TCC, the valet opened their doors and greeted them. Rachel went first and stepped into the lobby. The entire place had been decked out with pumpkins, lights, faux spiderwebs and a witch's cauldron, and the entry to the bar and billiards room had a fog machine to really set the stage and showcase guests as they entered.

Searching the sea of costumes, she didn't spot Matt. There were so many faces she recognized, mostly the men she'd photographed, but disappointment settled in. He'd said he was coming, so he'd be here, right? Besides, she was here to chat up the upcoming auction. That was her main focus.

Rachel maneuvered through the crowd, passing a Queen of Hearts, a couple dressed as Belle and the Beast, and another couple dressed as eggs and bacon. Everyone looked so amazing, and suddenly she didn't feel so insecure in her dress, especially considering the lights were low and there were so many people around. The music blared from the DJ's stand at the far end of the room and there were several people on the dance floor already.

This was definitely a fun, festive party. Somehow,

though, she'd lost Gus and Alexis. Rachel sighed and eased her way around people to squeeze into a slot at the bar. A nice glass of wine would hit the spot. She rarely drank, but she'd love to have a nice white.

"Buy you a drink?"

Rachel glanced over her shoulder. Matt had a wide grin on his face and had donned a fireman's costume sans the big coat. The red suspenders over the white T-shirt really accented just how in shape he truly was. Granted she'd seen, felt and tasted those fabulous muscles, but now they were all on display.

"I thought you were joking about the costume," she told him.

He raised a brow and leaned in closer. "Want to play with my hose?"

She couldn't decide to laugh or roll her eyes...so she delivered him both. "That line was terrible the first time you said it. Move on."

"That was pretty lame," he admitted. "But, do you?"

"Shut up."

She laughed again as she turned back to the bar and waited for her drink. Matt ended up with a bourbon and paid for both drinks before taking her hand and leading her toward the opposite side of the room from the music. He found a table in the corner that was empty. A slow song had come on and most couples were dancing.

"You look so damn hot."

Rachel crossed her legs beneath the table and toyed with the stem of her glass. "Thank you. I wasn't sure about this costume, but Alexis refused to let me try anything else on."

His eyes dropped to her lips, her chest, then back up. "Remind me to buy her a drink, too."

Rachel had to admit she was glad she'd bought this

costume now. The way Matt looked at her was well worth whatever she'd spent. She hadn't realized she was worried what he'd think until now. Pleasure rolled through her at the fact she might just have the upper hand here.

"That's some getup you have, too."

This fireman's costume was sexy as hell. His dark hair and dark lashes eluded to a man of mystery, but she knew all about Matt Galloway. Knew he'd do anything for her, including sacrifice his feelings for nearly a decade. And she also knew he was fabulous with her daughter and that before ever meeting her, he'd put her needs ahead of everything else.

"I borrowed all this from a friend," he stated, then inched closer as his gaze dropped to her lips. "I've missed you."

Her heart fluttered in her chest. Those three words held so much potential. She wasn't sure what to ask as a follow-up. Had he missed her in general or missed her as in he was just horny? Was there a tactful way to ask?

He curled his fingers around his tumbler and settled his free hand on her thigh. Instant warmth and tingles spread through her. Damn it, she'd missed him, too. She didn't want to get too attached, not in any way other than friends. But when he touched her, when he looked at her, she couldn't help but want so much more.

And that was dangerous ground for her to be treading.

"How's Ellie?"

Surprised at his question, and touched that he was even asking about her daughter, Rachel replied, "She's good. I'm trying to plan a first birthday party for her and work on the auction, so things are a little hectic. I know she won't remember the party and we aren't even in our own home, but I'd still like to do something special."

"Has she been to a beach?"

"What?"

"Why don't we take her to Galloway Cove? She can play in the sand, splash in the ocean, put her face in a cake if that's what you want. We'll take my jet and there will be no pressure on you to do something extravagant. I can have my staff on hand to do whatever you want or I can tell them to leave us. Totally your call."

Rachel blinked. Was he serious? Spending her daughter's first birthday with Matt on his island seemed way, way too familial.

"I didn't think you wanted more with me than…"

Matt smiled and inched closer, his hand sliding higher up her thigh. "Sex? I definitely want that, but we're also friends. Why wouldn't I want to help ease your worries and spend more time with you?"

Rachel shook her head. "I don't know."

"Think about it."

Now that he'd planted the seed, she had no doubt that's all that would occupy her spare thoughts. Part of her wanted to jump at the chance to take a relaxing, fun trip with Ellie to celebrate her first birthday. But the realistic side kicked in and sent up red flags telling her that might not be the best idea.

Rachel caught a flash of white from the corner of her eye. Alexis headed out a side door leading to the hallways and about a second behind her was a man wearing a black Zorro mask. Interesting. Who was Alexis slipping away with? Rachel didn't need to ask, honestly. Her friend wasn't so discreet at keeping the secret of the man she was infatuated with.

Well, maybe others didn't notice, but Rachel knew

her friend pretty well. Whatever Alexis wanted, Alexis would get.

"Dance with me."

Matt came to his feet and pulled Rachel up with him.

"I figured you'd want to stay hidden in the corner and make out," she joked as they headed for the dance floor.

He slid his arm around her waist and whispered into her ear, "Maybe I want to feel that beautiful body against mine instead."

Oh, when he said things like that he made her wonder how she never realized how he'd felt. Granted he'd stayed away from her for the past year because he'd worried about her emotions and his restraint. That right there told her how much he cared. She had been upset at first, and she still hated that she'd missed an entire year with him, but he'd been trying to protect her from getting caught up in more emotional upheaval.

Damn it. She was falling for him. There was no denying the glaring fact staring her in the face. At this point all she could do was hope his feelings started shifting, as well. If he'd cared about her for so many years, then perhaps he would want more.

Rachel sighed. She couldn't get her hopes up or hinge her future happiness on a man who clearly wasn't in it for the long haul. Above all else, she had to protect her little family and do what was right for them.

Before they hit the dance floor, Rachel pulled away. Matt glanced back at her and she merely nodded her head toward the side exit. Once she slipped out, Matt joined her.

"What's wrong?" he asked.

The thumping bass from the music inside pounded through the night. "I don't think it's a great idea for us to be seen dancing together. Talking is one thing, but grinding on the dance floor is something else entirely. You are the main event for the auction."

Her heart ached the moment those words left her mouth. But the truth was he was the big draw, and it was her job to promote the auction and help bring in as much money as possible. Matt Galloway would give some other lucky lady a very nice fantasy date.

"I think we need to call this quits after the auction, too." She had to guard her heart and try to keep some semblance of control here.

Matt crossed his arms over his broad chest, which only went to showcase his perfectly sculpted biceps straining against the short sleeves.

"And why is that?" he tossed back. "You think whoever bids on me will, what? Steal my heart or make me forget you?"

That was precisely what she thought, but she sure as hell wasn't about to express her insecurities.

"I think that for as long as this lasts, we should enjoy it," she corrected, closing the distance between them. "Then when the auction comes, we go back to Matt and Rachel. Friends."

"Friends."

The word slid out like he had sandpaper in his throat. His arms snaked around her waist and a second later she was flattened against his chest.

"You're bidding on me."

With her palms resting on his chest, Rachel shook her head. "I'm not. You know I'm right about this. The sex is muddling your mind, but I'm a package deal and you're not looking for a family. You're not even looking for a girlfriend, so we need to put a stop date on this."

*Or else my heart will get broken yet again.*

His lips thinned as he stared down into her eyes. "Fine, but you're all mine until then."

Matt's mouth covered hers. A whole host of emotions swept through her and she couldn't decide if it was because of the kiss or the promised threat of being his. Matt clearly had territorial issues…another aspect that aroused her for reasons she couldn't explain.

Oh, wait. She could. Never in her life, not even with her husband, did she feel this wanted, this valued. Matt made no qualms about his current feelings. But what would happen later? When he was done with the good times and the sex? She had to be the one to put an ending to this story.

Rachel lost herself in his kiss, wrapping her arms around his neck and threading her fingers through his hair. She was a woman with wants and desires, and Matt was all too eager to help her check those boxes. She couldn't stop this onslaught of emotions even if she wanted to.

His hands settled on her ass as he squeezed and had jolts of arousal spiraling through her.

The sound of a car door slamming had Rachel pulling back and glancing around. Nobody had pulled into this side lot. She took the moment to pull in a deep breath. When she glanced back to Matt, he had red lipstick smeared all over his mouth.

Reaching up, she swiped the pad of her thumb below his bottom lip. His tongue darted out and Rachel stilled, her eyes locked on his.

"Come to my suite tonight," he told her in that husky voice that practically melted her clothes right off. "I need you, Rachel."

"I can't. I have a baby back at Lone Wolf Ranch."

"Then I'm coming to you," he threatened. "I have

to be with you. So either get Ellie and bring her—I still have that baby equipment from our dinner—or I'll climb up the damn trellis and come into your bedroom."

She had no problem imagining Matt scaling his way into her bed. "There's no trellis outside my window," she joked, trying to lighten the moment before she stripped him out of this damn costume and begged him for anything he was willing to give.

His hands gripped her backside, grinding her hips into his. "What's your decision?"

As if she had one. She wanted him; he wanted her. This was an age-old song and dance. But nothing about this was typical or normal or…hell, rational.

"You better come to me. Ellie will be asleep when I get home."

"Then leave a door unlocked or meet me out back and sneak me in." He nipped at her lips. "And I'm staying the night."

Oh, mercy. She'd just made a booty call date with her best friend and she was sneaking him into her temporary housing. Classy. Real classy.

Her hormones didn't seem to care, though. The anticipation of the night's events only had her body humming even more.

What was she going to do when it was time to call it quits?

# Thirteen

"Where the hell are they?" Gus demanded.

Rose shook her head and sighed. "They've both been missing from the party for nearly an hour."

Alexis and Daniel had snuck out. There was no other way to spin this. They were purposely trying to sabotage the auction and totally go against their family's wishes. Gus couldn't stand the thought of a Clayton stealing his sweet Lex away.

Gus turned back to Rose. He'd sent her a text to meet him in the back gardens on the other side of the clubhouse and away from the party so as not to be seen. He'd gone out and she'd come about five minutes later.

As he stared at her, with the moonlight casting a glow over this elegant, vibrant woman, Gus couldn't ignore the punch of lust to his gut. He'd had that same heady reaction multiple times when they'd been younger, but he couldn't afford that now. Those days were gone, decades had passed. Lives had been changed.

Besides, he flat-out didn't want to feel anything for her. Things were much simpler if he could just go on thinking of Rose Clayton as the enemy.

But she'd come to the party dressed from the Victorian era and he couldn't deny how stunning she was. Even though they weren't together, never would be and he still had that anger simmering inside of him, he could freely admit she was just as breathtaking as ever. The dip in her waist only accented the swell of her breasts practically spilling over the top of her emerald-green dress.

Damn it. He needed to focus and not think of her tempting body…or her at all. One wrong turn in his thoughts and he'd fall down that rabbit hole of memories he'd vowed never to rehash.

"So what do we do?" she asked. "I called Daniel, but he didn't pick up."

"I did the same with Alexis."

Rose smoothed her white curly wig over one shoulder. "On the upside, he has agreed to be in the auction. Just make sure you get your granddaughter out of the way of bidding when he hits the stage."

"I know my part," he growled, frustrated over the missing couple and agitated with himself for that niggling of want toward Rose. "Alexis won't be around even if I have to fake a heart attack."

Rose's eyes widened. "Don't joke about something like that."

Was that…care in her tone? *Whatever.* He wasn't giving that a second thought right now. He had a mission and he couldn't deviate from it.

"I'll text Alexis and tell her I'm not feeling well," Gus stated, pulling his phone from his baggy pirate pants. He hated this damn costume. He'd rather have dressed up as a rancher, but Alexis had forbidden him to wear his everyday clothes. "We came together so I'll have her meet me in the lobby. Surely that will get a response."

Rose nodded. "Good."

Gus shot off his text and held his phone, waiting. Silence curled around him and Rose, and the tension seemed to grow thicker with each passing second. There was so much he wanted to say, so many things he'd bottled up over the years, but what would be the point? Yes, he wanted answers. Hell, he *deserved* answers. But learning the truth of what happened all those years ago didn't matter now. Nothing mattered but stopping their grandchildren from falling in love...or whatever the hell they called it. The thought of his sweet granddaughter hooking up with a Clayton irritated the hell out of him.

Alexis deserved better and he was going to steer her in the direction her life needed to go. If that was meddling, well then he wasn't the least bit sorry. He only wanted what was best for her, and that certainly wasn't Daniel Clayton.

The phone vibrated in his hand. "She's going to meet me in the lobby in ten minutes."

Rose's shoulder sagged a bit, as if she'd been holding her breath. Considering they were both on the same page as to how much they *didn't* want Daniel and Alexis together, he was kind of glad Rose was his partner in crime here.

"I'll slip out and go back to the party," she told him. "Don't come out yet."

"I know how to do this," he snapped.

Rose jumped and guilt instantly flooded him. Damn it. Working with her was just supposed to be a way of keeping their families distanced for good. Instead, the more time he spent with her, the more his mind kept playing tricks on him and making him believe he was intrigued once again by her.

But that was absurd. Rose had been his first love; it was probably some residual emotions that had simply never gone away. He simply hadn't been around her this much in…well, decades. That's all. He was just mesmerized and captivated momentarily by her timeless beauty and her tenacity. Then he remembered it was that beauty and tenacity that had pulled him in and spat him out so long ago.

"Good night, Rose."

He dismissed her, feeling like an ass but needing to get out of here. Just as he started to pass, Rose reached out and put her hand on his arm. Gus stiffened at her unexpected touch. He didn't look over at her—he couldn't.

"We don't have to be enemies," she murmured softly.

Gus swallowed and fisted his hands at his sides. Nothing he said at this point would be smart. What could he say? They were enemies, after all, and that was all on her.

Choosing to remain silent, he kept his eyes on the exit and walked away. Whatever was going through her mind, he didn't want to know. They couldn't get distracted by anything, sure as hell not each other.

Gus pushed Rose from his mind and headed toward the lobby. He had to get Alexis out of here and away from Daniel. There wasn't a doubt in his mind that the two had snuck off together. If his granddaughter knew he had concocted the auction to keep her away, she'd never forgive him. Which was why she could never find out and why he needed to limit his face-to-face time with Rose.

And that was just one of the many reasons he had to curtail his alone time with the woman who had once crushed him.

\* \* \*

How long should she wait? More importantly, why had she agreed to this preposterous plan of letting Matt into Lone Wolf Ranch?

Rachel sat on the back porch swing and blew out a sigh. She hadn't agreed—not in words, anyway. She'd kissed and groped all over the man instead. Clearly giving him the silent answer he wanted.

Clutching the baby monitor, Rachel pushed off the floor of the porch with her toe to set the swing in motion. There was something so calming, so soothing about country life. To hear the crickets, to see the bright stars, to know that your neighbor wasn't right on top of you was so freeing, and she valued the privacy. She really should start looking for a home of her own. She loved Royal and knew now with 100 percent certainty that she'd be setting her roots here. Ellie would love the park, love the farms, the community.

Rachel couldn't deny she also wanted a bit of distance from her in-laws. First, they'd wanted her to move in with them so they could care for her and Ellie. Then they'd wanted her to let Ellie stay there so Rachel could finish school and find a home. Her mother-in-law had called this evening, but Rachel had let it go to voice mail. She knew they meant well, and understood that they would forever grieve Billy's death, but when Rachel spent any time with them, she got sucked into that black hole, and she couldn't afford that…not if she wanted to move on to the life she and her baby needed.

An engine caught her attention and for a split second Rachel thought Matt was here. But the headlights and sound came from the direction of the barn where the hay was stored.

Confused, Rachel kept her gaze on the vehicle as it

slowly came down the drive toward the exit. There was no mistaking that truck. She'd seen it before.

As the vehicle passed the house, she got a glimpse of a profile and, yup. That was definitely Daniel Clayton. Rachel bit the inside of her cheek as her gaze went back to the darkened barn. Looks like she wasn't the only one sneaking around to be with a man tonight. Rachel just hoped Matt wasn't spotted by Alexis. That was a conversation she didn't want to have with her roommate.

The low rumble of another vehicle approaching had her heartbeat kicking up. Matt pulled his truck around the back of the house and parked like he had every right to be here. Something about his arrogance—or confidence, as he'd called it—only intensified her attraction.

Why did this have to be the man to get her attention? Why was she able to push anyone else aside, but Matt Galloway demanded her everything and suddenly she had no control? As he closed the distance between them, the shadows surrounding him only added to the intrigue. Considering he'd had a thing for her for years and she'd just discovered it, she wondered if there was anything else he kept from her.

Rachel came to her feet. Without a word, he mounted the steps and she held the door open. Moving quietly through the house, Rachel took his hand and led him toward her own suite she'd been given. Thankfully, it was away from the other bedrooms and large enough to have a sitting room.

As soon as she entered, she turned the baby monitor off, since the crib was in the far corner near the sofa. The bed was on the other side of the suite, but Rachel wasn't comfortable doing this with her baby in the room because…well, because.

She hadn't thought this through very well. Obviously her need for this man had overridden any common sense on the realities of her sleeping situation… not that Ellie was old enough to know if there was a man in her mother's bed, but still.

Rachel held a finger to her lips, grabbed the monitor and urged Matt into the bathroom. She flicked on the light and slid the pocket door closed once he was inside.

"I guess I wasn't thinking that I share a room with her." Rachel shook her head and let out a humorless laugh. "If you want to go, I completely—"

His mouth was on hers, his arms wrapping her up and hauling her against his hard body. Rachel melted. Or, she felt like she had. The more time she spent with Matt, the more she wanted…well, everything.

His hands were all over her at once, stripping her clothes away before pulling his own off. Stepping over the pile of unwanted garments, Matt tugged her toward the wide glass shower. How could she want him this much when she'd already been with him twice? When would this ever-pressing need go away?

Rachel wasn't sure, but she knew she needed to enjoy this while it lasted…because the end wasn't far off.

# Fourteen

"Did you have a sleepover last night?"

Rachel glanced up from the office she'd been using at Lone Wolf Ranch. Alexis stood in the doorway with a wide smile on her face.

"Hey, I'm not judging," she immediately added before stepping in and closing the door. "I just saw a truck in the drive before I went to bed, and then this morning I heard it leave."

Ellie held on to her baby-doll stroller and pushed it around before falling back onto her diapered bottom. She'd just started walking, so there were still a few tumbles.

"I'm not the only one who had an evening visitor."

Alexis pursed her lips and took a seat on the sofa near the window. "I didn't come to talk about me. I'm here for you. Tell me that was Matt Galloway. I'm not even upset that we'll have to take him off the auction block. I'm just so happy you're dating…or whatever."

Off the auction block? Rachel wasn't going that far, and Matt never acted like he wasn't ready to strut his stuff—he just wanted her to bid on him.

Rachel really didn't have any reason to hide her current situation from Alexis. It wasn't like Alexis was going to wave her paddle when Matt came onstage or run out and tell anyone. She sure as hell wouldn't tell Gus, because her grandfather wanted Alexis to bid on Matt. Mercy, this was one complicated web they were all ensnared in.

Besides all of that, Alexis definitely only had eyes for one man, and it wasn't Matt.

"Things are complicated." Understatement of the year. "But, he's still in the auction."

"What on earth for?" Alexis jerked back, almost appalled at the statement. "He's clearly interested in you."

"We've snuck around a little," Rachel admitted. "But, like I said, things are complicated."

Alexis let out a little squeal. "I knew it! And, honey, there is nothing complicated about that man. He's obviously infatuated."

Sex was one thing, her strong emotions were another…and she had no clue how he truly felt. All Rachel knew was that he'd be going back to Dallas soon and they'd return to the friend zone. Would he put more time between them like he had before? Because she didn't want to lose him. If she could only have him as a friend, then she'd take it.

Falling in love had never been part of the plan… not that there had been a plan. Every bit of her reunion with Matt had been totally unexpected, yet blissfully amazing.

"You're falling for him." Alexis moved her legs up

onto the sofa when Ellie toddled by. "I can see it plain as day."

"Don't be absurd," Rachel denied. She wiggled her mouse to bring her screen back to life so she could finish the social media graphics for the auction. "Matt and I have been friends for years. He was Billy's best friend. He's still going to be the headliner for the auction, so don't worry."

"Oh, I'm not worried about that. Because you'll be bidding on him if he insists on staying in."

Rachel groaned. "Why do you all think that's how this has to play out?"

"You know you don't want another woman bidding," Alexis laughed. "I take it your guy wants you to stake a claim on him, too?"

Throwing a glance over her shoulder, Rachel eyed her friend. "He's not my guy. I'm working on creating a countdown for the social media sites. Don't try to distract me with all this nonsense."

"I think hooking up with your friend several times in as many days isn't nonsense."

Ellie fell over once again, taking the stroller with her. Alexis eased down onto the floor and helped Ellie back up.

"I am not doing this," Rachel said, turning back to her screen. "But, if you'd like to discuss what happened in the barn with Daniel, I'm all ears."

Silence filled the room. Rachel bit the inside of her cheek to keep from laughing. Daniel's grandmother and Gus had been sworn enemies for years according to the chatter Rachel had heard. The two had once been so in love, but then they'd fallen apart and married other people. There was no way Rose or Gus would want to see their grandkids together.

If Rachel thought her personal life was a mess, she had nothing on Alexis.

"I know you're sneaking around." Rachel clicked on a different font, trying to make this conversation casual to get her friend to open up. "I also know why, so if you want to talk, I'm here."

"Nothing to talk about."

Rachel's hand stilled on the mouse. She didn't blame Alexis for not wanting to confide in her, but at the same time, she wished her friend would talk. She'd probably feel better if she had someone to spill her secrets to. Granted that person might be Daniel right now.

Ellie let out a whine. Rachel spun in her chair in time to see her daughter flop down onto her butt and rub her eyes.

"I guess it's naptime," she stated, pushing up from the desk chair. "Since we both know what's really going on, but we need these guys for the auction, let's just keep this to ourselves."

Alexis stared back at her and simply nodded, which was all the affirmation Rachel needed to know her friend was indeed keeping a dirty little secret. At this point in Rachel's life, she was the last person to judge someone's indiscretions.

Rachel scooped Ellie up and kissed her little neck, warranting a giggle from her sweet girl. Then Ellie rested her head on Rachel's shoulder and she realized there was nothing more precious or important than this right here in her arms.

"You're lucky," Alexis murmured with a sad smile. "I want a family one day."

Patting Ellie's back, Rachel focused on her friend. "You'll have one. Just make sure you find the right guy first."

"You make it sound like Billy wasn't the right guy."

Rachel swallowed the lump of guilt. She didn't want to speak ill of her late husband and she would never say a negative word to Ellie about her father.

"Billy was a great guy," Rachel said carefully. "I think we married too soon and confused lust for love, then expected that emotion to carry us through the rough patches."

Rachel wasn't ready to admit her fear of infidelity.

Alexis stepped closer and rested her hand on Rachel's arm. "Which is why you deserve this second chance. Bid on your man before someone else comes along and takes him from you."

There was no response Rachel could make at this point. Matt was hardly her man, and bidding on him wouldn't secure that spot in her life. Then again, she didn't want to bid on anyone else.

Rachel headed back to her room to lay Ellie down for her nap. Stifling a yawn, Rachel figured she might as well lie down, too. She didn't regret the lost sleep last night. In fact, she'd worried about Matt staying, but having him next to her had only made her realize she wanted him more.

Why had she let this happen? She'd warned herself going in that there was no room for emotions. Matt was the almighty ladies' man; there was no good ending to her getting this invested in their time together. Intimacy had clouded her judgment at first, but now she saw a clearer picture. Did she even risk her heart, her soul, by holding out hope that he'd love her back?

Could she even move on if he did?

The guilt had settled in long ago; at this point she had to remind herself she was young and it was okay to move on. But moving on with Matt? A man who was not in the market for a ready-made family? Maybe not the smartest choice she'd made. He'd never made any indication that he wanted a family life in Royal or that he wanted more than sex and friendship.

Rachel grabbed Ellie's favorite stuffed toy and silky blanket and laid her little girl down in her crib. The first few months of Ellie's life had been rough with trying to get her child to sleep. Between the grief over Billy and an insomniac baby, combined with her schooling, Rachel had nearly lost her mind.

Thankfully, she was on break and Ellie embraced the naps…for the most part.

After placing Ellie in her crib, Rachel tiptoed away and headed toward her own bed. She'd just lie here and stretch out for a bit. She had to meet with the new landscaper who was working at TCC for the auction. He had her list, but they hadn't spoken in person. She'd feel better if she went and discussed her plan.

Her cell vibrated in her pocket. Stifling a yawn, Rachel pulled it out and glanced at the screen. Her brother-in-law was calling. She couldn't keep dodging them.

With a quick glance to Ellie, Rachel eased out into the hallway and slid her finger across the screen.

"Hello, Mark."

"Rachel." He sounded relieved that she'd answered. "Glad I finally caught you. Is this a good time?"

Was there ever a good time when trying to dodge an uncomfortable conversation? She'd never felt a real connection to Mark and his wife, Kay. They were nice people; Rachel just didn't have anything in common with them.

She rubbed her forehead, feeling the start of a headache.

"I just laid Ellie down for a nap," she replied. "What's up?"

"When are you coming home?" he asked.

*Home.* Right now she didn't have one to call her own. If he meant Dallas, well, she wasn't going back there. No way was she going to stay with her in-laws again. It was well past time she find a place of her own. Not that she hadn't appreciated their help, but Royal felt more like home than Dallas.

"I'm actually helping with a charity auction here in Royal," she explained. "I'm not sure when I'll be back in Dallas."

Mark let out a sigh that slid through the line and wrapped her up in yet another layer of guilt. She hadn't lied, but she couldn't flat out tell him, either.

"We miss Ellie…and you."

Rachel didn't need the added compliment. She knew full well they all missed Ellie, and she wouldn't deprive them of seeing her. She would visit Dallas soon, but she wasn't moving back.

"I'll text you soon and we can all meet up for dinner. I start back to my classes next week and the auction is taking up much of my spare time. But…soon."

That sounded so lame. The struggle to do what was right for her daughter, Billy's family and herself was seriously real.

"We just want to help," he added. "Kay and I…we just want to help you."

"I know," Rachel conceded. "I appreciate it. Maybe you all could come to Royal for dinner one night."

"I'll see what we can do. I'll text you."

Rachel gripped her phone. "Sounds good. Bye, Mark."

She disconnected the call and leaned back against

the wall next to her bedroom. Her headache had come on full force now.

Closing her eyes, Rachel willed for some sign to come…something to give her clarity as to what the right answer was for her future.

Finishing her degree and finding a home of her own had to be her next steps. Her feelings for Matt couldn't override that; her guilt toward her in-laws couldn't interfere, either. At the end of the day, Ellie's needs and providing a stable life for her were all that mattered.

Suddenly, she wasn't so tired anymore. She peeked into the room, pleased when she saw Ellie was fast asleep. Rachel rushed to the office she'd been using and grabbed her laptop before returning to her room. She popped a few ibuprofen to help with her headache since she wanted to try to get some work done.

Over the next hour she polished up the multiple ads that would lead up to the auction. There was so much that went on behind the scenes: social media images to create, newspaper articles to write to draw interest beforehand, radio commercials to schedule and so many other things. This was exactly what she was meant to do. Her love of photography would only help her with her marketing career.

She couldn't wait to do this on a regular basis for an actual paycheck once her degree was in hand. Hopefully she could do some work from home and stay with Ellie. She hated the idea of finding a sitter, but she'd cross that bridge when she got to it.

The phone vibrated again in her hand, causing her to jump. Rachel's pulse skipped as a text from Matt lit up the screen.

Be at my penthouse at 7 for dinner. Bring Ellie.

She sighed. Her headache hadn't completely vanished and she still wasn't feeling that great. She settled onto the sofa in the sitting room of her bedroom. She didn't reply to Matt; he didn't expect one. He wanted her there and they both knew she'd go. Ignoring her need for him wouldn't make it go away.

Perhaps she should just rest while Ellie was still asleep. Perhaps when she woke she'd feel better and would be able to go to Matt's. Their time was limited and every day that passed brought them closer to being put back in the friend zone.

# Fifteen

Matt ended the call and resisted the urge to throw his phone across his suite. He'd been arguing with Eric once again, only this time over the price. Matt knew what his 51 percent was worth and he wasn't taking a penny less. It wasn't like he had to sell for financial reasons. No, this move came strictly from an attempt to save his sanity and take the time to discover something that would make him feel whole.

The knock on his door had him jerking his attention toward the entrance. It was twenty minutes after seven, which also had put him in a bad mood because he'd convinced himself Rachel wasn't coming. She hadn't replied earlier and he hadn't spoken to her.

The concierge had set up quite the spread of food along the wall of the living area. Matt had literally ordered everything off the menu and even asked for specialty items for Ellie. He'd done a bit of research on babies to see what she could eat. He knew she only had three teeth, so he ordered extra cheesy mashed potatoes and some pureed fruit for her.

Matt raked a hand through his hair and pushed thoughts of his business woes aside. Rachel was here and he wasn't going to let anything ruin his evening.

As soon as he opened the door, he found himself reaching for Ellie as he took in Rachel's state of disarray.

"What's wrong?" he demanded as he held Ellie against his chest and ushered Rachel inside.

Her hair was in a messy ponytail, her shirt was wrinkly and she hadn't a stitch of makeup. She was still stunningly beautiful, but definitely not herself.

What dragon did he need to slay for her? Because the thought of anything wrong with Rachel did not sit well with him.

"I'm not feeling well." She closed the door behind her and turned back to face him. "I fell asleep while she was down. I started working and the next thing I knew I was waking up, she was gone from her crib and my laptop was still in my lap. Alexis had taken Ellie out and I didn't hear a thing."

She was pushing herself too hard. Trying to do it all on her own, and Matt was done with this.

"Sit down," he demanded. "I'll get you some food."

"Don't fuss," she stated, but still made her way to the sofa and practically melted down onto it. "You're always trying to feed me."

"Because someone needs to take care of you."

Ellie smacked her little hand against the side of his face and rattled off some gibberish he was pretty sure wasn't real words.

"Has Ellie eaten dinner?"

"Gus said he gave her some pears and Alexis had

the cook make some eggs earlier." Rachel laid her head against the back of the couch and let out a frustrated groan. "What kind of mother am I that I didn't even hear her when she woke up or someone came in and took her from the room?"

Matt turned from the array of food and crossed to her. Still holding on to Ellie, he eased down on the cushion beside Rachel.

"You're a mother who is trying to do too much and is going to make herself sick," he chided gently.

Ellie reached for her mom and Matt let her go, instantly realizing he missed the warm cuddles. When had he started craving holding a baby? He'd been so consumed with his yearnings for Rachel, this had crept up on him.

"I just needed a nap, that's all." Rachel smiled to Ellie and smoothed her blond curls off her forehead. "Since someone started walking, I'm constantly on the move."

"When do your online classes start back up?" he asked.

"Monday."

Matt rested his hand on her knee. "I'll hire you a live-in nanny."

Rachel jerked her gaze to his. "You'll do no such thing."

"Why the hell not? You need the help."

"Mae, the Slades' chef, has been helping so much, and I'm not letting you pay for my family."

Her family. She kept him at an arm's length—which was what he'd thought he wanted. So why, then, did it irk him so much right now?

"Billy would want me to help you."

Rachel grunted. "That was a ridiculously low blow."

Yeah, it had been. "You're my friend and I want to help. Don't make this more than it is."

"We're fine," she declared through gritted teeth. "Maybe I should've canceled. I'm tired and cranky."

*And not going anywhere tonight.*

"Which is all the more reason why you need to be here so I can pamper you."

She slid him a side-glance. "I'm not here for sex."

"I don't always think that's why you want to see me…though I'm flattered to know getting me naked is clearly on your mind."

Rachel rolled her eyes. "You're impossible."

She turned her attention back to Ellie and lifted her up before settling her back on her lap. "Uncle Matt is silly," she told her daughter.

The whole Uncle Matt reference seriously grated on his last nerve. He didn't want to be Ellie's faux uncle. He wanted…

Hell, he didn't know what he wanted.

In an attempt to pull himself together, Matt made up a plate for Rachel and a small one for Ellie.

"Come to the table," he told her.

Matt took Ellie and sat down with her resting on one of his thighs. "I have no clue if this is okay, but hopefully she'll like what I ordered."

Rachel glanced around at the spread. "I'd hate to see your bill when you check out."

Whatever his bill was would be worth it. He'd buy the damn hotel if he wanted just to make sure Rachel was comfortable and cared for. Anything to make her life easier.

"Talk to me about the auction," he said, spooning up a bite of potatoes.

Ellie put her hands right in the bite, then put her

fingers in her mouth. Well, whatever. He'd discovered feeding a baby wasn't a neat and tidy process.

"We added a couple new faces. I'm supposed to shoot their pictures on Tuesday morning."

The growl of disapproval escaped him before he had a chance to stop himself.

Rachel smiled as she stabbed a piece of filet mignon. "Easy there, tiger. It won't end like *your* photo shoot did."

It sure as hell better not or he'd have a little one-on-one with those guys. Jealousy wasn't an emotion he'd ever been familiar with, and he sure as hell didn't want to experience it now. Rachel had made it clear they were back to friends as soon as the auction was over, so he knew he had no right to get all territorial.

"Gus is loving all of this and is constantly looking over the sheet of eligible bachelors," she laughed and shook her head, causing more golden strands to fall from her ponytail. "The two I added today piqued his interest and he's ready for Alexis to place her bid."

Matt gave Ellie a bite of mashed-up strawberries. "Does Alexis have her eye on one?"

"I'm pretty sure there's only one bachelor she's got her eye on, but she's keeping him a secret."

Matt raised his brows. "Kind of like us."

Rachel tipped her head. "Not exactly. Alexis has tried to brush me off when I broach the topic, but she has a thing for Daniel Clayton. They've been sneaking around."

"Why would they sneak? Just because of the auction?"

"The Slades and the Claytons make the Capulets and the Montagues look like playmates."

Interesting. No wonder Alexis had to sneak to see her

guy. If Matt didn't have this damn title hanging over his head and hadn't been roped into starring as the headliner for the auction, he wouldn't have to sneak around with Rachel, either.

"Sounds like a mess," he said.

Ellie swatted at the spoon full of strawberries and it flung back onto his gray T-shirt.

"Oh, Matt, I'm so sorry." Rachel jumped from her seat and grabbed her napkin to dab at his shirt. "Let me get that."

"It's a shirt, Rachel. Relax."

There she went again trying to do even the simplest things for other people. She had a plate full of food still, and she looked like she was about to fall over.

"I've got this and Ellie," he informed her. "Your job is to eat. That's all."

Slowly, she sank back into her chair and dropped the napkin on the table. "Sorry."

"Stop apologizing." Damn it, he wished she'd see he was trying to help. "I've got this, really."

Rachel finished eating and Matt ignored the stained shirt and the fact it had soaked through to his chest. Once Ellie was done, he picked her up and grabbed the diaper bag.

"I assume she needs a bath?" he asked, shouldering the bag.

Rachel nodded. "I can do it when we get home."

"You're staying here tonight."

Those doe-like eyes widened. "I can't stay here."

Considering she looked like a soft breeze could blow her over, Matt didn't even consider this a fair fight.

"You're staying and I'll give Ellie a bath."

Rachel smoothed her stray hairs from her face and

smiled. "You're joking, right? If you think dinner is a mess, you should see bath time. She loves splashing."

"It's water," he retorted. "I'll live."

Rachel eased her seat out and crossed her arms, leveling her gaze his way. "Don't do this, Matt. I can't…"

"Can't what? Let a friend help?"

"You know what I mean."

Matt shifted Ellie to his other side and couldn't deny his heart lurched when she put her head on his shoulder. How could he not fall for this sweet baby girl? She was innocent and precious and, with no effort on her part, had worked her way into his heart. Perhaps it was because she was his last connection to Billy or perhaps because she was a mirror image of her mother. Matt wasn't sure, but he knew for certain he wanted them both to stay here with him tonight.

"You can supervise," he told her. "Let's go."

Rachel got the water ready to the proper temperature and then started to remove Ellie's clothes. Rachel sank down next to the edge of the garden tub and sat Ellie in the water. Matt grabbed a cloth and a towel and sat next to Rachel.

Ellie patted her little hands on the water and giggled as she splashed herself in the face. Matt glanced for the soap and wondered if there was something special he needed to use.

"I have her soap in the diaper bag," Rachel stated, as if reading his mind.

She stood up and went to the vanity to her bag. Matt kept his hand on Ellie's back, not caring one bit that he was already getting soaked. Ellie's dimpled smile was infectious, and this familial moment was something he'd never thought he wanted.

Did he want it, though? Doing this one time was a far cry from being a permanent family man.

Damn it. He was getting too caught up in his thoughts and letting his heart guide him. He'd never let that happen. If he'd let his heart and hormones lead the way toward decision-making, he never would've become the successful businessman he was today…then again, he wasn't too happy with that job. At the end of the long, dragging days, he still felt lonely, empty. No matter how many mergers he secured, there was still the fact he came home to a quiet house.

Rachel came back with the soap, and after some more splashing and giggles, they finally got Ellie all washed up. Rachel grabbed a spare outfit from the bag and dressed her daughter while Matt cleaned up in the bathroom.

When he turned to face her, he realized her clothes had gotten soaked, as well. He didn't need that clingy fabric to remind him of how her waist dipped in and her hips flared. Those curves were made for a man's hands…his hands.

"Let me get her a bottle," Rachel said, pulling him from his thoughts. "She's going to be ready for bed."

"Why don't you take a relaxing shower or bath or whatever?" he suggested. "Get a bottle for me and I'll get her to sleep."

Rachel patted Ellie's back and smiled. "You're really determined to do this, aren't you?"

Matt reached for Ellie. "I'm determined to make sure you're safe and healthy, so if I have to feed you, bathe your child, make sure she gets to bed so you can rest, then that's what I'll do."

"We can't stay here," she argued, though there wasn't

much heat to her voice. "Ellie still gets up at night to eat, and she'll wake you—"

Matt put his index finger over her mouth to silence her. She slid her tongue out, moistening her lips, but she brushed the pad of his fingertip. Heat coiled low and it was all he could do not to forget their responsibilities.

Her eyes widened, clearly when she realized what she'd done.

"I'll be fine," he growled. "Now, get that bottle and let me get her to bed."

Rachel finally nodded and Matt eased his hand away. By the time she came back with a bottle, Ellie had started fussing and was rubbing her eyes. The crib was still set up in the living area, so Matt dimmed the lights. He settled in the leather club chair and attempted to find a comfortable position to get into. Rachel stood in the distance and stared, worry etched on her face.

"Go on to bed, Rachel. I'll stay in here with her."

"I won't win this fight, will I?"

Matt smiled. "Good night, Rachel."

He stared back down at Ellie and wondered how the hell he'd gotten to this point. He never invited a woman to stay all night, and here he was about to spend his second night with Rachel because he couldn't bear to be away from her. He was getting her child to sleep like some fill-in dad. What the hell kind of poser was he? This wasn't what he'd meant to do. He never wanted to fill Billy's shoes.

Billy. His best friend and the man who had been cheating on his wife just before his death. The secret weighed heavy on Matt's mind. Rachel deserved to know, but on the other hand, why would he want to put her through more pain?

He didn't like lying by omission to her. He also didn't like the way his entire life was turning on its axis because he didn't even recognize himself anymore.

Most Eligible Bachelor in Texas was now playing house with a woman he shouldn't want, but couldn't seem to be without.

He was so screwed.

# Sixteen

Rachel hadn't spent the night with any man other than Billy, but waking in Matt's bed didn't fill her with regret. If anything, she felt...complete. Having Matt take care of her when she felt bad, having him not mind looking after Ellie one bit only made Rachel fall for him even more.

She rolled over and checked her phone and was shocked to see it was well after nine. She'd missed a text from Billy's mother, but she'd answer her in a bit.

Rachel flung the covers back and rushed out to the living room. "I am so sorry—"

She stopped short when she spotted Matt reclined in the corner of the L-shaped sofa. He had pillows propped around him, Ellie sound asleep on his chest and his head tipped back against the cushions. He was completely out.

Well, if that didn't make her heart take another tumble, nothing would. She knew the friend side of Matt, the one that joked and was always there to lend a hand. Then she'd discovered the deliciously sexy side of him when he'd taken their relationship to a new level.

But seeing him hold her child, mimicking the role of a father, had her questioning just how deep she'd gotten with him. How could she ever reverse such strong feelings? Love was about as deep as it went, and there was no magical switch to just turn it off.

Rachel tiptoed toward them, but Matt stirred. He blinked a few times before focusing on her. A sleepy smile spread across his gorgeous face. This was the sexy side, the side she would never tire of seeing. She only wished they could take the day and spend it in his bed, forgetting the world and doubts and fears.

"She got up really early," he whispered. "I tried not to wake you, but I guess we fell back asleep."

"How early, and why didn't I hear her?"

Matt shifted, holding on to Ellie as he sat up a little more. "I was up working and it was around five."

Good grief. Here she'd slept like the dead and hadn't even noticed. That was the second time in as many days.

"Are you feeling better?" he asked softly.

Rachel nodded. "I can't believe I slept that long."

"You clearly needed it."

Ellie started squirming and Rachel stepped forward. "Let me take her."

Before she could reach her, Rachel's cell vibrated in her hand. She glanced down and frowned at the second message from Billy's mother.

"Everything okay?"

"Billy's family wants to come visit since I'm not getting back to Dallas fast enough," she sighed and sank down onto the couch next to Matt, taking Ellie from his chest. "I haven't told them I'm staying here permanently. They want to take Ellie so I can finish my degree. They've made it clear they can give her a good life."

Rachel kissed her baby on her head and nestled close. "I appreciate the sentiment, but there's no way in hell that's happening. Do they honestly think I'll give her up?"

"Have they seen her much since Billy's death?"

Rachel shrugged. "Some. They've just been hovering, and honestly, they're one of the main reasons I want to move. I can't handle being under their microscope. The calls, the texts—it's all day long."

Matt moved the pillows from between them and leaned in closer. His rumpled hair and the baby food on the shoulder of his T-shirt made him look like the opposite of the Most Eligible Bachelor in Texas. Yet he'd never looked hotter or more desirable. And she knew she was treading some very dangerous water here. Not only had she opened her heart to him, she'd let him in with her daughter, and that was an image Rachel would never be able to erase.

"Ellie is their only link to Billy," Matt said, resting his hand on her knee. "They just don't want to lose everything. Maybe you guys could come to some sort of visitation schedule that works for everyone."

"Mark and his wife asked me for full custody. Can you believe that?"

Matt shook his head. "Clearly that's a no, so sit down and talk with them. Tell them you'll be living here and see about letting them come to see Ellie. This doesn't have to be ugly, and it shouldn't be a fight. If you need, I have an excellent attorney I keep on retainer."

Rachel shook her head. "No. You're right. We can work through this. I'll call her in a bit."

When Ellie perked up and glanced around the room all bright eyed, Matt laughed. "At least she wakes up pleasant."

"She's usually a happy baby. I'd better call down and order some breakfast."

"I actually need to head over to the farmhouse and get a few things done," he told her as he came to his feet. "How about you meet me for lunch in town at the Royal Diner around one?"

Rachel smiled. "I'd love to. Are you sure you don't want me to order you something?"

He leaned down and kissed her. "I want you to stay as long as you like. In fact, why don't you stay with me while I'm in town? I want you in my bed, Rachel."

As much as she'd love to stay in his bed each night, she couldn't for so many reasons. Though that heated look he pinned her with had her questioning those reasons.

"If word got out that I was sleeping here with you, how well do you think that would go over at the auction?"

He stood straight up and cocked his head, smiling wide. Her toes curled and her belly tingled. "The auction where you'll bid on me and then take me home to have your wicked way with me?"

Rachel rolled her eyes and extended her leg to kick him slightly on his thigh. "Get out of here and take that ego with you."

But that's exactly what she wanted and he damn well knew it.

Holding on to her baby, Rachel eased to the corner of the sofa Matt had just vacated. She couldn't contain the smile and she wasn't even going to try. Maybe she would bid on him, but she had limited funds and probably wouldn't be able to compete with the other women of Royal and the surrounding area.

But what if she did bid and win? Then, when the auction was over, she'd tell him how she truly felt. If she had learned anything from Billy's death it was that tomorrow wasn't promised. Rachel never thought she'd feel such a strong pull toward another man, but everything she had inside her for Matt was completely different than her feelings for Billy.

And maybe she'd just have to let him in on her little secret.

Gus and Alexis had taken Ellie to the park for a picnic and to play. Rachel figured it was because there was a bit of tension swirling between the two Slades over the auction, but Rachel had her own issues to worry about.

She pulled up early to meet Matt at the diner. With a deep breath, she pulled out her phone and dialed her mother-in-law. Matt was right…the sooner she discussed this situation, the better off everyone would be. It wasn't fair to deprive Ellie of her grandparents. They obviously loved her, and that was at least the mutual ground they'd need to build from.

The phone rang twice before Alma Kincaid answered. "Hello?"

"Alma? Um, it's me. Is this a good time?"

"Rachel," the woman practically squealed. "Of course, of course. How are you? How's our sweet Ellie-bug?"

Rachel gripped her cell and watched as a family of four went into the restaurant. "We're all doing great. I'm sorry I missed your calls. These past couple weeks have been busy. I'm working on a charity auction and

I start back to class on Monday. My last semester before I earn my degree."

"That's wonderful," Alma praised. "You sound so swamped, though. Ellie is more than welcome to stay with me until your load lightens."

"That's one of the reasons I called to talk to you." *Please, please let this go smoothly.* "I know you guys miss Ellie and I'd like to see if we can come to some sort of agreement on a visitation schedule. My plan is to move to Royal...for good."

"For good?" Alma repeated. "Well, um, okay. I wasn't expecting that. But, I understand staying in Dallas might bring back some painful memories. Billy's death changed us all."

Wasn't that the truth?

"I'm just so thrilled you're going to let us see her," Alma went on. "I was so worried after he died that you'd shut us out. I tried to talk him out of going to that divorce lawyer and told him to work on your marriage. I mean, you were pregnant, and that certainly was not the time to end things."

Stunned, Rachel stared at the American flag flapping in the wind across the street at the courthouse. "Divorce lawyer?"

"I couldn't believe it myself," she added, oblivious to the bomb she'd just dropped. "But I love Ellie and I love you like my own, Rachel. I would love to come up with a visitation schedule. Whatever works best for you and Ellie. I'm willing to drive to Royal as often as I can."

Suddenly shaking, Rachel couldn't think. Billy had been ready to divorce her? She knew they'd been arguing, that they'd started growing apart, but that word had never been thrown around.

"Alma, I need to call you back. Will you be home this evening?"

"Of course, dear. It's so good to hear from you. Give Ellie-bug a kiss from Gran."

Rachel disconnected the call and rubbed her forehead. Pulling in one deep breath after another, she willed her breathing to slow.

The tap on her window had Rachel jerking in her seat. Matt stood outside her car with a smile on his face and opened her door.

When she slid out and looked up at him, his smile vanished. "What happened? Is it Ellie? Are you feeling bad again?"

She was feeling bad, almost nauseous, in fact. "I just got off the phone with Alma."

Matt's brows drew in. "Did she not agree to your idea? I can call my lawyer now—"

"No. We didn't even get to discuss the schedule. She was just glad I was letting Ellie be part of their life since Billy—uh—had already gone to a divorce attorney."

Matt eased back, his eyes showing no sign of shock. In fact, Rachel only saw one emotion, and that was acknowledgment.

"You knew?" she whispered hoarsely.

He slid a hand over the back of his neck and started to reach for her. "Listen—"

She slid from between him and the car to avoid his touch. "No. How dare you know and not tell me!"

Matt glanced around when she shouted, then took a step closer. "You don't want to do this here."

"I don't want to do it at all," she growled through gritted teeth. "You betrayed me."

Matt gripped her shoulders and came within a breath of her. Although she wanted nothing more than to shove him away, she didn't. Causing a scene wouldn't repair what had been done, wouldn't piece back together her shattered heart. She'd trusted him. Damn it, she'd fallen in love with him.

For the second time, she'd laid her heart on the line only to have it crushed and her trust betrayed.

"When did you want me to tell you?" he asked, lowering his voice. "I just found out the day he died. We were on the boat and he mentioned it, then I tried to talk to him. The accident happened so fast, then you were distraught from the loss. At what point should I have caused you more pain, Rachel?"

She closed her eyes, trying to force the truth away. Learning her most trusted friend had kept something so pivotal from her only exacerbated the pain he referred to.

When she focused back on him, Rachel's heart lurched. The way he held her, the way he looked at her all seemed so genuine and full of concern. But everything had been a lie.

"You knew this information and then you dodged me for a year," she accused. "I understand not telling me immediately, but did you ever think of reaching out to me after that? Is that why you really stayed away, because you wanted to keep your friend's secret? Did everyone know he didn't want me? Didn't want our baby?"

Damn, this hurt. The idea that she and Ellie were going to be tossed aside crushed her in ways she hadn't thought possible. And the fact that Matt knew and remained silent…well, she had no label to put on that crippling emotion.

"I never wanted you hurt," he ground out.

Rachel looked into his eyes, searching for answers she might never have. "Would you have ever told me?"

Matt's lips thinned as he remained silent. That told her all she needed to know.

"Let me go," she murmured. "I can't do this anymore."

"Rachel." His grip remained as he pulled her against his chest. "Let's go somewhere and talk. You have to know I never meant to hurt you."

"Yet you did."

He rested his forehead against hers. "Don't push me out. Let me explain."

"What else have you lied about?" she asked, her voice cracking, and she damned her emotions for not staying at bay until she was alone. "Did you actually want to be with me, or was this just because Billy—"

"None of this is because of Billy," he demanded. "I've wanted you for years, Rachel. You can't tell me you didn't feel it when I kissed you, touched you. Made love to you."

Rachel started to protest, but Matt's mouth covered hers. Their past kisses had been frenzied, intense, but this one could only be described as passionate and caring. He took his time as he framed her face with his hands. Despite everything, Rachel started to melt into him because she couldn't disconnect her heart from her hormones.

"Perfect."

They jerked apart at the unfamiliar voice. A young woman stood next to them with her phone, taking a photo.

"Mr. Galloway, can you comment on your relationship here?" the woman asked, whipping out a small notepad and pen. "Are you officially not the Most Eligible Bachelor in Texas anymore? And what about the charity auction? Rumor has it you're the star of the show."

Rachel backed away as Matt took a step toward the journalist.

"Delete that image now," he demanded. "And there will be no comment."

The lady's eyes widened as she slid her paper and pen back into her oversized purse, then she turned and ran. Matt cursed as he raked a hand through his hair. No doubt the woman was on her way to post the steamy picture on any and every social media site she could.

Dread racked through her. What had she been *thinking*? She couldn't kiss Matt on the sidewalk in broad daylight. He was the main attraction for the auction. Who else had seen the kiss?

None of this was going to work. She and Matt were nearing the end, and that reporter just solidified the fact. Rachel had a baby to look after; she had a career to get started and a new life to create. She needed to provide stability and a solid future for her and Ellie.

Matt's lie, even by omission, and now the fact she'd be all over social media in seconds…damn it, the forces pulling them apart were getting stronger.

Her mind scrambled in so many different directions. She couldn't stay here. That much she was certain of.

Rachel turned toward her car and opened the door.

"Wait," Matt commanded. "Don't go."

She threw a look over her shoulder. "We're done, Matt. And now I have to go do damage control to save you in this auction."

She settled behind the wheel and started to close the door.

"You can't run from us, Rachel," he called out.

One last time, she glanced up to him. "There is no us."

# Seventeen

"The press conference is scheduled for tomorrow evening."

Rachel heard Gus's words, but she didn't look up. Since the debacle two days ago with Matt, social media had exploded. Between the media speculation about Texas's most famous bachelor being taken off the market and the biggest draw for the auction in question, Rachel figured the only way to combat this cluster was to hold a press conference. That way she could field questions and make a statement, focusing on the bachelors for the auction, including Matt, and putting to rest any claims that he was off the market.

He certainly wasn't hers—no matter how much she wished he was.

Rachel put another block on top of Ellie's and Ellie promptly kicked them down.

"Listen, darlin', I know you think your man betrayed

your trust, but sometimes men do stupid things in the name of love."

Rachel jerked her attention toward where Gus had taken a seat in the leather recliner. "Alexis told you?"

"She gave the important details." He took off his Stetson and propped it on his bent knee. "Don't be upset with her. She's worried about you and so am I. You're like family to us now."

Rachel couldn't suppress her smile. "You guys feel the same to me."

"As much as I wanted my granddaughter to bid on Matt, I have a feeling he's off the table."

Rachel shook her head and handed Ellie another block. "He's still on," she corrected. "Whatever we had, it's over."

"Because he didn't tell you your husband was going to leave you?" Gus blew out a sigh and eased forward in his chair. "If Matt cared about you even a little bit, he wouldn't want you hurt more than necessary."

Rachel didn't want to argue about this; she didn't want the voice of reason to enter in. Because as far as she was concerned, she had every right to be angry at Matt for keeping the truth from her. Especially after learning that he had no intention of ever telling her. Had his loyalties to her late husband been that strong? Had everyone known Billy was leaving but her?

"I'm sure your mind is racing," Gus went on. "But if you don't listen to anything I say, listen to this. Love doesn't always come around twice in a lifetime. Trust me on that. Very few are lucky enough to get another chance. If you feel anything for Matt, you need to tell him."

Rachel came to her feet and leaned down to pick Ellie up. "Gus, I've come to love you like my own grandfather, but right now I can't handle this. Matt isn't mine, and I'll be sure to emphasize that tomorrow at the press conference. Now, if you'll excuse me, Ellie needs a nap."

Rachel didn't want to sound rude, but she just needed to not talk about Matt or her feelings or anything to do with why she should forgive him. Billy had destroyed her by the hints of infidelity and then rejecting the pregnancy. Now she was going through betrayal all over again with Matt. She never expected him, of all people, to lie to her.

Rachel carried Ellie upstairs and took her time getting her to sleep. She rocked her, sang to her, held her after her breathing had slowed and she was out. Rachel just wanted to hold on to the one person in her life she treasured more than any other.

Finally, Rachel laid Ellie into her crib and went over to the desk in the corner. She pulled up the screen on her laptop, ready to start looking for a home. It was time she pushed forward and made a life for herself and her daughter. Everything that happened before this moment didn't matter. She would finish her degree, find a house and make good on her promise to allow visitation with Billy's family.

But the second her computer came to life, she remembered she'd been working on a large spread with a photo of each bachelor. Her eyes instantly went to Matt. There was no competition as far as she was concerned. The image she'd used of him in the waterfall made him stand out and beg for attention…just like she'd intended.

Only her plan had backfired, and she had to stare at the photo knowing full well that only seconds after it was taken, her life had irrevocably changed. There would be no going back to friends, no matter how much she would miss him. Because, damn it, her heart hadn't gotten the memo that things were over. She still cared for him, still *loved* him. But how could she ever trust him again?

Rachel couldn't look away from the image. The longer she stared, the more mesmerized she became by that dark stare, those heavy lids, that white cotton shirt plastered in all the right areas.

But Matt wasn't just the sexiest man she'd ever known. He'd been her friend; he'd come to her defense in front of Billy more than once when her late husband had disrespected her. Matt had kept his needs to himself for a decade. Who the hell did that?

Were those the acts of a man in love? Had he loved her in that way? She didn't even know how to analyze all of this information without going absolutely insane.

Right now she had to push her emotions aside, no matter how difficult the task might be. She had a speech to prepare and bachelors to introduce tomorrow during the press conference. Damage control was just part of marketing, and this whole situation sure as hell gave her much-needed experience…she just wished her heart hadn't been part of the experiment.

Matt pounded the hammer once more, driving the nail home. He came to his feet and surveyed the brand-new porch and roof he'd spent the better part of two days installing.

And no matter how much demolition or renovation he did of his grandfather's home, nothing had exorcised those demons from him.

Rachel still consumed every part of him. He missed the hell out of her. But it wasn't just Rachel; he missed sweet Ellie. The two females had slithered right into his heart and taken up so much real estate, he had no idea how he'd ever lived without them.

He did know one thing: he'd managed to sell off his 51 percent early this morning when Eric finally came up to Matt's asking price. The weight lifted somewhat, but still there was something missing.

The sale would take time to finalize, but Matt wasn't worried about it falling through. He'd make sure it happened so he was free to move on to…whatever the hell he wanted.

Who knew? Maybe he'd take up residence here in Royal and make this old homestead his farm.

Something akin to a blast erupted inside of him, and Matt's breath caught in his throat. He'd called off his contractor, stating he wanted to do the initial work himself. He wanted the grunt work, the outlet for his frustrations, and a way to get back to his roots when he'd bonded with his grandfather. He would have his guy come in and take over soon enough, but for now, this was his baby to nurture.

He'd brought Rachel here and she'd helped. The most precious times of his life were spent right here in Royal…both past and present.

How the hell had he not seen this before now?

Matt stared up the two-story home once again, now looking at it in a whole new light. He instantly saw the place transformed. He imagined Ellie on the steps playing with dolls and Rachel swinging on the porch with her belly swollen with his child. He saw love and he saw a family he never knew he wanted…but couldn't live without.

Matt checked the time on his cell and calculated. He had just enough of a span to put his plan into motion. There was no way in hell he was letting Rachel get away. He'd waited this long for her, and now that he realized his true feelings, the future he wanted with her, he couldn't let this opportunity pass him by.

She was his best friend, but he wanted more. He wanted everything, and Matt Galloway never stopped until he got what he wanted.

# Eighteen

Rachel set her notes on the podium in the TCC clubhouse. She'd opted to use the back gardens as the area for the auction, and that was still being revamped. She wanted to keep the reveal of the changes a surprise. But she'd peeked in when she'd first arrived, and Austin Bradshaw was doing a fabulous job. She couldn't wait to see the end result.

As she glanced over her notes once more, she cursed her shaky hands. She just wanted to get this press conference over with so they could focus on what was important. The actual charity event. If they didn't bring in the projected goal, Rachel would never forgive herself. She only hoped she hadn't blown it with the whole kiss scene that had been plastered all over.

"All set?"

Alexis came up the aisle of chairs with a wide smile on her face. Her long hair spiraled down around her shoulders and she had on the prettiest floral dress with boots. If she didn't watch out, some man would make a bid for her.

"As ready as I can be," Rachel stated, stepping down from the stage. "It's almost go time. Is anyone out there?"

Alexis laughed. "Honey, this is the hottest thing in Royal and any surrounding town right now. There are hordes of people from several media outlets, plus some prominent citizens outside those doors."

"Well, that didn't help my nerves."

Alexis closed the distance between them and took Rachel's hands. "I figured you'd want to know what you were dealing with."

With a shaky breath, Rachel nodded. "You're right. I'd rather know what I'm facing."

Alexis gave a gentle squeeze. "You know, it's not too late to adjust those notes and have sixteen bachelors instead of seventeen."

Considering Matt hadn't contacted her since she drove away, she'd have to disagree. Not that she'd reached out to him, either. Apparently they were truly over and she'd just have to suffer through the auction in a few months and watch some lucky woman buy him up and whisk him away.

"Whatever we had, it's over." Maybe if she kept repeating those words out loud, and even in her mind, she'd start to believe them. "He hurt me and I just think we started off like Billy and I did. Maybe I mistook lust for love."

*Liar, liar.*

"You love Matt and he loves you." Alexis dropped her hands. "If you don't bid on that man, I'll bid on him myself."

Rachel smiled. "Well, that would make your grand-father happy."

Alexis tipped her head. "He would be a gift to you."

"Then save your money or bid on Daniel."

Alexis stiffened. "There's nothing going on there. I wish you'd quit bringing it up."

Rachel shrugged. "Then drop Matt and we'll call a truce."

After a long pause, Alexis nodded. "Fine. But you have nothing holding you back from taking what you so clearly want. You might never get a chance like this again."

Her friend turned and headed toward the doors leading into the clubhouse. Rachel closed her eyes and willed herself the strength to get through this press conference. She needed to sound convincing when she laid her claim that she and Matt were friends and the kiss was nothing.

Perhaps they wouldn't know she was lying to save her own ass.

Moments later the loud chatter enveloped her, and Rachel pasted a smile on her face as guests took their seats. This was the most pivotal moment before the auction because she would be quoted. And, to take the pressure off her and Matt and the scandal they'd created, she had visuals of the bachelors to hopefully get the media to focus on the auction and not the infamous kiss.

A kiss she was still feeling. Because no matter how much she tried to ignore her emotions, she couldn't get Matt out of her mind, and every moment she thought of him, her body heated.

Damn man had too much power over her. She fell in love with him easily; maybe she could fall out of love just as effortlessly?

If only flipping emotions on and off were a possibility, she could save herself more heartache.

Once everyone was seated, Rachel glanced toward the back of the patio area as Alexis closed the doors and gave her the nod to begin.

Gripping the edge of the podium, Rachel cleared her throat. "Good evening, ladies and gentlemen. I appreciate you all taking time to be here this evening. I have several points to address, but I promise to keep this short.

"There has been some chatter and misinformation spreading like wildfire," she went on. "I'd like to address that first." She took a deep, bracing breath, then continued. "Contrary to what you may have heard, Matt Galloway is still in the bachelor auction. We are thrilled he's contributing, and not only is he offering up his time for a fantasy date, he's also writing a check matching the winning bid for him."

The crowd murmured and a few clapped, just as she'd hoped. So far, so good.

"The picture of Matt and I kissing was harmless," she added with a fake smile as she lied through her teeth, but she pushed on. "We have been friends since college and he'd invited me for lunch to catch up."

*After I'd spent the night in his bed.*

"The timing was unfortunate and we do hope this will erase any doubt about him being in the auction. That kiss was meaningless and—"

"Nothing about that kiss was meaningless."

The crowd gasped in unison as they turned toward the back of the patio. Rachel shifted her focus as well and spotted Matt striding down the aisle. His dark suit screamed power and she wished she had her camera to capture that intense look on his face…a look all for her.

Her heart thudded even faster. What the hell was he doing here, and why was he sabotaging her press conference?

He stepped up to the stage and stood right next to her, reaching for the mic and angling it toward him.

"What Ms. Kincaid meant to say was there will now only be sixteen bachelors in the auction because I am removing myself."

"What the hell are you doing?" she whispered through gritted teeth.

Completely serious, he shot her a glance. "Saving us."

All at once, reporters shouted questions and came up out of their seats. Rachel glanced at the hyper crowd and in the very back stood her best friend with a wide smile on her face.

"I will take questions, but one at a time, please," Matt requested with so much dignity and authority, she wanted to smack him for...well this. How could she do damage control and hate him for lying when he was literally standing up for her?

"How long have you and Ms. Kincaid been seeing each other?" one reporter shouted.

Behind the podium, he reached for her hand. That was solely for her benefit, she knew, because nobody could see his actions.

Her heart tumbled.

"Like she said, we've been friends for years. We recently reconnected when I came to Royal for a get-away."

"Are you two getting married? Will you both live here?"

Matt laughed and the low, sensual tone sent shivers of arousal through her. He was making things nearly impossible for her when she just wanted to be angry. Why couldn't he let her be?

"Well, you're jumping the gun," he replied. "I have every intention of asking Rachel to marry me, but I'd hoped to get her alone."

The crowd erupted in cheers and Rachel froze. "You what?" she croaked out.

Matt turned toward her, ignoring the loud crowd. "I want to marry you, Rachel. I want to raise Ellie with you. I want to stay in Royal with you."

He threw those statements out like he was serious. He looked at her like she was the most precious thing in the world. The way he held her hands and waited for her to say something…was he serious?

"Matt—"

"Give me another chance, Rachel. I'll still make a donation to the charity—just name the amount. I love you, and I don't see a future without you in it. Without our family. I want to have more children with you and I hope you'll help me with the farmhouse, because I think it's the perfect place for us."

Well, now he'd gone and done it. Rachel's eyes swelled with tears and she glanced down to their joined hands. "I love you, too," she whispered. "But how can I trust you?"

She realized the room had gone silent. No doubt every reporter had their phones out trying to record this moment, but Rachel couldn't worry about them or what they might or might not put out to the masses.

"I'm terrified," he admitted, resting his forehead against hers. "I've never done love before, but I want to do it with you. There's nobody else, Rachel. You're it. You can trust me with your heart, because I'm trusting you with mine."

The tears slid down and she could do nothing to stop them at his bold, heart-flipping statement.

"I've never known you to be afraid of anything," she laughed. "What about Dallas?"

He tipped her chin up so she looked directly at him. "Nothing matters but you saying yes."

"What exactly are you asking me for?"

That signature heart-stopping, toe-curling smile spread across his face. "Everything."

She slid a glance to the crowd only to find each and every person had scooted closer to the stage. Rachel laughed as she turned back to Matt.

"I need to finish the press conference."

Matt's eyes studied her, but then he took a step back. Rachel turned back to the podium, glanced down to her useless notes and flung them in the air.

"Bachelor Seventeen is officially off the auction block," she declared.

The hoots and shouts were deafening and Rachel squealed when Matt wrapped his arms around her and kissed the side of her neck as he spun her around.

"I knew you'd end up with me." He smoothed her hair back from her face. "I hate to say I told you so, but..."

Rachel wrapped her arms around him and smacked his lips with a kiss. "I don't mind. You're mine, Matt Galloway. My very own bachelor."

He kissed her back, pouring promises and love into each touch.

"As you can see, we've lost another bachelor."

Rachel laughed against Matt's mouth at Alexis's statement to the crowd.

"I assure you all, we will have plenty of available men to choose from," Alexis went on, her voice echoing into the mic. "Rachel prepared a wonderful presentation, but she and Matt will be slipping out, and I'll be taking over and answering any questions."

Matt wrapped his arm around Rachel's waist and ushered her down the steps. They attempted to wade through the aisle, but kept getting high fives and hugs and smiles from each guest. Rachel wasn't sure how she'd gone from explaining why Matt was the greatest bachelor for the auction to removing him and agreeing to be his wife in the span of ten minutes.

That pretty much summed up their courtship, though, didn't it? He'd swept back into her life, dredging up emotions she never even knew she had and then forced her to see this second chance she'd been given at a lifetime of happiness.

Of course, to her this had been fast, but to him, he'd had feelings for a decade.

Once they reached the inside of the TCC clubhouse, Matt pulled her down the hallway toward the offices.

"Where are we going?" she asked.

"I have something for you."

Intrigued, she followed him into the office at the end of the hall. Matt closed the door and went to the desk.

"I brought this with me because I didn't want to wait." He pulled something from the drawer and turned back to her. "I'm sorry I hurt you, after Billy's death and again the other day. That was never my intention. Hell, Rachel, I'd do anything for you and Ellie."

The fact he always included Ellie warmed her heart. The small box he held in his hand had her heart catching in her throat.

"I didn't want to do this out there," he admitted, closing the space between them. "But I have this ring that belonged to my grandmother. I've had it since my grandfather gave it to me just before his death. He made me promise I would only give it to someone I loved."

Matt opened the blue velvet box and revealed a bright ruby with smaller diamonds flanking each side. Rachel gasped, her hand to her mouth as she tried to control her emotions.

"I know it's not the biggest or the flashiest," he went on. "I'll buy you anything you want. Hell, you wanted an island. I'll get you one of those, too."

Rachel shook her head, causing even more tears to spill down her cheeks. "No. I want this ring and I want your island."

Having something from his past made her feel even more special.

Matt pulled the ring from the box and slid the band onto her finger. "It fits," he said, relief flooding his tone.

"Of course it does." She admired the vibrant red stone. "We fit."

Matt circled his arms around her waist and tugged her against him. "Let's go get Ellie and head back to my penthouse."

"Were you serious about staying in Royal at the farm?"

Matt framed her face and placed a soft kiss on her lips. "If that's okay with you. We can escape to Galloway Cove any time you need a break, but I want you to finish that degree. Who knows, maybe we can start up a company together. What do you think?"

Rachel smiled. "I think we'd be a hell of a team."

\* \* \* \* \*

To my best friend, entrepreneur, aesthetician, makeup artist, proprietor of The Brow Snob, a cancer survivor and an all-around badass Tonie Jones. I'm thankful you just celebrated another cancerversary, and that we're still friends three states, two marriages, four children, two grandchildren and thirty-five years later.

To the amazing readers who faithfully read my books, fall in love with my characters and share your enthusiasm for my work with your friends and family online and off…I'm so grateful to have you as a reader. I honestly can't thank you enough.

# Prologue

"Benji? Oh, my God, is that you?"

Benjamin Bennett shifted his attention to the source of the husky female voice he knew as well as his own.

"Sloane." He hadn't seen Sloane Sutton in nearly a decade yet he recognized her instantly. The passing years had been good to her; she was even more beautiful than he remembered. "I wasn't sure you were coming to the wedding."

Sloane wrapped him in a hug that seared his skin and sent electricity skittering down his spine. He released her reluctantly.

"I just decided a couple of days ago." Sloane smoothed down the skirt of her brilliant blue, floor-length gown. It hugged her heart-stopping curves, showing off the glowing brown skin of one toned shoulder. "I didn't even tell Delia I was coming."

That explained why his sister hadn't mentioned it.

"Well, it's good to see you, Sloane. You look...incredible," he stammered, his face and neck warm. The passage of time hadn't lessened Sloane's effect on him. He was as tongue-tied in her presence now as he'd been at fifteen.

His crush on her began the moment he'd first laid eyes on her. He was five years old and Sloane was ten.

"Thanks." Sloane beamed. "You look pretty darned handsome yourself."

"Blake must've been glad to see you." Benji nodded toward the groom. He loosened the collar of his shirt, which suddenly seemed too tight.

"It's good to see Blake so happy." Sloane's gaze softened, but sadness suddenly crept into her voice and clouded her brown eyes. "Savannah seems really sweet, and their baby, Davis, is adorable."

"He's a cute kid," Benji acknowledged, shoving his hands in his pockets and shifting his weight to his other foot. "And Savannah is really sweet. You'll like her."

Getting to the altar hadn't been easy for his cousin and Savannah. When they'd first met, Savannah was on a mission to infiltrate the company founded by Blake's grandfather to prove that half of King's Finest Distillery belonged to her family. But somehow, they'd managed to move past the pain and distrust to find love and happiness.

Sloane caught the eye of someone on the other side of the room and nodded. She turned back to him. "I'd better go, but we'll catch up later."

"Count on it." Benji watched as she walked away.

*Sloane Sutton.*

Growing up, he'd adored Sloane. She and his sister, Delia, had been thick as thieves. He'd spent countless nights as a boy kept awake by their girlish giggles, heard through the thin wall between his and Delia's bedrooms. Sloane had been everything to him, but she'd seen him as an honorary little brother.

She'd been a beautiful girl, but she'd grown into a stunning woman. When they were young, she'd had the toned body of a farm girl who was no stranger to physical labor; her lean, athletic body had given way to softer, fuller curves. The hair she'd worn in a thick, black braid down her back was now cut short on the sides with thick, glossy curls piled atop her head.

A small, barely there diamond stud adorned her left nostril. And when she'd turned to walk away, he'd noticed shooting stars tattooed on the back of her neck. The tattoo disappeared beneath the fabric, which dipped low between her shoulder blades.

"Better close your mouth and stop drooling or everyone will know you've still got a thing for Sloane Sutton," Parker Abbott, his best friend and first cousin, said matter-of-factly.

"I didn't have a *thing* for Sloane Sutton." Benji straightened his navy tuxedo jacket, hoping he wouldn't be struck by lightning for the whopper of a lie he'd just told.

Of course he'd had a thing for Sloane.

He'd been a red-blooded teenage boy and she was… well, she was Sloane Sutton. Confident, beautiful, funny, slightly irreverent.

She hadn't thought him strange because he preferred *Star Trek* marathons and sci-fi books to spending time playing outside. Nor had she ridiculed him for his fascination with computer programming and astronomy or his love of data. Instead, she'd told him how smart he was, and that one day he'd change the world. She'd said it with such confidence, she'd made him believe it, too.

How could he not have had a thing for her?

"I know that reading people isn't my thing," Parker said, "but if *that* wasn't the very definition of having a thing for someone, I'll marry Kayleigh Jemison." He nodded toward the woman he'd escorted down the aisle during the wedding ceremony.

Parker and Kayleigh had been at each other's throats for as long as Benji could remember. But since Kayleigh was close friends with Parker's new sister-in-law, he'd been charged with escorting her down the aisle.

"Speaking of having a thing for someone." Benji chuckled.

"Me? Have a thing for Kayleigh?" Parker's cheeks colored, though he dismissed the idea with a wave of his hand. "You must've fallen and banged your head."

The wedding photographer beckoned them, indicating it was time to join the rest of the wedding party for some group shots.

Benji was thankful for the distraction. Still, he couldn't help scanning the crowd, hoping to catch another glimpse of Sloane.

Sloane nibbled the gloss off her lower lip as she studied Benji from across the room. He took another sip of his beer, then laughed at something Parker said.

She could hardly believe that the incredibly sexy man whose muscular frame filled out his fitted tuxedo in ways that did wicked things to her was the shy, sweet little boy she'd once known.

When his gaze captured hers again, an inexplicable warmth settled low in her belly and her breath caught.

"Are you all right?" Her best friend, Delia, tilted her head. "If I didn't know better, I'd say you were staring at someone at the bar."

Delia turned to look over her shoulder, but was distracted as her father approached with her daughter in his arms. The two-year-old girl was as beautiful as Delia and generally just as sweet. At this moment, though, she was crying hysterically, demanding her mother.

"Evie, what's wrong, sweetie?" Delia stood, taking her daughter into her arms.

"Your mother says she feels warm." Richard Bennett said. "We were going to offer to take her home with us, but she's insistent that she wants her mama."

"It's okay. Thanks, Dad." Delia kissed the girl's face and she seemed to immediately calm down. She leaned over and kissed Sloane's cheek. "Sorry about this, hon. We'll take up this conversation later. How long will you be in town?"

"I'll probably head back to Nashville tomorrow, but don't worry about me. We'll talk later. Just take care of Evie."

Sloane watched as Delia and Mr. Bennett made their way through the crowd. She sighed, eyeing her half-finished glass of bourbon punch.

With Delia gone, she felt alone—even in a room filled with people she'd known her entire life. Her family and the Abbotts didn't run in the same circles. She just happened to have hit it off with Blake Abbott and his cousin Delia Bennett when they were in grade school. Blake was preoccupied, and Delia was on her way home with little Evie.

There was no reason to stay.

Sloane gulped the rest of her drink, returning the glass to the table with a thud. She stood, bumping into a solid expanse of muscle.

*Benji.*

He gripped her waist to steady her.

"Sorry, I didn't see you there." She took what she hoped was a subtle step backward. Just out of his reach, but still close enough to savor his provocative scent.

"It was my bad." Benji revealed the sheepish smile that had been his trademark as a kid. He rubbed a hand over his dark brush waves.

Sloane couldn't help smiling, remembering how obsessed Benji had been with perfecting them.

"It was good seeing you again, Benji." Sloane turned to leave, but he placed his strong hand on her arm.

"You're not leaving already, are you? I've been patiently

waiting for a chance to catch up with you. My sister has been monopolizing your time all evening."

"You know how we are when we get together." Sloane smiled. "Not much has changed. We're still basically those same two giggling teenage girls."

"I'd say a lot has changed." Benji's heated gaze drifted down the length of her body, before returning to meet hers.

"I guess you're right." Sloane cleared her throat.

Some things certainly had changed.

Benji had always had a crush on her. There was nothing unusual about a little boy having a crush on his older sister's best friend. Back then, she'd thought it sweet. But Benji Bennett wasn't a little boy anymore. He was a grown-ass man and a fine one at that.

What she saw in his intense dark brown eyes wasn't the misguided admiration of a little boy. It was lust, plain and simple. The same feeling that crawled up her spine and made her heart beat faster.

His confident smile indicated that he could sense her attraction to him.

*Pull it together, sister. This is little Benji Bennett you're gawking at here.*

Benji had gone to college in Seattle, where he still lived. He'd started his own tech company in his junior year. A company he'd just sold for more than two billion dollars, according to Delia.

Benjamin Bennett was a catch by anyone's standards—even before you factored in his healthy bank account. But he was her best friend's little brother. And though he was all grown up now, he was just a kid, compared to her.

Flirting with Benji would start tongues wagging all over Magnolia Lake. Not that she cared what they thought of her. But her mother and grandfather still lived here. So did Delia, for most of the year. If the whole town started talking, it would make things uncomfortable for the people she loved.

Sloane tore her gaze from his and scanned the room. "I'd better go."

"Don't go. Please. Just one dance." Benji held up a finger, his eyes warm and pleading, his smile sexy and sweet. Then he extended his hand. The same one she'd held when she'd helped him across the street on the way to school when he was five.

Sloane looked at him, then glanced around the space as she nibbled her bottom lip, her heart racing. No one was paying attention to them. The other guests were wrapped up in their own conversations and enjoying the open bar, courtesy of the Abbotts, owners of King's Finest Distillery.

"I guess one dance won't hurt." She placed her hand in his much larger one and let him lead her onto the dance floor.

Benji walked to the center of the dance floor and held her in his arms. He swayed to Jeffrey Osborne's smooth vocals on L.T.D.'s "Love Ballad."

"God, your parents loved this song. They played it so much that your sister and I hated it. Which is a shame, because it's a pretty perfect song."

"It is," he agreed. "You still working for the record company in Nashville?"

"I am. I love what I do, but I've got my eye on a spot on the management team."

"You're the most determined girl I've ever known." Benji smiled. "If you've set your sights on it, it's as good as done."

"Is that a nice way of calling me stubborn?" It was a familiar put-down from the older folks in town.

"No." His tone was apologetic. "I hated when people said that about you." He sighed softly. "I liked that you were determined. You wanted to move to Nashville and work in the music industry, and that's exactly what you did. I'd say your determination has served you well."

Warmth filled Sloane's chest. Benji had grown up to be extremely wealthy and incredibly handsome, but at his core, he was the same sweet, thoughtful guy she'd always known. His gift for making her smile was still intact.

"Thanks, Benj. That means a lot." Sloane was slightly unnerved by his intense gaze. "Which reminds me, I haven't congratulated you on your big deal." She was eager to turn the conversation away from her. "I should be asking for your autograph. Never met a billionaire before."

The muscles of Benji's back tensed beneath her finger-tips and the light in his eyes dimmed. "I'm the same guy I was before I signed the big deal, Sloane. The same guy I've always been."

"I didn't mean anything by it." She'd only meant to tease him, but she'd struck a nerve instead.

"I know you didn't." He sighed. "I'm just a little fed up with people treating me differently. You wouldn't be-lieve how many obscure business ideas I've been pitched tonight."

She hadn't considered that there might be a downside to becoming a multibillionaire. But for her, never having to worry about how she'd pay second mortgages on her condo and their family farm would outweigh the disadvantages. "I'm sorry you've had to deal with that."

"Don't apologize. You're just about the only unattached woman in the room who doesn't see me as a golden lot-tery ticket." He nodded toward the gaggle of women in the corner of the room, whispering to one another and star-ing at him. "Not one of them would've given me the time of day back then. Their only interest in me was whether I could hook them up with one of my wealthy cousins. Now they've been stalking me all night. But you—I had to beg you to dance with me."

A knot tightened in her stomach. She had a good job and owned a cute little condo that she was slowly renovating in one of the hottest neighborhoods in Nashville. But she was in debt up to her eyeballs. Not because she was a frivolous spender addicted to retail therapy, but because she'd sunk every penny of her savings into helping her mother save their family farm. Then there were the bills that had been piling up since her grandfather's costly heart surgery.

Her budget was so tight it had practically squealed when she'd purchased the fancy dress she was wearing, despite finding it on the clearance rack at a designer dress shop.

If there was one thing she'd learned from her grandfather, Atticus Ames, it was pride. She'd work three jobs and sell plasma before she'd ask Benji or anyone else in this town for a handout.

"I told you that one day they'd regret ignoring you." Sloane grinned. She honestly couldn't have been prouder of Benji if he'd been her own flesh and blood.

"You did." A soft smile played across his handsome face. "I was an awkward kid trying to figure out my place in life. But you always made me feel that just being me was good enough. You said that everyone else was just slow to catch up. That eventually they'd figure it out. You made me believe it, too."

Sloane's heart swelled. She was moved by his confession. "You were a special kid, destined for great things. I always knew that. And look at you… You've exceeded my wildest expectations."

He smiled, looking bashful, yet deliciously handsome. Her heart beat a little faster; she needed to change the subject.

"Evie's gotten so big, and she looks just like Delia. I'm surprised your parents aren't urging you to settle down and give them more grandchildren."

"You know them well." Benji grinned. "My mother

sneaks it into the conversation whenever she can. Don't get me wrong. Evie's a cool kid and everything, but 3:00 a.m. feedings and dirty diapers just aren't for me."

Sloane understood exactly how Benji felt. The primary reason her ex had filed for divorce was because he was ready to start a family but she wasn't. Though, truth be told, it was just one of the many reasons their marriage had failed.

"What about you? Are Davis and Evie giving you baby fever, too?" Benji teased.

"Me?" She forced a laugh. "Between rehabbing my condo and being completely focused on my career, I forget to feed myself most days."

True. Still, holding little Davis, with his chubby little legs and sweet baby scent, made her think for the briefest moment about one day having a baby of her own. A thought she dismissed immediately.

Finally, the song ended.

"Thanks for the dance." Sloane slipped out of Benji's embrace, determined to banish the inappropriate thoughts that had commandeered her brain and made her body ache for the warmth and comfort of his strong arms.

Benji lowered their joined hands but didn't let go. Instead, he leaned down, his lips brushing her ear and his well-trimmed beard gently scraping her neck. "Let's get out of here."

It was a bad idea. A *really* bad idea.

Her cheeks burned. "But it's your cousin's wedding."

He nodded toward Blake, who was dancing with his bride, Savannah, as their infant son slept on his shoulder. The man was in complete bliss.

"I doubt he'll notice I'm gone. Besides, you'd be rescuing me. If Jeb Dawson tells me one more time about his latest invention—"

"Okay, okay." Sloane held back a giggle as she glanced

around the room. "You need to escape as badly as I do. But there's no way we're leaving here together. It'd be on the front page of the newspaper by morning."

"Valid point." Benji chuckled. "So meet me at the cabin."

"The cabin on the lake?" She had so many great memories of weekends spent there with Delia and her family.

"My parents hardly used it after they bought their place in Florida. I bought it from them a few years ago and Cole completely rehabbed it. I'd love for you to see it."

*Just two old friends catching up on each other's lives. Nothing wrong with that.*

She repeated it three times in her head. But there was nothing *friendly* about the sensations that danced along her spine when he'd held her in his arms and pinned her with that piercing gaze.

"Okay. Maybe we can catch up over a cup of coffee or something."

"Or something." The corner of his sensuous mouth curved in a smirk. A shiver ran through her as she wondered, for the briefest moment, how his lips would taste. "Meet you there in half an hour."

He disappeared into the crowd, leaving her missing his warmth.

Benji made two more cups of coffee and added creamer to Sloane's before setting the cup in front of her.

She thanked him and reached for her cup. But her eyes widened when she caught a glimpse of the time, flashing on her fitness watch when she flipped her wrist. "I didn't realize it was so late. You must be exhausted, and I'm keeping you up."

"You can't possibly think I want you to go." Benji placed his hand on hers. "The last two hours were the best time I've had since I've been back in town."

"Me, too." Sloane smiled. A deep, genuine smile. Then she frowned, a crease forming between her brows as she slipped her hand from beneath his. She stood abruptly, smoothing her dress over her hips. "Which is why I should go."

Benji stood, too, his eyes searching Sloane's. For the first time in his life, Sloane Sutton wasn't treating him like a little boy with a crush. Tonight, she saw him as a man. A man she desired.

He could see the passion in her brown eyes. Feel the heat that had been building between them all night.

When he was ten years old, he'd decided he was in love with Sloane because she was the nicest, prettiest girl he knew.

The passage of fifteen years hadn't altered his opinion. With her standing this close, her luscious scent washing over him, his boyhood conviction was reinforced.

He wanted to be with this woman. To hold her in his arms. To tease every inch of her gorgeous body. Make love to her.

Get her out of his system once and for all, so he could stop living in the past.

They hadn't seen each other in ten years. And in three days he'd be boarding a flight to Japan for the six-month-long consulting gig he'd agreed to when he sold his company. When it was over, he'd return to Seattle and Sloane would be back home in Nashville. Who knew when they'd see each other again?

*Speak now, Benj, or forever hold your peace.*

Benji stepped closer, his gaze locked with Sloane's. She inhaled audibly, her body tensing as he leaned down and cradled her face. The sound of Sloane breathing and the frantic beat of his heart filled his ears.

Sloane didn't object to the intimate gesture. Her pupils dilated, and her chest rose and fell heavily. He moved in closer, and she leaned in, too. She pressed a hand to his chest and her eyes drifted shut.

He kissed her, easing into it at first, reveling in the softness of her lips and the way her body nestled against his. Her lips parted on a sigh, granting his tongue access. Her mouth tasted rich and sweet. Like premium bourbon and pecan pie.

As the urgency of his kiss escalated, Sloane's response matched his intensity.

Eager. Hungry. Demanding.

His heart thundered in his chest, his need for her building. He hauled her closer and groaned with pleasure at the sensation of his length pinned between them.

Sloane slipped her arms around him and tugged his shirt free from the back of his pants. Her fingernails scraped gently against his skin.

Benji groaned, hardening painfully as the sensation—part pain, part pleasure—heightened the euphoric feeling that vibrated beneath his skin. Made him desperate to finally have her. He lifted her onto the table, nestling in the space between her thighs.

He swallowed her gasp in response to the sudden move, kissing her harder. Losing himself in the clash of lips and tongues and the delicious sensation of their bodies moving against each other, desperate for more contact than their clothing would permit.

He savored her intoxicating scent and relished the feel of her full breasts with their hardened peaks pressed against his chest.

She glided her fingertips down his stomach and fumbled with his belt buckle, loosening it.

"You have no idea how long I've been waiting for this," he whispered, his lips brushing her ear.

Sloane's hands froze. Her eyes opened and her gaze had shifted from one of intense desire to one of regret.

"Hey, beautiful." Benji traced her cheekbone with his thumb. "Did I say something wrong?"

"I shouldn't have come here, and we shouldn't be doing this." She lowered her gaze.

He was seconds away from making his boyhood fantasy a reality and he'd blown it, because he couldn't keep his stupid mouth shut.

*Way to go, Benj.*

"Why not?" He spoke calmly, trying to put her at ease. "We're consenting adults."

"I've known you since you were five. You're my best friend's little brother. I've introduced you as *my* little brother." She shook her head, her eyes still not meeting his. "This is bad. What would Delia say? And what would your parents think?"

"My mother will never believe anyone is good enough, and my sister adores you." Benji dropped a slow, lingering kiss on her lips.

"Because I'm her friend, who she trusts not to blow into town and screw her little brother." She jabbed him in the gut, but her lips parted to his tongue when he kissed her again.

"You're too young for me, Benji," she whispered against his lips as he slid the silky, blue material down her shoulder.

He kissed the shell of her ear. "Five years mattered then. It doesn't now."

"I'm not looking for a relationship, Benj." She pressed her hands to his chest, halting his movement as her gaze met his. Still, she hadn't moved an inch. Her legs framed his as she awaited his response.

"Neither am I," he said finally. "That doesn't mean we can't be together. I want you, Sloane. And I know you want me, too." He slowly tugged the zipper down her back. The silky, cobalt blue material slid from her shoulders, giving him better access. He trailed kisses down her shoulder and across the top of her breasts, exposed by a pale pink strapless bra. "Just for tonight."

She sucked in a deep breath and let the material slip down her arms and pool around her waist. Sloane unbuttoned his pants and inched the zipper down. The sound echoed off the solid oak floors and shiplap walls. She leaned in to kiss him. "Just for tonight."

Usually an early riser, Benji refused to leave the warmth of Sloane's curves. Her naked bottom was nestled against him, making him painfully hard. Which gave him hope they'd pick up where they'd left off just a few hours earlier when sleep had finally pulled them under.

Starting at her neck, he planted gentle kisses to the shooting stars that tattooed the length of her spine. By the time he reached the stars inked between her shoulder blades, she stirred.

"Mmm. Nice way to wake a girl."

He rolled her, so she was facing him. Her pebbled brown nipples betrayed her arousal. "I can think of an even better way to wake you."

"Bathroom first," she mumbled through the hand clamped over her mouth.

"Anything you need is in there." He nodded toward the adjoining bathroom before dropping another kiss on her shoulder. "Just hurry back."

When Sloane returned, he was seated with his back propped against the padded leather headboard. Her bashful smile slowly gave way to a determined one. Her eyes locked with his as she straddled him. Bracing her hands on his shoulders, she leaned in and kissed him, tentatively at first.

He fought the urge to take over. Instead, he let her dictate the pace and manage the heat building between them.

Sloane palmed his face and angled her head, her tongue gliding against his and her slick folds gliding along his heated flesh. She swiveled her hips, the pace and intensity of her movements more frantic.

Benji groaned with pleasure, losing all sense of control as he dug his fingers into the soft skin at her hip that bore a mandala tattoo with a rose at its center. He jerked her hips forward and then back. They were both getting closer to the edge, and he ached with the need to be inside her again. He flipped them over, so he lay atop her, and reached into the nightstand for a foil packet, fumbling to put it on.

He was desperate to get his fill of the woman who'd haunted his dreams since puberty. The only woman he'd ever really wanted.

Sloane wrapped her legs around him as he moved inside her. Her fingernails dug into his shoulders and her breath caught as she flew apart beneath him. His name rolled off her tongue as her muscles tensed, pulling him beneath the river of pleasure that washed over them.

Benji tumbled to the mattress, his skin slick with sweat and his breathing labored. He pulled her to him and kissed her damp forehead. "Come to Japan with me, Sloane."

The words he'd whispered impulsively into her hair took him by surprise. They'd agreed to one night together, not a six-month-long commitment.

*Smooth, Benj.*

His brain urged him to revoke the invitation. But everything below his neck desperately wanted her to say yes.

"Sure. It'll be a blast. We can eat sushi every day, sing karaoke every night and ride the bullet train on the weekends. Besides, seeing the cherry blossoms in bloom is on my bucket list. Just give me a few hours to throw a travel bag together."

"You'll come with me?" Abject terror and genuine excitement battled in his chest. The way they did during the seconds when a roller coaster made its painfully slow ascent to the summit before plummeting toward the earth.

"Wait…" Sloane lifted her head from his chest and blinked, her head cocked. "You're not serious, are you?"

His shoulders tensed. "Dead serious."

"Benji, I can't. I thought you understood that this was just…"

"A game?"

"Fun. A release. Two people being a little naughty for the weekend." Sloane pulled the sheet around her, suddenly self-conscious. She sat up, her back against the headboard. "But us getting serious? That can't happen. I thought you were clear on that."

"I am, and that doesn't have to change. But it was nice to wake up to someone who made me want to spend the day in bed." He shrugged. "I haven't had that in a long time."

"Neither have I, but—"

"Then why not keep doing it? In Japan," he added.

Sloane dragged her fingers through her messy curls and huffed. "And while you're working every day, what am I supposed to do? Lounge around, waiting for my sugar daddy to get home? No thanks, Benj. I'm not interested in being anyone's kept woman. Not even a billionaire's." She climbed out of bed, taking the sheet with her as she wrapped it around her body and rummaged on the floor for her bra and panties. "Besides, I have a job and responsibilities, and I don't have a passport. Never needed one."

Benji dragged the remaining covers up to his waist. "I wasn't thinking of the arrangement that way at all. We'd just be two friends hanging out."

"And screwing. On your dime." She looked at him pointedly. "Plus, you just called it 'an arrangement.' So if it looks like a duck and it quacks like a duck—"

She had a point.

He had just turned into *that* guy. The one who thought he could buy anyone and anything. Even the woman he adored.

"Point taken." He cleared his throat. "Like I said, that wasn't my intention."

"I know it wasn't. And I'm flattered you asked." Her tone and her gaze softened. She gripped her blue dress to her chest as she approached him and brushed a soft kiss to his lips. "If the situation was different…" Sloane wouldn't allow herself to finish the thought.

It was just as well. No point in musing about some alternate universe in which she would say yes.

Benji did the only thing there was left to do. He tugged her to him. Her dress tumbled to the floor, quickly joined by the pale pink bra and panties.

# One

*Six months later*

Benji inhaled the scent of the roses, lilies and snapdragons overflowing his arms as he approached Sloane's building.

The edge of his mouth curled in a faint smile. Sloane had always loved the scent of the snapdragons his mother grew in their front yard.

He halted in front of the red door and drew in a deep breath.

*It's just friends going out for coffee. No big deal.*

At least that was the first step of his grand plan. He'd invite her to coffee where they could have a discussion on neutral ground about the possibility of picking up where they'd left off before he'd departed for Japan.

He'd casually inquired about Sloane during his absence, but his sister had been unusually tight-lipped about her friend, so he didn't press. It would only raise his sister's suspicions about why he was so interested.

So he'd simply told Delia that he needed Sloane's address for his Christmas list. Not a lie, but not the primary reason he was asking.

Benji had considered picking up the phone and calling Sloane while he was in Japan. But she'd been so adamant that walking away was the right thing to do. There was no way he would've been able to persuade her with a long-distance phone call.

He'd kept himself busy with work, but when it was time to book his flight home, he realized he'd arrive on Valentine's Day.

It had seemed like a sign.

So instead of flying directly to Seattle, he'd booked a flight to Nashville. He needed to speak to Sloane in person.

Maybe he was crazy to believe there could be anything more between them. But dealing with Sloane's rejection would be a lot less painful than suffering a lifetime of regret.

Clutching the flower arrangement in one arm, he rang Sloane's buzzer.

"You looking for Sloane?" The woman in the unit across from Sloane's peered down from the balcony where she was sweeping. "She left a couple of hours ago, but if you have a delivery for her, I'll sign for it."

"Thank you." Benji tried not to sound as defeated as he felt. "But Sloane's an old family friend. I was hoping to deliver these in person."

"Then you're in luck." The older woman pointed toward a vehicle that had just turned down the lane next to the building. "That's her truck pulling around back."

Benji thanked the woman and made his way behind the building. Sloane had parked her car in the garage and was rummaging in her trunk.

He approached her silently, still replaying in his head exactly what he planned to say. Gripping the flowers in one arm, Benji stopped a few feet short of where she stood. He shoved his free hand in his pocket.

"Hey, Sloane."

"Benji?" Her body stiffened, and she glanced over her shoulder. "What are you doing here?"

Not the reception he'd hoped for. He forced a smile anyway.

"I wanted to surprise you for Valentine's Day. I thought that, if you don't already have plans, maybe we could do something together." He cleared his throat when she still hadn't turned around. "I flew straight here from Japan because I really needed to see you."

"You shouldn't have come." She turned back to the groceries in her trunk. "This isn't what we agreed to."

"I know it isn't, but—"

"You should go. Now. Please." She arranged the grocery bags in her trunk into two rows, her back to him.

"Can't we at least talk about this?" He hated that he sounded like a kid negotiating his bedtime with the babysitter. He was a grown man. A business owner. A self-made fucking billionaire whose business advice was in demand.

So why did he revert to a love-struck little boy whenever he was around Sloane?

"No." Sloane stood up straight, abruptly smacking her head on the raised deck lid. She swayed, her body going limp.

"Sloane!" Benji dropped the flowers to the ground and surged forward, catching her before she hit the concrete.

"I've got you." He hoisted her into his arms. She was noticeably heavier than she'd been when he'd carried her to his bed six months ago.

Is that why she didn't want to see him? Was she self-conscious about her weight gain? She should know him well enough to realize that would never matter to him.

"Sloane. Sloane! Honey, are you all right?" His heart beat faster.

She was breathing but unresponsive.

Benji carried her to the passenger side of her car and put her in the seat to drive her to the hospital. He stretched the seat belt to put it over her, his gaze trailing down to her burgeoning belly.

"Sloane, you're… I mean…are you—"

"Pregnant?" The word came out as more of a moan as her eyes fluttered open. One hand moved to her belly and rubbed it in a soothing circle. "Yes."

"Exactly how pregnant are you?"

"Very." Sloane forced a weak laugh, then winced. When he didn't react, she cleared her throat and her expression grew serious, too. Her response was little more than a whisper. "Six months."

"Is it… I mean…am I…" He felt as if he were suffocating, unable to get the words out. He swallowed hard and tried again. "Is the baby mine?"

"I haven't been with anyone but you since my divorce, so my money is on you. I'm not really the immaculate conception type."

He narrowed his gaze at Sloane. How could she joke about the fact that he was going to be a father in just a few months and she hadn't even had the decency to let him know. "Were you ever going to tell me?"

"Honestly? I don't know." The sarcasm she'd been using as a shield evaporated, and he noticed that the corners of her eyes were suddenly damp. Her gaze didn't meet his. "That weekend, you made it pretty clear that you weren't the daddy type."

"What do you—" He stopped midsentence, recalling their conversation about his niece.

*Evie's a cool kid and everything, but 3:00 a.m. feedings and dirty diapers just aren't for me.*

"I was speaking in hypotheticals. As in, I had no immediate plans to have children. Not as in, I'm such a cold-hearted bastard that I wouldn't want to know my own baby."

"Babies." Sloane emphasized the *s* at the end of the word as she reached up and rubbed the spot where the lid of the trunk had tagged her head. She grimaced.

"Twins?" Benji's voice reverted to the high pitch of a boy entering puberty. He cleared his throat and tried again. "We're having twins?"

Benji's gaze returned to her belly. For a moment he felt weak. As if everything was spinning around them.

"*I'm* having twins." Sloane's voice deepened as she gripped her belly and winced. "Hopefully not at this moment. It's too soon, but something doesn't feel right."

Benji felt the knot rising on her head, then touched her stomach, but drew his hand back. Despite everything they'd done that weekend, the simple act of touching her belly suddenly felt intrusive. Too intimate.

"I'm getting you to a doctor." He stretched the seat belt across her body and secured it, then demanded her keys.

She stared at him as if she wanted to give him the finger, but she reached into her pocket instead, and handed him the keys without a word.

Benji retrieved the bouquet he'd brought for Sloane from the ground and got into the driver's seat.

"Those are for me, I presume." Her voice was softer. Apologetic.

"Oh, yeah. Here." He handed her the flowers that looked the worse for wear after he'd clenched them in a Vulcan death grip and then dropped them to keep her from falling. "Happy Valentine's Day," he mumbled bitterly.

"Snapdragons." She whispered the word as she inhaled their scent. Suddenly tears were running down her face.

"Are you in pain?" He gripped her arm.

"Yes, but that isn't why I'm crying." She sniffled. "It's these stupid hormones and…" She sniffled again, louder this time. "You remembered that I like snapdragons."

Benji sighed and gave her a pained smile despite the anger that was burning inside his chest. "I remember everything about you, Sloane. No matter how damn hard I've tried to forget."

Benji's words hurt.

More than the physical discomfort of one of the twins bouncing on her bladder while her belly felt as if it was being squeezed in a vise.

He'd tried to forget her. Meanwhile, Benji had been all she could think of even before she'd learned she was pregnant—with twins, no less.

Because when she screwed up, she did it big.

She'd spent the two months after their night together regretting that she hadn't taken him up on his offer to join him in Japan, daydreaming about their incredible night together and wanting him. She'd been so preoccupied with work and thoughts of Benji that she hadn't noticed that she'd missed not one but two periods. Until the sudden, severe case of morning sickness she developed made it clear she was pregnant.

"I'm sorry you had to find out like this." Sloane stared out the window, not wanting to see the hatred and disappointment in his eyes.

"Why didn't you tell me?" His words vibrated with hurt and anger. Pain.

"I know I should've, but…" She turned toward him, needing to see that he was okay. She licked her lips, her throat incredibly dry. "This isn't what you signed up for. We agreed to a one-night stand, not an eighteen-year commitment as parents. Besides, you made it pretty clear that kids weren't something you wanted."

"I was speaking in generalities, Sloane." He clenched the wheel as he turned a corner.

"You said, and I quote—"

"I'm aware of what I said. I remember everything that happened between us that night." He took another sharp turn, following the directions of the GPS app. "But how could you think that meant I wouldn't take care of my own flesh and blood, or wouldn't want to know that I have a son or daughter somewhere out in the world?"

"It's both." She winced again, pressing a hand to her belly, trying to calm herself as the pain got worse. "A boy and a girl."

He glanced at her quickly before returning his gaze to the road. "Does this happen often? The pain, I mean?"

"Not like this." Tears stung her eyes, more from fear than from the pain. It was too early for the twins to be born. Not if they were going to be okay. She forced a laugh. "Usually it's just discomfort from your son bouncing his big head on my bladder and your daughter doing some kind of calisthenics. I swear, that girl is going to be a gymnast."

"Everything is gonna be okay." He reached over and squeezed her hand, despite the reserved anger in his tone. "First, we make sure you and the babies are all right. Then…"

"I'll tell you anything you want to know," she said, grateful to see the hospital sign come into view. "I promise."

Benji hadn't stopped pacing outside Sloane's hospital room since they'd admitted her.

He was going to be a father of two babies—a boy and a girl. He still couldn't wrap his head around it. He'd been responsible and used protection every time they were together.

How could this have happened?

Benji's phone vibrated in his pocket and he glanced at the screen. It was his mother. Probably checking to see if he'd returned safely from Japan. But he didn't dare answer the call. Not yet. Not until he'd gotten some definitive answers from Sloane about why she hadn't told him he was going to be a father. Regardless of what he'd said that night, he couldn't believe that was the only reason Sloane had kept something this important from him.

He respected the fact that it was Sloane who was carrying these babies, but they were half his, too. What about his right to know? And to be part of his children's lives? Sloane's father had left home when she was around ten. She understood the pain of living without a father. Why would she intentionally subject their kids to the same fate?

The door opened, and the doctor introduced herself and invited him into the room where Sloane was hooked up to an IV. She gave him an apologetic smile before lowering her gaze to her hands, which were pressed to her belly.

"Is Sloane okay? Will the twins be all right?" he asked Dr. Carroll.

The older woman placed a gentle hand on his arm. "Sloane is going to be just fine, Mr. Bennett. She's experiencing something called Braxton Hicks contractions. It's basically the uterus practicing up for child labor." Her smile deepened. "They're usually painless, but Sloane is experiencing particularly intense ones today. She's dehydrated. That likely contributed to it."

He nodded dumbly, his hands shaking and his head feeling light. None of this seemed real.

"Perhaps you should have a seat." Worry lines spanned the doctor's forehead as she indicated a sofa along the wall. She sat beside him. "Just take a deep breath. I realize this must seem very overwhelming, but everything is going to be fine."

"Sorry, this is all kind of a surprise."

"I know." The woman nodded gravely. "Sloane explained the situation to me. I can only imagine what a shock it must've been. But the good news is, you have the opportunity to be there for the birth of your children. And you and Sloane still have lots of time before the twins are born to hash things out." She looked pointedly at both of them in a firm but kind manner. "The twins are counting on you two to do that."

"Will she be released today?" Benji wasn't ready to talk about making nice. Not until he got some straight answers.

"I want to observe her for another hour. But as long as everything looks good, yes, she can go home. This isn't preterm labor, but I still want her to take it easy." The woman shifted her gaze to Sloane, and her tone and expression turned more serious. "Make sure she understands my instructions that she refrain from working. That includes not hauling groceries around. If she can't comply with my limited restrictions, I'll have to put her on full bed rest."

"I understand," Sloane said, her expression contrite. "I would never knowingly put the babies in jeopardy."

"I know you wouldn't, Sloane. But you're carrying multiples. That makes everything a little trickier. So let's err on the side of caution." Dr. Carroll moved beside Sloane and squeezed her arm briefly before making a few notes on the tablet in her hand and checking the monitor.

"Any other specific things she shouldn't be doing?" Benji was on his feet beside the doctor.

"Nothing strenuous. No lifting or high-impact exercise. Walking, swimming and gentle yoga should be okay." She turned to Sloane. "But you should monitor how you're feeling. Make sure there's no pain or unusual discomfort." She turned back to Benji with a sly smile. "And there are no restrictions on sex, within reason. If that's what you're asking."

Benji's cheeks heated and he sputtered, "No, that isn't what I was asking."

"Relax, Benj." Sloane and the doctor were laughing. "I have no intention of jumping you when we get back to my place."

Benji glared at her, not acknowledging her jab. He returned his attention to the doctor. "I was referring to the bump she took to the head. She passed out momentarily. Does she have a concussion? Will it impact the twins?"

"Relax, Mr. Bennett." Dr. Carroll's voice was patient and soothing. Like she was trying to convince a man in a straitjacket that he hadn't been abducted by aliens. "She has a little knot there, but no concussion. We applied an ice pack to reduce the swelling. Something she should continue to do off and on this evening. But if she suddenly seems woozy or disoriented, by all means, bring her back."

"Will the Braxton Hicks contractions always be this strong?" Sloane asked. Her voice was strained, the levity gone.

Benji quickly made his way over to Sloane and let her grip his hand. It seemed to ease her discomfort.

When he looked up at the doctor she was smiling, seemingly pleased by his instinctive need to comfort Sloane.

"If you stay hydrated, knock off strenuous activities and reduce your stress levels, hopefully they won't be as intense. In fact, you might not feel them at all." Dr. Carroll turned to Benji. "If they do become intense, give her fluids and get her to walk around a little. That should relieve them."

The woman handed him a pamphlet from her pocket. "I went over this with Sloane earlier. It outlines the difference between Braxton Hicks contractions and preterm labor—which can be dangerous for the babies at this stage. Study it. Memorize it. We want these babies to gestate until at least thirty-seven weeks, if possible."

"Benji doesn't live here. He'll be going back to Seattle," Sloane interjected.

"No, I won't. I'm not leaving your side until the twins are born. Not up for discussion," he added, glaring at her again when she opened her mouth to object.

She snapped her mouth shut and rubbed her belly.

"Good." Dr. Carroll nodded approvingly. "Because she's been trying to do this on her own for too long, and I've been worried about her."

Benji couldn't help the twinge of guilt in his gut at the doctor's remarks, despite the fact that he couldn't possibly have known that Sloane was struggling through this pregnancy on her own. The guilt quickly turned to resentment.

He should've been there, and he would've been, if only Sloane had given him the courtesy of a single phone call or even a text message.

"All right, I don't expect to see you again until your next *scheduled* visit at the office." Dr. Carroll raised one brow at Sloane before turning to Benji. "Walk me out, Mr. Bennett?"

He followed the woman into the hall.

"I know you must be angry and that you have many questions for Sloane." She pinned him with her piercing blue eyes. "I don't begrudge you for that. But she doesn't need any unnecessary stress. So keep that in mind as you search for answers and you two decide what comes next. Capisce?"

"Yes, ma'am." He nodded, shoving his hands in his pockets.

"Good." Her expression softened. She patted his arm. "Give her a chance to explain. And listen to all the things she's afraid to say. She's one tough lady, but deep down she's terrified of going through this alone. So don't let her fool you into believing that she doesn't want or need your help." Dr. Carroll reached out to shake Benji's hand. "You two take care of each other and the two little people growing inside her."

Benji sighed and nodded. "We'll figure it out."

When he returned to Sloane's room, she immediately tensed, her eyes not meeting his.

Benji sucked in a deep breath and pulled a chair up beside Sloane. He sat back in the chair. "Okay, let's talk."

# Two

Sloane's heart felt as if it were beating out of her chest. And despite all the water she'd been made to drink in the short time since she'd been admitted, it felt like she was swallowing sand.

Her hands shook, and it took everything she had to maintain his gaze.

He was angry and hurt. Disappointed. In her.

So different from what she'd felt when she'd stared into those brooding brown eyes six months ago.

Her reasons for not telling Benji about the pregnancy seemed honorable and self-sacrificing when she'd made the decision to keep it from him. But now, faced with his resentment, they felt like cowardly excuses to avoid this very moment. When she'd have to face him again.

"I didn't do this to hurt you, Benji. I honestly thought I was doing you a favor by keeping you out of the mess that I've made."

"It's not like you did this alone. I distinctly remember being there, too." He folded his arms.

A wave of heat came over her and her nipples prickled with the memory of what had happened between them that weekend. How he'd made her feel.

"So why in the—" He drew in a deep breath and closed his eyes for a moment. She could swear he was counting to ten under his breath. Finally he opened them again and released a long sigh. "So why on earth would you think you needed to handle this on your own?"

"Because I'm not twentysomething anymore. I'm old enough to know better. I should never have gone to your cabin that night. Never let you kiss me." Sloane shook her head, tears sliding down her cheeks. *Damn hormones*. She wiped away the tears with the back of one trembling fist.

"I'm not nine, Sloane." His voice was softer, though it still vibrated with controlled anger. "I don't need you to cover for me like you did when I broke Mom's favorite vase." A faint smile momentarily curled the edges of his mouth. "You don't need to shield me from the consequences of my actions. And money, obviously, isn't an issue. I can take care of you and the babies."

"That's just it…" The pain rising in her gut had nothing to do with the Braxton Hicks contractions and everything to do with the rumors that had swirled around Magnolia Lake her entire life. "Everyone back home will swear I got knocked up on purpose. That this was all some grand plan to secure my family's future by having a billionaire's baby."

"I know Magnolia Lake still feels like a little backwoods town." He practically snorted. "But even they understand how babies are made."

"I'm not joking, Benj." She rubbed her belly. "You don't understand because…" Sloane shook her head and lay back on the pillow, staring up at the ceiling. "Never mind."

"No, tell me." He sat on the edge of his chair. "You say

I don't understand, so school me on why rational adults would completely ignore my role in this and blame you."

"They'll say, like mother like daughter." Tears burned her eyes. Her life in Magnolia Lake seemed like a lifetime ago. Yet, the pain of that phrase uttered underneath folks' breath still hurt.

Benji was quiet, as if he suddenly remembered the cruel things folks in town had said about her and her mother. He cleared his throat. "You're not your mom, Sloane. No matter what they say—"

"What they say about her isn't true."

Sloane met his gaze. She didn't always get along with Abigail Sutton. Nor had she completely gotten over her resentment of her mother. But no one else got to talk shit about her. Especially when what they were saying was a bald-faced lie.

Sloane sat up in the bed and adjusted her pillows. "She didn't 'trick' my father into marrying her. She was young and stupid enough to believe he actually loved her. She was too naive to understand that the Suttons would never approve of a poor girl from the wrong side of town."

"Look, Sloane, I'm sorry for what a few busybodies might've said to make you feel that you were somehow inferior. But we both know that isn't true. I've never believed it. Nor does my family."

She wanted to tell him she knew his mother had never liked her. It was obvious from the coldness in her voice and in her eyes, despite the fake smile she always managed for Sloane's benefit. Constance Bennett had merely tolerated her, preferring that she and Delia spend time at their home, under her careful supervision.

But there was no point in reopening old wounds when there were fresh ones gushing bright red blood that needed tending.

"You have to admit, it'll seem odd that you returned

to Magnolia Lake a billionaire and suddenly I'm having your babies. Then there's our age difference." She pressed a palm to her suddenly throbbing right eye. "Your sister is going to kill me."

"Forget everyone else for a minute. This isn't about any of them. It's about me and you and..." His gaze was drawn to her belly before he raised it to hers again. "Our babies." He swallowed hard, leaning closer. "Do you mind if... I mean, would it be all right if—"

Her heart swelled with affection for this man. The sheepish look on his face as he struggled to ask for permission to touch her after the intimacy they'd shared that night was utterly adorable.

"Give me your hand." She reached out for his, guiding it to her belly between the two straps from the electronic fetal monitor that crossed her midsection. "Put your hand here."

"I don't feel any—"

"Shh..." She closed her eyes, her voice lowered. "Just wait."

They sat still, his hand on her stomach. The only sound in the room was the intermittent beeping of the IV pump.

Suddenly one of the babies kicked. Sloane smiled when she opened her eyes and saw the look of amazement on Benji's face.

"I can't believe it. I could really feel that. That's incredible." His voice broke slightly. "That's my...*our* baby."

Her chest tightened at his use of the phrase. She'd only ever thought of the babies as *hers*.

"That was your son." Sloane adjusted her position as the baby kicked again. "I don't know what my ribs ever did to him, but he's got it out for them."

No longer tentative, Benji pressed more firmly on the area where he'd felt the kick. He jumped, startled as the skin high on her belly shifted. Their baby girl started to roll.

"It's okay. The first time I saw that, I was pretty weirded

out, too." She smiled so much her cheeks hurt. "Looked like something straight out of one of your favorite sci-fi movies."

That seemed to relax him a little. Benji glided his hand to where her skin stretched and moved. He touched what looked like a tiny little shoulder. It protruded slightly from her belly, then disappeared from sight again.

He stood, staring at her stomach in awe for a few moments before he met her eyes again.

"I wasn't around during most of my sister's pregnancy, so I didn't see any of that." He indicated her belly. "It really is remarkable."

"Speaking of remarkable—" she pointed a thumb over her shoulder at the electronic fetal monitor "—I asked Dr. Carroll to turn the sound off before you came in the room. Turn that dial up."

Benji went to the machine and turned up the volume. His eyes sparked with recognition as he turned to meet her gaze again. "That's a heartbeat." He listened carefully, turning the volume up a little more. "No, it's two heartbeats."

She rubbed her stomach again. "That's right."

Benji dragged a hand over his head and sat beside the bed. His brows furrowed as the pain and disappointment returned to his face, forming hardened lines that weren't there before. "How could you not tell me?"

Sloane's phone rang. She swiped it from the table beside her bed, thankful for a respite from the withering heat of Benji's stare.

*Mama.*

Sloane hadn't thought to call her mother. But the last thing she wanted was to give her mom an excuse to come to Nashville and set up camp at her place. With her growing belly and all of the baby things she was collecting in duplicate, the place already felt too small.

She silenced the phone and turned it facedown. She'd

return the call once she was settled in back at her place. No need to worry her mother unnecessarily.

There was nothing to tell.

Except that the man her mother still referred to as "little Benji Bennett" was the father of her babies. And that wasn't a conversation she was prepared to have.

"Everything okay?" Deep worry lines creased his forehead.

"Everything's fine." She pulled the sheet around her and asked him to turn down the monitor again. "Now, about what you said when Dr. Carroll was in here."

"About me not returning to Seattle?" He raised a brow and narrowed his gaze.

"Yes, that." She refused to repeat the words that both terrified her and made her hopeful. "That isn't necessary. As Dr. Carroll explained, there's nothing wrong with me or the babies."

"I missed the first six months of your pregnancy. I'm not missing another minute."

It wasn't a question or even a suggestion.

"You've pretty much gotten the highlights. The first two months, I had no idea I was pregnant. Then there was four months of barfing my brains out before the morning sickness finally subsided." She settled back against the pillow.

"The morning sickness was that bad?"

"It bordered on spectacular. I had acute morning sickness, which, by the way, is a misnomer. There was nothing cute about not being able to hold down anything or work for the past four months."

A pained look crimped Benji's face. "You've been out of work for four months? How've you been paying your expenses?"

Sloane's cheeks stung with embarrassment. Her dire financial situation wasn't a conversation she wanted to have with the golden boy billionaire. She'd gotten herself into this mess and it was her job to navigate her way out of it. If there was one thing she'd learned in her thirty years, it was that when she got into difficulty, no one was coming to rescue her. She needed to figure this out on her own, just as she'd done her entire life.

"Sloane?" he prodded.

"I manage." She stared down at her ragged fingernails and fought the urge to chew on them.

Benji spoke after a few moments of awkward silence between them. "When you were filling out the hospital paperwork… I couldn't help noticing the past-due bills hanging out of your wallet."

"You snooped in my purse?" The heat in her cheeks turned to a butane-lighter-charged flame.

"I wasn't snooping. I just couldn't help noticing the words stamped in bold red capital letters." He raised his hands in self-defense, then sighed. "Sloane, what are you trying to prove? I have all this money. What good is it if I can't even help the people I care about?"

"That's not what you said at the reception." She folded her arms and glared at him pointedly. "You said you were tired of people treating you differently. Like you were a freakin' ATM. I couldn't bear for you, Delia or your parents to ever think I'm no better than the girls who stalked you at the wedding. That I looked at you and got dollar signs in my eyes. That I planned this to ensure I'd get a big ol' piece of the Benji Bennett pie."

"Sloane, no one will think that."

"I've been taking care of myself since I was sixteen. I worked a job, in addition to my duties on the farm. Paid my own way. I've never needed to ask anyone for anything." Tears formed in her eyes again. She swiped at them, but that didn't stop fresh tears from falling. "I should be able to take care of myself and the twins. Without help. But my life is falling apart at a time when I should be able to enjoy motherhood."

Benji pulled his chair closer to the bed and held one of her hands in his. He lightly kissed the back of it. "You don't need to do this alone. Accepting help doesn't make you weak." He squeezed her hand. "It took two people to make the twins. Stands to reason it'd take both of us to care for them."

She leveled her gaze at him. It wasn't fair. She was emotional and feeling vulnerable. His argument actually made sense.

"Don't do this out of a sense of obligation, Benji. If this isn't what you want, you can walk out of that door right now and no one else ever needs to know."

Benji slid his hand to her cheek and cradled it. His voice was soft. "Nothing in the world is more important to me than taking care of you and the twins. Are we clear on that?"

She nodded, and he leaned in and kissed her cheek. A kiss that was soft and sweet. Yet, it warmed her from the inside out.

He kissed her again, this time a closed-mouth kiss on the lips.

When he raised his eyes to hers, there was the same desire she'd seen there that night. The night they'd made the twins.

Except six months ago she'd been beautiful, and now she felt like a beached whale.

A sly smile curved the edge of his mouth and he leaned in to kiss her again.

"Should I come back later?" A male nurse hovered inside the doorway.

"No." Benji groaned, his gaze still meeting hers. "I'd liked to get her back home and settled in as soon as possible."

He moved to the sofa to give the nurse room to check Sloane's and the babies' vitals. The man put a blood pressure cuff on Sloane.

"Now's a good time to tell my mother and father they're going to be grandparents." He pulled out his cell phone.

"You're going to tell them over the phone?"

Sloane's pulse suddenly raced as she imagined Connie and Rick Bennett's reaction to the news. Rick would be mildly surprised, but Connie would be spitting fire, and she'd probably faint right on the spot. When she recovered, the woman would blame her for corrupting their son. Which she probably deserved.

And Delia. God, her friend was going to be angry with her. Delia already knew of her pregnancy. Only Sloane hadn't told her friend the whole truth about it. Like the fact that her little brother was the father.

"Why not tell them now?"

"I'm pretty sure that's the kind of conversation that should be had in person."

"We have to tell them eventually, Sloane." He kept his voice even.

"I know." Sloane frowned when the blood pressure machine beeped, and she saw the unusually high numbers. She turned to the nurse. "Can you give me a few minutes and take it again, please? I just got a little worked up. My numbers will go down in a few minutes, I promise."

The man nodded begrudgingly. "Be back in fifteen minutes."

She sighed in relief, then turned to Benji. "I know that we have to tell them, and we will. But don't you think it's better if we figure all of this out first?"

"All of what?" He sat beside her again.

"You said you're not going back to Seattle. Well, fine. But there isn't enough room in my tiny condo for me, you and all the stuff for the babies."

"So we'll sell your place and get a bigger one."

"I can't just sell my place. It needs a lot of work before I can put it on the market and…" Sloane chewed her lower lip. She didn't like talking money with Benji. Feeling as if she had her hand out.

"And?" He prodded.

"And I'm under water."

"You overpaid for the condo?"

She shook her head, her voice lowered. "I took out a second mortgage on the place." Sloane fiddled with the strap across her belly. "Don't look at me like that. I didn't spend the money on shoes or something. I took the loan out for a good reason."

"Which was?"

"I don't think that's any of your—"

"Sloane!" He inhaled deeply, then lowered his voice considerably. "Just tell me. Why did you need the money?"

"To save the farm. The crop yield hasn't been good the last few years. Plus, my grandfather needed bypass surgery last year and the insurance didn't cover everything. Do you have any idea how expensive medicine is for a cardiac patient?"

Benji stood and paced the floor. "Delia mentioned that your granddad had surgery." He turned to face her, the wheels in his head obviously turning. "Both your condo and your family's farm have second mortgages on them?"

"Yes." She whispered the word under her breath. "I had a plan. I didn't have much cash to spare, but I was paying my bills and theirs. And I was about to land the job as the creative director at the record company until…" She paused, sinking her teeth into her lower lip. She didn't want to make it seem as if she was blaming him or the twins.

"Until you couldn't work anymore because of the pregnancy." Benji slid into the seat beside her again. "I'm starting to get the picture."

They were both quiet for a moment. Then he leaned forward and gripped her hand. "Look, I know you think the worst of the folks in Magnolia Lake, but I plan to prove you wrong."

"What are you talking about?"

"Let me get the condo ready for sale."

"Even if I got top dollar for it, I'd barely break even with the second mortgage." Her grandfather had implored her not to do it, but she'd been determined to prove to him that she'd made something of herself, despite his predictions that she'd flop in "the big city." Not one of her better decisions. "Besides, if I sell my condo, where will I live?"

"You'll move to Magnolia Lake with me." His brown eyes were earnest, but his expression was neutral.

"I have no intention of moving in with my mother and grandfather." A shiver ran down her spine just thinking of it. "I'd rather live in a tent in the woods."

"Perfect. Then you'll move into the cabin with me."

A tiny ray of hope flared deep in her chest.

Benji was asking her to move into the cabin with him. Did that mean he felt something for her, too?

After their weekend together, she hadn't been able to get him out of her head. She couldn't stop wondering if a future for them was possible. But Benji was the first man she'd been with since her divorce. She cared about him too much to make him her rebound guy. Once she learned she was pregnant, she'd attributed her feelings for him to her wildly fluctuating hormones.

The same hormones that filled her body with heat as her gaze traced the sensual lines of Benji's strong physique. The same hormones that made her long for his hands to glide along her skin, the way they had when he'd made love to her.

Sloane pinched the bridge of her nose and squeezed her eyes shut, trying to shake loose the fine image of how

Benji's muscles had bunched beneath his brown skin. She needed to focus on the larger implications of what he was saying.

"You're asking me to move in with you?"

"We should get married first, naturally. For the sake of the twins." He released her hand and pulled out his cell phone, tapping out a message. "But it would only be temporary."

"The marriage?" Her heart had inflated and deflated in six seconds flat.

Not that she wanted to get married again. Ever. And she still had a modicum of pride. He wanted to marry her, but only because he felt obligated to, and now he was saying it would be some kind of temporary arrangement?

He looked puzzled, then frowned with realization. "No, not the marriage. Living at the cabin would be temporary," he clarified. "I'm shooting my cousin Cole a message now. We'd live at the cabin until Cole's company can build us a permanent home."

"Hold up there, Andy Griffith." She extended her palm toward him. "I'm not agreeing to a shotgun wedding. Do people really still have those?"

"You don't want to get married?" The poor thing looked bewildered, as if he couldn't possibly imagine why a knocked-up poor girl would reject the offer to get hitched to an incredibly handsome, impossibly sexy billionaire and commence having his babies.

"Because getting married strictly because of an unexpected pregnancy worked out so well for my parents and for your sister." Baby boy bounced his generous-sized head on her bladder as if in objection.

*Of course, you'd side with him. Traitor.*

Sloane rubbed her belly, hoping to calm the little one.

Benji's jaw tensed. "We're not either of them."

If he said that a few more times, she'd suggest he put it

on a T-shirt. But as things stood, she didn't want to aggravate him any more than she already had.

"No, we're not. They were in long-term relationships, but still couldn't make their shotgun weddings work. We had a one-night stand, Benj. A really incredible one, but still—"

"Then why not just keep doing it?" He winced and swiped a hand across his forehead. "I wasn't talking about sex…necessarily. I just meant being together. The night we spent together, it wasn't just about sex, not for me, at least."

"Not for me, either." She smiled sweetly. Or at least as sweetly as she could manage while baby boy played trampoline with her bladder and kicked underneath her ribs. "But one night of great sex and reminiscing over the past does not a marriage make. And I really do like you, Benji. Too much to watch our friendship turn into a strained, bitter relationship that'll make us and the twins miserable."

Sloane sighed, her heart twisting at the pained look on Benji's face.

He slipped his phone back in his pocket without sending the message to Cole and scrubbed a hand down his face. "You're sure about this?"

"I'm positive. Thanks for the offer, Benj, but if I ever get married again, it'll be for one reason and one reason only—that we're both head over heels in love."

# Three

Benji drove Sloane's car, the silence stretching between them. She'd pretended to be upbeat, like everything would be okay, until they'd sent her to the cashier's desk once she'd been released by the doctor.

The stress and embarrassment she felt were obvious when they'd asked how she'd pay her insurance co-pay. She'd almost whispered the words, "Bill me."

When Sloane had made one last stop at the restroom, Benji had gone back to the desk and paid the entire bill. After she came back, he'd handed the receipt to Sloane and, though she'd thanked him, her face had fallen. She'd been silent ever since, staring out the passenger window the entire drive.

"Are you angry that I paid the hospital bill?" he asked finally, gripping the steering wheel tightly. The tension rolling off her shoulders was contagious.

"I appreciate what you did." She turned in his general direction as they idled at the traffic light. "I'm just angry with myself for being in a position where you felt you needed to do it."

"I wish you'd reconsider my offer."

"Thanks, but no thanks on the shotgun wedding, Benj." She adjusted her seat belt. "I know you billionaires aren't used to people telling you no. But marrying me strictly for your progeny…that's gonna be a hard pass for me."

"I was wrong." He turned into the parking lot of her condo, recalling their conversation on the dance floor. "You're stubborn as hell."

She laughed and the tension between them eased a little. He couldn't help chuckling, too.

Sloane was wrong about him. He wasn't some asshole billionaire who expected strict obedience from the people surrounding him. But when it came to business, he knew what he wanted and made it happen, whether that was developing a new app, acquiring a new company or getting the very best price when he sold his.

He applied a thumb to people's pressure points and used whatever leverage he ethically could in order to negotiate the best possible deal. It worked every time. Even with hard cases, like the Japanese company that eventually purchased his tech start-up and the block of promising companies he'd acquired.

Why couldn't he do the same with Sloane?

It wasn't a tactic he'd use on the soon-to-be mother of his children, if she'd left him any other choice. But no way would he let Sloane struggle to care for his son and daughter in a run-down condo thousands of miles away. He had no choice but to do what he did best. Apply gentle pressure to get the desired results.

When they'd stopped to get her mail, there were more envelopes stamped Final Notice. He got her and the groceries inside, settled her on the sofa and put the groceries away.

"You really don't have to do that, Benji. You're the guest, and the contractions have stopped, so I'm perfectly fine."

He shot her a look that dared her to move from the couch. For once, she didn't object. She sat back and almost seemed relieved he hadn't taken her up on her offer.

Maybe it was the same with his marriage proposal. A proposal that made perfect sense given their situations. Sloane was proud and determined. She didn't want him trying to ride in on his white horse and save the day.

He got that. Her determined attitude was one of the things he'd always admired about Sloane. So maybe what he needed to do was sweeten the pot. Make her look like the winner in the deal. Give her an offer she simply couldn't pass on.

Benji got Sloane a glass of cold water to make sure she stayed hydrated. He handed it to her and sat in a chair across the coffee table from her. He drummed his fingers on his knees, running the words through his head.

"Whatever it is you want to ask me, Benj, just say it." Sloane put the glass down on a coaster and drew her legs onto the sofa, sitting cross-legged. She rubbed her belly again.

Every time her hand drifted there, he couldn't help recalling how it'd felt when the babies moved beneath his hand. Or thinking about the fact that he was going to be a father in just a few short months.

He slid to the edge of the chair. "I'd like to make a proposal."

"Please, don't get on one knee, Benj. That'll just make it awkward for both of us. My answer hasn't changed. No shotgun wedding."

Sloane had no qualms about battering his poor ego. If he'd been afraid that the money and women chasing him would go to his head, Sloane Sutton was a sure antidote for an overinflated ego.

"I'll fix up your condo and get you top dollar for it." He cleared his throat as he studied Sloane's face. Her eyes widened with surprise, then narrowed as if she didn't like where the conversation was going. "You can keep all of the proceeds of the sale, plus I'll write you a seven-figure check, just as a way to compensate you for—"

"Having my own kids?" She was more than a little indignant as she clutched her belly protectively. "I'm not your surrogate, Benji. These are *my*…" She released a long, slow breath. "These are our twins."

"I didn't mean it that way, Sloane. It's just that I realize what a burden this has been for you trying to handle it all on your own. I just want to help."

"But let me guess, the 'price' of this help is agreeing to become Mrs. Benjamin Bennett." She gave him a pointed look, like she couldn't have possibly been more disappointed with him. Then she stood suddenly, steadying herself on the arm of the sofa before shuffling into the kitchen. "So being rich has changed you."

Her cell phone rang, and he glanced at the screen. It was the same toll-free number that had called two or three times already. Each time she'd looked at the phone and gotten agitated before sending the call to voice mail.

He sat at the kitchen island, where she was scooping ice cream into a bowl.

"Having money hasn't changed me, Sloane. I'm a businessman. It's my job to make deals and get results—in a way that's fair to both parties. That's what I'm trying to do here. Do what's best for everyone."

"You don't get to show up in my life after ten years and assume you know what's best for me." She snatched a bag of salt-and-vinegar potato chips from the pantry, opened them and crumbled chips over her ice cream.

He was pretty sure a little of his lunch tried to crawl back up his esophagus, but he made a point not to cringe.

This woman needed 24/7 supervision and a nutritional intervention.

"Okay, Sloane, maybe you're right," he said calmly. "But I can see that you need help right now, and I want to be there for you. Not just because of our son and daughter, but because you're a friend. I care about you."

She looked at him, just as she stuffed an overflowing spoon of the ice-cream-and-potato-chip concoction into her mouth. Her eyes suddenly welled with tears and she dropped the spoon back into the bowl.

"A year ago, I completely had my shit together." She poked an accusing finger at him. "Then I had to take out those loans and things were tight, but I was managing it and, dammit, I had a plan. And it was working. Hell, that promotion was as good as mine." She wiped away tears angrily and huffed, shaking her head. "I will not marry you, Benji. Especially not for money."

*Pressure points.*

He cared for Sloane, but what he was doing was for the good of her *and* the babies. They belonged with him back in the place they'd both known as home.

Benji leveled his gaze with hers. "You're completely opposed to us getting married, that's fine. Then just come back to Magnolia Lake with me and stay at the cabin until the twins are one year old. At the end of the year, we can have a home built in Magnolia Lake, here in Nashville or wherever you want. If you still want to walk away, no harm, no foul. But I'll still help you sell the condo. And I'll pay all of your expenses while we're living together."

Sloane looked as if she were turning the idea over in her head. She chewed on the corner of her lower lip before slowly shaking her head.

Benji came around to her side of the island and faced her. "I'll pay off the farm, too. Free and clear."

Now she paused. "Why would you do that?"

"Because I want to be with you and our children. And it'll give me a year to show you that this relationship can work for all of us."

Sloane licked her lower lip and glanced at the envelope printed with the angry red letters on the counter.

"And what if at the end of that year, I still want to walk away?"

It pained him that she'd asked, but he forced a half smile, shoved his hands in his pockets and shrugged. "Then you walk away with the seven-figure check and zero debt. Your family's farm will be paid off and you can buy a house with a yard for you and the twins. And, of course, I'm going to take care of them, regardless of what choice you make today."

Sloane nibbled on one nail as she thought. She sighed. "And you won't try to take them away from me?"

"I would never do that to you." He hadn't meant it as a dig at her and the fact that she'd chosen not to tell him about the twins. But from the way she'd lowered her gaze, she'd taken it that way.

Fine. If he had to play to the guilt she felt over what she'd done, so be it. Whatever it took to get her to yes.

"You'd pay everything off at the end of the year?"

The tension in his chest eased a bit. She was almost there. "No."

She frowned. "How much longer would I need to wait?"

"You wouldn't have to wait at all. You just say the word, and I'll make a call right now."

"Why wouldn't you wait until the end to pay them off in full?"

"Because I trust you, Sloane." He lifted her chin and gave her a faint smile. "And I don't want you to spend the rest of your pregnancy stressed about the condo or the farm."

She stepped backward, as if she needed air and space. Sloane stared at him for a moment, then pressed a hand to her stomach. "If I do this, I'm doing it for my mother and grandfather. And the twins, of course. I don't want anything for myself."

Benji swallowed hard and agreed, but deep down he hoped that it wasn't true. By the end of the year, he was determined to make her realize that they should be a family.

"One more thing…" She raked her fingers through her curls. "If we do this, I need you to understand that this doesn't make us a couple. We're simply co-parenting the twins. I think it's best if we don't complicate things."

He nodded and forced a smile, hoping he'd managed to hide his disappointment. "Agreed. But I have a stipulation, too."

She tilted her head. "Yes?"

"Don't tell anyone about our deal."

Sloane frowned and rubbed her back. "My mother and grandfather are going to realize the truth as soon as the calls and threatening letters stop coming. It won't be hard for them to figure it out."

"Okay," Benji conceded. "But even they don't need to know that it was part of our deal. And ask them to keep everything low-key and not tell anyone where the money came from."

"And what about Delia?" Sloane frowned, her expression pained. "I don't like keeping secrets from her. These past six months…not being able to tell her the truth… It was hard." She shook her head. "I don't know if she'll ever forgive me, and the last thing I want to do is make it worse by keeping this from her."

"You didn't seem to have a problem keeping it from me."

*Okay, so maybe that one was on purpose.*

"All right." A deep frown still pinched her features. She nodded. "I'll move into the cabin with you until the twins' first birthday."

"Finish your ice cream." He winked. "We've got a lot to do."

\* \* \*

"You sure she's pregnant? You know, I saw this episode of—"

"I'm positive." Benji cut his always-skeptical cousin Parker off before he could launch into another "women can't be trusted" story.

Benji adjusted the volume on the airport rental car's Bluetooth as he turned into the entrance to his parents' community in Vero Beach, Florida. He hated to leave Sloane by herself, but she'd been right. This was a conversation he needed to have in person.

"Are you sure they're yours?" Parker, known for his bluntness, sounded apologetic, which meant he was making a real effort.

"Yes." Benji's tone lacked conviction. He didn't doubt that he was the twins' father, but he had no solid evidence to prove it.

"Okay, let's say you are the father. Do you think Sloane did this on purpose?"

"No, you know that's not Sloane's MO. I had to beg her to let me take care of her and the twins. I asked her to marry me, and she turned me down."

"You asked her to marry you?" Parker sputtered as if he was choking on whatever he'd been drinking. Knowing Park, it was probably coffee. "Are you insane?"

Benji wasn't sure how to answer that, either.

"Look, I have to go." His parents' house came into view. "See you in a week."

"Benj, it doesn't sound like you've thought this through. There are too many variables you're not accounting for. What if—"

"Goodbye, Parker." Benji ended the call and parked in the drive. He got out and put his coat on.

Delia and little Evie were spending the winter in Vero Beach, so it was the perfect time to tell his entire family. Sloane had insisted she should be there, but just talking about it had stressed her out. He'd overruled her and set out to tell his family on his own. But now that he was here, his feet felt as heavy as cement blocks as he trudged toward their front door.

"Benji? What on earth are you doing here, son? I had no idea you were in town." Rick Bennett hugged him. "Come on in. Your mother and sister will be thrilled you're here."

"That's why you didn't answer my call," his mother said, her face lighting up when she saw him. "You planned to surprise me." She hugged him tightly.

"I actually do have a surprise." He shoved his hands into his pockets when she finally released him. "Not that that's what I'd intended, it's just that it all came as a shock to me, too."

"What are you babbling about, Benji?" His sister trotted down the stairs and hugged him. "And don't wake your niece. I just put her down for a nap."

"Perfect, because I need to talk to you guys about something."

"What is it, Benji? You're scaring me." His mother frowned.

"Why don't we have a seat in the sunroom." He guided his mother to her favorite space in the house, a room filled with light that faced the pool.

"This is gonna be bad, isn't it?" His mother looked to his father for confirmation.

"Relax, Connie. Whatever Benji has to tell us, I'm sure it'll be fine." His father took a seat beside his mother on the sofa.

Delia squinted at him, her head cocked. "Oh…my… God."

"What, what is it?" His mother was in full panic mode.

"You knocked someone up, didn't you?" She was practically giddy with delight.

"How'd you know?" His face stung with heat and his heart raced.

"That's the same look I had on my face when I had to tell Mom and Dad I was pregnant with Evie. Halfway between extreme nausea and gut-wrenching terror."

That pretty much summed up how he felt. Which was ridiculous, because he was a grown man with more money than he knew what to do with. He glanced at his parents.

"So, it's true?" His mother pressed a hand to her cheek. "We're going to be grandparents for the second time?"

Benji held his forehead. "And third."

"Wait, you're having twins, too?"

"What do you mean, *too*?" His father, who'd barely reacted to his news, turned to his sister. "You're not pregnant again, are you?"

"No, I'm not." She practically sang the words. "But a friend is."

"Benji, I didn't realize you were dating. Did you meet someone while you were in Japan?" his mother asked. Suddenly she turned toward Delia. "One of your friends is pregnant with twins? Why haven't I heard about this before?"

"I was too busy working to meet anyone while I was overseas," Benji assured his mother. "And, no, I haven't exactly been dating."

"She wasn't prepared to share it with the world because she's not with the guy," Delia responded almost simultaneously.

"So you're not in a committed relationship with this girl." His mother frowned. "What if she won't allow us to spend time with the kids? And, worse, what if she's only done this to get money from you?"

"Why does everyone in this family automatically assume that if a woman gets pregnant, it's part of some nefarious scheme?" Benji paced the floor. "Some things just *happen*."

"Benjamin Darnell Bennett." Delia folded her arms and pinned her stare on him. "Who is it that you just *happened* to knock up six months ago, before you left for Japan?"

The recognition was there in his sister's eyes, before he uttered the name. "Sloane Sutton."

His mother, father and sister all spoke at once. His mother looked like she was going to faint, his father was at least mildly interested in the entire conversation and his sister was fit to be tied.

"Benji, how could you sleep with the Sutton girl, and at your cousin's wedding?"

It wasn't like he'd taken Sloane on the dessert bar amid the miniature peach cobblers and strawberry-rhubarb pies. But he didn't think his mother would appreciate his sad attempt at humor, so he didn't respond.

"Isn't she quite a bit older than you, son?" His father almost seemed impressed.

"Half of the single women in town were after you that night. Yet the one person you chose to sleep with was my best friend?" Delia looked as if her head were about to explode. "And then you both lied to me about it."

"We didn't lie to you," Benji corrected her. "We didn't tell you, because it wasn't any of your business."

"When I asked Sloane about her babies' father, she said it was a meaningless hookup. That it had been a huge mistake. Was that a lie, too?"

His sister had hurled Sloane's words back at him, knowing that they'd pierce flesh and nick bone like a sharpened blade. He gritted his teeth.

"None of that matters now, Delia. The only thing that matters is that I'm going to be a father."

"I don't trust that girl." His mother's voice trembled. "Never did." She turned to his father. "I told you we shouldn't have had Sloane over. We should've forbidden Delia to see her."

"You're really going to blame this on me?" His father rubbed a hand over his balding head. "Besides, it seems to me that you tried that, and it didn't work."

"Why would you say that, Mom?" Benji winced. "Sloane has never given us reason to distrust her."

"Like mother, like daughter." Benji's mother shook her head. "She barely came back to town while her grandfather was sick. Then she comes to Blake's wedding and she's all over you? I'll bet this was her plan from the start. She gets herself pregnant and she never has to work another day in her life."

"I can't believe you would say that about Sloane, that you'd even think it. She was right, you've never liked her."

"She's a better judge of character than I thought."

"Delia, Connie, I know you're both upset, but you're being much too hard on the girl. Regardless of what you might think of her mother," his father objected, "Sloane has always been smart and independent. A hard worker. Doesn't sound like the kind of woman who'd set a honey trap for some unsuspecting man. Least of all, Benji."

"That farm of theirs has been bleeding money. Now suddenly Benji comes to town rich and she's carrying his children? I don't believe it. Not until I see proof." His mother turned toward him. "We need to hire an investigator to find out exactly what Ms. Sloane has been up to since your night together. See if she's ever pulled this before. And the moment the babies are born, we're doing a paternity test."

"That isn't up to you, Mama." Benji strained to remain civil with his mother. "I'm not seeking your permission. I'm giving you an update on what's going on out of courtesy and respect."

"We appreciate that son—" his father was saying.

His mother interrupted. "But obviously, when it comes to Sloane Sutton, every ounce of the good sense you were born with flies right out the window."

"Sloane said you all would react like this. I didn't believe her, but she knows you better than I do." Benji laughed bitterly.

"Or maybe we know her better than you think you do." Delia's eyes were shiny with tears.

"What are you talking about?"

"Ask Sloane what she said would be the solution to all of her financial problems?"

His skin vibrated with anger. His jaw clenched so tightly it ached. "Why don't you tell me, since you seem so eager to?"

"About a year ago, she and I were joking that a couple of rich husbands would be the solution to all of our problems." Delia swiped at the corner of her eye. "I guess she wasn't joking, after all."

"Stop it. Both of you." Benji looked from his mother to his sister. "Whether you like it or not, Sloane Sutton will be the mother of my son and daughter. And I've invited her to move into the cabin at the lake with me."

Delia and his mother started talking at once.

"I don't want to hear any more about this. I'm *not* investigating her, I don't need a paternity test and she *is* moving into the cabin with me. So, if you'd like to meet your grandchildren and your niece and nephew, I suggest you find a way to treat her with respect, beginning with an apology."

Benji turned to Delia. "Maybe Sloane didn't handle this the way she should've, but I believe she did it for what she thought were the right reasons. She's your best friend, Delia, and she's always had your back. Too bad she can't say the same of you."

He left, slamming the front door behind him.

# Four

"Thank you again, Benji." Sloane shifted in her seat, adjusting the seat belt as they made the drive from Nashville to Magnolia Lake. She was grateful, of course, for everything Benji had done for her and her family.

As promised, he'd gotten on the phone right away, contacted his accountant and made arrangements to pay off both properties immediately. Then he'd gotten on the phone with his cousin Cole Abbott to see if he could either send a small crew to Nashville to work on Sloane's condo renovation or recommend a local crew.

That night, he'd helped her pack her luggage and hired movers to pack up the rest of the space and put her furniture in storage.

Within forty-eight hours, a crew had started renovating her condo. Benji had put her up at a hotel while he flew to Vero Beach to see his parents.

Sloane was grateful. How could she not be? But there was also a part of her that hated that she'd allowed Benji to do any of that for her. That she hadn't been in a position to do it herself.

The older women back in Magnolia Lake had called her independent, as if it were a bad thing. She carried that designation like a mantle of honor. She was glad they thought of her that way. The very opposite of how she'd always viewed her own mother.

Abigail Sutton had been dependent upon one man or another her entire life. Sloane's father. A succession of live-in boyfriends. Sloane's grandfather.

Sloane had vowed that she would never be like her mother. Though she loved her, she'd found it hard to respect her once she'd become a teenager and truly understood her mother's relationships with her boyfriends. She'd accepted their poor treatment as long as they'd paid the bills.

Sloane would never be that woman, yet the arrangement she had with Benji made her feel that she was teetering dangerously close to becoming just like her.

"I was happy to do it, Sloane." Benji's response brought her back to the moment. His words were kind, but he'd been in a foul mood since he'd returned from Florida. He refused to talk about what had happened with his parents, other than to say things had gone badly.

He'd advised her not to bother calling Delia. But Delia had been her best friend since they were ten. She was her only close friend. So she'd tried calling anyway. Each call had gone straight to voice mail.

Her friend hated her, Benji was at odds with his family and all of it was her fault.

"I know you said you don't want to talk about how things went at your parents' house—"

"Still don't." His jaw tensed, and he gripped the wheel tighter.

She had the overwhelming desire to hold him and whisper in his ear that everything would be all right. But aside from the constraints of the car he'd rented, there was the reality that they weren't in a relationship and didn't share that kind of emotional intimacy.

It was just as well.

In her experience, that kind of intimacy made one incredibly vulnerable. She'd been ass up in stirrups at least once a month since she'd learned she was pregnant. That was more than enough vulnerability for a lifetime.

"Let's talk about baby names instead." A smile curved the edge of his mouth, the first she'd seen since he'd returned from Vero Beach. "We need a boy's name and a girl's name. Got any prospects?"

She shrugged. "Not really."

He furrowed his brow. "I'm no pregnancy expert, but I thought that dreaming up baby names was one of the things moms-to-be spent their time doing."

"No one has ever accused me of being typical." She laughed bitterly. "And I didn't say I hadn't given their names any thought. It'd be nice to call them something other than Little Dude and Buttercup. What I said is that I don't have any prospects, as in I haven't settled on anything."

The one male name that Sloane felt strongly about was Benjamin. But back when she'd intended to keep Benji's paternity a secret, there was no way she could've risked naming the baby after his father without creating speculation. Now that their families and the entire town of Magnolia Lake would know, there was no reason Little Dude couldn't be a junior.

"What names have you considered?"

She was quiet for a moment. "For her? Scarlett."

"As in O'Hara?"

"As in Johansson."

Benji nodded thoughtfully. "I do like a woman who can play a badass Marvel superhero. What else you got?"

"Vivian."

"As in Leigh?"

"No, as in Julia Roberts' character in *Pretty Woman*." Sloane grinned. "Do we need to talk about your obsession with *Gone with the Wind*?"

"It's my mom's favorite movie." Benji shrugged, frowning at the mention of his mother. "And do I need to spell out the reasons I'm diametrically opposed to naming my daughter after a character that was a prostitute?"

"Hey, sex workers are people, too." Sloane poked his bicep. "But point taken. What about Bailey?"

"I love the name Bailey for a girl." He nodded. "Let's stick a pin in that one. And for Little Dude?" He gave her a sarcastic grin.

"Phillip, Beau or maybe Benjamin." Sloane looked straight ahead, but her cheeks warmed as Benji looked over at her briefly before returning his eyes to the road.

"I'm honored that you'd propose making him a junior. But I've never liked the idea of putting additional pressure on a boy to be like his father. I want our kids to do or be anything they want. And I'm grateful they'll have the resources to do that."

"Me, too." She glanced over at him, realizing for the first time how grateful she was that her children would never struggle like she and her mother did.

He squeezed her hand and gave her a warm smile before putting his hand back on the wheel and changing lanes. "I like Beau. It goes nicely with Bailey, don't you think?"

"Beau and Bailey." She repeated the names softly. "What do you think, Little Dude and Buttercup? Do you think you can deal with Beau and Bailey? Think carefully before you answer. You're going to have those names your entire lives. Unless you become actors or strippers." When Benji's eyes widened, she laughed. "Relax, I'm kidding."

He sighed, shaking his head. "If your way of cheering me up is supposing that our daughter might become a stripper, I'm gonna need you to work on your cheering-up game."

"Who said I was talking about her? I could've been re-ferring to him. Just think, our son could grow up to be the next Magic Mike."

"If you weren't carrying Beau and Bailey, I'd put you out on the side of the highway and make you walk the rest of the way to Magnolia Lake." He laughed.

Both the babies moved.

"They just responded to the sound of your voice," she told Benji, then spoke again, projecting her voice down to-ward her belly as she placed her hands on either side of it. "Does that mean you two like your names?" When there was no movement, she told Benji, "Say their names again."

"Beau and Bailey, this is your father. You two okay in there?"

Beau seemed to stretch his legs and Bailey responded by doing the same.

"I think we have a winner." Sloane rubbed her hand in a circle over the babies, her heart full and her eyes sting-ing with tears. "Beau and Bailey, it is. Though I think it should be something like Beaumont. Beau should just be his nickname."

"I like it." Benji nodded, his handsome face animated with a genuine smile. "And since their first names begin with the same letter as mine, we should pick middle names that begin with the letter *S*."

"I like that idea." Sloane smiled. "God, please tell me that co-parenting will be this easy for the entire eighteen years."

Benji looked uneasy. He shifted the conversation to a different topic. "So about the twins' room. I thought, while we're at the cabin, that they could share a room. That would make middle-of-the-night feedings and diaper changes easier. That'd also leave one guest room and a room for the nanny."

"A nanny?" Sloane laughed. "I'm not really the nanny type, Daddy Warbucks. Besides, I'm not working right now, so I can handle it."

"I'm renting some space and setting up a satellite office in town, but I'll try to be there as much as I can in the beginning. Still, I think you're underestimating how challenging it is to take care of one baby, let alone two."

"Delia managed with Evie."

"She only had one baby to deal with." The corners of his mouth tugged down at the mention of his sister. "And my mother lived with Delia and her new husband for the first two months to help out. If you ask me, she helped them right out of their marriage."

Sloane refrained from agreeing with Benji, though there was some truth to what he'd said. "Their relationship was never on solid ground because they got married for the wrong reason."

Delia and Frank's marriage had been strained and volatile from the start. He'd resented her family for pressuring him to marry Delia once she got pregnant. She'd been angry because their life together wasn't the domestic fantasy she'd been dreaming of her entire life.

"True." And just like that, Benji was back to growling one-word answers.

"If you don't want to talk about what happened down in Florida for me, then do it for Little…for Beau and Bailey. This silence and the suspense are completely stressing me out. Which means it's stressing the twins out, too."

Benji sighed heavily. "Okay, since you're determined to talk about it…you were right. My mother didn't take the news well. In fact, she questions whether the twins are mine."

"She thinks I'm lying?" Sloane's chest tightened. She

knew Connie Bennett wasn't her biggest fan, but even she hadn't seen that coming. "How could she believe I'd do something so horrible?"

"I don't know." He shrugged. "But, at the very least, she questions your motives. She's overreacting, I know, but what my sister said only confirmed her suspicions."

Her heart squeezed in her chest. Connie not being thrilled that she was the mother of Benji's twins wasn't a surprise. And though she knew Delia would be upset that she hadn't told her the truth right away, she certainly wouldn't have imagined that her best friend would turn on her and give her mother more ammunition.

"What did Delia say?" The sound of her own heart thumping filled her ears.

"Did you say that finding a rich husband would be the key to solving your financial worries?"

Sloane nearly denied it, but the memory of their conversation over drinks that night came back to her.

"I was joking. We both were. Delia knows that."

Benji's expression was stoic. "Now she thinks maybe you weren't kidding."

It hurt that her best friend could think for even a moment that she'd purposely done this. That she'd used her brother and would use her own children for financial gain.

"And what do you think, Benji?" Sloane asked softly, studying his profile as he focused on the road that stretched ahead of them.

"I told them that didn't sound anything like the independent woman I've always known. And that if they hoped to ever meet the twins, they needed to apologize for how poorly they'd treated their mother."

Her heart soared momentarily. He'd defended her to his mother and sister, had taken her side over theirs. Then her heart crashed nearly as quickly, as she realized she'd driven a wedge between Benji, his mother and sister.

The thing she'd always admired about the Bennetts was how close they were. Nothing had been able to come between them. Nothing except for her.

The guilt lay in her gut like a rock, beside the two precious babies she was carrying.

"Thank you for believing me, Benj. I really appreciate you standing up for me. But I don't want to be the cause of contention between you and your family."

"That was their choice," he said abruptly, frowning. "And they can choose to apologize whenever they're ready." He heaved a sigh. "Enough about that. Let's talk about something else."

"Like what?"

"Like what it feels like to be growing not one but two human beings inside you."

Her mouth stretched in an involuntary smile. "It's incredible." She massaged her tummy, prompting movement from Beau. "I never really aspired to be a mother. Not even during my marriage. That's one of the reasons it ended."

"Why didn't you want children?" His tone was tentative. As if, he wasn't sure he wanted to know the answer.

"It's hard to get that corner office when you have to take off for maternity leave and OB appointments. Sucks, but it's true." The record company hadn't been overt about it, but there was a reason most of the women who worked there were young and unattached. "Besides, I didn't think I had it in me to be self-sacrificing and I'm the last person on earth who should be dishing out life advice."

"What made you change your mind?"

"Because from the moment I've known about them, they're all I think about. I even dream about them. I know I won't be a perfect mom by any stretch of the imagination. But I'll try my hardest, because that's what they deserve."

She wiped away the tears that leaked from her eyes.

"You will be, Sloane." Benji's voice was as soothing as

a warm hug, the kind her grandmother used to give her as a little girl.

"I just hope they appreciate the fact that I've sacrificed my four-cups-of-coffee-a-day habit and my long, hot soaks in the bathtub." She spoke to her belly again. "If you're considering how to reward Mommy, how about sleeping through the night by two months. I'd really appreciate that."

Benji and Sloane laughed.

"I get why you had to give up the coffee. But why'd you have to give up baths?"

"It's not that I can't take them at all. It's just that the water shouldn't be too hot, and I'm not supposed to soak for too long. More practically, there's the concern that once I'm in the tub, I won't be able to get out. The hazards of living alone." She forced a laugh.

He squeezed her hand and smiled. "Thankfully, living alone won't be an issue anymore."

*Dammit.* The waterworks were starting again.

Benji got Sloane settled in at the cabin and went out to stock the place with groceries. He'd asked Sloane if she wanted to come along, but she wasn't quite ready to make her Magnolia Lake pregnancy debut. He understood, and, to be honest, he was grateful for a little time alone to process what had happened over the past few days.

He was a doer. He saw what needed to be done and he made it happen. Those were the moments when he felt most in control. Even before he'd signed the multibillion-dollar deal for his company, he'd been the kind of take-control guy who knew how to get shit done, despite whatever obstacle was thrown in his way. He loved it when a competitor or investor dismissed him, insisting that what he wanted to do was impossible. He thrived on the challenge of making doubters eat their words.

But that was business. What was happening between him and Sloane was deeply personal.

His instincts and emotions were magnified because it was Sloane Sutton—his longtime crush. Seeing her again for the first time in nearly a decade, dancing with her, kissing her, making love to her... All of it had created feelings exponentially more powerful than anything he'd experienced.

It had hurt like hell when Sloane had rejected his offer to travel to Japan with him.

So when Parker, his mother and his sister had attacked Sloane, he'd taken it more personally than he would've if the attack had been directed at him.

He'd defended her, and he'd meant every word. He believed in Sloane, believed that she'd never do the things his family was accusing her of.

But when all was quiet, small doubts crept in, making him wonder if he hadn't been as charming or as lucky as he imagined himself to be. Had Sloane's dire financial situation been a factor in her decision to spend the night with him? If so, maybe their birth-control failure wasn't an accident at all.

He massaged his throbbing forehead and dismissed the ugly thoughts.

"Benji, I didn't realize you were back in town." Nanette Henderson, owner of the Magnolia Lake General Store, approached him with a wide smile. "How long you in town for?"

She and her husband, Ralph, had owned the town's general store for as long as he could remember.

Benji leaned down to give the kindly woman a big hug. "I'm moving back home. Not to the old house, but out to my cabin. Until I can get something built in town."

"That's fantastic news! It'll be good to have you back around here." She grinned. "You have to come out to the house and have lunch with me and Ralph one afternoon. I'll show you the scrapbook I'm keeping of all the magazines you've been in."

This was the kind of thing he missed about being home. People who were genuinely happy for you when you succeeded. Who didn't see you as a threat. He just hoped that Sloane would feel the same about returning to their roots and giving Beau and Bailey a life here.

"Yes, ma'am, that sounds nice. Only I didn't know you read business and tech magazines." He grabbed a shopping cart.

"Can't reveal all my secrets." She chuckled softly. "I might be an old bird, but that doesn't mean I can't learn a few new tricks." She winked at him. "Just let me know if you need anything."

The woman walked away to greet another customer in the store.

Benji grabbed everything they might possibly need, including a few items he'd seen in Sloane's bathroom at the condo: shampoo, conditioner, bodywash and lotion.

When he rolled his cart down the baby aisle, he got lost reviewing the endless formulas, baby food, diapers, bottles and pacifiers.

It'd be a while before they needed those things. Still, it wouldn't hurt to be prepared with a few essentials. He grabbed two packs of newborn diapers and some bottles with nipples that the package claimed were ideal for newborns. Then his eye was drawn to another item. He smiled and dropped it in the cart.

It was strange to be in the cabin alone while Benji was in town. This would be her home for the next year and three months. Benji had told her to make herself at home, but it still felt like she was intruding.

He'd given Sloane her choice of bedrooms and she'd selected one of the larger guest bedrooms that had lots of light and an unobstructed view of the lake. It was next door to the bedroom they agreed their infant twins would share.

"Beau and Bailey." She said their names again as she stood by the window, staring out onto the lake. Was it silly that she already missed calling them Little Dude and Buttercup?

The sound of tires on the gravel drive and the slam of a door indicated that Benji had arrived with the groceries. She put on her coat and shoes and went outside to help.

"You'll catch a cold. Besides, I distinctly remember Dr. Carroll telling you not to lug around groceries."

"I'll take the light ones." Hopefully, there was a bag of salt-and-vinegar potato chips in there somewhere.

"No." Benji's answer was firm and his stare indicated he didn't intend to address the subject again. "If you want to help, stay inside and start putting the refrigerated goods away."

"Fine," she muttered under her breath and went inside, where the warmth of the wood-burning fireplace greeted her. "You can't blame a girl for trying to help."

"Do you want to end up on full bed rest?" His patience was wearing thin.

"God, no."

"Then cooperate or I'll be on the phone with Dr. Carroll before you know it."

"I've decided to switch to a doctor who's closer. So, sadly, she won't be my doctor anymore."

"I'll tell the new guy." He carried in an armload of groceries and set them on the counter. "No reaching high into the cabinets, either." In response to her eye roll, he added, "Don't make me take you over my knee."

"Sounds fun." She emptied the contents of one of the bags onto the counter.

His eyes darkened, and he bit his lower lip. "You're intentionally trying to drive me mad, aren't you?" He turned and headed back outside.

"Maybe," she whispered under her breath.

"I heard that." He held up a finger on his way out the door.

Sloane laughed. Living with Benji might not be so bad, after all.

Sloane wiped down the counter and turned on the dishwasher. She'd sliced her thumb while cutting onions with the super sharp, chef-worthy knives, but she and Benji had survived her first attempt at cooking dinner, so she counted the meal as a success.

It wasn't that she was incapable of cooking. After all, she could read a cookbook as well as the next person. But her execution was lacking due to limited practice. Before she'd found herself out of a job, she'd had very little time for cooking. Her job kept her busy. Most days she just stopped at one greasy spoon or another late at night when she was dragging her tired behind home.

Once she was pregnant, she'd spent the majority of those months at home subsisting on the limited foods that she managed to keep down, due to the acute morning sickness that lasted throughout the day and most nights. She hadn't been in any hurry to cook a fancy meal.

But tonight was the first night she and Benji spent in what would be their home together for the next fifteen months. It seemed like a good time to make the effort.

Now she was exhausted. She just wanted to take a hot shower and hit the bed. She turned off the kitchen light and headed toward her room. Sloane knocked on the open door of the master bedroom.

"Hey, Benj. I just wanted to say good-night," she called, not seeing him. The scent of lavender and bergamot filled the room, but she didn't see a candle burning.

Benji stepped out of the bedroom, his shirtsleeves pushed up to his elbows. He was drying his hands on a towel.

"Actually, I have a surprise for you. Come here." He reached his hand out to her and she took it, following him inside the master bathroom.

The most divine scent rose from the tub filled with water.

"You said you missed taking a bath and I saw this bath bomb in the grocery store, specifically for pregnant women. It's designed to help you relax. I would've done it in your room, but this is the only tub in the cabin."

"Thank you, Benji. This was sweet of you."

His sheepish smile deepened. "I made sure the temperature isn't too hot. Just don't stay in the water more than forty-five minutes and everything should be fine. I'll help you in and when you're ready to get out you can holler. And I'll keep my eyes closed, I promise."

"You've seen the entire package up close and personal, so I don't think we have to worry about that." She smiled. "Not to mention how much of me you'll be seeing when I go into labor. That is, if you'd like to be in the room with me when they're born."

"I wouldn't miss being there for anything in the world." He smiled faintly.

"Good." Sloane hadn't realized until now how much she wanted Benji to be there. "I need to grab a few things from my room first, but then I'll be back."

Benji waved his hand at a stash of items beside the tub. The bottles were too full to be hers, but they were the hair- and body-product brands that she used.

"You don't miss anything, do you?"

"Not when it comes to the people and things that are important to me." His gaze held hers.

Sloane was sure her heart skipped a beat. Her body, already filled with heat, reacted to him. His sweet words. His thoughtful actions. And to the memory of when she'd last stood in this bathroom, his hungry gaze sweeping over her.

She wanted him—more now than she had then.

But she was full of hormones going wild so her judgment was not to be trusted. It wouldn't be fair to toy with his feelings, knowing that when the fog cleared they might both feel very differently.

She excused herself to grab her pajamas and robe, needing to escape the magnetic power of those penetrating brown eyes.

Benji reviewed his email at his bedroom desk. A college basketball game played in the background with the sound turned down low. Even after his assistant screened his emails, he had countless requests for consulting gigs, business proposals and messages from potential investors who wanted to get in on the ground floor of whatever project he planned to take on next.

His parents had thought he'd settle down and retire at the ripe old age of twenty-five. Travel the world and perfect his golf swing. But the truth was, he'd be lost without his work. Not because his work defined him, but because he loved what he did. Playing with data, creating programs that would solve problems. He'd never even considered slowing down, let alone retiring. But seeing Sloane again had changed everything.

Since their encounter six months earlier, he hadn't been able to get their night together out of his head. Nor had he been able to dismiss the idea of picking up where they'd left off that night at the cabin. But now he was even more enamored with her.

He was only twenty-five and at the height of his career. Being a father and settling down to raise a family were the last things on his mind. Yet, when he'd seen Sloane's belly, round and full, her skin glowing, an unfamiliar feeling had gripped his chest. He was overcome with the need to take care of and protect her and their babies. Even if he was forced to do so on her terms.

Maybe he'd been impetuous to suggest marriage, but he was on the clock. Because at the end of their agreed-upon fifteen months together, he was determined to make Sloane see that he truly cared for her and that they should raise the twins together.

"Benj, would you do me a favor?" Sloane called from the bathroom.

"Anything. What is it?" He approached the open door tentatively, sensitive to respecting her privacy.

Sloane sat with her hands and arms covering her breasts and her knees drawn up. She handed him her soapy bath sponge. "Would you mind washing my back? I can't reach that part in the middle and it's been dry and itchy all day."

"Sure." He pushed his sleeves up farther and leaned over her, scrubbing her back. It produced so many suds that he hated to waste them. He scrubbed her arms, then her legs and her feet.

"Thanks. I think it's time for me to get out now."

"Right." He grabbed a towel and held it up for her, averting his eyes as she stood and wrapped it around herself. He helped her out of the tub.

"Thank you. You don't think about things like taking a bath or how difficult it is to dry your legs and feet when you can't even see them."

"Let me." He grabbed another towel and dried her lower legs and feet, painfully aware of how close he was to the space between her thighs. The memory of her warmth and taste washed over him, making his movements stilted and uncoordinated.

Regardless of all the things he'd accomplished in his life,

there was something about Sloane Sutton that still reduced him to a bumbling, inexperienced teenager.

"All done." When he stood, she gazed up at him with the same heat in her eyes he'd seen that night. She licked her lower lip and his shaft instantly hardened.

He honestly hadn't drawn her a bath as a prelude to taking her to bed. He'd done it because it was something she missed. And after their long drive from Nashville and the delicious meal she'd made for them, it was his way of showing his appreciation.

But he couldn't tear his gaze away from her lips. Couldn't stop wanting her.

With one hand, she still clutched the towel around her. With the other, she grabbed his shirt and pulled him closer as she lifted onto her toes.

He leaned down and claimed her mouth with a hungry, raw kiss, his tongue gliding along hers.

His arms slipped around her waist, though he was careful of her belly, which was pressed against him.

Sloane let the towel slip to the floor, and his hands glided along her silky, smooth skin. He caressed the curve at the small of her back, gripped her firm bottom.

He'd appreciated the undulating curves of her fit body six months ago. But now her curves were fuller—her belly firm and round, her hips and bottom wider than they were before. And her full breasts with their darkened peaks and larger areolae were the most sensual things he'd ever seen.

The remarkable changes to her body made her sexier. Every one of those changes, and the babies growing inside her, had stemmed from the seed he'd planted six months before.

Nothing he'd ever done had made him feel more powerful than this. Knowing he'd started life inside her.

She tugged his shirt free from his pants, and her hands

roamed his bare chest. Her thumb flicked his nipple, making him painfully hard.

He groaned against her mouth.

"I want you." Her warm breath skittered against his skin.

"You know I want you, Sloane, but you're hormonal." He'd spent the plane ride between Florida and Nashville reading about what to expect during pregnancy. "I don't want to do anything you'll regret in the morning."

Her eyes twinkled, and one edge of her mouth turned up in a naughty smile that did wicked things to his body.

"I promise you, I won't regret it." She broke away from him and headed toward the bedroom, calling over her shoulder. "And neither will you."

The last vestige of his control snapped when she turned and strode into his bedroom wearing nothing but the ink on her brown skin. She sat on the edge of his bed, one leg crossed over the other.

"I'm the only one naked. There's something very wrong with this picture." Her dark eyes flashed.

He couldn't disagree.

Benji stripped out of his clothing, titillated by Sloane's obvious admiration as she watched him.

He stepped forward, following her as she scooted up the bed and lay on her back, drinking in his hungry gaze.

Benji kissed Sloane before trailing kisses down her neck and chest. He worshipped the hard, fat brown peaks, laving them with his tongue as she writhed beneath him. He palmed the heavy globes, sucking on her beaded tips until she moaned with pleasure.

He kissed his way down her body and over her belly. There was honestly nothing sexier than Sloane Sutton in all her pregnant glory.

Benji kissed her mound, shielded by a patch of dark curls. He tasted her, reveling in her scent and her escalating whimpers as he teased her with his tongue.

She rested her hands on either side of his head and moved against his mouth. He gripped her thighs, opening her wide as he varied the speed, pressure and placement of his tongue. Sloane's body tensed, then she cried out his name. Her body trembled and her core pulsed.

The sight was enough to make a weaker man come undone.

He climbed up beside Sloane and held her with her back pressed against his chest. Benji buried his nose in her damp hair, losing himself in the warmth and fragrance of her soft skin. He inhaled the notes of lavender, bergamot and frankincense.

"You've always been beautiful, Sloane, but never more than you are right now." He kissed her ear, resting one hand above her belly and the other below it on the other side.

"Funny, because I feel like a double-wide trailer." She laughed, placing her hands over his. "But I do appreciate your willingness to pretend otherwise."

"I've never lied to you, Sloane. So trust me when I tell you that your body is amazing."

She turned to face him. "Really?"

"Really." He kissed her.

"Good." She climbed on top of him, planting her hands on his chest. "Because I need to feel you inside me, Benji."

His palm rested on the tattoo on her hip as she guided him to her entrance. Her eyes fluttered, and her breath hitched as she sank down, taking him deeper.

The sensation of being buried in her wet heat sent waves of electricity up his spine. They moved together, their pace building, until they'd both found their release.

He held her in his arms, hoping this was the first step to convincing her to stay.

# Five

Benji rolled over and threw one arm across his face to shield it from the sunlight creeping in through the window. It had been a month since Sloane had moved in. He loved sharing his home with her and having her in his bed at night. But each night, after he'd fallen asleep, Sloane returned to her own bed. No matter how many times he'd invited her to stay.

There was a knock at his bedroom door. "Benj, can I come in?"

It was a funny question, when he'd never wanted her to leave his bed in the first place.

"Yeah," he grumbled. He turned onto his stomach and calculated how many more minutes of sleep he could squeeze in before his 9:00 a.m. business call. "Come in."

She practically waddled into the room, her full stomach visible before he caught a glimpse of her lovely face. Her odd expression alarmed him.

He sat up quickly, wiping the sleep from his eyes. "Is everything okay?"

"I'm fine." She pressed a hand to her forehead. "But there's a guy here who claims to be trying out for a chef position."

"Shit." Benji looked at his watch. He'd forgotten that he'd set up an appointment with a personal chef. He was supposed to be cooking them breakfast right now. "His name is Marcellus. Can you show him in and tell him to get started?"

A loud clang came from the kitchen.

"Sounds like he's already setting up." Her tone and expression registered annoyance.

"Something wrong?"

"No, of course not." The twist of her mouth contradicted her words.

"Remember our deal. You be straight with me, and I promise to do the same." Benji patted the bed beside him and stretched while she tried to find a position that was comfortable. "So what's with the face? You don't like Marcellus?"

"I don't have any reason not to like him. I don't know him. Which is why it's kind of weird to have him in my... our kitchen, cooking my breakfast."

He chuckled. "You don't share the same opinion about Caitlin coming in twice a week to tidy up and do the laundry."

"True," she conceded. "But having someone else clean the bathrooms and fold the laundry doesn't feel like an assault on my domestic skills."

"You're insulted that I hired Marcellus? I thought you'd be thrilled."

"Tell me the truth. Is my cooking that bad? I mean, I

know I probably lean a little too heavily on the chicken surprise casserole, but it's good, isn't it?"

"It's delicious, babe. It's just not much of a surprise anymore." He chuckled, pulling her into his arms and kissing her cheek. "I just thought it was important that we add some variety to our diet. Make sure that you and the twins are getting some balanced nutrition."

"You're right. I've got a dozen cookbooks. I can find something else to cook."

"I've watched you in the kitchen cooking. You get tired and your back hurts from standing." He rubbed her back, and she practically cooed with pleasure and melted against him. He kissed her ear, then her jaw. "Let me do this for you." He added with a big smile, "For us."

"Ha, ha, ha." She punched him in the gut. "Fine. I'll eat Marcellus's cooking. But I don't have to like it."

"Fair enough. And if you don't, we'll send him packing. But give him a fair chance. Say...two weeks?"

"Okay." She shuffled toward the door.

"Where are you going?" He caught her hand in his, hoping to talk her into sleeping in with him for a few more minutes.

"If we're having company for breakfast, I'd like to look a little less like a disaster." She indicated the peanut-butter-and-jelly stain on her robe.

"Speaking of company... Blake and Savannah have been trying to get us to come to dinner for the past two weeks. Savannah's starting to think you don't like her."

"I don't dislike her. I just don't know that I'm ready to be paraded through town like the resident harlot."

"You're not being fair, Sloane. Give them a chance. I don't think folks here are nearly as judgmental as you believe."

"I'll consider it." Sloane shrugged. "Have you decided when we'll get started on the twins' room?"

Home improvement wasn't his gift. And what was the point of being a billionaire if you still had to do all of the tasks you hated yourself? But Sloane didn't see it that way. She wanted the twins' room to be special and bear their personal touch.

"Which reminds me…" He reached into the bedside stand and dug out his wallet. "There's a new interior decorator in town. She's looking to build her portfolio and she has some really great ideas for the twins' room." He handed her a business card.

Sloane's expression sank as she studied the card. "I know you don't think I can paint the room myself, which I totally could, by the way."

"What part of 'no strenuous activity' are you not getting, Sloane Sutton?"

"You didn't seem to mind last night when I was on top."

Her defiant gaze made him want to both spank her and toss her onto the bed and make love to her. Right now, he wasn't sure which feeling was more dominant.

Benji climbed out of bed, determined to keep his cool. "You're not painting the room and I suck at stuff like that. Cole is sending over one of his guys as soon as he can."

"I know this won't be your permanent home, but the twins will be in that room for at least a year. It's where they'll begin their lives. I want it to be special."

"Of course you do, and it will be, I promise." He picked up his phone and opened his calendar. His schedule was clear for the afternoon. "Tell you what. Why don't we do some shopping for Beau and Bailey this afternoon? We'll drive into Gatlinburg and go to the mall. When we get back, Marcellus will have dinner ready."

"Okay." She didn't look nearly as thrilled about the prospect as he'd hoped, but at least she wasn't talking about painting anymore.

\* \* \*

Sloane sat on the floor in the middle of what would eventually become the twins' room. She looked around at the shiplap walls and the window that overlooked a pretty wooded area.

Benji had the movers remove the guest bed and store it in a shed out back. The twins' cribs, still in their boxes, rested against the wall. Sloane put more of the adorable little graphic onesies on hangers and hung them in the closet. All of the clothing on the left side of the closet was for Bailey, all of the clothing on the right for Beau. A growing stash of baby toys, furniture and other items lined the floor of the closet. Pairs of little shoes were on the shelf above.

Sloane sat in the chair in the center of the closet. Benji had insisted she keep it there after she made the mistake of sitting on the carpeted floor, sorting clothes, and then required his help to get up.

She'd been living with Benji in the cabin for the past six weeks. They'd eaten breakfast and dinner together every day, and thanks to Marcellus's mouthwatering culinary skills, she didn't have to cook or do the dishes. Sloane didn't have to do any major cleaning, thanks to Caitlin. And she'd had time to binge-watch all of the shows she'd missed when she was working crazy hours for the past few years. She should be a completely content lady of leisure.

Then why was she bored out of her mind?

The babies would be here soon enough, and they'd keep her busy. Her mother had reminded her often enough how "lucky" she was to be with a man who "was swimming in cash" *and* adored her and their unborn babies. As if she'd hit the lotto.

But she wasn't "with" Benji. True, they lived together temporarily. And they'd slept together frequently. But she'd always returned to her own bed. They weren't a couple, and this wasn't a fairy tale. When the calendar turned on the twins' first birthday, they would go their separate ways.

She wasn't like her mother. She wouldn't rely on one man or another to take care of her and the twins. Sloane had made it on her own just fine before. Once she could find another job, she'd do it again.

A tightness gripped her and she gasped. She rubbed her hand in a circle on her abdomen.

The discomfort was unlike anything she'd felt before.

"No need to be alarmed." She whispered the words under her breath.

It was probably just more Braxton Hicks contractions. She hadn't felt them in a while. Not since Benji had appointed himself her personal water and nutrition dictator. Still, she glanced at her fitness watch. She needed to make note of the time, just in case it happened again.

She got up and moved back into the twins' room, opened a box of diapers and began stacking them in the pretty changing table they'd purchased the week before.

The walls still hadn't been painted, nor had the cribs been assembled. But the room was slowly beginning to take shape. Besides, they still had more than a month to get everything done.

Another bout of pain racked her, taking her breath and nearly making her drop to her knees. She stumbled forward, her weight on the changing station as she gathered herself. She looked at her watch. It'd been a little over ten minutes since the last one. Her new OB, Dr. Miller, had advised her to call him if she had four or more contractions in an hour—a possible indication of preterm labor, which could be dangerous for her and the babies. If the contractions continued at this rate, she'd call Dr. Miller, just to be safe.

She inhaled deeply, her eyes drifting closed, and slowly released her breath. As she did, she tried hard to let go of the tension and stress that built in her chest.

Sloane put aside the diapers she'd been stacking and went to the kitchen to get a glass of water. She poured the glass and downed it, quickly pouring another for herself. She checked her watch. Just a few more seconds and she'd know whether the contractions were coming at a consistent clip.

She howled, dropping the glass, which crashed to the floor and shattered. Her eyes watered from the intensity of the contraction.

Sloane drew in a long, slow breath through her nose and released it.

Benji had flown to New York for a meeting and was scheduled to be back later in the day. He'd suggested that her mother stay with her during his three-day trip. Or that she stay at Blake and Savannah's house in his absence. But she'd grown tired of being fussed over and treated like she was incapable of doing anything for herself.

It was just three days and she wasn't expected to deliver for another six weeks, at around thirty-eight weeks. Only, she was beginning to wonder if the twins had gotten the memo.

Sloane held her belly as she moved to the sofa, thankful for the private, in-home childbirth coaching Benji had insisted that they go through.

*Breathe in. Breathe out. Breathe in. Breathe out.*

No need to call the doctor and alarm everyone until she was sure there was just cause.

She closed her eyes, lay back on the sofa and kept breathing, wishing that Benji was there to hold her hand and assure her everything would be all right.

But as the pain moved through her, something felt very wrong.

Benji sprinted through the tiny local airport to his waiting car as fast as his legs would carry him. Marcellus had called to tell him that Sloane was experiencing preterm labor and he was taking her to the hospital.

He should never have left her alone, regardless of what she said. It was his job to protect her and the twins, and he was failing. He only hoped that his failure hadn't put Sloane or the twins in jeopardy.

He shouldn't have taken no for an answer. He should've either insisted that her mother come and stay with her or packed her up and carted her to Blake and Savannah's place, even if he'd had to carry her, kicking and screaming.

It was a mistake he wouldn't make again.

The rubber on his tires peeled as he took off for the hospital.

Sloane's skin was flushed, and it felt like it was one hundred degrees in her hospital room, thanks to the magnesium sulfate being pumped into her veins via the IV stuck in her arm.

She was little more than thirty-two weeks. Her doctor was determined to hold off delivery as long as safely possible, to give the twins more time to develop. Which was why she was also being given steroids to help develop their little lungs, in the event that the magnesium couldn't slow the preterm labor enough.

She was agitated and cranky. Most of all she was terrified. More for the babies than for herself. If something happened to either of them, she'd never forgive herself. Benji wouldn't forgive her, either.

How many times had he reminded her to keep her cell phone charged? And hadn't he insisted that she shouldn't be alone? She hadn't listened. She'd thought Benji was overreacting. Being melodramatic. But he'd been right all along.

Thank goodness Marcellus had come to prepare dinner for her, despite her insistence that it wasn't necessary.

The twins weren't even born yet and she was proving to be an incompetent parent.

"I'm starving, Marcellus. Can't you smuggle something in here?"

Sloane had discovered, in the weeks since he'd worked for them, that the mostly quiet man was a culinary genius and a gentle giant. He was built like a linebacker but wore his weight well.

"Benji would kill me." His kind smile always warmed her, mostly because of its rarity. Marcellus's expression seldom revealed emotion. "You'll be asleep in a few hours. Then tomorrow you can eat whatever you'd like."

"You're lucky I'm hooked to this IV. Otherwise, I'd try to turn you upside down until a piece of that beef jerky you've always got stashed on you shakes loose."

Now the man chuckled, a deep rumble that filled the room. She was pretty sure it was the first time she'd ever heard Marcellus laugh.

"Guilty." He patted his breast pocket and smiled. "But the doc says no food for you tonight, so guess what? No food for you tonight. I promise to make up for it once you're cleared to eat again and you and the babies are safe and sound. And you will be, because everything is going to be fine. Okay?"

Sloane nodded, rubbing her belly. She was glad to feel Bailey and Beau moving more than they had been during the preterm contractions.

"Thank you for bringing me here, but I'm sure you have other clients you're supposed to be taking care of today. I don't want to keep you from whatever you had planned. I'm in good hands with Dr. Miller, I promise."

"I'm not leaving here until Benji or your mom arrive." Marcellus's stony expression had returned, though his eyes twinkled.

"I'm here." Benji rushed into the room and went directly

to her bedside. He clutched her free hand and clasped it between both of his. "Is everything okay? Are you all right? Are the babies?"

Sloane explained everything as the doctor had explained it to her. They were trying to stop her early labor so she could get as close as possible to bringing the twins to term. But they were preparing the baby's lungs, just in case.

Benji thanked Marcellus profusely. Once the chef was gone, Benji sat beside the bed. He held her hand in one of his, the other gently pressed to her abdomen.

"Are you sure you're okay?"

Something about the sincerity with which he asked the question crumbled the walls of bravado she'd erected.

"No, I'm terrified." She wiped away tears. "If anything happens to them—"

"It won't. I promise." He kissed her hand.

It was a promise he had no power to keep, but she appreciated his confidence in making it just the same.

Somewhere along the way she'd come to need him. Not because of what he could do for them, but because of quiet moments like this.

Benji was here, and everything was going to be all right. That was enough for now.

Benji checked the calendar. Sloane's preterm scare had been three weeks ago. Since coming home, she'd been on complete bed rest.

He'd convinced her to sleep in his room so he could monitor her at night. Sex wasn't an option while she was on bed rest, so it seemed to relieve her of any anxiety about spending the entire night in his bed.

They'd read, watched TV and chatted every night until she finally drifted off to sleep. He'd held her in his arms and rubbed her belly. He'd felt the twins growing stronger as they moved inside her.

Nothing would've convinced him that he'd be this man, doting over two unborn babies and falling harder and deeper for the woman carrying them.

He cradled Sloane to him. The scare they had a few weeks before had turned him inside out.

What if something had happened to her or to either of the twins?

Neither he nor Sloane had planned this, but she'd been the only woman he'd ever really wanted. He'd known that since he was ten years old. Now that he had her back in his life again and they'd been given this incredible gift, he wouldn't squander the opportunity. He'd do whatever it took to convince her that they should be together, if only for the sake of the twins.

A gush of wetness spread beneath him and Sloane awakened with a gasp.

"Oh, my God. My water just broke. It's happening. We're going to have the babies."

His heart raced and panic gripped his chest, but she needed him to be her strength. She and the twins were counting on him.

Benji kissed her ear and squeezed her tight. "It's okay, baby. Everything is going to be all right. I promise."

It was a promise he kept. Twelve hours later he held Bailey and Beaumont Bennett in his arms.

# Six

Sloane was hungry and exhausted. She'd never done anything harder than giving birth to the twins. But as she watched Benji standing by the window, rocking their son in his arms and telling him how glad he was to finally meet him and his sister, it was worth every single moment of pain, exhaustion and terror.

There had been a moment, after she'd delivered Beau, when she'd thought she wouldn't make it. That she couldn't hang on a minute longer. She was in pain and terrified as the doctor reached in and tried to turn Bailey so she'd come out headfirst. Benji had been there, had kissed her and held her hand. He'd whispered in her ear that she was stronger than any woman he'd ever met and assured her she could do this.

"Just hang on a little longer," he'd told her, "and you'll be able to meet our daughter."

He'd breathed with her through the pain. Encouraged her to push once it was time again. Praised her once she'd safely delivered Bailey, too.

She held her daughter, inhaling her sweet scent as she kissed her little forehead. Then she glanced lovingly at the father of the two incredible miniature human beings she'd just given birth to.

Now Benji was rocking Beau, who'd gotten a bit fussy, and singing "Hush Little Baby" in the same deep, throaty, hypnotic drawl that had captivated her the night they'd made the twins.

Her eyes burned with tears, and an involuntary smiled tightened her cheeks. This man was beautiful and sweet. Loving and generous.

Benji still embodied the essential heart-melting qualities she'd loved about him when she'd known him as the sweet kid who was her best friend's little brother. Now, though, there were the new and unfamiliar elements of Benjamin Bennett, the fine, grown-ass man she couldn't seem to get enough of.

As she watched Benji softly singing to their son, her heart felt as if it would burst. There was a part of her that wanted nothing more than to curl up in his arms, holding their beautiful twins. Another part of her feared what would happen once the glow wore off and they were just two people struggling to raise demanding infants.

There was an old, floral photo album in her mother's cabinet with a picture of her father, holding her in his arms and smiling as if he were the proudest father in the history of Magnolia Lake. Yet, her memories of him were of a man who resented her, a man who'd had no interest in being a father and a husband.

She wouldn't put Benji in that position, wouldn't take a chance on waking up one morning and seeing that kind of bitterness in his eyes.

"He's finally gone back to sleep." Benji grinned proudly as he returned Beau to the clear acrylic bassinet marked

Bennett, Beaumont. "How's our girl?" He nodded toward Bailey, dozing in Sloane's arms.

"I fed and burped her, and she just fell asleep." She handed the baby to Benji, and he tenderly kissed the infant's cheek before laying her in her own designated bassinet.

Benji sat in the chair beside Sloane's bed and squeezed her hand. "You were amazing today. What you did… God, I'll never make the mistake of thinking that men are the stronger sex."

"Thank you for being here." She kept her gaze on their joined hands, afraid of getting lost in his deep brown eyes. "I couldn't imagine trying to do this without you." She finally met his gaze. "You were pretty amazing today, too."

Benji cradled her cheek and smiled, pressing a soft kiss to her lips.

"Enough of that, you two. That's how you ended up with these two gorgeous babies in the first place." Abigail Sutton swept into the room, a big grin on her face.

She'd been at the hospital earlier, but she'd had to leave to take Sloane's grandfather to a cardiologist appointment.

"Hey, Mama." Sloane lay back on the pillow, reluctantly pulling away from Benji's touch. "How'd Granddad's appointment go?"

"The cantankerous old thing will probably outlive all of us." She kissed Sloane on the forehead, then crossed the room to give Benji a hug. "He wanted to be here, but after the drive there and back, he was tuckered out."

Her mother was a terrible liar, but Sloane appreciated the effort. Sloane still couldn't shake the look of disappointment on Atticus Ames's face when she'd returned to Magnolia Lake to tell them about her pregnancy. He wasn't happy that she'd unwittingly followed her mother's path. Learning that Benji Bennett was the father had only solidified that stance.

She'd given up trying to please the old man a long time ago. Still, his abject disappointment hurt.

"The twins are sleeping," her mother complained, taking a seat on the sofa near the window. "I was hoping to hold them."

"Go right ahead," Benji said, just as Sloane was going to ask her to let them be. He winked at her. "Your mother came a long way to see the twins. I don't think it will hurt for her to hold them for a bit."

Sloane sighed and gave a reluctant nod.

Her mother moved to the sink and washed her hands up to her elbows before standing over the sleeping infants in their bassinets, trying to decide which one to pick up first.

"How about if Grandma visits with you first?" She carefully lifted Bailey from her bed and cradled her in her arms.

The girl made only the slightest indication of being perturbed by the move before falling back asleep.

"She's beautiful. The spitting image of you as a newborn." Abigail Sutton beamed as she held little Bailey in her arms.

"Really? I'd love to see Sloane's baby pictures." Benji grinned, obviously amused by the prospect.

"Please don't trot those out." Sloane groaned. "We'll take your word for it."

"Not me." Benji chuckled. "I need to see proof."

Sloane shifted the pillow behind her back as her mother started to coo at her brand-new granddaughter, quickly getting lost in a baby-talk conversation with the sleeping infant.

Sloane lowered her voice and leaned closer to Benji. "That reminds me… I know you said that you trust me, and I appreciate that, but I won't object to a paternity test to prove that the twins are yours."

He shifted his glance to where Abby sat, oblivious to their conversation as she cooed at her granddaughter. His smile hardened into a straight line, but he didn't respond.

"It's okay." She ran her fingers through her hair. "I realize that you need to do this for your own peace of mind and to settle any doubts your mother and Delia have."

The mention of his mother and sister elicited a deep frown that marred his handsome face.

God, Beau looked so much like him. Same mesmerizing brown eyes and strong chin.

"No." His tone conveyed absolute conviction, but something in his tortured expression belied the certainty in his voice. "What my mother and Delia believe or don't is their problem. We don't need to prove anything to them."

"But if it would ease their minds and erase any doubt, why not?"

"Because I don't need it. I know Beau and Bailey are mine. I could feel it the instant I looked into their eyes." He looked back at her. "Data and numbers are essential to my work, but the reason I've been successful is because I always trust my gut." He patted his stomach. "I know the truth in here. I trust that feeling. And I trust you. I only wish you'd do the same."

"I'm trying." Sloane turned her attention to her hands, perched on her still-swollen belly. "I really am."

"That's all I ask." He squeezed her leg, then stood, turning to her mother. "I'm going to get a real cup of coffee. I don't think I can tolerate another drop of that dreck from the cafeteria. Can I get you anything, Ms. Sutton?"

"We're family now," her mother said, returning Bailey to her bassinet and moving toward Beau's. "Call me Abby. And yes, I'd love a cup of coffee. Nothing fancy. Just black with a couple of packets of sugar."

"Yes, ma'am… I mean…yes, Abby." He leaned over and pressed a chaste kiss to Sloane's forehead, as if he was a nervous teenage boy pinning a corsage on her chest on prom night beneath the watchful eye of her gun-toting grandfather.

He was adorable.

Benji pressed a quick kiss to the forehead of his infant son, lying in Abby's arms, and then left.

"I can't believe that handsome man was once little Benji Bennett." Her mother grinned, sitting beside her and rocking Beau, already sleeping, in her arms. "And I can't believe you're not trying to get him to marry you. He's obviously fond enough of you, he adores these babies and he can give you anything you'd ever want."

Was that what her mother wanted for her? To be with a man who was simply "fond enough" of her? Both she and her mother had married men who were "fond enough" of them, though they'd married for very different reasons.

She'd run off to Nashville with Allen Dickson not long after her eighteenth birthday. He was a session musician who played electric guitar like he'd been born with the thing in his hands. They'd bonded over their common interests—escaping their dysfunctional families, finding careers in the music industry and putting Magnolia Lake firmly in their rearview mirror.

Once those shared grievances were stripped away, there was little substance to their relationship, and they wanted different things from life. Allen had wanted to settle down and start a family. But what he'd really meant was that she'd settle down and raise the kids while he spent the majority of the year on the road, touring the world with one musician or another.

Eventually, her marriage to Allen had ended, like her parents' had. It was a mistake she wouldn't repeat, especially now that she had Beau and Bailey to think about.

"We both know better than most that marrying a man for money isn't the smart move." Guilt tugged at Sloane when her mother's expression deflated. She shook her head. "Sorry, Mama. I shouldn't have said that. I'm just really tired. Maybe now isn't the best time to discuss this."

"Maybe not." Abby Sutton nodded once and turned her attention back to her sleeping grandson. "But there is one thing I want to say... Benji ain't nothin' like your daddy. He's a sweet boy, and he clearly loves Beau and Bailey."

"I know, Mama." Sloane was tired, and she just wanted to sleep. "But it's just not that simple."

*We both know better than most that marrying a man for money isn't the smart move.*

Benji had gone back to Sloane's room to ask if she'd like him to bring her some real food. Now the words he'd overheard played in his head again and again as he made his way to the parking garage.

After all they'd been through—their history together, the last months of her pregnancy and the birth of their precious twins—was that all she saw in him? That he was a man with money?

Supporting Sloane through the delivery and witnessing the birth of their children was the most amazing experience of his life. He'd been left with a profound connection to her. He thought she'd felt the same. Was he simply seeing what he wanted?

Benji left the hospital, picked up coffee for himself and Abby, then grabbed some food.

He obviously hadn't convinced Sloane that she and the twins were his family as much as his parents and sister were. Not wanting to pressure her, he'd been too subtle, too laid-back.

*Time for a bolder approach.*

He pressed the voice-command button in his vehicle. "Dial Kamilla Price."

When Benji returned to the room, Abby was holding Bailey again, who'd awakened in his absence. Sloane was breastfeeding Beau. The pained look on her face indicated that the process wasn't going well.

"Everything okay?" he asked her as he set Abby's cup of coffee on the table beside her. She thanked him.

"Other than the fact that I'm questioning whether this one was born with teeth—" she nodded toward Beau in her arms "—everything is good." She sniffed the air and looked at him hopefully. "Please tell me that's a Kick-Back Burger and Rocky Top Potato Skins from Calhoun's."

He lifted the grease-stained bag with a slight grin. "What else?"

"Thank God. It wasn't the epidural that made me queasy, it was that food they were trying to pass off as edible," she grumbled. Then she grimaced in pain. "Ouch, ouch, ouch. Take it easy, Little One. Mama's gonna need those when you're done."

Benji's face flushed with heat. He cleared his throat. "I'll save it for when you're done." He avoided the chair beside the bed and sat next to Abby on the sofa instead. "Got something for you, too, Abby. I guessed, so I hope you like it."

"That's mighty thoughtful of you, Benji. I'm grateful for whatever you brought. I'm not picky, so I'm sure it'll be just fine."

He nodded, glancing at Sloane and Beau, hoping everything would be just fine.

# Seven

In the week that Sloane had been in the hospital with the twins, Benji's Range Rover SVAutobiography had arrived from Seattle. As they drove the final stretch of road home from the hospital, she looked over her shoulder in the baby mirrors perched over each twin in the back seat. They were both still asleep. Good.

Maybe she could get in a long nap before they both woke up hungry. Breastfeeding was a struggle, but Benji had been encouraging. He'd even hired a lactation consultant, which she honestly hadn't known was a thing. The nurse and mother of four—including a set of twins—had shown her how to breastfeed the twins simultaneously using a double football hold and a twin nursing pillow. Sloane was still less than confident.

"Everything okay?" Benji tapped her leg, drawing her attention back to him. He'd been wearing the same big grin from the moment the doctor had released them from the hospital. She only wished she felt as ready as he did to begin this thing in earnest. To be the full-time parents of two little people who were dependent upon them for everything.

This was something she couldn't afford to screw up. The stakes were much too high.

It had been easy to judge her own parents. To play Monday-morning quarterback and point out all the ways in which they'd failed. But now that the responsibility was hers, she felt the enormity of the weight upon her, even as her heart expanded with love for the twins and affection for their father.

"Yes." She nodded. "I'm just a little tired. That's all. Hopefully, they'll sleep for a couple of hours so I can get a nap in. Maybe take a hot shower."

Benji frowned, his hands tightening on the wheel. "You said you were tired of lying in bed all day at the hospital. And before that you'd spent so much time isolated at the cabin. I thought maybe you'd want to—"

"You thought maybe I'd want to do what?" She looked up as they approached the cabin. There were five or six cars parked in the long drive.

Sloane recognized several of the vehicles. Delia's car and Rick and Connie Bennett's SUV were notably absent.

"You invited all of these people here as soon as we got home?" Her face flushed with heat and her spine tensed. She raked her fingers through her hair, which was just short of a hot mess after her hospital stay.

"They wanted to welcome you, Beau and Bailey home." He sounded so apologetic that she shifted the focus from her rising anger to how he must be feeling.

Sloane shut her eyes momentarily and took a deep breath. "This was thoughtful of you, Benj. Really."

"Are you sure? Because if you just want to crash, I'm sure they'll understand. I'll explain that I hadn't considered that you'd be wiped out."

"It's okay. I know they're eager to meet the twins. I'll catch up on my sleep later."

He smiled uneasily and nodded. "Okay, great. Because everyone is excited to see you, too."

He pulled in front of the cabin and parked, then came around the car to help her out, refusing to allow her to carry the babies' car seats.

He ushered her inside where her mother, Blake, Savannah and Blake's sister, Zora, warmly greeted her. Her grandfather hung back, seated on the sofa watching television and drinking a beer, wearing his typical frown. Parker greeted her with a curt, but polite nod, then went out to help Blake and Benji bring in the babies in their car seats, her bag and the collection of baby things they'd gathered while in the hospital.

"So how does it feel being a mother now?" Zora asked, guiding her to take a seat on another sofa. "It must seem surreal, right? Especially since you weren't really expecting it."

Sloane had always appreciated that Zora was pretty straightforward. She was similar to her brother Parker in that way. But Parker's directness often made him come off as an arrogant asshole, particularly to those who didn't know him well. Zora's honesty, on the other hand, had the charm and sweetness of the lone girl raised in a house full of boys.

"It was a strange but also kind of wonderful experience." Sloane smiled as her mother and Savannah lifted the babies out of their car seats and fussed over them. "I've been talking to them since the first time I felt them move. But once I saw their little faces…" Tears stung her eyes and her voice broke, but her smile deepened. "Well, it's just really hard to explain."

"Not to me." Savannah sat beside her holding Bailey. "I know exactly what you mean. Davis was completely unexpected and the situation between me and Blake was so dire when I learned I was pregnant. I'm thrilled that everything worked out between me and Blake." She smiled at him adoringly as he helped Benji and Parker carry items to the nursery. "But even if it hadn't, I could never regret having Davis. Blake is the love of my life. My rock. But Davis is my heart. And Blake feels the same."

"You guys seem very happy." Sloane was glad for her friend Blake. He'd had a relationship go terribly wrong a few years earlier, then his relationship with Savannah had nearly blown up when he discovered who she really was—the granddaughter of a man who believed he rightfully deserved half of the Abbott family's distillery.

Despite all of the drama over Savannah having surreptitiously come to town to exact revenge on the Abbotts, they'd managed to reconcile. They'd been mature enough to realize that despite the circumstances, they were meant to be together. And little Davis was a happy surprise.

"Speaking of Davis, where is he?" Sloane looked around the cabin.

"He's with his Grandpa Duke and Grandma Iris. They're spoiling him to death, I'm sure. I guess it pays to be the first grandchild in a family this big."

Sloane watched her mother fussing over Beau. It had been sweet seeing how much she loved and adored the twins. Sloane couldn't ever remember having a relationship like that with her own grandfather. Even in her earliest memories of him, he was wearing the same scowl he wore now as his gaze periodically drifted in her direction.

"My grandfather isn't going to make his way over here, so I guess I'll go over and say hi to him." Sloane groaned, slowly getting up from the sofa. Her body was still sore.

"While you're gone, maybe Savannah will share the baby since she's already got one of her own." Zora eyed her sister-in-law, who brushed her lips over little Bailey's forehead.

"They're so sweet and they smell so good at this stage," Savannah said dreamily. "Makes me want another one."

"We have a spare, so you can always borrow one." Benji

grinned, approaching them. He held a hand out to Sloane. "Hey, come here. Let me show you something."

She slipped her hand in his, conscious of everyone else in the room watching them and of the knowing looks they shared.

"I was just about to say hello to my grandfather. Give me a sec?"

"Sure." Sloane could tell he was trying not to sound disappointed. "Meet me in the nursery when you're done."

She nodded, then made her way across the room to the other sofa and sat beside her grandfather, who hadn't even looked up to acknowledge her approach.

"Hey, Granddad."

"Sloane." He polished off a little meatball on a toothpick. Marcellus had outdone himself putting together this little spread for their guests. "Glad you and the twins made it home and that you're all okay."

"Thanks, Granddad." She swiped one of the little meatballs, a fried ravioli and a potato-cheese-and-onion fritter. They were all foods that Marcellus knew to be favorites of hers.

Her grandfather gave a disapproving groan but didn't object. With his dietary restrictions, he shouldn't be eating half of the food on his plate.

"No more beer," she admonished sternly. "Or do you want me to text your doctor a picture of your plate?"

He grunted more loudly this time. "Fine."

It was as close as Atticus Ames was going to get to saying he loved her, a fact of life she'd accepted and convinced herself she was okay with. But she was moved by how deeply and immediately her mother had bonded with the twins. And by hearing Savannah gush about the relationship little Davis had with his grandparents.

Would her life have been different if she'd had that kind of relationship with her grandfather?

"I notice those uppity Bennetts still haven't come around yet." He added an indignant humph. "They always did think that girl of theirs was too good to be friends with you. Connie is probably about to pop an artery because her grandbabies share a bloodline with the likes of us."

"We're surrounded by their relatives and the subject is a sensitive one for Benji, so please refrain from badmouthing them here." Sloane glanced around the room to see if any of the Abbotts had overheard their conversation. "You and Mama can bellyache about my choice of in-laws in the truck on the way home."

"Unless you two stopped at the local magistrate on the way here, them ain't no relatives of mine."

Sloane wondered how long it would take her grandfather to bring up the fact that she and Benji weren't married. She wouldn't take the bait. Not today.

"I have to see what Benji wants." She swayed a little as she stood. Her grandfather nearly dropped his plate to steady her.

Sloane thanked him and headed down the hall to join Benji in the nursery. If Atticus Ames was willing to sacrifice food that good to keep her from falling, maybe he cared a little more than she thought.

Benji snapped a photo as the nursery door opened and Sloane stepped inside.

Her mouth fell open and she pressed her fingers to her parted lips. A range of emotions played out on her lovely face as she surveyed the room, which had still been undone when she'd been admitted to the hospital to have the twins.

"Oh, my God. It's completely finished." Her voice relayed surprise, but none of the joy he'd expected. "It's beautiful."

Her smile seemed forced as she ran her fingertips along the edge of one of the handcrafted cribs made from locally sourced birch. He'd commissioned them from Zora's best friend, Dallas Hamilton, a local who'd turned his passion for making handcrafted furniture into an international, multimillion dollar business.

Benji had stalled on finishing the twins' nursery because Dallas's commissioned pieces were in high demand, and there was a long waiting list.

The cribs were placed against one wall, separated by a different changing table than the one they'd previously purchased. The shiplap walls had been primed and painted a soft green, and there was a new mural of birch trees, similar to the ones outside of the nursery window. Each of their names was spelled out in handcrafted wooden letters that appeared to hang from the branches of the trees in the mural over their individual cribs. Bailey's letters were painted pink and Beau's were blue. Luxe two-toned silk was suspended over each crib from a rustic cornice, also made from birch. The fabric fanned out to form an elegant little canopy over each crib.

The dressers and changing table were also constructed of matching birch. A luxurious half rocker upholstered in a sage-green fabric completed the furniture in the room. Every piece of furniture in the room was a Dallas Hamilton original.

"I don't know what to say," she said finally, standing in the center of the room and turning slowly as she took it all in. "It's very different from what we'd discussed…but it's beautiful. More so than anything I could've come up with." There was almost a hint of sadness in her voice.

"But you like it, right?"

"It's stunning. How could I not like it?" Her expression was neutral, as if she were stating an indisputable fact. She looked at the cribs again. "What happened to the cribs I bought?"

"They were really nice. But when Zora mentioned that

Dallas does custom cribs, I thought it'd be really special to have heirloom pieces made just for them."

"And they're lovely," she agreed, her arms folded. "But you didn't answer my question."

"Since we weren't using them, I thought you'd want them to go to someone who could. I donated them to a women's shelter in Gatlinburg." He took a few steps toward her, trailing his fingers down the outside of her arm. He could feel the tension vibrating off her. "Is something wrong?"

She shook her head, but her eyes looked watery. "They were just wood veneer, purchased at a discount retailer. These are much better."

She stepped beyond his reach and surveyed the room again with her back to him. As if she needed the space. "How'd you come up with the design?"

"I brought in Kamilla Price, the new interior decorator I told you about. She shot a few ideas past me. I liked them, so I gave her carte blanche to do whatever she liked, as long as she could get it completed before you were released. I'm glad I did. It's better than anything I could've imagined."

Sloane turned to him wearing a polite smile. "Thank you for taking care of everything, but we'd better get back to our company. Beau and Bailey are probably ready for another nap, so we can take their new cribs for a test spin."

She gave him an awkward hug and a kiss on the cheek.

He followed her back to the great room to get Beau and Bailey and they put them down for a nap. Then they returned to the impromptu celebration of the twins' arrival home, both pretending it didn't hurt that Benji's parents and his sister weren't there.

# Eight

Sloane lifted her head and checked the clock beside the bed. It was almost noon.

She nearly fell off the bed scrambling to get out of it. The last thing she remembered was feeding the twins in the early morning hours, before the sun rose. But that was several hours ago. Why hadn't she heard their cries?

The proximity of her room to the nursery was the primary reason she'd returned to her own bed rather than sharing Benji's. But since they used state-of-the-art video baby monitors, Benji didn't seem convinced by that argument.

Sloane slid her feet into her slippers and shuffled to the bathroom. Teeth brushed, hair tamed, she made her way to the twins' room next door.

Beau and Bailey weren't in their beds. Her heart raced. *Don't panic. I'm sure Benji has them.*

She peeked into his bedroom. He wasn't there. Sloane stepped out into the hall and heard someone singing softly, but it was a female voice. And not one she recognized.

Sloane padded down the hallway quickly but cautiously. She peered into the kitchen. The babies were in their carriers, perched on the kitchen counter. A woman with long, blond hair pulled into a single messy, one-sided braid was singing to them as she stirred something on the stove.

"Who the hell are you, and what are you doing with my kids?" Sloane edged closer, casing the room for something she could use as a weapon in case this chick was some batshit crazy stalker who was here to steal her babies.

"Please don't be alarmed, Sloane." The woman held her hands up, her shoulders tensed. "You probably don't remember me, but I'm Olivia Henderson—Mrs. H's niece from Chicago. But please, call me Livvie."

Sloane's hackles went down, but only slightly. She vaguely remembered the girl who'd spent a few weeks visiting her aunt during summers growing up. The woman before her bore no resemblance to the gangly, awkward girl with braces and bad skin who sometimes helped her aunt out at the general store.

"Well, Livvie from Chicago, that doesn't explain what you're doing in my kitchen with my children." Sloane was standing a few feet from the woman. She'd quickly surveyed the twins to make sure they were fine. They both seemed content.

"Maybe it would be better if Benji explained."

"Since he's not here and you are, maybe *you'd* better explain." Sloane didn't like the idea that Benji and this woman shared some conspiratorial secret.

"I had an appointment to meet with both of you this morning, but you were sleeping so soundly that he didn't want to wake you."

"If the appointment was with both of us, why is this the first I'm hearing of it?"

Sloane moved in closer, struck by how beautiful the girl was. She was closer to Benji's age than hers. Her blue eyes were stunning, the color of the Caribbean Sea. And her bronzed skin glowed as if she'd spent more than her share of time on a sandy beach. Her teeth were brilliantly white and perfectly straight.

The braces had obviously paid off.

"Benji wanted to surprise you, I think," the woman explained. "He had to make a quick run into town, but he'll be back shortly."

"What was the appointment about?" Sloane pressed. Her tone made it clear she expected a direct answer.

"Surprise." Livvie shrugged her shoulders, her expression racked with apprehension. "I'm your prospective nanny."

"You're my what?" The blood pumped through her veins more quickly.

"Your prospective nan—"

"I heard what you said, obviously." Sloane clenched her teeth. "But Benji and I talked about this. I was clear that I didn't need a nanny."

Sloane pressed a hand to her forehead and paced. She felt hot and cold at the same time and her hands were shaking.

First there was the housekeeper, then a chef and now a nanny?

Was this what their year together would be like? Benji would call all the shots under the guise of surprising her, while completely ignoring her input?

"I'm sure it would've come off better had he been here to explain himself," the girl said apologetically, returning to the stove. She stirred the pot, inhaling the savory scent.

Beau got fussy and started to cry.

"Hello, handsome." Livvie smiled as she turned off the stove.

She wiped her hands on a rag and reached for the baby, but Sloane stepped in and lifted him from his seat.

"Hey there, Bubba. Did you miss your mama?" She cradled him in her arms. The tension drained from her shoulders when one side of his mouth seemed to pull into a grin. Sloane was fully aware that it was probably just gas. Still, the timing of the pseudo smile made her feel much better.

Sloane kissed Beau's forehead and slipped her finger into his little hand. Despite being barely more than one week old, Beau had quite the grip.

"Since I was sleeping, they must've been given the supplemental formula." Sloane didn't look up at the girl. Instead, she smiled at her son, who studied her face with wide eyes. "When were they last fed?"

"I arrived a little before eight o'clock, and I was here for about two hours before Bailey got fussy. Benji fed her, and I fed Beau. I'd say that was around ten thirtyish." Livvie shrugged.

"Not very precise." Sloane met her gaze momentarily before returning it to Beau's. Maybe she couldn't remember whether she was coming or going, let alone exactly when the babies had eaten last, but this woman was purporting to be a nanny. Shouldn't she have a system for tracking such things?

"Actually, there's an app designed to help multiple caregivers keep track of feedings. I planned to download it to my phone as soon as I got a free moment." Livvie grabbed cheese from the fridge and sprinkled a generous amount into the pot on the stove before returning it.

The woman seemed a little too comfortable in the space. As if she already lived there.

"Are you hungry? Benji said savory cheese grits are your favorite breakfast." She spooned some in a dish. "So I made plenty."

"I'm not hungry right now, but thanks," Sloane said. Her belly grumbled loudly in protest. She pretended not to notice Livvie's smirk.

"Well, I'm gonna have a bowl. If you need me for anything, I'll be right here." Livvie dropped into a seat at the breakfast bar, took a bite and made an exaggerated "mmm" sound.

Sloane's belly grumbled again, and little Beau gave her another smirk.

Okay, so she was a liar, and both her belly and her baby were calling her out on it.

"Maybe I will have a little before it's time to feed them again," she murmured, strapping Beau back in his chair beside his sister.

"Sit down, I'll fix you a bowl," Livvie said with a broad smile.

When Livvie placed a serving of grits in front of her, she tasted it and nodded. "Not bad for a Chicago girl."

Livvie winked. "My mama's from the South, too, don't forget."

Sloane didn't respond, not wanting to get too friendly with the girl, whom she planned to send packing as soon as Benji returned.

When she'd finished eating, the twins were fast asleep. She didn't want to rely on an expensive nanny or a private chef or a housekeeper. After all, she wouldn't have any of those luxuries once her year with Benji was up. It was better that she didn't get too dependent. But since Livvie was here, and the babies were asleep…

Sloane rinsed her plate and put it in the dishwasher. "They'll probably sleep for twenty minutes or so. Would you mind watching them while I take a quick shower?"

"Keep an eye on these two little angels?" Livvie smiled as if Sloane had asked her to be her new best friend. "I'd be glad to. You go on and take your shower. I'll clean up in here."

Sloane took a shower and washed her hair. When she emerged from the bathroom, she recognized Benji's distinctive knock on her bedroom door.

She opened the door and glared at him.

"You're upset. Let me explain." Benji frowned.

"I'm listening." She tightened her grip on the towel wrapped around her. "But I can't, for the life of me, understand why you'd leave our newborns with a complete stranger."

"Liv isn't a stranger. She's Mrs. H's niece. We became good friends when I worked summers at the general store." He placed his hands on her shoulders. "But I'm sorry I wasn't here when you awoke. I hope it wasn't too upsetting."

"I thought she was some crazy stalker who'd killed you and was here to take the babies." Sloane pulled out of his embrace and rifled through the dresser drawers for something to wear. "But, hey, other than that, no big deal."

"That wasn't a good look, and you have reason to be upset. I scheduled time for us to meet with Liv this morning, but you were so exhausted you slept in. Then I had an emergency work call, but I needed a document I'd left at the office. I tried to wake you before I left, but you were dead to the world."

"Why didn't you leave a note?"

He retrieved a piece of paper from beneath the glass of water on her nightstand and waved it before handing it to her.

"Oh." Sloane quickly scanned the note, which explained everything he'd just said. She raised her eyes to his, clutching her clothing in one arm. "Why didn't you tell me about the meeting in advance?"

"Honestly?" Benji sat on the edge of the bed. "Because I knew you'd say no if I asked."

"So you simply chose to ignore my wishes." She crumpled the note and tossed it onto the nightstand.

"You didn't want a housekeeper or a personal chef, but I doubt you'd want to live without either of them now." He sighed when she didn't respond. "Look, it's not as if I've already hired her. I just wanted you to get to know Liv. I figured that would make the prospect of a live-in nanny less intimidating."

"I'm not *intimidated* by your little friend in there. I simply don't need her. There are two of them and there are two of us. I think we can handle a couple of infants on our own." She gathered her clothing and slipped inside the bathroom, shutting the door.

"You were exhausted when we arrived home from the hospital yesterday." The exasperation was evident in his voice, despite the door between them. "And today you were practically in a coma."

"But you clearly didn't just contact what's-her-face this morning." She realized she was being childish and petty by pretending not to know Livvie's name, but she didn't care. This was the second instance in as many days of him making decisions where the twins were concerned without consulting her.

It took him so long to respond Sloane wondered if he'd walked away.

"You're right. Livvie and I keep in touch. She graduated a couple of years ago with a degree in early-childhood education. She'd been working at a premier day care in Chicago, but she wanted a change."

"So you just hired her? How do you know they didn't fire her for losing someone's kid or pushing a toddler down the stairs?"

"Again, I haven't hired her, and I won't if you don't give the okay. And I had her background pulled the moment we discussed the possibility."

"Yet, you still didn't think to tell me you were considering hiring her." Sloane gave up struggling into a pair of pre-pregnancy jeans. She opened the door and strode past Benji. She grabbed a pair of leggings from the dresser drawer and put them on instead.

"It was a surprise," he said, as if that made everything better.

"So are ambushes." She turned around to face him, pulling her top down over her still-rotund belly. She folded her arms. "Don't think just because you're handsome and rich and you smell incredible…" For a moment, the point she was trying to make completely escaped her. "Don't think I won't call you out when you're full of shit. You didn't consult me on this because you knew I'd never agree to it."

"Yes, I was pretty damn sure you wouldn't go for the nanny. But I also knew that we needed the help. Just like we needed Caitlin and Marcellus." He sank onto the edge of the bed. "My job has always been to get results. I identify deficiencies and find solutions."

"I've been a mother for all of a week and already you think I'm deficient?" She planted her hands on her hips, her voice wavering slightly. "Thanks for the vote of confidence."

"I'm not saying you aren't doing a good job, Sloane. But neither of us has ever done this. We have not one but two infants to care for, and we're learning on the fly here. Is it so bad if we have a little help? It's not as if we can't afford it."

He'd mentioned the money again.

A little of the air deflated from her lungs. She remembered her father screaming at her mother that he made the money so he called the shots.

She clenched her fists at her sides. "I didn't have Beau and Bailey so someone else could raise them."

"And what would you have done if you'd been on your own and had to return to work at the end of maternity leave?" Benji didn't wait for her response. "You would've dropped them off at day care every day or hired a sitter. How is this different?"

She hated him a little for being so goddamned smart.

"I would've been doing it out of necessity." She folded

her arms, not looking in his direction. "Not because I preferred to sleep in."

"This isn't a judgment of your ability as a mother." He lifted her chin and forced her eyes to meet his. "You've been so stressed. I just wanted to take the pressure off so we'll have time to enjoy Beau and Bailey. That's all."

"Then why do I feel like you've just subcontracted my duties as a mother to someone else?"

He sucked in an audible breath and released it.

"You know that isn't true. You're a great mother."

"Then have a little faith in me. I'll learn to manage on my own. Millions of women do it every day. Our parents didn't have a chef, a housekeeper and a nanny, and we both turned out fine."

Okay, maybe she was only *relatively* fine, but now wasn't the time to split hairs. Especially when she was finally making a few valid points of her own.

"I know this isn't the way you or I grew up, sweetheart. But I won't apologize for having the means to give our kids a better life than we had."

That she understood.

Sloane hated that Benji's money had become a factor in the conversation again, but the truth was, she wanted a better life for Beau and Bailey, too.

"It would've been nice if you'd consulted with me rather than ambushing me with Goldilocks out there."

"It's easier to ask for forgiveness than it is to get permission." He shoved his hands in his pockets. "Something else I've learned in business. I anticipate the needs of my clients and employees. When I see a need, I fill it. Even though my team might not be on board yet."

"I'm not your client or your employee."

He furrowed his brows. "It was just a comparison."

"I've barely gotten used to living with you and having Marcellus and Caitlin here part-time. Livvie being here takes things to a whole nother level." Sloane felt claustrophobic just thinking about it. "What if I don't like her? What if Beau and Bailey don't like her?"

"Livvie's sweet, and she was great with Beau and Bailey this morning. Give her a chance, like you did with Marcellus. If you don't like her, she goes. No questions asked." When she reluctantly agreed, he kissed her forehead and turned to leave.

"Benji…" She grabbed his arm and sighed. "I don't mean to seem ungrateful, and I appreciate everything you've done. But I'm not used to this…being so dependent on someone else. It feels like I'm constantly adding to my tab."

She hated saying those words. Hated admitting that she'd become like an extra appendage. He wanted the twins in his life and she got thrown into the bargain.

"I'm not keeping a tab, Sloane." He frowned, seemingly perturbed by the implication that he was. "I don't care about the money, and I don't want you to think about it, either. You, Beau and Bailey are all that matter. Got it?"

She genuinely believed that he meant it in the here and now. But would he eventually come to resent her for all the ways she was indebted to him?

"Got it."

Sloane pushed the unnerving thought from her head and followed Benji out to interview Livvie Henderson about becoming their nanny.

# Nine

Benji pulled his Range Rover into the driveway of the cabin and parked. His five-day business trip to Japan had been far more successful than he'd hoped and had resulted in an incredible offer, one he'd be crazy to pass up. It was also the longest period he'd been away from Beau and Bailey. Though they'd video chatted nearly every day of his trip, he'd missed Sloane and the twins like crazy.

He hauled his luggage and laptop inside and inhaled the savory scent of a delicious home-cooked meal. If the heavenly aroma was any indication of how the meal would taste, Marcellus had outdone himself.

"I thought I heard you come in." A broad smile spread across Sloane's face when her eyes met his. "I just put the twins down after feeding them, but they're awake, and I know they'll be glad to see you."

He met her in the middle of the room and kissed her softly on the lips, something he hadn't done in a long time.

The twins had turned three months old the day before

he'd left for Japan. Those months had been a blur of feedings, diaper changes, doctor's appointments and incredible firsts. And despite that first rough week after the birth of the twins, he and Sloane had grown closer through it all.

"God, you're a sight for sore eyes." He grazed her cheek with the back of his fingers and inhaled her scent, as fresh as sunshine and summer flowers. Her mop of dark curls was still damp from the shower. She wore a short, belted, button-down dress. It was casual. Nothing fancy, but it hugged her ample curves in all the right places.

"I'll bet you say that to all the mothers of your children." She grinned, adding, "Just kidding," before he could object. Sloane took his hand and led him toward the bedrooms. "Come on. I've got a surprise for you."

His heart thumped a little faster in anticipation. She'd welcomed his kiss and embrace for the first time in months, so clearly she'd missed him. Did that mean she was ready to resume their physical relationship?

Sloane stopped at the twins' room instead, easing inside quietly in case they were asleep.

They weren't. Beau saw him first. He smiled and made a little gurgling noise, slobber rolling down his chin and cheek.

"There's my boy." Benji picked him up, remembering when he'd thought any slobbering child was too gross to touch. Now he leaned in and kissed his son's sloppy cheek without reservation. He gave the boy his finger and let him squeeze it.

"He's gotten stronger." Benji was endlessly amazed by the twins' rapid advancement. It seemed as though they hit some new milestone every day, which was why he'd hated to miss an entire week with them.

"I discovered that when he caught a strand of my hair a couple of days ago." She picked Bailey up, kissed her forehead and handed her to Benji, too.

He sat down in the wide half rocker with both the babies in his arms, talking to them in soft, cooing tones. Though, at Sloane's insistence, he avoided gibberish baby talk.

"What is it?" He couldn't help smiling when he caught a glimpse of Sloane standing in the corner staring at them.

Her eyes shone. She swiped a finger beneath the corners of her damp eyes. "Nothing's wrong. They missed you. I could tell. And they seem so happy to see you. Even at this age, it's obvious how much they love you. I can't believe I ever considered not telling you about them." She shook her head, suddenly choked up with emotion. Her cheeks were wet with tears.

"Don't beat yourself up over something neither of us can change." It was a thought that often plagued him. One he'd rather not explore.

She wiped at her face angrily. "I need to get started on the fried pork chops and check on my macaroni and cheese."

"Wait, you cooked?"

He didn't mean to sound so shocked. But the truth was, despite her early objections, she'd become quite fond of Marcellus and had fallen in love with his cooking. Even on the weekends when Marcellus wasn't there, they barely ever cooked. He usually ordered something.

"Still don't trust my cooking?" she teased, one hand on her hip.

"No, it's not that. It's just that I know how much you love Marcellus's cooking. He usually makes us something for Friday night."

"I know, but today I didn't want him to cook. I asked him to walk me through cooking dinner. We've been doing that a lot lately, since I have more time on my hands with Livvie being here and everything."

A smile curled the edge of his mouth and she wagged

a finger at him. "Don't you dare gloat. It's still way too soon for that."

"I don't know. I'm starting to get a little jealous of Marcellus. I'm beginning to think that aside from Beau here, he's your favorite man in this house."

Her eyes twinkled, and she tugged her lower lip between her teeth as the edge of her mouth turned up in a sensual smile. "We'll see how things go tonight."

She winked at him and laughed as she sashayed from the room.

Benji finally forced himself to push back from the table once his stomach was so full the top button of his khakis was in danger of shooting across the room. Sloane had made juicy, tender fried pork chops, mouthwatering macaroni and cheese, moist, delicious corn bread and spicy collard greens. She served it with chilled sweet tea spiked with King's Finest Bourbon and served Tennessee Jam Cake.

"You put your foot in that meal, girl." He patted his gut, barely able to move. All he wanted to do now was sit on the sofa and catch up on his favorite TV show until he faded into a food coma.

"Thank you?" She laughed, injecting a singsong inflection at the end of the phrase. "That's one of those uniquely Southern phrases I completely understand, but I always think to myself… God, that sounds incredibly gross."

Benji chuckled, pulling her onto his lap and wrapping his arms around her. "Well, it was a damn fine meal, babe. And I'll say it any way you'd like."

"How about like this?" She leaned in, a mischievous smile on her face, and pressed her lips softly to his.

He splayed one hand against her back, desperate to erase the space between him and those lush curves.

She parted her lips to him and he licked the inside of her

mouth, savored the taste of Tennessee Jam Cake and sweet tea—hers without bourbon.

Her soft moan made him as hard as steel. His body ached with the desire for her that had been coursing through his veins these past months without release.

His hands moved to the front of her dress as he fumbled to undo the buttons, which were far too large for the buttonholes for his liking.

He could have hiked up her dress and reached underneath it, but he wanted to see every inch of the body he'd grown to love so. To feel the weight of her firm breasts in his palms and soothe the nipples that had suffered such abuse in the weeks after the twins were born and just learning how to latch onto their mother. He wanted to worship her gorgeous body from head to toe with his tongue and then start all over again.

He'd unbuttoned the uncooperative garment down to her navel when the unmistakable cry of their son blared from the baby monitor sitting on the table behind her. The sound was soon followed by the quieter, more delicate cry of his little princess.

Sloane broke their kiss and sighed, pressing her forehead to his. "So much for the after-dinner cordial I had in mind."

He laughed hard, a belly laugh that reminded him that he'd stuffed himself like a Christmas hog. "Adorable little party poopers."

"Those are your children." She pointed a finger at him. "It's time for their next feeding, so I'll go and get them. Just leave the dishes, I'll take care of them when I'm done."

"You cooked. It's the least I can do. Now go ahead before my poor babies get laryngitis."

She stomped her foot, stood ramrod straight and saluted him before saying in the sexiest voice he'd heard her use to date, "Anything for you, Captain."

He laughed heartily and slapped at her bottom while she skittered away. Then he collected the dishes and carried them to the kitchen.

*Damn.* He'd been bamboozled. The food had been delicious, but Benji was pretty sure every dish they owned was in that sink, many of which required hand washing.

He turned on the water, rolled up his sleeves and got to scrubbing. At least he'd burn some of the calories he'd just consumed.

Sloane sat in the chair in the nursery and breastfed both the twins. She hated to admit it, but she didn't know what she'd have done without the lactation consultant Benji had hired. In fact, she couldn't imagine having done any of this without his support.

The financial support was appreciated, of course. After all, it cost a small mint to clothe, feed and diaper one baby, let alone two. But the money came a distant second or third to the emotional and physical support Benji so willingly gave.

They were a team.

It wasn't a platitude, it was a fact. Benjamin Bennett wasn't just a good man, he was an amazing father and an incredible partner. Perhaps the circumstances weren't ideal, but she couldn't imagine herself going through this experience with anyone else.

She loved being a mother to the twins. Loved growing into this crazy life with Benji by her side. Sloane honestly didn't think she could blame it on the hormones anymore, but nothing brought her to tears like seeing Benji interact with their son and daughter or watching how they reacted to him.

It was love, in its purest, rawest form.

But nearly as quickly as she was overcome with joy over her life with Benji and the babies, she was gripped by the throat with fear.

What would happen when the novelty of being a father wore off? Would he resent her? Would he resent the twins?

Part of her realized it was an irrational fear. Benji wasn't her father and shouldn't be judged by his standard of failure. Still, that fear had appointed itself as guardian of her heart. And it seemed safer to let it do just that.

# Ten

Benji's eyes fluttered open. His neck was stiff and his body unusually warm. The light from the television flickered over the otherwise dark great room of the cabin. His left arm, partially numb, was pinned between the back of the sofa and Sloane's sleeping form nuzzled against his chest.

He glanced around the room. The twins were sleeping in the double bassinet against the wall. His gaze swept the rest of the room and a soft smile curled the edges of his mouth. When they'd first moved in, the cabin had been a high-end bachelor's getaway. Now it looked like a baby-goods store had exploded and the random pieces had landed around the space.

Yet he was completely content with how the place had changed. It was warmer, more lived in. Now, it wasn't just a cabin. It was a home. Their home.

He gently rubbed Sloane's back. She stopped snoring softly and repositioned herself, but didn't wake up.

Benji slipped from beneath her. He took Beau, then Bailey to their cribs, and turned off the television.

He stood over Sloane. She looked so comfortable, he considered tossing a throw over her and letting her sleep. But as comfortable as the couch was to sit on, she'd be far more comfortable sleeping in her own bed.

He squatted slightly, sliding his hands beneath her and lifting her into his arms, cradling her against his chest. As he carried her down the hall, she lifted her head, her eyes fluttering as she came back to awareness.

"No," she said, halting him in his steps.

"Hey, it's okay," he said gently. "You fell asleep on the sofa. I'm taking you to your room so you can go back to sleep."

She wiped the sleep from her eyes, her gaze meeting his. "I don't want to go back to my room. I want to go to yours." A sensual smile slowly curved her lips. "And the last thing I want to do is sleep."

Benji stood still, stunned. A part of him wondered if he'd heard her correctly. If maybe she was dreaming, or maybe it was him who was caught inside a dream.

"Make love to me," she whispered in his ear as she cradled his beard-roughened jaw. Sloane pressed her open mouth to his, slipping her tongue inside.

He considered asking her if she was sure, but the insistence of her kiss made it clear that she was fully aware and quite determined.

Benji carried her to his bedroom, stripped off the pesky button-down dress and helped her slip from the pretty but simple nursing bra and panties. Then she helped him out of his clothing until they'd dispatched every barrier between them.

He lay her down, kissed her shoulder, nibbled on her neck and blew a stream of warm air across her skin. "God, you're beautiful. I can't believe how lucky I am."

"I'm glad you're home. We missed you."

"I'm glad Beau and Bailey missed me." He kissed her again and again, his fingertips tracing the stars tatted along her spine. "But I'm especially glad Beau and Bailey's mama missed me. Because I missed her, too."

"Really?" Her lips curved in a mischievous smile, then she sank her teeth into her lower lip. The erotic motion caused his shaft to tighten. "How much did you miss me?"

He reached beyond her, into the nightstand and retrieved a black velvet box, hoping she'd be receptive to the gift he'd deliberated over so intensely.

Benji pulled out the necklace he'd purchased in Tokyo and opened the clasp. He slipped the chain around her neck and let the charm fall between her breasts as he pressed a kiss to her ear. "This much."

He turned on the light so she could see. It was a family necklace with entwined white-gold hearts, each with an emerald suspended near the top of the heart. One heart was engraved with Beau's name and the other with Bailey's. Diamonds were embedded in the remaining surface of the hearts.

She fingered the necklace and turned it so it faced her. Her eyes went wide, and tears spilled down her cheeks. "It's beautiful, Benji. Thank you. I don't know what else to say."

*Say you'll marry me* were the words that sounded in his head.

"Don't say anything," he whispered. He kissed her, gliding his tongue between her lips as his body moved against hers.

She pressed a hand to his chest. "Benj, don't forget..." She nodded toward the nightstand.

The last time they'd made love she'd been eight months pregnant, so pregnancy wasn't an issue. Now they had to go back to the dreaded barrier between them.

He nodded, reached into the nightstand, sheathed himself and turned the light out again. He kissed her mouth and neck. Trailed kisses down her chest. Ran his tongue over her beaded tips as he reverently held the heavy globes in the palms of his hand. He was gentler with her hardened nipples than he'd been the first time they'd made love. Now he lavished them with delicate kisses and the swirling of his tongue as she squirmed beneath him.

He rained kisses down the valley between her breasts and across her soft belly.

She tensed beneath him, her squirm no longer signaling desire and anticipation, but rather apprehension. As if she were self-conscious about the stretch marks and fullness that the twins had left behind.

"This…" He placed her hand on her belly beneath his as he pressed kisses to the narrow stripes on her skin that were badges of honor. They represented the sacrifice she'd made to have their babies. "This is now my very favorite part of your body. I'll never forget the first time you placed my hand here so I could feel Beau move." He eased their joined hands higher on her stomach. "Or when I first saw Bailey's little shoulder right about there."

He released her hand and kissed lower, to the edge of the small patch of curls over her mound before gliding his tongue along the slick, swollen flesh.

"Or watching you give birth to our children from here." He licked her again. She shivered beneath him and made a little humming sound that made him so hard it hurt. "Then again, maybe this is still my very favorite part."

Wrapping his arms around her thighs, he spread her open with his fingers and delved inside her, licking, sucking and teasing her until she shattered on his tongue. She tensed, her body convulsing as she slowly came down.

Benji kissed his way back up her body, enjoying the way she tensed and relaxed in response to each kiss as she shivered beneath him.

Gripping the base of his shaft, he glided the tip between her slick folds. Something in his chest roared at the delicious feeling of being inside her again. At the way he felt, when she called his name.

*Be gentle. Take it easy.*

It was their first time together since the birth of the twins, and he didn't want to hurt her. He desperately fought the urge to go hard and fast. Battled the driving need for release after months of not having her.

He strained to move his hips slowly. Deliberately. Despite the fire that burned inside him, screaming for release.

Her body softened beneath him as she moved with him, her fingers digging into his hips. Her breath quickened, coming in hot little pants that made him think about all of the naughty things she could do with that mouth. And how much he'd enjoy them.

He tensed his muscles, trembling as he squeezed his eyes shut and tried to slow his ascent toward climax. He was determined to bring her over the edge one more time. To give her body the intense pleasure it deserved.

Benji lifted her legs higher, changing the angle of entry, grinding his hips slowly and intensifying the friction against her swollen clit.

She cried out his name as she stiffened and her inner walls clenched and unclenched around his heated flesh. He released a primal groan of his own, his back arching as he plunged deeper inside of her.

He hovered above her for a moment, both of them panting as they caught their breath and came down from the peak they'd just been driven to.

He would happily spend the rest of his life making love to this woman. Showering her with gifts. Raising their family together. And he'd never been prouder in his life than he'd been the day their twins were born. Or more content than he'd been falling asleep on the couch with Sloane and their babies surrounding them.

All of those words came to him as he stared into her eyes. But they lodged at the back of his throat.

The feelings this woman engendered in him raged in his chest. Made him crazy with want and need and the closest thing he'd ever felt to love.

But he'd asked her to marry him and she'd flatly turned him down. Had the months since that rejection changed things for her? Or deepened her feelings for him, the way his feelings had deepened for her?

One night in his bed didn't mean Sloane was suddenly ready to commit to a life with him. Nor did it wipe out the lingering pain and the hint of resentment he worked so hard to hide. But it was a start.

He tumbled onto the mattress beside her and gathered her into his arms. Kissing the side of her face, damp with sweat, he cradled her against his chest, one arm behind his head.

They lay in silence for several minutes before he finally spoke.

"Sloane?"

"Hmm." She sounded like she was in that hazy glow just before sleep.

"Promise me something."

She was silent for a moment as she ran her fingers through the hair on his chest. "If I can."

"Tonight…don't go back to your room. Stay with me. I want to wake up to this beautiful face." He kissed her again.

"I promise," she said without hesitation. He could hear the smile in her voice. "In fact, I was wondering if maybe…" She seemed to lose her nerve momentarily, before she cleared her throat and finally forced the words from her lips. "Would it be okay if I moved in here with you?"

His heart thumped against his breastbone as the weight of her request registered.

Not wanting to sound too eager, he waited a beat before responding. "Yes, I'd like that very much."

Sloane awakened, sprawled across the king-size bed she'd shared with Benji the night before. He was gone. Now she understood the disappointment of awaking to a cold, empty bed when expecting to still be wrapped in the warmth of a lover's embrace.

She dragged a hand through her hair, wondering just how crazy she'd looked when he got up. Or perhaps her tendency to be a wild sleeper had driven him from the bed.

Sloane sighed, staring at the ceiling, one arm thrown over her forehead. She'd spent the night in his bed. Asked to move into his room. A terrifying move she'd been considering during the final days of his trip.

In the scheme of things, five days didn't amount to much at all. But, during those five days, Sloane had discovered something unequivocally.

She'd missed everything about Benjamin Darnell Bennett.

His smart-ass mouth and nerd-boy humor. His innate sense of when she needed him to take control. The heart-melting love and adoration he had for their babies. His incredible body. His friendship and the unique partnership they shared.

Sloane had tried breaking herself of her growing need for Benji. Tried to convince herself that they were co-parents and they needn't be anything more.

But during his first long business trip since the birth of the twins, she'd realized the truth. She wanted to be with Benji, but only if he truly loved her, not because he felt some noble sense of obligation.

Sloane fingered the lovely necklace Benji had gifted her

the night before. It was the only item she was wearing besides the sheet she'd pulled up to her chest. Sloane appreciated the necklace, but she appreciated the thoughtfulness of the gift even more.

She'd taken a chance by asking him to make love to her. It had been her way of letting him know she wanted more with him. She wasn't sure how things would end between them, but she was ready to consider taking another step forward in their unconventional relationship.

He'd asked her to stay the night with him, rather than slinking off to her room in the wee hours of the morning. But she'd hoped for something more. That perhaps he'd tell her he had *real* feelings for her. Not lust or a boyhood crush, but the kind of true, deep feelings she was slowly realizing she had for him.

But she'd seen the devastating shift that happened in a relationship where one person loved unequivocally, and the other wielded all the money and power. She'd seen how that kind of dynamic eroded not only the relationship but damaged everyone in it. Sloane didn't want that for herself or the twins. Nor could she bear to watch the man she was growing to love turn into a bitter, resentful monster.

Sloane got up, showered and dressed. She was greeted by smiles from the twins as she leaned over their cribs. Beau and Bailey were her main priorities, and she needed to focus on them.

She'd keep her feelings for Benji to herself for now.

# Eleven

Sloane inhaled deeply, her stomach in knots, as Benji pulled into the driveway of Blake and Savannah's home. Benji seemed to instinctively realize how stressed she was. He threaded their fingers together.

"Relax. It's only Blake and Savannah. We're going to have a great time."

"Of course." She shrugged, as if she didn't have a concern in the world about their lunch date slash playdate.

Sloane glanced over her shoulder where Beau and Bailey lay asleep in their car carriers. The motion of the SUV seemed to put them both to sleep instantly.

At five months now, the twins were already starting to get so big, and they each had their own distinct personalities.

They parked and got the twins out of the car, then Benji went back to get their portable playpen. Blake and Savannah's little boy, Davis, was now nearly eighteen months old and fascinated by the "babies," which he said often and gleefully. He was clearly glad not to be the baby of the family anymore.

They fed the children and shared a delicious meal prepared by Blake—who, Sloane was learning, was quite the cookbook aficionado. He'd prepared a roasted vegetable antipasto plate, a delicious salad and the best eggplant parmesan she'd ever eaten, all served with a lovely Chianti she couldn't have because she was still breastfeeding. For her, there was a yummy hibiscus ginger punch instead.

Once the kids were down for a nap, the adults were able to move to the beautiful den with two walls of windows—one overlooking the lake and the other the mountains.

She'd agreed to drive home later so that Benji could enjoy Blake's stash of King's Finest Premium Bourbon while they watched a movie. She and Savannah sat on the other side of the room, taking in the pretty views.

"So, how is not-quite-married life?" Savannah's smile was warm and teasing.

Sloane smiled and sneaked an involuntary glance at Benji, who was laughing with his cousin. Her smile deepened. "Things are good. Really good."

"Wedding bells good?" Savannah prodded as she folded one leg over the other and leaned forward in her chair.

Sloane nearly choked on her punch. She covered her mouth and coughed, using the time to formulate her response.

"I don't think either of us has even considered that yet. Not seriously," she added, thinking of Benji's perfunctory proposal when he'd first learned of her pregnancy. "I know that how we're doing things isn't the traditional Magnolia Lake way. But right now, it's working for us."

"Humph." Savannah looked thoughtful as she leaned back in her chair.

Sloane clearly saw the trap Savannah had laid out, but like a cartoon mouse, she couldn't resist taking the bait.

"All right, I'll bite. What's the humph for?"

Savannah shrugged and sipped her Chianti. "Maybe I'm allowing my own experience to color the situation," she acknowledged, "but what I hear is fear. I couldn't help noticing the deep connection between you two that day we were all at the cabin. Even though you were obviously a little miffed that you'd been ambushed with a party after your release from the hospital."

Sloane frowned. "Was it that obvious?"

"Maybe not to everyone." Savannah laughed. "But it wasn't that long ago that I had a baby myself. I remember feeling gritty and exhausted. I just wanted to take a hot shower, relax in my own bed and enjoy my time with Blake and our baby. I'd probably have had a meltdown if I'd been presented with a party. Believe me, you handled it well."

Sloane breathed a sigh of relief. It was bad enough that Benji's immediate family wasn't part of his and the twins' lives. The last thing she wanted to do was alienate his extended family. The Abbotts had been warm and welcoming to her. The only person who seemed to regard her suspiciously was Parker.

Then again, no one in Magnolia Lake would use the terms *Parker Abbott* and *friendly* in the same sentence.

"The bond between you two seems even stronger now." Savannah nodded toward Benji. "It's obvious how much he adores you and the twins."

Sloane sighed, feeling a little more at ease with Savannah. "I care for him. Very much. Still, there are a lot of issues we both need to work out. One of which is, despite what he says, I often wonder if he'll ever fully trust me since he had to find out about the twins on his own. Sometimes, when he looks at me, I see it, that pain and resentment. Him imagining what would've happened had he not shown up at my place in Nashville that day." Sloane swallowed hard. "It made so much sense in my head when I made the decision. Now it just seems cowardly and self-ish. I don't blame him for being angry."

Savannah nodded sagely. "You know the story of what happened between me and Blake and why I really came to Magnolia Lake?"

Sloane nodded apologetically. She hated to admit that she—and everyone in the town or who had relatives here—had heard the story.

"And yet here we are. Together. Happy. And truly in love." An absent smile lit her eyes as she talked about Blake. Then her gaze met Sloane's again. "I hate to sound like one of those annoying newlywed couples, but I honestly feel... No—" she shook her head "—I know that Blake is the man I was meant to spend my life with. The way we came to be... I'll always bear some pain for my role in deceiving him in the beginning. But if I hadn't come here, hadn't done what I did, there would be no us. And we wouldn't have learned the truth about the role my grandfather played in King's Finest."

Sloane glanced over at Benji. Could they, too, have a happy ending despite their inauspicious start?

"I honestly want to believe that Benji and I could have the kind of relationship that you and Blake have, but..." Sloane looked over at Benji, who seemed to be having a more serious discussion with Blake now. "I don't know. Especially with him being estranged from his family. They didn't even come back to Magnolia Lake this summer the way they typically do. I'm hurt and angry about their reaction to me and Benji. Delia, especially. We've been best friends since we were ten years old. I can't believe she'd think, even for a minute, that I'd ever do anything to harm or take advantage of her brother."

Savannah's hazel eyes were filled with sympathy. She placed a hand on Sloane's arm. "I'm sorry that the Bennetts are being so unfair to you. Iris feels horrible about it," she said, referring to her mother-in-law, who was Benji's aunt. "She's tried talking to her sister, but Benji's mother won't budge."

"I appreciate it. And as furious as I am with Delia and Connie, it's mostly because of what it's doing to Benji. He doesn't like to talk about it, but I can see how much it hurts him." Sloane took another sip of her punch and shook her head. "I hate being the wedge that drove Benji and his family apart. They've always been so close."

"He sided with you over his own family." Savannah looked at her pointedly. "And you think that man isn't serious about you?" The question didn't require a response. "Take things as slowly as you need to. Don't mind busybodies like me trying to rush you to the altar." Her smile widened and they both laughed. "I know Benji has reasons to be hurt, just as Blake did. But if he's trying this hard to get over it, he obviously wants this. Don't give up on him. Give him time. He'll get there."

Sloane hugged Savannah and thanked her.

She didn't know where things would go between her and Benji, but she felt more hopeful about it than she ever had before.

Benji and Blake had volunteered to bundle up the kids, put them in strollers and take Blake's two dogs—Benny the Labradoodle and Sam the greyhound—for a walk around the lake. But the real reason for the walk was that Blake wanted to talk to Benji. It was a conversation Benji wasn't sure he wanted to have, mostly because he already knew he wouldn't have answers to many of the questions his cousin would ask.

Where did things stand with him and Sloane? Were they a bona fide couple now?

The answers were that he didn't know and he didn't think so, though he felt more hopeful that it was possible.

As far as he was concerned, it wasn't a conversation worth packing up three children and two dogs.

After they covered the basics, Blake asked him a pointed question. "Do you love her?"

Benji frowned at his cousin.

"Does that mean no, or is it that you think I've broken some unofficial bro code by asking you about your 'feelings'?" Blake made a flourish with his hands when he said the word.

"The latter." Benji stared out onto the lake instead of looking at his cousin.

Blake chuckled. "Well, put your big-boy pants on and try to make an exception just this once." Blake elbowed Benji in his side, then indicated the spit-up dribbling down Beau's chin.

Benji wiped his mouth and secured the blankets around the twins, who both seemed to enjoy the venture into nature. Likely because Livvie often took them for walks around the lake by their cabin.

"Yes," Benji said finally.

"Yes, what?" Blake wasn't going to let him get off with the bare minimum. He was determined to throw a little torture in with his cousinly advice.

"Yes," Benji said, pausing. "I think I love her."

"You *think* you love her?" Blake was like Benny with a bone. For a fleeting moment Benji wanted to knock that self-satisfied smirk off his older cousin's face.

"Anyone ever tell you that you can be kind of an asshole?" Benji gritted the words through clenched teeth, his voice low enough that none of the children could hear him.

Blake laughed harder than Benji thought the situation required.

"Yes," his cousin said. "But usually only people I'm related to by blood."

Now Benji chuckled, too.

"Okay, fine," he said finally. "I do. I love her. I've never felt this way about anyone before. I honestly think I've been in love with her since I was ten years old. When I saw her again at your wedding—God, I thought I'd gotten over that puppy-love crush. But the second I saw her...it was like I'd been hit by a ton of bricks."

"Well, you certainly know the mother of your children better than I do," Blake said, carefully prefacing his next statement. "But the Sloane I've always known is a tough nut to crack. She's got issues with her mom and her dad. She doesn't like to need anyone or anything, and she's slow to let people inside. But if you can ride out the storm and prove that you're worthy, that you won't let her down like so many people in her life have... Man, it's worth it. She's a good person. And you two could be really good together, if you're both willing to work for it."

"That's just it." Benji halted on the path as Blake's house came into view. "I've been trying to show her. There's obviously friendship and affection between us. Fire," he added, his cheeks heating slightly. "I just don't know if she's ready to commit to something permanent."

"Have you told her how you feel about her?"

"I asked her to marry me."

"And she turned you down? When was this?" Blake looked stunned, but when Benji gave him the rest of the details, Blake shook his head and whistled. "Man, no wonder she turned you down. That wasn't a marriage proposal, it was a business proposition. Sloane isn't the analytical kind who would make a decision like that based on logic alone." He patted his chest. "The girl's all heart. If you want her to love you, to really be willing to risk her heart for you, you're going to have to strap on a set and lay it all out there, Benj."

Blake started walking toward the house again, but Benji tugged him by the elbow. "What if she doesn't love me the way I love her? What if she never will?"

"Then it's better that you swallow that bitter pill sooner rather than later," Blake said gravely. "But for what it's worth, I don't think that's it at all. If Sloane is the one for you, just keep showing her how you feel until you're ready to tell her."

Benji nodded and they resumed their final journey back to the house.

Sloane was the woman for him. He was as sure of it now as he had been when he was ten. Only now it wasn't based on a childish infatuation. It was based on something real and true.

Still, sometimes it was hard to turn off the nagging little voice in the back of his head. The one that pointed out that if he hadn't gone looking for Sloane, she might never have revealed the truth. The one that reminded him that if he hadn't made a deal to pay off her family's debt, she wouldn't be with him now. And the ticking of the clock reminding him that in seven months she planned to take their twins and walk away.

# Twelve

Sloane sat at her mother's farmhouse kitchen table savoring her first cup of coffee in more than a year. The twins had just turned seven months old and were completely weaned. Sloane's grandfather was mesmerized by the twins—both of whom adored him. And Bailey had a special bond with the old man. The first time Atticus Ames held her in his arms and she tugged at his wiry gray beard, she'd had him wrapped around her tiny little digit. And she'd brought her big brother along for the ride.

Now he couldn't get enough of the twins. He visited them often. He even accompanied Livvie when she took the twins for their daily walk around the lake in their double stroller, weather permitting.

Beau was crawling across the floor, playing with one of the countless musical baby toys that drove Sloane crazy and made her consider sabotaging them.

Bailey was in her favorite spot—standing on her great-grandfather's lap and trying to swipe his glasses off his face. She was fast and occasionally she succeeded.

For which the old man never so much as gave her a sideways glance. Instead, his deep chuckle filled the room. "You got 'em again, Bailey. PawPaw has got to be quicker."

"He was never that kind and understanding with me," Sloane grumbled, keeping her voice low enough not to travel the short distance to the family room where her grandfather and the kids were. She poured a generous amount of creamer into her second cup of coffee. "If it was me, I'd be on the floor doing baby push-ups or something."

"Honey, you really shouldn't exaggerate about your grandfather that way. He wasn't as bad as you make him out to be. He loves you and you know it."

"He's always had a damn funny way of showing it," she muttered under her breath, and nibbled on another one of her mother's homemade cinnamon rolls. Which didn't help her goal of losing that last fifteen pounds of baby weight.

Okay, maybe it was twenty. But Marcellus was a darn good cook.

"I know he was hard on you, but he regrets that." Her mother sighed heavily, taking another small bite of her cinnamon roll. "I suppose I'm the one to blame for that. He felt he failed with me, so he was determined that you were going to be that perfect little girl that I wasn't." Her mother's voice was small, her eyes sad.

Sloane reached over and squeezed her hand. Being a mother herself had given her new perspective on the enormous duty of raising a child—or in her case, two. Her mother had been little more than a child herself when Sloane was born. She'd done the best she could with the skills and experience she had.

Sloane didn't agree with the choices her mother had made, but she respected the fact that she'd made those choices because it was what she felt she needed to do in order to take care of her.

"Granddad's grand plan for me didn't exactly work out." Sloane forced a bitter laugh. "I guess we're both incorrigible."

"Wouldn't say that exactly." He was standing over them holding Bailey, who chose that moment to say, "Ma, Ma, Ma!"

"Nice, Bailes. You couldn't have given me a heads-up *before* you guys got in here?" Sloane teased her daughter. Bailey laughed, whether she understood what was going on or not.

Sloane's mother got up from the table, a sad smile on her face. "I'd better check on Beau. I'll take Bailey, too." She put Bailey in the playpen and then picked up Beau, who was absolutely a grandmama's boy. His face spread into a gummy smile, showcasing two top teeth and one on the bottom.

Her grandfather sat at the table, both of them quiet until Sloane couldn't take the silence between them anymore.

"Look, about what I said, Granddad. I'm sorry. I shouldn't have said it." There, she'd apologized and hadn't lied by saying that she hadn't meant it.

"That's how you feel, and I can't change that." He tapped the table rhythmically. Then he raised his eyes to meet hers. "But I can apologize and try to explain why I was so tough on you."

Sloane tipped her head, her brows furrowed. Who was this contrite man who was putty in the hands of precocious infants and willingly offered apologies?

"All right," she said simply.

"I never got to be that doting grandparent with you because I was as stupid and wrongheaded as Benji's family. I'd insisted that boy marry your mother, but that didn't make me like or respect him. So I kept my distance. Missed most of the first year or two of your life. Never got to bond with you the way I've been blessed to have bonded with these two." He pointed in the direction of the playpen in the other room. "Then when I did come into your life, I could see how smart and determined you were. How much potential you had. I didn't want you to squander it the way I felt your mother had. So I took the hard line. Tried to make you the person I thought you should be. And it only got worse when your father left, because I was trying to be your father and your grandfather. Prepare you for the world."

"And how'd that work out?" Sloane interjected, needing to add some levity to the tense situation.

He shook his head and chuckled bitterly. "Problem was that you and I are too goddamned much alike. You fought me tooth and nail. You were determined to be whoever the hell you wanted to be, which was deliberately the complete opposite of what I wanted for you."

There may have been some truth to both those statements, but she wasn't inclined to admit to either at the moment. Nor was she inclined to give him a you're-excused-for-sucking-as-a-grandfather pass so he could go back to happily playing peekaboo with the twins, as if the way he'd treated her back then was no big deal or as if it hadn't shaped the choices she and her mother had made.

"Why are you telling me this now?" She held back the anger that trembled just below her carefully controlled surface, like only the tip of an iceberg showing above the cold, icy waters that doomed the *Titanic*.

"I only wanted to prevent you from making the mistakes your parents made. I didn't want you to run away from responsibility and family the way your father did. Or go chasing after the wrong men like your mother. But my hard, cold demeanor pushed you away. Prompted you to do both." His voice broke slightly.

When she met her grandfather's eyes, there were tears

in them. The sight shook her, like a two-ton wrecking ball crashing against an old, dilapidated building. Suddenly he didn't look like the old man who'd tried to ruin her fun at every turn. He was sad. Broken. Remorseful. None of those were words she'd ever used to describe him.

He pulled a hanky out of his pocket and quickly dabbed his eyes as he shook his head.

"Maybe there's nothing I can ever do to change how you see me. But I can't let you ruin your life and theirs without at least speaking up about it." He stuffed the hanky back in his pocket.

"What do you mean?"

"If your plan is still to take the twins and walk away after their first birthday, it'd be a huge mistake that none of you will likely ever recover from."

"You're being a little melodramatic, Gramps." Sloane's gaze dropped to the cup of cooled coffee in her hands.

"Benji's a good man, Sloane. And he's one hell of a father. Regardless of what brought you two together, you've been blessed with each other and the twins. Don't take that gift for granted." His voice was tender.

In that moment, the dam she'd spent her entire life building around her heart, brick by brick, cracked.

It was jarring to see Atticus Ames in a new light. Yet, it relieved a little of the constant pressure that she'd felt in her chest for as long as she could remember.

Not trusting herself to speak, Sloane nodded to acknowledge that she'd heard her grandfather's wise words. She stayed silent and pretended she didn't feel the wetness that fell from the edges of her eyelashes and stained her cheeks.

But as for what would happen between her and Benji... that wasn't only up to her.

# Thirteen

Benji whistled as he entered the Magnolia Lake Bakery on Main Street in town. The twins were nine months old and had both learned to pull themselves into a standing position on the furniture during their recent two-week visit to his place in Seattle.

He'd run through the house excitedly to tell Sloane, who'd been soaking in the tub, about Bailey's latest feat. By the time Sloane had gotten out of the tub and padded with damp feet into the family room, Beau, who refused to be outshone by his younger twin, had also pulled himself up on the couch.

They'd both been so excited and Sloane, a videographer and editor by profession, had grabbed her ever-present camera to record the twins' latest development.

It was a week later, and while he and the twins were back at the cabin, he'd treated Sloane and her mother to a few days at a luxury spa resort in the mountains, about forty minutes outside of town.

Benji still couldn't stop grinning like a fool. Because all was right in his world. Granted, neither he nor Sloane had said those three little words. Nor had they formalized their relationship. But they were closer to it every day. He could feel it, knew it as certainly as if they'd signed their names to a contract written in blood.

They were a family. He and Sloane recognized that the twins needed them both. And that they needed and wanted each other.

He was ready to take the plunge, to lay his heart on the line and ask Sloane to marry him again. Only this time he'd do it right. Let her know that the reason he wanted to marry her had everything to do with her being a beautiful, intelligent woman who made him laugh and with whom he enjoyed spending time. She was the person he felt closest to in the world, and he could no longer imagine his life without her.

He'd already purchased the perfect engagement ring. He just hadn't decided when and how he'd ask Sloane to be his wife.

"Hey, Park." Benji slipped into his seat and turned over his coffee cup, indicating to Paige, the waitress, that he'd like a cup of coffee.

"You look happier than a pig in slop," Parker remarked bluntly. "I would've preferred it if you weren't so happy this morning."

Benji frowned. He was used to his cousin's odd comments that sometimes bordered on rude, but it seemed harsh even for Parker to say he wished he wasn't so happy.

*Shit. This can't be good.*

Benji suddenly wondered if he should ask the waitress to top his coffee off with a little bourbon to make whatever hell Parker was about to rain down on him go down a little smoother.

Taking a sip, Benji waited for the strong, piping-hot

coffee to hit his system before he asked the next logical question.

"What the hell are you talking about, Parker?"

"I have two things to tell you, and I don't think you're going to like either of them," his cousin said matter-of-factly.

Benji's heart crumbled in his chest. Parker wasn't given to histrionics. If he indicated that the news was bad, it was. Unequivocally.

"All right, Park," he said after another hit of coffee. He set his mug on the table and met his cousin's eyes. "What is it?"

"Yesterday I stopped into Kayleigh's shop to look for something for my mother's birthday."

"Why would you go to Kayleigh's shop? You don't even like her, and she's certainly no fan of yours." Benji chuckled. Parker and Kayleigh Jemison's love-hate relationship dated back to when they were all kids. Once close friends, he'd chosen the popular kids over her during a very un-Parker-like time in his young life. Kayleigh had never forgiven him and wasn't very fond of the Abbotts in general.

"My mother and sister like her jewelry pieces. They've been requesting them as gifts for the past couple of years," Parker informed him, clearly agitated by the subject. "But that's not the point. The point is that she does like you. Always has. So she felt the need to make me aware of a few things."

"Such as?" Benji's gut churned. He was already growing weary of this little song and dance.

"Did you know that Sloane's family's farm was *this close* to being repossessed?" Parker peered through a tiny space between his forefinger and thumb.

"Yes."

"And did you know her condo in Nashville was in jeopardy of being repossessed, as well?"

He nodded once, sipping his coffee. "I did. The question is how does Kayleigh know all this? Sloane and her family's finances are their business. Not fodder for this town's gossip mill."

Suddenly he understood Sloane's reluctance to return to Magnolia Lake. The low crime rate and quiet, relaxing pace of life left folks with an awful lot of free time on their hands. Not all of them used that time well.

"Why does any of this matter?"

"Because Sloane gets pregnant by you—a very wealthy man who she just happens to know has always had a crush on her. She hasn't attended a funeral or wedding in this town for years, but she's there at Blake's wedding, knowing you'll be there, and suddenly you two tumble into bed? Does any of this really seem like a coincidence to you, Benj?"

"Why can't it be?" Benji wanted to believe it with all his heart. He could forgive a lot of things, but he wouldn't be able to countenance having been Sloane's "mark." He shook the thought from his head. Sloane wasn't the type. He knew that as well as he knew himself.

"You know my philosophy on coincidences, Benj." Parker drank some of the espresso that kept his intricate mind fueled all day, since the man subsisted on three or four hours of sleep.

Benji did know Parker's theory on coincidences. He also knew how skeptical Parker was about the fact that he and Sloane had gotten together than night and conceived twins, despite using preventive measures.

But he didn't want to hear any of Parker's theoretical bullshit this morning. Benji was only a few steps up the ladder of maturity from plugging his fingers in his ears and singing "la-la-la-la" until Parker got the hint and shut the fuck up.

"You're a smart, sensible guy, Benj. So I know that at the very least, you took a paternity test."

His nostrils flared, and his pulse quickened, as anger filtered through his bloodstream.

He glared at his cousin. "Beau and Bailey are nine months old. Why are you bringing this up now?"

"It's not like I haven't brought it up before," Parker reminded him. "You just weren't receptive. Probably because it was your mother who insisted on the paternity test. But in light of this new information, the question seems valid. I don't suppose I need to ask if you're the reason Sloane and her family are no longer in debt."

"How I choose to distribute my finances is my own damn business." Benji's muscles tensed as he gripped the mug. "You're the chief financial officer at King's Finest, not mine."

"I can't understand why you'd be willing to lay out that kind of cash without irrefutable proof that…" Parker's eyes widened and he pointed a finger at Benji. "You're afraid they're not yours. That this entire world you've built with Sloane is going to come crashing down at your feet like a house of cards."

"Back off, Parker. This is a road you don't want to go down. Trust me."

Parker, who, for all of his intelligence, wasn't the best at reading people, had chosen today to exhibit insight. If he hadn't been the subject of Parker's scrutiny, Benji might've actually been proud of his cousin.

It wasn't that he had any real doubts about the paternity of the twins. Besides his gut feeling, both Beau and Bailey possessed plenty of his physical features. But perhaps there was a tiny, dark part of his heart that entertained the accusations his mother had made against Sloane.

"And despite her joking with your sister about needing a sugar daddy to dig herself out of her family's financial

mess, you choose to believe this was all just a serendipi-
tous coincidence?"

"Yes."

"Even though Sloane told Kayleigh at the reception that
she had *a plan* to get out of debt?" Parker stared at him
incredulously and pushed his expensive designer glasses
up the bridge of his nose. "Seems to me like that plan was
you."

"Dammit, Parker." Benji slammed his fist on the table
and the dishes and silverware clattered. "I'm only going
to say this once, so listen up. Sloane has already admitted that she *and* Delia joked about the sugar daddy thing,
well before I sold my company. She was kidding, Parker. I
know that's a concept you aren't very familiar with—" he
shouldn't have taken that jab at his cousin, but he was more
than a little pissed at Parker's determination to "save" him
from himself when it came to Sloane "—but she was no
more serious about it than Delia was. It was a joke. Would
you want people taking everything you've ever said literally, even things you said in jest?"

"I don't generally have time for jesting, so yes." There
was zero humor in Parker's response.

*Great.* Benji had forgotten for a second exactly who he
was dealing with. Parker was literal and stone-cold serious
about everything. Not that the guy never laughed, but his
cousin wouldn't have to worry about laugh lines anytime
soon. Parker had little use for humor or sarcasm, which
often went over his head.

"Okay, for once in your life, don't apply that question
to yourself. Think in terms of the broader population of…
you know, human beings." He was usually Parker's biggest
defender, but right now he was furious with his cousin.

"And her grand plan for getting out of debt?"

"I don't know." He shrugged. "I only know it had nothing to do with me."

When Parker didn't respond, Benji asked, "We done here?"

"No. There's one more thing. Aunt Connie asked me to relay a message. She wants you to bring the twins for a visit. Whether they're biologically yours or not, you've chosen to raise them. That makes Beau and Bailey her grandchildren, and she wants to get to know them."

"My number hasn't changed." Benji stared out the front window of the bakery onto Main Street. "If she has something to say to me she could always call. Better yet, she could come here and talk to me face-to-face. Show me the same courtesy I showed them. And I'm not bringing the twins to visit her if their mother's not welcome, too."

"Fair enough." Parker drank more of his espresso. "If your family wanted to talk, maybe even apologize, you'd welcome that conversation, right?"

Hurt and anger roiled in Benji's gut. The same anger and frustration he felt when he recalled his family's reaction to his announcement about Sloane and the twins.

He ordered a King's Finest Coffee—one part bourbon, one part cream liqueur, a splash of hazelnut liquor and a whole lot of strong coffee, dressed up with a flourish of whipped cream.

"Well?" Parker was clearly impatient with Benji's reluctance to give him a yes or no response. "Look, I may not be the most sociable guy in the world, but even I recognize the importance of family. As happy as you've been with Sloane and the twins these past months, you're equally torn by how much you miss your own family."

"That was their choice, not mine."

"I know," Parker said quietly. "But you've been at an impasse for months. If they're humble enough to admit they bear some blame in this, would you be big enough to accept it?"

In the beginning, it was a question he wouldn't have

needed to think on. The answer would have been a re-sounding *yes*. But the longer their stalemate had gone on, the more difficult the question had become to answer.

"The twins will be one in a few months. They've never met their grandparents, their aunt or their first cousin." There was a soft pleading in Parker's voice that Benji had never heard before. "That's not how we were raised, Benj. We're family. Yeah, we do stupid things and sometimes we screw up. But we forgive each other, and we move on."

"I'll think about it." Benji shrugged as Paige set the steaming glass mug of King's Finest Coffee in front of him.

Parker's eyes sparked with recognition before returning his attention to Benji. He nodded to something behind him. "You'd better think quick."

Benji turned and looked up as he took his first sip of the frothy, bourbon-laced coffee.

"Hi, Benji." Delia stood over him, her expression pained. "Do you think we could talk?"

# Fourteen

Benji narrowed his eyes at his cousin and released a heavy sigh. He returned his spiked coffee to the table and indicated that Delia should take the seat Parker currently occupied.

"Oh, right." Parker jumped up from his seat and reached into his back pocket for his wallet.

"Forget it, Parker." Delia slid into her cousin's recently vacated seat. "This one's on me."

Parker thanked her and grinned. "Hey, Paige, would you mind adding a couple of sticky buns and another cup of coffee to my tab. Delia's paying."

"Cheapskate."

Benji and Delia uttered the word simultaneously. Neither of them laughed, but their expressions softened and Benji saw a flash of one of his big sister's dimples.

"So, you asked for this meeting," Benji said finally, sipping the hot coffee and enjoying the warmth of the bourbon that slowly spread through his chest.

"I'll have one of those, too, Paige." Delia nodded toward Benji's drink.

"Coming right up." The waitress nodded knowingly.

Delia removed her coat before folding her hands on the table and looking up at him.

"Benji, you're my brother, and I love you. I'm sorry for how I handled things. Sloane is…was my oldest, dearest friend." She unwrapped the napkin from the silverware and dabbed the corner of her eyes. "I was hurt that she'd sleep with my little brother and then not even tell me that you were the father of her twins."

He didn't respond, and he resisted the urge to comfort his sister in any way. Delia had been cruel to Sloane, and she needed to feel the pain. To sit there and wallow in the enormity of her accusation against her friend.

"I can't speak for Mom, but I made this entire thing about my friendship with Sloane. That wasn't fair to you or to my niece and nephew. And it wasn't fair to Sloane. She's always been there for me. I should've been able to get past my hurt feelings and do the same." She dabbed her tears again. "Guess it's obvious which one of us is the better person."

Paige set Delia's coffee on the table and gave them both a worried glance before excusing herself.

"I appreciate your apology, Delia, but I can only accept on my own behalf. You'll need to talk to Sloane yourself. I'm sure she'd be glad to hear from you."

A flash of something crossed his sister's face as she shifted her gaze from his and rubbed her ear. There was something she wasn't telling him.

"I miss you, baby brother." Delia's big brown eyes met his again. "And Evie misses her uncle Benji."

"I miss you guys, too." His estrangement from his family had caused many sleepless nights. "How are Mom and Dad doing?"

"Honestly? Mom's miserable and things haven't been great between her and Dad. It was Dad who finally insisted that we all come here and talk to you. I think he might actually be growing a spine."

"Better late than never, I guess." Benji shrugged. "So they're in town, too?"

"They will be in about an hour." Delia checked her watch. "I arrived last night."

"Thanks for the heads-up," he said. An awkward silence settled over them for a moment.

"Fatherhood looks good on you, Benj. You were a good uncle, but you're an incredible dad." Delia's voice broke and she dabbed at her eyes again.

"How would you know?"

Delia released a heavy sigh and bit her lip. "First, promise me you won't get angry or go back on your word."

"To whom?" There was a sinking feeling in his gut.

"Sloane." Delia whispered her name.

"You talked to Sloane?"

"Not exactly. But she's been talking to me through this private blog where she keeps kind of a video journal. It's one of those mommy blogs where she shares cute little stories about your life together and posts pictures of you guys and the twins. It isn't public, and she doesn't use your real names. She refers to the twins as Little Dude and Buttercup. Sloane sends me the link whenever a new entry is posted."

"Let me see this blog." He held out his open palm.

Delia retrieved her phone, pulled up a website and handed it to him.

Benji scrolled through the photos of Beau and Bailey. Played a couple of the videos showing various stages of the twins' development or Sloane openly gushing about what a good dad he was.

He was angry she'd kept this from him. Trust was already a sore spot in their relationship, and this was one more secret between them. Yet, he couldn't help being moved by the touching things she'd said about him.

He rubbed his jaw as he watched small clips of one video after another. Benji sent the blog link to his phone via text message, then returned his sister's phone. Suddenly the last part of Delia's request came back to him.

"You said not to go back on anything I'd promised her. Does that mean she told you everything?"

His sister nodded. "She told me about the condo and the farm. She felt guilty about keeping it from me, and she was afraid that hiding it only made my accusations seem warranted. So she wanted me to know. Even if it meant you would go back on your arrangement, it was a chance she was willing to take. She couldn't bear being the cause of the rupture in our family. Told me to do whatever I wanted with the information."

"Did you tell Mom and Dad?"

"I haven't told anyone. But you know it won't sit well with Mom. She'll think it only proves what she already believed. That Sloane did this for the money."

Gossip was easy to come by in a small town. If his sister said she hadn't told anyone, he believed her.

"I know Sloane wouldn't have put that on the blog."

"No, she included that in the first email to me. I've never responded to any of her emails or calls."

"If you're telling me all this, why not?"

"I wasn't ready to forgive her, and to be honest, I'm still a little hurt. But I miss my friend, and eventually, I'll be ready. But for right now, I knew I needed to reach out to you and make amends."

Delia reached for his hands across the table. She seemed relieved that he didn't withdraw them.

"I know the world sees you as a powerful, successful businessman, and I couldn't be prouder. But part of me still sees that sweet, naive little brother that I need to protect."

"Noted, but I'm a big boy now. I can take care of myself, and you." He gave his sister a faint smile.

"One more thing." Delia took a sip of her coffee. "I know I was dead set against the relationship, but you two seem really good together. I'm pretty sure she loves you just as madly as you love her."

"She tell you that in the email, too?"

"She didn't need to. Your love for her and the twins is apparent in those videos. And the love she has for you… It's obvious when she gushes about you." Delia drank more of her coffee. "I'd love to believe that the primary reason Sloane reached out to me was to salvage our friendship, but the truth is…she did this because she cares deeply about you. You've been living together for a year. Don't you see it?"

He did see that Sloane cared for him, and he appreciated her heartfelt desire for him to reconcile with his family. But he couldn't help feeling she'd betrayed him again.

He'd sworn her to secrecy about their financial agreement. If Sloane had felt so strongly about telling Delia, she should've discussed it with him, instead of going behind his back and hoping for the best.

Benji cared deeply for Sloane, but if they were going to have any kind of future together, he needed to be able to trust her.

Right now, he wasn't sure if he could.

# Fifteen

"I could get accustomed to living like this." Abby Sutton sank deeper in the tub of mud beside Sloane's. Both of them had their hair wrapped in microfiber turbans.

"Well, don't." Sloane sighed, luxuriating in the warm mud as it melted the tension from her shoulders. "This was an unexpected surprise."

"I hope Benji unexpectedly surprises you again soon." Her mother took a sip of her smoothie.

Sloane's phone, sitting beside the mud bath, vibrated. She reluctantly pulled her hands from the mud, wiped them off and picked up the phone. There was a knot in her gut as she stared at the caller ID.

"Who is it?" her mother asked, noting her alarm.

"It's Delia."

"I thought Benji's family wasn't talking to you, and he wasn't talking to them."

That's why she was so surprised to see Delia's call. She didn't tell her mother that she'd been sending communications to Delia for months now, though Delia had yet to respond. The call rolled over to voice mail before she could answer, and Sloane was relieved. But it immediately started to ring again. This time she answered. "Hello, Delia."

"Sloane." Delia seemed surprised to hear her voice. "I wasn't sure you'd want to talk to me. If you didn't, I wouldn't blame you. We've been terrible to you."

Stunned, Sloane didn't respond.

"I'm sorry," Delia said. "I should've led with that. Sorry for all of the awful things I accused you of. I know you too well to think you'd ever knowingly hurt my brother."

"But?" There was hesitance in Delia's voice.

"But I'm not completely over it. I'm hurt that you kept this from me, that you were going to keep it from him. To be honest, that's what hurts the most. That you even considered doing that to Benji." Delia's voice wavered. "He loves those babies so much, and you were going to deprive them of their father."

"I know. He's such an amazing dad." Tears slid down Sloane's cheek and she sniffled. "I often think of what their lives would've been like if he hadn't come to Nashville that day. I would've ruined their lives and his, and I don't know if I can ever forgive myself for that, either."

"I believe you, and though you were completely wrong to keep this from him, I believe you thought you were doing the right thing." Delia sniffled again. "I'm not ready to make up today, but I wanted you to know that I'm trying because I miss my best friend."

"Me, too." Sloane couldn't stop the tears from falling.

"One more thing," Delia said. "This isn't an official Bennett apology. I'm only speaking for myself. My mother... Let's just say that she's not ready to make nice."

Sloane closed her eyes, more tears sliding down her cheeks when her friend disconnected the call.

It was the first step to repairing the friendship that had

been a lifeline for most of her life. Not having Delia in her corner for the past year had hurt.

"I know this is painful, honey, but it's progress." Her mother's voice was reassuring. Sloane wished her mother could hug her right now.

The phone rang again.

"Delia again?" her mother asked.

Sloane checked the caller ID. "No, it's Garrett Hyatt."

"Your old boss from the indie record company in Nashville? What does he want?"

Sloane had no clue. She answered the phone, trying to avoid getting mud on it.

"This is Sloane Sutton."

"Hey, Sloane. This is Garrett. It's been a while since—"

"You fired me?"

"You resigned," he said quickly, not mentioning the part where the company had asked her to resign. "Anyway, I just wanted to catch up and see how things have been going. I saw the pictures of the twins that you sent Natalie. Beau and Bailey are adorable kids. What are they now...about twelve months?"

"They're nine months, and thank you." Sloane inquired briefly about his wife and children and the rest of the team.

Abby mouthed, *What does he want?* and Sloane shrugged in response.

Garrett was telling a story about the latest antics of the lead singer of one of the label's most profitable acts when she cut him off. "Garrett, I'd love to catch up some other time, but I'm literally up to my elbows in mud right now. Is there something in particular I can do for you?"

"Yes, you can come and get your job. The one you earned and we should've given you in the first place."

"The creative director position? What happened to the woman you hired away from the big label?"

"She had the talk down, but the walk, not so much.

Maybe it would've worked if we'd had her old label's budget, but she couldn't adjust to how we do things here, and she wasn't amenable to learning."

"That's too bad." Sloane studied her mud-caked nails, but didn't acknowledge his invitation.

"So what do you think?"

"About?"

"C'mon, Sloane. Don't be that way." Garrett was a brilliant record executive, but a mediocre human being. "So, about my offer—"

"I'm not in Nashville anymore," she said coolly. "I moved back to Magnolia Lake. On account of not having a job."

He cleared his throat again. "Like I said, I'm sorry about that whole ugly business. But if you take the creative director position, you'd be making twenty percent more—"

"Nope."

"Twenty-five percent—"

"Uh-uh."

"Thirty per—"

"If you're not offering at least a fifty percent increase and a signing bonus, I can just get back to my spa mud bath."

"You're at a spa right now?"

"Are you offering, or am I hanging up now?"

"Okay, okay. Look, I have to level with you here. We've got two major artists we're trying to re-sign. They're with the same agent and they're insisting that without you, there's no deal. Things here have been kind of crazy for the past few months. So I really need your help."

"Is that a yes on the money or are we moving the negotiation number higher?" She wiggled her toes in the mud.

"Yes, fine. Now will you come back?"

"Let me think about it. I need to consult with my family.

I'll get back to you in a few days. Bye, Garrett." She hung up the phone and slipped down in the mud again.

"You've learned a lot from that wonder boy of yours, haven't you?" her mother laughed. "Gotta say, he'd be pretty proud of the way you handled yourself."

All of the tension returned to Sloane's shoulders. She'd gotten the job she'd always wanted at the salary she wanted. And she'd already found the perfect day care for the twins before she'd been fired.

But she couldn't have the job she wanted in Nashville and the life she'd made in Magnolia Lake with Benji, too.

She'd have to choose.

# Sixteen

When Benji pulled into the driveway at the cabin, Atticus Ames's weathered pickup was parked in the driveway. The old man frequently visited the twins, and Beau and Bailey had their beloved PawPaw wrapped around their tiny little pinkies. But Benji had been agitated since his conversations with Parker and Delia, and he was in no mood to be cordial.

Sloane's grandfather sat in the great room bouncing Beau on his knee. The infant's adorable laugh filled the space, and Benji couldn't help smiling, despite the anxiety in his chest.

"Mr. Ames." Benji shook the older man's hand.

"Been thinking…" The man cleared his throat, his focus still on Beau as he continued to bounce him on his knee. "There's no need to be so formal. We're practically family."

Little Beau reached eagerly toward Benji, chanting, "Da, Da, Da."

"Hey, buddy." Benji ruffled his young son's soft, curly

hair and lifted him over his head, garnering more chuckles from Beau before he kissed his chubby cheek.

He turned back to Mr. Ames, not acknowledging the remark. He'd known the man all his life and always called him Mr. Ames. They weren't close enough for him to call him Gramps, as Sloane did. And he certainly wasn't going to call him by his first name.

"Is there anything I can get for you, sir?" Benji asked, despite his eagerness to spend some time with his son and daughter.

The man stood up and stroked his gray beard. "Just a few answers."

"About?" Benji raised a brow as he dodged Beau's slobby little hand grabbing for his beard.

"What are your intentions toward my granddaughter?" The old man yanked his pants up by the belt loops, hiking them higher on his waist. "I've kept my peace because Sloane, and Abby, asked me to stay out of it, but it's been a year. I gotta wonder, if my granddaughter is good enough to play house with, why ain't she good enough for you to marry?"

Sloane obviously hadn't told her grandfather about his earlier proposal, though given how he'd proposed, he couldn't blame her. But if she hadn't told him, it wasn't Benji's place to tell him now.

"Mr. Ames—"

"You've been extremely generous to our family, and I appreciate everything you've done for us. You've proven yourself to be a good man and a good provider. And it's obvious you have feelings for my granddaughter. But I won't stand by while you use Sloane and then toss her aside."

Okay, now he was getting pissed.

"I'm not using Sloane, and I have no intention of tossing her aside. I've always valued her and recognized what an amazing woman she is."

The older man lowered his gaze, not missing the verbal throat punch Benji had delivered.

"I haven't always been the best grandfather, but it wasn't because I didn't love her. I wanted the very best for her, but I went about it all wrong. I've apologized to Sloane for that."

The man sat down again, as if the weight of the confession was too heavy for him to bear.

Livvie came into the room with Bailey on her hip. Benji kissed his smiling daughter, then asked Livvie to take the twins to their room so he and Mr. Ames could talk.

Once the door of the nursery clicked shut, Benji sat beside the old man on the sofa. "Look, I shouldn't have said that. It wasn't my place, and I'm sorry."

"I'm no fool, son. I know who I am. Who I've been. That I failed both Sloane and Abby. But I'm grateful that I've been afforded the opportunity to make amends." His expression was filled with pain and regret. "The bypass surgery I had, it gave me a new perspective on life. And these incredible kids of yours, they've given me a chance to finally get things right."

"I'm thankful you and Abby have been there for us from the beginning without question." Benji thought about his own family. "And I'm glad the twins have had the opportunity to get to know you."

"There's no doubt you love those kids, and I believe you love my granddaughter, too."

"I do love her." His voice was strained and there was tension in his neck and shoulders.

"Sounds like there's a *but* rattling around in there somewhere, son." The old man indicated Benji's chest.

Benji released a deep sigh. "Sometimes I wonder if I'm the only one emotionally invested in this relationship."

"You don't think Sloane cares about you?" Atticus asked incredulously. "Why else do you think she's here?"

Benji looked at the man pointedly.

"You're a man of means who can give my granddaughter anything she wants," he acknowledged. "But Sloane has never been one to mince words. If she didn't want to be here, son, you'd know it. And if she didn't care about you, you'd damn sure know that, too."

"Even if it was in her best interest to make me believe she did?" Though he'd defended Sloane to his cousin, Benji hadn't been able to let go of Parker's accusation.

"You obviously don't know Sloane very well." The old man stood and headed toward the front door.

"I do know Sloane, and I care for her and the twins more than anything in the world." Benji stood, too. "I honestly couldn't imagine my life without them. But it's hard to ignore the circumstances and what people around town are saying."

"Humph." Atticus turned back to him, his expression disapproving. "I actually believed you were a strong enough man to not let the gossips get inside your head. Evidently, I was wrong. If you'd think—even for a minute—that Sloane is capable of that kind of underhanded trickery…" He dragged a hand through his thinning, gray hair. "Well, maybe it's better if the two of you do part ways. For Sloane's sake, I hope it's sooner rather than later. Before she gets in any deeper."

"Mr. Ames… Atticus." Benji caught up with him on the porch and placed a hand on the man's shoulder, halting him. "I really do love Sloane, and I want to be with her."

The older man turned around, his gaze searching Benji's. His tone and expression softened. "Then let me offer you a bit of unsolicited advice, son. Don't make the mistakes I did. Don't leave Sloane wondering if you really love her. And don't try to control her. She'll fight you every step of the way, and I guarantee you'll be the one to lose."

With that, he shoved a baseball cap onto his head, got in his truck and drove off.

As the old man drove away, his shrewd advice replayed in Benji's head, already spinning from the day's events. One thing became abundantly clear: he and Sloane needed to sort things out. And it couldn't wait until her return.

Sloane slipped on her hotel robe and hurried to the door. Someone was knocking like a lunatic and it was well after ten at night. It had to be an emergency.

She peered through the peephole and quickly opened the door. "Benji, what's going on? Are Beau and Bailey okay?"

"They're great. I fed them and put them to bed for the night before I left them with Livvie."

"Is my grandfather okay?"

"He's fine." Benji closed the door behind him and entered the suite. Taking Sloane's hand, he led her to the sofa.

Sloane's heart still slammed against her chest. Something had to be very wrong.

"So what is it that you had to come all the way out here to tell me in person? It must be pretty important."

Benji inhaled deeply, and for a moment she thought he might hyperventilate. Finally, his gaze locked with hers.

"Sloane... I..." He cleared his throat and tried again, taking her hand in both of his. "Sloane Sutton, I love you. You and the kids, you're everything to me, and I don't ever want to be without you. I know I gave you until the twins' first birthday to decide whether you wanted to stay, but I couldn't wait any longer to tell you how I feel."

His meek smile reminded her of the little boy she'd first met all those years ago.

"You look stunned." He frowned. Lines spanned his forehead.

"Benji, I love being with you and raising the twins together, but as much as I love the family we've made, I can't ignore the damage I've done to yours." She wiped away tears with her free hand, and shook her head. "You've tried to hide it, but the pain of being alienated from your sister and your parents... It's always there."

"Is the rift between me and my family what's holding you back?" He cupped her cheek. "Honey, you can't blame yourself for that. Besides, Delia and I talked today."

"I know, and I'm hopeful about our relationship, but your mom hasn't budged."

He dropped his hand from her face. "Delia showed me the blog, told me about the emails. Why would you risk telling her about the money and being in breach of our agreement?"

"Because I broke your family. Just like I broke mine." Sloane wiped her face with the back of her hand. "I seem to have a gift for that."

"What are you talking about?" Benji frowned.

"When my mother got pregnant with me, it damaged her relationship with Gramps, and destroyed my father's relationship with his parents. And I'm the reason you've been estranged from your family this past year. When I heard the pain in Delia's voice today..." Sloane shook her head. "I can't live with being the one who destroyed the Bennetts. And as long as we're together—"

"You'd be willing to walk away to fix things with my family?" Benji's voice grew quiet. "I appreciate how much you care for me, but Sloane, I'm a grown man. I made the choice to be with you, just like my mother and sister made their choices."

"You feel that way now, but what happens in two years when you look at me and see the woman who tore your family apart? Will you still love me then? Or will you wake up one day and hate me, the way my father did?"

"Honey, I could never feel that way about you or the twins." He held her in his arms as tears slid down her face, wetting his shirt. "I love you. I always have."

"That wasn't love, Benji, it was a crush." She freed herself from his embrace and turned to face him. "Sometimes I worry that's still what this is."

"Sloane." He pulled her onto his lap. "I know you don't believe it, but I honestly have been in love with you since I was ten. Back then, I didn't really understand how I felt. I just knew you were one of the most important people in the world to me, and that you always would be. Our past year together has only confirmed what I've always believed. We belong together."

She stared into his warm brown eyes, her heart full. There was so much she wanted to say, but the words wouldn't leave her mouth.

"Thank God for Blake and Savannah's wedding, for the weekend we spent at the cabin, for the twins…" he continued, undeterred by her silence. "Otherwise, I wouldn't be sitting here, holding you and telling you the thing I've always wanted to say. That I love you, Sloane, and I want to be with you. No matter what."

"I love you, Benjamin Darnell Bennett." She smiled as she leaned in to kiss him.

He cradled her face as his tongue met hers, heat building between them. Sloane unbuttoned his shirt, gliding her hand along the strong muscles of his hard chest.

Benji broke their kiss. His apologetic gaze met hers. "There's something else we need to talk about. At the wedding, when you told Kayleigh Jemison that you had a plan to get out of debt—"

"She thought I was talking about you?" Sloane asked incredulously. She and Kayleigh weren't close, but they knew each other well enough for it to sting that she would believe that of her. "Is that why she's been acting so weird whenever I see her around town?"

"Probably, but please don't be angry with her. She only mentioned it because—"

"She was afraid I was taking advantage of you." Sloane

narrowed her eyes at Benji. "Wait... Is that what you think, too? That getting knocked up by a billionaire was my debt relief plan?" She scrambled off his lap and scampered to her feet.

When he didn't respond and his eyes didn't meet hers, it felt like he'd stabbed her in the heart.

"Sloane." Benji grabbed her hand and pulled her back onto his lap when she turned to walk away. "No, I don't believe you could be so cold and calculating. But I wouldn't have believed you'd keep the twins a secret from me, either."

She lowered her gaze. "I know it was wrong, but I honestly thought I was protecting you."

"Like you did when you broke our agreement and revealed our financial arrangement to Delia?" His voice was tense.

"I didn't want her to find out from someone else, and I couldn't stand being the reason you two weren't talking."

"If you felt that adamant about it, you should've talked to me so we could work through it together." He blew out a frustrated breath. "Look, I love you, Sloane. But if you want me to trust you implicitly, you need to start trusting me. We need to be equal partners in this relationship. I don't want the kind of relationship my parents have. Where one person exerts all the control and the other is just along for the ride."

He was accusing her of behaving like his mother. Worse, she'd given him valid reason.

"Benji, I'm sorry." Sloane squeezed his hand. "I didn't realize that's what I was doing. That's not what I want for us, either. I convinced myself I was only doing it for you, but maybe part of it was me trying to take back some control of my life. I went from being my own person to you suddenly calling all the shots. Maybe I was a little resentful."

"And for that, I apologize." He wrapped his arms around her and pulled her closer as he leaned back against the sofa. "Guess I was overcompensating, not wanting to be too passive like my father. I was also trying too hard to show you that I'm not that little boy you still feel the need to protect."

"We've got issues." Sloane smiled, and they both laughed.

"I'll tell you what, let's make a promise here and now that we won't keep secrets from each other and when it comes to our lives together, we're a team. So no more nanny ambushes, unexpected chefs or surprise interior design. Deal?"

"Deal." She pressed a quick kiss to his lips and smiled. "And you're absolutely sure this is what you want?"

"Never been more sure about anything." The humor in Benji's expression was gone. What she saw in his eyes was a love deeper than any she'd ever known. A love she couldn't bear to be without.

The solution to her Garrett problem was suddenly very clear. Her life in Nashville had been good, but the life she, Benji and the twins were building together in Magnolia Lake was far better.

Sloane opened her mouth to tell Benji about the job offer, but he kissed her again. A kiss that built slowly, but ignited a flame that quickly consumed them both.

He made love to her, and when she fell asleep in his arms, she knew without a doubt that this was exactly where she belonged.

# Seventeen

Benji had an early breakfast with Sloane and her mother at the resort before heading back to the cabin to check on the twins. After spending a few hours with Beau and Bailey, he drove over to his parents' house.

He climbed the stairs of the home he'd lived in as a kid. His mother had already prepared the flower boxes on the porch.

*Snapdragons.*

He smiled, thinking of the bouquet of flowers he'd brought to Sloane on Valentine's Day when he'd returned from Japan. The day he'd first learned of the twins and had felt them moving inside their mother. A day he'd never forget.

Benji took a deep breath and pressed his thumb to the doorbell.

His father came to the door. A slow smile spread across the man's face and his eyes shone in the sunlight.

"Benji." Rick Bennett grabbed him in a bear hug and patted his back. "Son, it's so good to see you."

"You, too, Dad."

His father had emailed him, sent text messages and made the occasional call. All of it behind his mother's back, which had only made him angrier with his father for not taking a stand...until now.

"Delia showed me pictures of Beau and Bailey. They're beautiful, son." His father's eyes were watery. "I can't wait to meet them."

"We'll see how things go, Dad." Benji shoved his hands in his pockets as he followed his father inside the house.

"No." Rick Bennett turned around and pressed a palm to Benji's chest, halting him. "This ends today. This has been complete madness, and I've indulged your mother far too long on this. Regardless of what happens between you two, I'm ready to make my peace with you and Sloane. I want to see my grandbabies. *Today.*"

"Okay, Dad. Relax." Benji placed his hands on his father's shoulders. His dad had always been laid-back. It was strange to see him so fired up. "Where's Mom?"

"In the sunroom, pretending she didn't hear the doorbell." His dad jerked a thumb over his shoulder and frowned. "Good luck."

Benji didn't need luck. He'd never been so determined about anything in his life.

As long as Benji and his mother maintained this stalemate, he and Sloane would agonize over it in their own ways. And from what Delia had told him, things were just as bad for his mother and father. So he wouldn't take no for an answer.

When Benji entered the sunroom, his mother didn't look up from her crocheting. He leaned against the wall by the door. "So you're sending Parker to do your dirty work these days?"

"Benji." She spared him a brief glance, ignoring his statement. "I see you came alone."

"Why would I bring my family where they're not welcome?" He folded his arms.

She grimaced, as if his words had caused her physical pain. "Seems you and Sloane have created your own little family. One you prefer over ours."

"Only because you made me choose," he said without apology.

She sighed quietly, raising her eyes to meet his after a few moments of silence between them. "Sit down, please. This is still your home, you know."

"Doesn't feel like it anymore, Mom." Benji sat on the sofa across from her. "Because home, for me, is wherever Sloane and the kids are."

Tears welled in his mother's eyes.

"Sloane certainly has cast a spell on you, hasn't she?" She set her work in the basket and turned her full attention to him. "I know you've always had a little crush on her, but I never imagined it would turn into something like this."

"I think the term you're looking for is *love*. I love Sloane, I love our kids, and I love our life together. And I wouldn't give it up for anyone or anything in the world. They mean everything to me, Mom."

"Sounds like you're all quite happy, then."

"We are, except for one thing that keeps looming over us. Sloane loves me, Mom. And she can't bear thinking that she's the reason you and I aren't talking."

"Well, she is," she said matter-of-factly.

"No, she isn't. That was the choice that you made." Benji scrubbed a hand down his face. "Whether you like it or not, Sloane is the woman I choose to be with. She and the twins make me happier than I've ever been. There is only one person who seems determined to destroy that happiness, and that's you."

"I just don't want to see you being taken advantage of by a girl like that."

"By a girl like *what*, Mom? Why is it that you hate Sloane so much? What has she ever done to deserve your distrust?"

"She was a bad influence on Delia."

"Seriously? You think Sloane was the bad influence?" Benji laughed bitterly. "It's time you and Delia have a heart-to-heart talk. If anything, you should be thanking Sloane for keeping Delia from getting in a lot more trouble than she did."

"I don't believe it."

"Talk to Delia, then get back to me." He stood up and headed to the door. "One more thing, Mom. The woman you believe is a gold digger… I asked her to marry me the day I learned about the twins, but she turned me down cold. And as recently as last night, she was prepared to walk away rather than come between you and me. *That's* love."

His mother seemed genuinely stunned by both revelations. "Benji, what about Beau and Bailey? I'd really like to meet them."

"Once you've apologized to Sloane, I'd love for you to meet the twins." He turned back to her, his jaw tense and the sound of his heartbeat filling his ears. "That hasn't changed."

"Benji." She grabbed his arm before he could turn to leave, tears sliding down her cheeks. "I let this feud between us get out of hand, and I'm sorry, but you're my baby and… You've always had such a big heart. I just didn't want to see anyone take advantage of you."

"I know you only want what's best for me, Mom." The tension in his jaw eased a little. "But you need to trust that I know what that is."

She nodded, dabbing tears away. "Do you think tomorrow morning would be convenient for Sloane and I to talk?"

Benji gave his mother a quick hug and sighed. "Yes, I think that can be arranged."

* * *

Sloane paced the floor in the great room. She'd given the twins their baths, fed and dressed them. Now Livvie was entertaining them in the nursery.

Benji had offered to cancel his conference call so he could be there to give Sloane moral support. She'd insisted that he didn't need to coddle her. She'd be just fine. But now she wasn't so sure.

The doorbell rang and Sloane took one last deep breath before she opened the door and smiled. "Hello, Mrs. Bennett. Come in. Have a seat, please."

It felt odd welcoming the woman into the cabin they'd once owned.

"The renovations Benji made really do make it look completely different now." The older woman glanced around the space. "Cole's crew does excellent work."

"They certainly do. They did a fantastic job renovating my…" Sloane paused, realizing that wasn't a topic she wanted to discuss with the woman who already thought she was only with Benji for his money.

"About a year ago, my sister inadvertently mentioned that Cole had sent a crew to renovate a condo in Nashville. I suspected it was for you." It seemed to pain the woman not to make further comment about it. "But that's not why I'm here."

Sloane offered Mrs. Bennett coffee, water or sweet tea, but she declined. They both had a seat on the sofa in the great room.

"Look, Sloane, I was wrong," Benji's mother began without preamble. "And I fear I've always been wrong about you and your mother. I was so sure that you were going to bring my girl down. But from what Delia tells me, you were my secret ally, reining her in as much as you could."

"Delia was like a sister to me. It was my job to look

after her," Sloane said, once she got over the initial shock of the apology.

"And as Benji's mother, I was only trying to do the same when I feared that you were taking advantage of him." The woman looked weary.

"I would never do that to him or to anyone." Sloane sat taller, determined to keep her cool.

"Benji believes that's true, and I've promised to trust his instincts about you."

"Thank you, Mrs. Bennett. That means a lot."

"It appears that you and my grandchildren mean the world to him." She smiled faintly. "Benji's never stood up to me like that before. I truly do believe he's been in love with you since he was a little boy. Leave it to Benji to find his soul mate at the age of ten."

"He told you that?" Sloane laughed, even as tears welled in her eyes.

"He did. I've learned quite a bit in the past twenty-four hours, and I've gotten to see you in a whole new light. Perhaps, I have been too hard on you all these years. I can't promise I'll change overnight, Sloane. But I do promise to give you a fair chance."

"That's all I ask." Sloane wiped away her tears. "By the way, I've spoken to Benji, and I'd really like to do a paternity test on the twins to put to rest any lingering doubts you may have."

"I appreciate the offer, Sloane," she said with a tight smile. "But I've seen pictures of Beau. He's the spitting image of his father. So please, don't go to any extraordinary lengths on my account."

Sloane nodded, her heart beating rapidly. She felt fiercely protective of her babies and a little nervous about Connie Bennett finally meeting them. Sloane stood, wringing her hands. "Would you like to meet the twins?"

Fat tears welled in the woman's eyes, too, as she nodded. "I'd like that very much."

Sloane went to the nursery and she and Livvie returned with her sweet babies. "Constance Bennett, I'd like you to meet your grandson and granddaughter, Beaumont and Bailey Bennett."

Benji's mother took them both in her arms and hugged them, her face wet with tears.

# Eighteen

It had been more than a week since Benji's mother and father had met the twins. Two days ago, his sister and Evie had come to visit them, too. His niece had been enamored with her younger cousins and he'd never seen his sister or Sloane cry so many happy tears.

Benji checked his watch. He'd sent Sloane on an errand to Gatlinburg to give him time to finalize a few arrangements. Now, he'd been pacing the floor for more than twenty minutes and he'd already changed his shirt twice.

Everything had to be perfect.

He'd gone over the words he wanted to say to Sloane and the order in which he should say them. Debated whether he should start with his big ask or by telling her his big news.

He checked on the twins again, corralled in a large, colorful playpen so they couldn't get into anything.

Finally he heard the tires of her SUV crunch along the gravel up their drive and then the door slammed.

"Hey, babe. How was your trip into town?" He helped her bring in a few items.

"Great." She kissed him. "Did the twins give you any trouble?" She picked up each of them and kissed their little cheeks before returning them to the playpen. Then she went to the kitchen to start putting things away and he followed.

"Everything okay?" She narrowed her gaze at him. "You're acting a little weird."

*Take it easy and relax.*

"Everything is fine." He took her hand and led her to the couch. "I just need to tell you about an offer I got."

"Okay." She looked a little nervous.

He took a deep breath. "The company that bought mine, they want me to come back to Japan to help them work on a new project."

"Another six-month-long contract?"

"This time it'll be a year, and the money they're offering me to do this is insane."

"Wow, that's great." Her voice and expression indicated the exact opposite. "An entire year. Wow."

*Opening and closing with a wow... Not good.*

"Remember when I asked you to go to Japan with me and you listed all the things we could do together there? Well, here's our chance. And Beau and Bailey will get to travel the world before they're even two years old."

"That's a really incredible opportunity." She walked over to the fireplace, her back to him.

"Then why do you seem so miserable about it?" He followed her, wrapping his arms around her waist from behind. "Do you regret turning down the offer at the record company?"

"I don't regret choosing you, Beau and Bailey over fifty-hour work weeks. But maybe there is a little part of me that wishes I'd gotten to spend a little time doing the job. They came crawling to me, and I negotiated a fair salary. You would've been proud," she added faintly.

"I am proud of you, honey. You worked hard for that creative director position and they offered it to you. So yes, I'm damn proud of you. And if you've reconsidered the offer, I'll support you one hundred percent."

"There's no way we can be together if I'm in Nashville and you're in Tokyo." She sank onto the sofa, glaring at him as if he'd gone insane.

"Don't worry, babe. We'll work it out." He sat beside her and traced her cheekbone with his thumb. "Trust me."

"That sounds awesome. Except for the part where it's completely impossible. Either you win, or I do. There's no way we both get what we want."

"Then it's simple. We move to Nashville. You take your dream job, and I'll become your incredibly rich househusband."

Sloane punched his arm playfully and laughed, laying her head on his chest. He draped an arm over her shoulder and pulled her against him.

"Don't be ridiculous. Your offer is probably worth more than I'd earn in a hundred years."

She wasn't wrong, but that didn't mean what she wanted wasn't important. He didn't need to work another day or do another deal ever. They'd still be fine and so would the kids.

"I've already achieved my holy grail."

"Building a company from scratch and selling it for two-point-five billion is a pretty hard act to follow."

"Not talking about that." He grinned. "I meant finally being with you. That's all I've ever wanted. So as long as I have you, Beau and Bailey, nothing else matters. I want you to go out in the world and do whatever it is that will make you as happy as you've made me."

"C'mon, Benj. Be serious."

"I am." He got on one knee and pulled out the diamond ring he'd been waiting to give her.

"Oh, my God." She pressed trembling fingers to her mouth. "It's beautiful, Benji. I love it."

"And I love you, Sloane. I've loved you most of my life. But what I feel for you now isn't a silly crush or lust or obligation or any of the things you were so worried this was. I genuinely love you. And I'm so lucky to have you in my life."

"I love you, too." She kissed him. "Just promise me that all of our crazy family issues won't become our issues."

"That I can promise you." He kissed her hand. "Say you'll marry me, Sloane. And we can live anywhere you want. Do whatever you want. As long as we're together."

She nodded eagerly, tears sliding down her cheeks. "Yes, yes, absolutely yes. I love you so much, Benji."

He slipped the ring on her finger and kissed her. Then he stood, pulling her into his arms.

"I can't believe we're finally gonna do this." She smiled, admiring the beautiful platinum-and-diamond solitaire ring flanked with smaller diamonds.

"Which reminds me." He pulled out his phone, sent a group text message, then returned it to his pocket.

Suddenly Sloane gripped his arm and pointed.

"What is it?" He looked where she was pointing. Bailey stood in the middle of the playpen, teetering on unsure legs.

"That's great, babe. But we've seen her do that lots of times."

"Shh…" She slipped her hand in his. "Wait for it."

Arms spread, Bailey looked up at them and smiled. She

took three steps toward them before falling onto her bottom again.

"I just saw my baby girl's first steps." He picked up the infant and kissed her plump cheek. She drooled on him and giggled.

Sloane picked up Beau, not wanting to leave him out. "Don't worry, sweetie. You'll be chasing your sister around the playpen in no time." She kissed his cheek, too.

Suddenly her eyes lit up.

"What is it?" Benji asked.

"I know where I want to live."

"Nashville or Tokyo?"

"Neither." She grinned. "I want us to build a house right here in Magnolia Lake, where the twins can grow up surrounded by our friends and family."

"So we pass on both opportunities?" He put Bailey, who was eager to try out her newfound skills, back down in the playpen.

Sloane put Beau down, too.

"It'll take at least six months for Cole to build our house here, right? It'd be nice to get some decent sushi and see the cherry blossoms while we're waiting."

"Are you sure about this, Sloane?"

She nodded. "Positive."

"You, soon-to-be Mrs. Bennett, are a genius." He hauled her against him, wondering if they had enough time to put the kids in their cribs and sneak off to their bedroom for a private celebration.

The front doorbell rang. *Apparently not.*

Marcellus carried in insulated food warmers and Benji went out to help him. Before they were done, his sister, niece and parents arrived. Then Abby and Atticus arrived in their truck, followed by Blake, Savannah and Davis. Zora, Parker, Max, Cole, and his uncle Duke and aunt Iris arrived soon after. Livvie and Mr. and Mrs. H filled out the rest of the party.

Benji watched as his parents fussed over the twins and Sloane showed off her ring.

They'd be very happy indeed living in Magnolia Lake.

\* \* \* \* \*